The Good Time Girls at Christmas

Fiona Ford

The Good Time Girls series

First published in Great Britain in 2022 by

 **embla books**

Bonnier Books UK Limited
4th Floor, Victoria House, Bloomsbury Square, London, WC1B 4DA
Owned by Bonnier Books
Sveavägen 56, Stockholm, Sweden

A CIP catalogue record for this book is available from the British Library.

ISBN: 9781471415388

Thi s book is typeset using Atomik ePublisher

Embla Books is an imprint of Bonnier Books UK
www.bonnierbooks.co.uk

For all the saga readers out there who keep the
importance of social history alive.

Prologue

December 1931

The Christmas tree towered above her, bathed in twinkling fairy lights, the tiny bulbs shining as brightly as the Star of David. Studded in between each flash of light stood a carefully chosen ornament, each one hand-picked, selected for its beauty rather than sentimentality. In pride of place at the top of the tree stood, not an angel as was traditional, but a tiny dancer's shoe complete with high heel trimmed in gold.

As Renee Newsham stood in the centre of her parlour looking up at the tree that seemed to take over half the room, she was transfixed. This tree was one of the most beautiful things she had ever seen. Gingerly she reached out and touched one of the branches, afraid for just a second that her touch would destroy the magic. But in that moment she had to check that this perfect vision of Christmas was real. Feeling the stubby pine needles against the smooth skin of her palm, she shivered with pleasure – perhaps this Christmas all her dreams would come true? Perhaps, despite her misgivings at the situation she found herself in, newly wed to a man she despised to settle an old score of her father's, well, perhaps things might turn out all right. Perhaps there might be a little Christmas magic in the air.

Growing up, money had been sparse. And there had never been much at Christmas time. Other than the tangerine she and her sister Lizzie enjoyed every Christmas Day, there had never been any treats to savour and enjoy. At the thought of Lizzie she smiled. Her younger sister was her best friend and confidante. The only woman in the world who shared her story and understood all that she had endured.

This Christmas, her first as a married woman, would be different. This time there seemed to be plenty to go around, with her husband already promising to shower her and her sister with gifts as well as providing a goose with all the trimmings. Now, this huge tree she had just finished decorating with ornaments Ronnie had chosen and paid for gave Renee a flash of hope. Catching sight of the shoe in pride of place, she smiled. This hadn't been an ornament Ronnie had chosen, this shoe was Renee's touch, and it meant so much to her. Seeing how the gold glinted in the last of the afternoon light, she hoped her husband would be delighted with her creative flair.

Hearing footsteps behind her, she jumped in surprise before she felt Ronnie's slim hands snake around her waist.

'What do you think?' she murmured, his whiskery chin burrowing into the soft skin of her neck.

'I think it's beautiful,' he whispered. 'But not as beautiful as you, nothing is ever as beautiful as you, Reen.'

As her husband peppered her with kisses, Renee tried to relax as she gazed at the tree. For once her husband seemed pleased with her. It didn't happen often, but she was getting used to judging his moods. As Christmas Day was in just two days' time, she hoped she could help him remain in a good mood. All she wanted was for this Christmas to be perfect.

As Ronnie continued to press against her, Renee tried to quell the feelings of nausea that were never far away when he touched her. She had been forced to marry this man, this infamous criminal, to settle her late father's debt, and in the three months they had been wed she had felt nothing but resentment burn deep inside of her. But now, as she looked up at the Christmas tree, she found herself pushing aside the old resentments. Maybe it was time to learn to love this man. Perhaps this Christmas would be the making of them, and given how affectionate he was being with her now, she was sure it would be a day they would never forget.

Suddenly, Ronnie stopped kissing her neck and as he lifted his chin away from her body Renee gave in to the familiar tension that was never far away when her husband was nearby.

'What's that?' he asked in a low voice.

Renee followed his gaze. Ronnie was staring at the tree just as she had been moments earlier. Only, instead of a look of awe and wonder, Ronnie was wearing a look that could kill.

'What?' She gulped.

She knew why he was upset. Renee had been sure to follow Ronnie's every instruction. He had been very clear about how he wanted the tree decorated and she had made sure she had done as he asked. Not only had she painstakingly ensured every single light faced the same way, she had ensured that each ornament hung equidistant from the other, with every colour coordinated with its neighbour. Ronnie always expected the best and Renee had been determined to ensure he got what he wanted.

But when it came to the shoe she had been unable to resist. The precious, pretty shoe that meant so much deserved a place on the tree, and she had hung it knowing deep down it was likely to cause trouble.

Only now, as she caught the look of anger in Ronnie's pale grey eyes, she felt a flash of fear. She weathered each of Ronnie's emotions like a roller coaster and now, sensing the tell-tale clench of his jaw and the narrowed slant of his eyes, she braced herself for trouble.

'Everything all right, Ron?' she asked in as breezy a tone as possible.

Ronnie said nothing, and, as he stepped away from her and

walked towards the tree, for a moment Renee thought she had imagined the smile that broke out on his face.

'What's this?' he asked again, gesturing towards the shoe on the top of the tree.

Renee let out a shaky breath. 'Me . . . mother gave it me. You remember when I went up to Blackpool for the first time and came second in the Shield? She bought me this shoe as a consolation prize. Course, I've never had a chance to use it until now . . .'

Her voice trailed off as she became aware she was babbling. Turning her gaze away from the tree and back towards Ronnie, her stomach turned over as he approached her.

'Did I say you could put that on the tree?' he half growled, half whispered.

Renee shook her head and took a step back.

'So, why is it there?'

'As I said . . . Because my mother gave it me.'

For a moment Ronnie was silent as he stared at her.

'Because your mother gave it to you?' he mimicked.

As Renee stared into his cold eyes she cursed herself for her stupidity. Of course, Ronnie did not like her thinking for herself. Of course, he didn't want her sharing something of her own that meant so much. He hated the fact she was a dancer, that she drew admiring glances from every dance floor she frequented. He only tolerated it because she had a following in the North West – if she disappeared completely from view, suspicions would be raised. In public, Ronnie could play the proud husband, he could sing her praises whenever she won a dance contest. But in private it was different. She should have known that to not only put something of her own on the tree, but to put something connected to her precious dancing would be asking for trouble. What had she really been expecting? That because it was Christmas he would have a change of heart?

'I'm sorry, Ronnie,' she began. 'I just thought it would be nice—'

'Nice?' Ronnie threw his head back and roared with laughter now. 'You thought hanging a bit of tat off this tree, which I paid a small fortune for, would be *nice?*'

Renee nodded, but it was too late.

Slowly, her husband walked towards her and grabbed her by the wrist. The deftness of his grip surprised her, but Renee knew better than to cry out in pain. They may only have been married a few short months but she had already learned that the best way to ensure Ronnie kept his episodes of terror short was to say nothing.

'Why do you do this to me?' he jeered, leaning his face into hers. 'Here I am, taking you in when you've got nothing. I give you the world and this is how you repay me? I bought an angel for that tree, a beautiful golden angel, yet you've chosen some cheap-looking bit of rubbish instead.'

His breath felt hot and heavy against her cheek and Renee tried not to recoil as she caught the smell of whisky.

'I'm sorry, Ronnie,' she offered, her pulse racing as she tried to delay what she knew was coming. 'I'll take it down.'

'*I'll take it down,*' he mimicked again, imitating her sing-song Liverpool accent, one that he himself had managed to lose. 'No. *I'll* take it down.'

With one hand still gripping her wrist, he reached for the ornament in one fluid motion.

'See this?' he said, jabbing the heel of the ornament dangerously near her face. 'I never want to see this again.'

'Just give it me, Ronnie,' Renee begged. 'It was me mam's. I won't put it on the tree again, I promise.'

Ronnie said nothing. Instead he fixed his cold eyes on hers.

She tried to read him. Had her apology meant something? Had she been able to fend off his anger?

But then she felt the full force of the heel against her cheek.

'Ow!' she squealed, the stab of pain darting across her cheek.

At the noise, Ronnie laughed. Dropping the ornament to the floor, he gave her one sharp shove and pushed her against the beautifully decorated tree.

As the decorations toppled down, leaving her tangled up in strings of fairy lights and streamers, Ronnie stood over her and laughed.

'Clean this up.'

He stalked out of the room leaving Renee lying in a crumpled heap, breathless and wounded.

Feeling blood trickle down her face, Renee managed to sit up. As she did so, her eyes landed on the little shoe.

As she reached for it Renee felt a fire inside her burn. Gripping the precious ornament in her palm, she vowed that, like this shoe, she would survive this Christmas and beyond. No matter what.

One

December 1940

'No, no, no,' the voice shrieked across the dance hall of the Palais. 'How many times? It's slow, slow, quick, quick, slow.'

From her position in the centre of the maple-sprung dance floor, Nancy Blum groaned inwardly.

She was watching her mother-in-law, Edna Goldstein, lead a lunchtime practice session for the dancers in the pen. To say it was a shambles was putting it mildly.

Once a champion dancer in her own right with a successful teaching school, Edna had been the toast of the Hammersmith Palais de Danse. But now she was frail and seemingly confused as she attempted to lead the dancers in a quickstep that was more slow than quick.

Nancy was no dancer but she understood what it took to be a good leader. In the months she had been in charge of the Palais, while her husband Alex, the previous general manager of the Palais had been serving in the army, Nancy – the former front desk manager – had stepped up. And although she barely knew a waltz from a foxtrot, she did know that as a leader you needed to give clear instruction – something Edna was having a hard time understanding.

She glanced across at her new chief dance instructor, Temperance Adams, who was doing her best to encourage the girls alongside Edna, but it was clear she too was struggling.

'Why don't we take a little break, huh?' Nancy called in her distinctive New York drawl.

Getting to her feet, she stalked across the dance floor in her low-heeled court shoes and felt Edna's eyes bore into her.

'Nancy, dear. You *never* interrupt a practice session – if you've learned nothing else, you should know that by now,' Edna said coldly.

Doing her best not to bridle at her mother-in-law's criticism, Nancy offered a smile instead. 'I appreciate that, Edna, but I think the girls need a break. Besides, the tea dance starts in less than an hour.'

Lifting the pale-pink sleeve of her jacket to check the time, Edna sniffed. 'Very well, then. But girls, I expect better of you next time.'

Shooing them away, as if they were a herd of cats rather than professional dancers, Edna turned to Nancy.

'You really must give me more notice if I am to get these girls anywhere up to my standards,' she said.

'The girls are talented, as you well know,' Nancy said with a sigh. 'There's no need for you to give instruction at all, that's Temperance's job. I thought you were going to take more of a backseat role now.'

'I'm here to help,' Temperance said eagerly. 'I got top marks in all my dance exams, I understand the more modern dances and I've been learning some of the new American-style dances, too, as well as the Latin.'

As if to demonstrate, Temperance executed a series of small, perfectly timed steps that even Nancy with her untrained eye could tell made up the rumba – a new Latin dance sweeping the dance halls in New York.

Edna curled her lip in disdain. 'There is no place for dances like that at the Palais.'

Temperance stopped, but rather than look contrite she lifted her chin a little higher and met Edna's gaze.

'With respect, Mrs Goldstein, the new dances from around the world are becoming very popular. The customers want to see them and the dancers want to dance them.'

At that, there was a chorus of approval from the dancers who were watching the exchange with interest.

Edna folded her arms, her coiffed, grey hair as stiff and serious as the glint in her eye. 'You have only just qualified as a teacher. I have more than fifty years of experience in this business. I think I know more about it than you, my dear.'

'You're an incredibly gifted teacher,' Temperance began smoothly, a flash of pink just beginning to creep across her cheeks. 'But times are changing, and if the Palais wants to continue to thrive we have to showcase these new dances as well as honour the old. We can't just keep doing tempo variations on the old foxtrot, not when dance halls across the country are offering something different. If Renee were here—'

'Which she is *not!* That thieving trollop!' Edna snarled.

Nancy got to her feet. Whenever the Palais' former chief dancer was mentioned, Edna became very upset. Nancy understood, after all, Renee had stolen from the Palais, but she had done so with good reason. Not that the reason made any difference to Edna. She was blinkered when it came to Renee, and Nancy could see that this argument was in danger of getting out of control, which was the last thing she needed. Later that afternoon, she had a meeting with the catering manager from the national chain of department stores, Howell & Smart, and she wanted to remain calm.

'That's enough,' she said smoothly, ushering the dancers away with a small jerk of her head and a smile.

Glancing at the warring women Nancy suddenly felt very old. There was so much on her shoulders. Temperance was a marvellous teacher, but she had a lot to learn before she could ever hope to be in the same league as Renee Hammond.

Just thinking about Renee filled Nancy with sadness. She had done her best to keep Renee's theft of hundreds of pounds' worth of cigarettes and alcohol from the Palais a secret. However, she had made the mistake of confiding in her husband, Alex – taking care to explain that Renee had felt backed into a corner, that she felt she had no choice to steal in order to raise money to pay off her tyrannical husband so that she could be free of him, once and for all. Alex had then gone on to write to his mother and tell her how worried he was about the future of the dance hall with a thief like Renee working her way into Nancy's affections.

Despite the fact that Renee had paid back a lot of what she'd stolen, after her sister, Lizzie, died, she stopped working at the Palais. Instead she had left for a fresh start – a dance hall in Manchester. But still Nancy found her own skill as a leader and judge of character being called into question. If it was just her that was suffering, it wouldn't be so bad, but Edna's air of superiority was making everyone else miserable, too. In recent weeks Edna had almost taken over Temperance's role, accused Violet of getting the filing wrong in her new position as office clerk, and made Maisie – the cloakroom assistant and Violet's sister – cry when she told her she needed to smile more.

The only person Edna hadn't taken on was Betty Millington – Violet and Maisie's mother – who was now also working full time at the Palais, in the office. For some reason Edna seemed to revere Mrs Millington – perhaps something to do with the fact that Betty was older than the rest of the Good Time Girls. But, if truth be told, Nancy wasn't sure how long that respect would last. For Edna, all that mattered was staying in the Palais board's good books, and if they told her to jump, Edna would always ask how high. Nancy knew that the Palais played a huge part in both Edna's and her son's life. But since Renee had gone, Edna's interest had really gone up a notch, with her wanting to be kept abreast of every development on and off the dance floor. Nancy wasn't sure why, and although she had tried to find out, her enquiries had always been met with a hard stare.

'Let's not start all that again,' Nancy said now, curtly. 'The matter has been dealt with and that's the end of it.'

Seeing a flicker of annoyance cross Edna's face, Nancy decided to take advantage of the fact that her mother-in-law was quiet for a change.

'I wanted to talk to you both about Valentine's Day.'

At the mention of another festivity just after Christmas, Temperance looked wrong-footed. 'What about it?'

'Well, I know it's going to be tough this year, what with the war on, but I don't think that should stop the Palais making sure everyone has as good a time as possible. The Palais needs to serve as a refuge, where people forget their troubles.'

'The show must go on,' Edna agreed, crisply.

'Precisely,' Nancy said, surprised that for once they were of a like mind. 'So, as well as the Christmas Eve and New Year's Eve dances, I want to give people something to look forward to in the coming year. We could do a ladies excuse me, and a ladies choice, and perhaps a couple of extra exhibition dances. Offer discounts for sweethearts that met at the Palais, and maybe even find a guest band.'

'But it's just six weeks after New Year. We won't have time,' Temperance protested.

Nancy opened her mouth to disagree, when she saw Edna's expression soften as she peered past Nancy's shoulder. Turning around to see what had caught her attention, Nancy saw the latest recruits to the Palais and smiled. Siblings Ruth and Peter had found a way into her heart from the moment they arrived, straight from Dovercourt by way of the Kinder Transport. Dressed in their grey-and-white school uniforms they looked worried, a look that had rarely left their faces since they had moved into the Palais last month.

'What are you guys doing here?' she gasped. 'Shouldn't you be at school?'

'It's finished for the holidays,' Ruth said, her dark hair swishing gently across her shoulders.

'And it's finished permanently for me,' Peter said, standing a foot taller than his sister.

Nancy frowned as she took in his words. 'Whaddya mean?' she asked, reverting to her fast-talking New York brogue. 'You just started a month ago.'

Peter shrugged. 'I'm fifteen. I can leave now, the school said.'

Nancy narrowed her eyes. 'And do what? There's a war on in case you hadn't noticed.'

The moment the words were out of her mouth, she regretted them. If anyone knew there was a war on, it was these two. Peter and his sister, who was twelve, were Austrian refugees. They had no idea if their parents were alive or dead as Hitler rampaged through their homeland.

Ever since she'd first heard of their plight, Nancy had been desperate to take the siblings into her home and have the Palais help heal them, as it had so many lost souls before. But in the six weeks they had been living with her, Peter and Ruth had rarely looked happy or relaxed, and it made Nancy ache with sorrow. Every day, she'd thought of the mother they had left, and wondered if she was still alive. Although she had never been blessed with children herself, Nancy felt bonded to these children and had made a silent promise to the family they had left behind in Europe that she would do the very best she could for them.

'So, why do you want to leave school, honey?' Nancy tried again, recognising patience was likely her ally in this battle.

Peter looked at her, his dark eyes glistening.

'I want to learn a trade,' he said. 'When I was growing up, my papa said I'd make a good apprentice. I know I can't do that now, but I was hoping you'd take me on as a trainee at the Palais.'

Nancy's eyes widened in surprise. This was a lot to take in. She knew of course that Peter and Ruth's father had run a successful soap factory back in Vienna, but she had no idea that Peter had hoped to follow in his father's footsteps. She bit her lip and tried to be more forgiving of herself. The children had only been living with her for a few weeks, she couldn't possibly be expected to know their entire life stories already.

Still, she wanted to do right by them, and felt caution in this moment was best. 'That's lovely, honey, but soap's a world away from dance. What sort of a trainee would you wanna be? The best place for you is school, surely you can see that?'

But Peter shook his head. 'School's no good to me with a war on. I want a trade, so when this is all over I've earned enough money to go back to Austria and find our family.'

For a moment Nancy felt stung. She had been working so hard to give Peter and Ruth a home, but she understood. She thought of her own family back in New York and how she ached to see them.

'I think that's a lovely thing to want to do,' Temperance put in gently. 'I think Nancy's just worried about you. You can learn things about the world at school that will help you. What do you want to do?'

But Peter stood firm, shaking his head, and as he then exchanged a look with Ruth, Nancy noticed his eyes were glistening with excitement.

'I want to do what you do here. I want to manage a dance hall.'

Two

Upstairs in the office of the Palais, Betty Millington was doing battle with torn-up newspaper and scissors while her younger daughter, Maisie, looked on in disdain.

'What are you doing, Ma?' she hissed.

'What does it look like I'm doing? Making paper chains to try and bring a bit of Christmas cheer into the office,' Betty said sharply.

She glanced around the dark, cramped office she shared with Nancy and Violet and sighed. She had come to love working at the Palais, but as with so many entertainment venues across the country, the place kept the glamour strictly front of house. With tatty blinds, badly scratched furniture and peeling wallpaper, the office of the Palais needed a complete overhaul, not a couple of newspaper chains. Still, Betty thought, as she continued licking the paper ends to make the decorations, every little helped. With Christmas just a few days away now, she was determined to bring some sort of cheer to the place. Everyone seemed so miserable lately, including her youngest.

She glanced at the clock and saw it was well past five in the afternoon.

'What are you doing up here, anyway?' she asked Maisie. 'Shouldn't you be at home minding your father? Your shift finished an hour ago, didn't it?'

Maisie grimaced. 'I'm supposed to be meeting Nancy. We're going to talk about me joining the dancers' pen occasionally. Temperance said she'd put in a word for me.'

Betty put down her strips of newspaper and made the sign of the cross on her chest. Although she had gotten over the fact her daughters worked in a dance hall, even to the point she had chosen to join them, Betty drew the line at one of her own becoming a dancer and cavorting about with men for a sixpence.

'I don't think that's a good idea,' she ventured. 'You get all sorts on that dance floor. Sure, didn't the MC have to break up a fight last week?'

Maisie rolled her eyes at the mention of Bill Cain, their resident Master of Ceremonies. 'He broke up a fight between two lads fighting over a girl, it had nothing to do with the dancer.'

Betty picked up her paper chains and said nothing. Maisie would do as she pleased, she had always been headstrong, and Betty knew to pick her battles. She also knew that someone should be with her husband. George hated being alone since he'd come back from Dunkirk, and Betty was feeling fractious about the situation at home.

'Can't you talk to Nancy about this tomorrow?' she tried again. 'Your father needs someone.'

'Where's Nan?' Maisie said, folding her arms. 'He's *her* son.'

'And he's *your* father,' Betty snapped. 'You promised to be more responsible and help me look after him a bit more when I took this job on. You know we need the money, Maisie, please . . .'

As her voice tailed off, Betty was pleased to see that her daughter's face softened. Of all her children, Maisie adored her father and would do anything for him. She had been devastated when he had joined the war effort at the age of forty-two earlier in April. Yet when he returned home bloody and battered with his arm blown clean off, Maisie had been stoic, offering support to not just her father but to Betty, as well.

The largest problem was that Violet hated George, and,

privately, Betty couldn't blame her. As for Betty's mother-in-law, Queenie, she too had lost all respect for her son, choosing only to speak to him if she had to, and preferring to be out as much as possible, always citing WVS business.

Betty more than understood. The truth was that Betty hadn't taken a job at the Palais because she needed the money – George's army pension was enough to take care of their simple needs. No, the truth was Betty couldn't stand to be in the house with her husband. For all these years, marriage between them had worked because Betty had put up with a lot from George, believing that as a wife it was her duty to do so. But after George returned from France, he had been a shell of his former self. As a loyal wife, Betty had vowed to help him, remembering her wedding vows – in sickness and in health. But the revelation he had fathered another child with Renee's sister had floored Betty. All she wanted to do was run away and get far away from Hammersmith. But that was impossible. And so Betty did the only thing she could: she got a job, meaning her waking hours with her husband were limited, which in some small way gave her the strength to continue with her marriage. She had worked hard to become a respectable wife and mother, she wouldn't lose that because of George's infidelity.

Glancing at Maisie, Betty felt a pang of guilt and set down the newspaper strips. Reaching for her bag and coat, Betty realised she didn't feel able to ask anything more of her daughter, not today.

'It's time for me to go, anyway,' she said, getting to her feet. 'If I leave now, hopefully he won't have got into too much mischief.'

At the gesture, Maisie's face visibly relaxed and Betty knew she was doing the right thing. She was just about to leave when Nancy burst in, her face beaming with pleasure.

'Everything all right?' Betty asked, surprised to see Nancy looking so happy.

When she had seen Nancy earlier, after Peter had announced

he wanted to leave school, the manager had looked like she was bearing the weight of the world on her shoulders.

'I've just had a very exciting meeting,' Nancy said, stalking across the room towards her desk and pulling out a notepad.

'About me joining the dancers' pen?' Maisie asked, hopefully.

At the question, Nancy paused and looked confused, her pen hovering over her pad. 'No, honey, this concerns your mother. Betty, have you got a minute?'

'Of course,' Betty replied.

She set down her coat and bag. George would just have to wait.

'I've just had a visit from Nora Lovell, from Howell & Smart,' Nancy explained.

'The chain of department stores?' Betty asked.

'Exactly.' Nancy nodded. 'When war broke out, they set up staff canteens so that, no matter what happened, their staff would have access to a hot meal.'

Betty knew of the scheme. She had a friend that worked at the Harlesden branch, who had been delighted that she could get something hot to eat for almost nothing when rations were so low.

'What's that got to do with us?' Betty asked.

'They want you, Betty,' Nancy declared, her eyes flashing with excitement.

'Me?' Betty echoed in disbelief.

'Yes, you! They were so impressed with the way you managed the community event here at the Palais, that they want your help with their latest idea. They wanna roll out this thing called "National Restaurants". Basically, a place for everyone to get a hot meal for next to nothing. It's to help those that have been bombed out.'

'Don't the WVS do that?' Betty asked, thinking how Queenie was always complaining that she was ladling out bowls of soup to the needy and ungrateful.

'They do,' Nancy agreed. 'But this would be on a much

bigger scale and they want the Palais – and you, of course – to be involved.'

'But how does this help the Palais?' Maisie asked.

Nancy frowned at the question. 'It shows we're about more than just getting a dollar . . . a *sixpence* . . . out of a customer. It shows we care about the country.'

Maisie cocked her head to one side, her golden curls bouncing on her shoulders as she did so. 'It's not a bad advertising idea, I grant you.'

'Maisie!' Betty admonished, as Nancy laughed.

'She's right, Bet. It does make us look good, and at very little cost to us. Howell & Smart will pay for all the food and resources, but they need manpower to help manage the scheme,' Nancy said.

'I see.' Betty nodded.

'So how do you feel about helping Nora manage this operation, Betty? Are you happy to take it on? I know you have a lot to do, but the girls and Queenie could help you out, right?'

At the mention of helping out more at home, Maisie's face turned to thunder. But at that particular moment Betty didn't care. The idea of being a part of something real to help the nation was tantalising. Maisie would just have to lump it, and Violet – though Betty knew it was a lot to ask – might help, too, if only to just pop round to help with the housework while George was in bed. That was assuming, of course, that her eldest daughter felt better. Violet had been looking ever so peaky lately, so much so that Betty had pressed a bottle of malt extract into her hands, insisting it was a cure-all.

She began to have second thoughts, suddenly realising how much she was going to have to take on.

'I'd be proud to help, but, to be honest, would it eat into much of my time?' she said.

Nancy shook her head. 'I wouldn't ask you to work any extra

hours, and the hours you were with Howell & Smart we would pay you for, anyway,' she said, persuasively.

'Oh, right,' Betty said, brightening again to the idea. 'Well, perhaps I'll reconsider . . . Thank you very much.'

'Great,' Nancy said, looking pleased. 'We've a meeting with Nora's team in Oxford Street on Saturday, if you can make it. I think this is something the nation will really get behind, and it's exciting for all of us to be a part of it.'

As if to demonstrate the point, the telltale sound of the air-raid siren sounded in the distance and Betty's heart sank. Heaven only knew what time she would get in now.

Exchanging frustrated glances with the girls, they trooped in silence down to the basement of the Palais, seeking shelter. They were almost there when Maisie piped up, 'Can we talk about the dancers' pen now, Nancy?'

Three

Tracing her fingertips over the envelope, Renee Hammond smiled as she took in the sight of the familiar handwriting. Since moving to Manchester three months earlier, she found herself looking forward to her old friend Temperance's weekly letters, full as they often were with Palais news, such as what Bill and Edna had done now to upset Nancy and the rest of the dancers – and, in the process, the customers. Sometimes, though, Temperance would simply write pages filled with questions about dance, which gave Renee more pleasure than she could ever have imagined. For Renee there was no greater joy than talking about her great love in life – ballroom dancing.

There had been many casualties when she had left London for a new start, including her name. Now no longer known as Renee Hammond, she was Goldstein. Not only did it help keep her safe, but it was a tribute to her old friend Nancy, who would have used the name as a married woman if she hadn't stuck to Blum.

When Renee had moved from London, she had known she would miss her old life. But she hadn't expected to miss it as much as she did. At the Palais she had found a team of people she considered real friends, and although she recognised she hadn't treated them as well as she could have done, they didn't mean any less to her.

All her life, Renee had found herself backed into a corner, forced to do things she didn't want to do. At the Palais, she had felt as if there were times she could be her true self, and that was someone she hadn't been since she was a child. It had been a comfort, and now she had been forced to move, Renee clung to the memories she had made at the Palais like a child saying goodbye to its mother. But it had been losing her daily chats with Temperance that had been one of the hardest crosses to bear.

Renee had loved seeing her friend change. Having once been a timid, shy mouse, Temperance had emerged into a roaring, confident woman, and a dance instructor in her own right. Renee only wished she could have stayed in London to spend more time with her friend before she left, but it hadn't been possible – and that was Renee's biggest regret.

Now their weekly exchange of letters meant the world. There was nothing Renee loved more than the familiar sight of her friend's handwriting decorating her doormat. This Friday morning, four days before Christmas, Renee had got up in the only one-bedroom flat she could afford in Deansgate, which was luckily a stone's throw from the large dance hall she now worked in as chief dancer, and been delighted to find a letter from Temperance amongst the usual bills.

Tempted to dive in then and there, instead Renee had put the letter into her bag and got ready for work, promising herself she would enjoy half an hour with her friend during her tea break.

Now, as she nodded her good mornings to the general manager and MC, she hurried to the practice rooms ready to take her first class of the day.

'Hiya, everyone,' she said, just in time to welcome her pupils through the doors. 'As Christmas is just around the corner, I thought we might have a go at something new.'

'Like what? Giving Hitler the bum's rush?' one of the women, Irene, shouted.

Renee chuckled. As much as she loved the feisty Londoners, there was something about a strong northern woman that made her feel right at home.

'I think we'd all like a go at that, queen.'

'He wants stringing up,' Irene continued, warming to her theme. 'What he did to Coventry was shameful. He'll be coming here next, mark my words.'

Renee pinched her nose as the room erupted into mass chatter.

'I heard he was going to bomb the entire north,' someone else called.

'No, he's got his sights on bombing London first, till there's nothing left. What happened in Coventry was a warning.'

'A bloody warning?' Irene's pal, Rita jeered. 'I should give him a bloody warning, him or any of those filthy Jerries come this way, I'll knock seven bells out of 'em.'

'And where's the Yanks, eh?' said Irene. 'The Canadians are entering the war next week, sending their troops over here. Why ain't the Yanks joining 'em?'

''Cos they're a bunch of bleedin' cowards,' someone else chimed in.

'But I do love a Canadian,' another of the women said, a dreamy look on her face. 'I reckon they're ever so dishy.'

'All right, that's enough,' Renee said, clapping her hands together and rapidly losing the will to live. 'How about we forget Hitler and his band of merry men and concentrate on some dancing instead?'

Reluctantly, the women shuffled into order and Renee smiled, her nerves beginning to feel a little less frayed as the chatter ground to a halt.

'As Christmas is next week, I thought we'd do something a bit lively. So let's start with a quickstep.'

'That'll keep the Canadians on their toes,' Irene piped up again.

'It will as long as you're not treading on 'em,' Rita said, earning a peal of laughter from everyone else for her trouble.

Wordlessly, Renee walked over to the gramophone and

started to play something uptempo by one of the big bands. Turning the volume up as loud as she could, she was grateful that the women had started to pair up and begun to dance.

'Lovely, ladies, let's just warm up a bit,' she said, letting the music soothe her.

As she watched her pupils rotate clockwise around the floor, Renee tried not to think about how the Manchester dance hall was a world away from the Palais in London. True, the Manchester Crystal – as it was officially known – was certainly a draw, but her heart would always belong to the Palais. She wasn't sure if it was the people, the music, the space or just the atmosphere, but she'd felt she belonged there the moment she walked across the maple-sprung floor. But for now, the Crystal was home, and it wasn't a bad home, either: purpose-built with vaulted ceilings, large sash windows decorated with red velvet curtains and, just like at the Palais, a maple-sprung floor that was routinely packed at the weekend with dancers wanting to forget their troubles.

It was a beautiful space, there was no denying it. Not only that, Renee worked with a largely female team, including a wonderfully warm and witty MC named Janice Dobson. Janice knew just how to get a crowd in the mood on a Saturday night, no matter how many bombs Hitler dropped.

Judging from her pupils' comments, it was clear nobody had forgotten the devastating raid on Coventry last month. Hitler's brutal bombing campaign seemed to have wiped out the entire town, destroying the legendary cathedral and killing thousands of people. The lesson had been a harsh one, not just for Coventry but the whole country, as everyone realised Hitler was intent on bombing the life out of the entire country.

Consequently, the cities were on high alert which meant that when evenings rolled around, tensions were high. Most took out their frustrations on the dance floor, tuning into the waltz or a frantic quickstep with their partners. But, more recently, fights had broken out on the floor, which Renee had to admit had been expertly handled by Janice, who wasted no time throwing the troublemakers out on their ear.

An hour later and the dance class finished with as much energy as it had started. As Renee bade her pupils goodbye, she sat in the windowsill, enjoying a sudden burst of late December sunshine. Reaching for her bag, she fished out one of her trademark Craven A cigarettes, and, as she did so, her fingertips brushed against the envelope from Temperance. Delicately opening the letter she smiled, pleased to see her dear friend had written plenty of news.

12ᵗʰ December 1940

Dear Renee,

How are you? Hope you've settled into your new flat now and got that hob working. There's nothing nicer than a hot drink when you get in from work, is there? Though I expect you made do with a gin after a shift, as you usually did when you were here.

So much seems to happen in between these weekly letters that I think I ought to start writing daily! Firstly, Edna and Bill are still thick as thieves. Edna's started taking over my dance lessons in the pen, saying I haven't got enough experience! I know, I can hear you now, calling her a cheeky cow – I suppose she is, but she's right, I haven't got anywhere near as much experience as she has.

Nancy has stood up for me, but you know what it's like when Edna teams up with Bill – it's pointless trying to take 'em on. Nancy thinks it's only a matter of time before they start courting. We had a raid the other day nearby and the two of them were apparently cosying up to each other in the public shelter while we were all down in the basement. How true that is, I don't know, Reen – but when has the truth ever got in the way of a good story?

What I can tell you is that all hell broke loose that same day because Peter told Nancy he wants to leave school. She's gone mad. Refused to let him. But he's desperate. I think if he wants to leave, he should. He says he wants to be an apprentice at the Palais, learn everything from the ground up, but Nancy wants him to have an education. Bill's stepped in and said he thinks it's a good idea, as well, but I don't really think he means it – he's just seen an opportunity to get one over on Nancy!

As you can imagine, the atmosphere is icy. I'm sure the customers have sensed something too, but times are hard and I think everyone's just glad of an escape and that's what the Palais is.

I'm doing all right. There are some days I manage to forget what's happened, if you can believe it. Then I remember, and I feel so guilty that for a second it's like I'm losing Eamon all over again. I feel bad bringing this up, but I think you're the only one that really understands. Like me, you lost a sibling that awful night, and I can't stop picturing what happened to Eamon and worrying if he was hurt, if he was in pain, or if he was afraid. I know he had Violet with him, and that comforts me more than I think it probably comforts her. She looks haunted, Reen, properly haunted by what happened. I've tried talking to her, but she clams up. She's still living at Auntie Winnie's place but I think she should be at home. She needs her family around her. I've tried getting Maisie to talk to her, but she's got her own problems since she found out your Lizzie was pregnant with her dad's baby.

Not only that, there's practical things to think of. Eamon's wages are missed. Mum's putting a brave face on it all and saying she can manage, but I don't bring in enough, even with the tiny pay rise I had when I was promoted. I dunno what to do. Aunt Winnie says it'll all work out, but I'm not sure.

Otherwise, it's business as usual. Customers are still paying their sixpence for a dance in the pen. The girls are falling over themselves to learn the new dances. Daisy says she's sick to the back teeth of dancing the waltz with fellas that can't do a reverse turn. I've got a new lady that wants one-to-one lessons with me. She's the wife of a fancy hotelier who's got a hotel up west. They're both ever so nice to me, and Mrs Henshall says her dancing's come on leaps and bounds since she started with me. Mr Henshall's really pleased, too, and they've invited me round to their fancy hotel for a drink one night as a thank you! Can you believe it?

Anyway, I'll let you get on. That's all the news for this week. I hope to hear from you soon about what you've been doing. You stay safe and don't be a stranger.

Your friend,

Temperance xx

As Renee finished reading, she felt a surge of worry for her friend. Temperance really had been through a horrendous time following the loss of her brother. But as she pressed the letter to her heart, Renee felt a surge of gratitude that Temperance had at least been given the promotion she deserved and would find solace in dance. As Renee closed her eyes she could almost feel the heat of the Palais and smell the sweat of the dancers after they'd finished a turn around the floor. With the note still clutched to her chest, she looked out of the window at the industrial landscape of the city centre. Much to her surprise, the Palais had felt like home. Would this new city ever creep into her heart and take its place?

Four

Back in London, Friday morning dawned bright and clear and, as usual, Temperance had leaped out of bed determined to be the first one on the dance floor. Now, as she threw back the blackout blinds and snapped on the lights, she took a moment to admire the view. It was a scene she never tired of. Hammersmith Palais de Danse wasn't just the most luxurious dance hall in London, or even the country. It was the most prestigious in Europe and standing at the edge of the maple-sprung dance floor, Temperance could easily see why. When the former tram shed was transformed first into a skating rink – and then in 1919, the Palais – the architects involved were determined to create an ambitious Chinese theme. In homage, above Temperance stood the giant pagoda roof, complete with brightly coloured silk lanterns that hung from the ceiling. Elsewhere, lacquered-glass panels, each one elegantly decorated with Chinese scenes, were flanked by tall black columns with intricately painted gold lettering. In the middle of the floor stood an elegant, show-stopping mountain range. But it was the replica temple at the front of the dance hall that was the Palais showstopper. It was the perfect stage for either of the Palais' resident band leaders, Harry Leder or Oscar Reyburn. And visiting bands loved the novelty and luxurious setting that proved the Palais was pure glamour.

It was Renee who had introduced her to the magic of the Palais' empty dance floor. When Temperance had first started working there, Renee had taken her by the hand one evening, held her finger to her lips and shown her the true thrill of having the dance hall to herself.

'Here you can be the queen of your own destiny, and of all this splendour,' Renee had said, before gliding out to the floor and showcasing a series of steps she had been working on – a new tempo for a waltz, even one of the new American or Cuban dances, the rumba. Temperance had watched her from the shadows, lost in her own world and in her own steps. From then on, Temperance revelled in the freedom to experiment with her choreography, with no one else around, just the history and glamour of a world-class dance hall for company.

Temperance so appreciated everything Renee had taught her and she just wished her friend and mentor was here to share it with her. She knew that she was a talented instructor, but it was Renee who had championed and encouraged her, who had made sure she got the opportunity to prove her worth.

Not for the first time that day, she missed her friend. With Christmas now just four days away, emotions were running high for everyone. It was a tricky time of year at the best of times, with so much forced jollity. But this year would be tough without Eamon, and Temperance knew that Renee would be finding life difficult without her sister for the first time, no matter how much she tried to put a brave face on things. United in the loss of their siblings in the same wretched blast, Temperance and Renee had formed an unspoken but unbreakable bond.

Resolving to write again later, during her tea break, Temperance was just revelling in having the floor to herself for a few minutes, when she heard a rustling sound. She paused for a moment. To her left, near the bar, she heard it again.

'Hello,' she called, heart pounding. 'Who's there? We're not open yet.'

She tried not to give in to panic. She had been attacked in the Palais less than three months ago, and although she had tried hard to forget the assault she had endured at the competition dance, the memory still plagued her.

Slowly, a figure emerged from the shadows, and Temperance let out a sigh of relief. It was her friend and colleague, Violet.

'What are you doing down there?'

Violet gave a shaky smile. 'Just helping with a stocktake.'

'At eight in the morning?' Temperance said with a hint of incredulousness. She reached for her friend's hand and helped her to her feet. As she did so, she drank in Violet's appearance. She looked so pale. Her skin was almost grey, while her eyes had lost their familiar sparkle.

As always, Temperance's heart went out to her. Violet and Eamon hadn't been together long, but it was clear to everyone how much they loved one another. Temperance mourned for her brother every day, as did her mother, Enid, and her Aunt Winnie, who was now at their house so much she might as well have moved in.

Despite their grief, they had all started moving forward. Enid had found purpose in doing her bit for the war effort, throwing herself into her WVS work, together with Violet's grandmother, Queenie. The two of them regularly helped out with clothing drives, make-do-and-mend workshops and first-aid demonstrations. It was just what Enid needed to help her cope with the loss of her son so soon after losing her husband. Winnie, too, had thrown herself into work, ensuring that the West End theatre she ran operated like a well-oiled machine. And Temperance had committed to her dance duties, sailing through her exams to make her brother proud, and now working as hard as she possibly could to not just be a successful dance instructor but a successful black woman, too. Temperance took her responsibility as a woman of colour to show the world just what she could do very seriously.

But Violet was struggling. She was listless, tired and didn't seem to find joy in anything. When she had first joined the Palais in April of that year, she had talked about never being reliant on a man and wanting to carve out a fulfilling career for herself. But now, although Violet was always punctual, Temperance could see that she found no joy in her work anymore. She was not living so much as just existing, and Temperance was desperate to reach out and offer help.

As Violet turned away, Temperance reached for her hand. Spinning her friend gently towards her, she looked into her eyes.

'Vi, please talk to me,' she tried. 'I know you're heartbroken but I just want to help.'

Violet gazed at the floor. 'You can't help. Nobody can.'

'That's not true, Vi,' Temperance said. 'If Eamon could see you now, he'd be devastated. He'd hate seeing you like this.'

'I know,' Violet whispered.

At this admission, Temperance blanched in surprise.

'I hate myself,' Violet continued, as if Temperance wasn't there. 'I hate myself for feeling that I can't carry on, when I know one of the things Eamon loved about me was my strength.'

The words touched something in Temperance's heart and she reached for Violet's hand once more.

'He would still love you, no matter what. Don't hate yourself, you're grieving.'

'So are you,' Violet shot back. 'And you're not carrying on unable to get through each day, not like me. I'm pathetic.'

'Violet, that's the last thing you are,' Temperance insisted. 'You're hurting, and we all cope with that hurt in different ways.'

Violet only shook her head, and Temperance knew that nothing she could say would help, at least not now.

'Look, just know that I'm here, all right?' she tried again. 'We all are.'

At that Violet looked up at her, and for one brief moment, Temperance hoped that Violet might talk to her.

But just as Violet opened her mouth to speak, the sound of footsteps echoed behind them.

Whirling around, Temperance came face to face with Ann and Nigel Henshall, who were looking apologetic.

'I'm sorry . . . are we early?' Nigel said hesitantly.

Temperance collected herself and shook her head. 'Not at all. Why don't you make your way to the practice rooms and get set up.'

As Temperance gestured for them to make their way along the corridor, Violet walked over to her coat, which was lying over a barstool. She shrugged it on and then walked out without a backward glance. Temperance watched her go, wishing once again that she could find some way to help. After all, there wasn't just Violet to think of.

Making her way to the practice room, her heart heavy, Temperance fixed a smile on her face as she greeted the Henshalls. Mrs Henshall was the only private client she had and she knew how much it meant to Nancy that she had been able to secure this piece of business. The hope was that if they liked what Temperance did, the Henshalls would direct some of their guests towards the Palais, and she was only too happy to try and help.

'So, we've got the Valentine's Day dance coming up in February,' Temperance said brightly, now. 'How about we make sure you have mastered the foxtrot by then, Mrs Henshall? You could confidently swap partners for that one, then.'

At the idea, Mrs Henshall looked flustered and her husband laid a hand on her shoulder to calm her down.

'That's a wonderful idea, sweetheart. Something to aim for.'

'Do you really think I could do that?'

'Temperance wouldn't have suggested it if you couldn't,' Mr Henshall said firmly.

'Excellent,' Temperance beamed.

Flipping though the records she used to teach her lessons, she slipped on something joyful by a big band.

'Now, I want you to show me how you've been practising your footwork,' she called above the music.

Eagerly, Mrs Henshall got to work, demonstrating all Temperance had taught her. As she watched the older woman concentrate on keeping her head straight and her elbows high, Temperance felt Mr Henshall sidle up beside her.

'She's doing well?' he asked.

'Very well,' Temperance confirmed.

'Will she be ready for Valentine's Day?'

'Of course,' Temperance assured him. Turning to look at the hotelier, she could see he looked worried. 'Why?'

'We've got some important guests coming over and we have promised to take them to the Palais, give them a good night out.'

'I see.' Temperance nodded. 'Well, then, let's make sure you and Mrs Henshall can put on a show for your guests.'

Relief passed across the hotelier's face and Temperance felt concerned.

'Is everything all right?'

'Fine.' Mr Henshall gave a brief nod of his head. 'Well, you know what the entertainment business is like these days. Hard for all of us with this damned war. I'm not sure how we'll survive if things keep going like this.'

'Things aren't that bad, are they?' Temperance asked in alarm.

'No, I'm sure they're not . But it's hard, what with rations hitting us at every turn. We're a luxury hotel, our overseas guests have standards . . . expectations . . . And while they're very accommodating, you try telling a Georgian oligarch he can't have eggs for breakfast because they're rationed. Then, of course, we're having to turn down certain guests. In the past we have always welcomed German and Italian visitors, now we can't host them any longer. I don't know where it's going to end. We were promised this war would be over by last Christmas, but now look at us.'

As Mr Henshall brought his impassioned speech to a close, he looked stricken.

'I'm sorry, Temperance, I shouldn't have said all that.'

'Not at all,' Temperance replied, a feeling of knowing eating away at her. 'Trust me, it's better to get things off your chest. Secrets eat away at you.'

Five

Nancy sat in the bar area of the Palais that Friday night, trying to allow the music to lift her spirits. As she raised a glass half full of gin and orange, she watched the dancers whirl around the floor in a simple veleta that never failed to make the customers smile. If only it would have the same effect on her. Despite her anger, she had tried to be supportive of Peter since he'd made his shock announcement last week. At first, she'd tried to reason with him to stay in school, but he wouldn't have it, and Nancy knew she couldn't make him, no matter how much she thought he was making a mistake. Besides, she couldn't find anyone to back her up.

Taking another sip of her drink, she thought about her husband, Alex. Would things be different if he was here? Would Peter have had more respect for a man's word over hers? She shrugged. Who knew? The simple fact was that Alex wasn't here. And if she was truly honest with herself, he hadn't really been 'present' in the two or three months before he had joined up, either. When they had first met, ten years earlier, Nancy and Alex had been inseparable. Before that, she had always thought she would return to her native New York, but somehow with him in her orbit, she'd felt as if she would never need to be anywhere else, with anyone else, again. Not as long as she had Alex by her side.

They laughed at the same things, enjoyed the same food and music, looked at the world the same way, and crucially they both adored the Palais, wanting nothing more than to give it their all and make it the very best dance hall in the world. Alex hadn't been sure about Nancy working, but he had never stopped her, and they'd both assumed that when they had a family things would change. They had expected to have children, of course, but for some reason it had never happened. And much as Nancy hated to admit it, she knew that this had driven a small but silent wedge between them. The effort of pretending that they were enough for one another without children was becoming harder over the years. Of course they were still committed to and enjoyed the same things, but something between them had shifted. When Alex had been called up, her first thought had been one of relief, quickly followed by guilt, but she hoped that time apart might give them a chance to miss one another.

And so, in her letters to Alex, Nancy had tried to be more loving and supportive. Not only did she tell him how much she missed him, but she confided in him about matters regarding the Palais, hoping that would bring them closer together. When she wrote to tell him how she was taking in Ruth and Peter, Alex had been delighted. For the first few weeks, she could hear the excitement in his voice as he chatted about these new additions to the family in his letters back to her. Yet as time passed, the familiar distance returned, and then Alex suggested that if she had problems she should talk to his mother.

Nancy would rather stick pins her eyes than talk to the old cow that was her mother-in-law, but of course she didn't say that to Alex. Then again, she thought, watching Violet move slowly across the floor towards the ticket booth, perhaps she should? She would love to see Alex's face. But honestly, she would rather just have the support of a husband that loved her no matter what.

Shaking her head free of these thoughts, Nancy picked up her glass and now that the dance had finished, made her way over to the ticket booth to talk to Violet, who was standing with Maisie.

'Everything all right tonight?' she asked them.

As usual the Millington sisters were working silently away together and the sight tugged at Nancy's heart. When they had started work at the Palais in April, they had been so full of life and excited about all the possibilities ahead of them.

But so much had changed in the last few months.

Violet lifted her head and gave a ghost of a smile as she nodded. 'All quiet. No air-raid sirens tonight, either, which has kept everyone in a good mood.'

'Yes, I'd hoped we might have a free night tonight as it's been so foggy,' Nancy said.

Lifting the lid of the ticket booth, she watched Maisie rifle through the ticket stubs and felt another pang of sadness. With Renee gone, Eamon's death and the almost nightly raids in the city, it was hard to find the strength to keep going some days.

'Anyway,' she said, wanting to get to the point. 'I was hoping you would be able to help me with Peter.'

Violet frowned. 'He's leaving school, isn't he?'

Nancy nodded. 'That's right. He's going to be starting an apprenticeship here and I thought he might start with you next week, Maisie, in the ticket booth.'

'All right.' Maisie beamed, a look of delight passing across her features. 'I'll show him how to make sure Helena never gets lumbered with old Mr Jennings.'

Violet laughed and the sight was such an unexpected tonic that Nancy couldn't resist joining in. 'Old Twinkle Toes? Yes, Renee always ended up with him, didn't she?'

'And now that she's not here, he always asks for Helena.' Maisie laughed. 'She said she'd kick him in the shins if she had to dance with him again.'

'No, Maisie, she said she'd kick *you* in the shins if she had to dance with him again,' Violet pointed out wryly.

'Well, whatever she said, I think the ticket booth would be a good place for Peter to learn,' Nancy continued. 'I've got him with Eric the storesman, lifting and carrying, then I thought he could help you out in the afternoons, Maisie.'

'All right,' Maisie nodded. 'We're busier than usual now, 'cos of Christmas, so it'll be nice to have some help. And of course if I'm in the pen as a dancer then an extra pair of hands here would be welcome.'

Nancy smiled wryly. Maisie Millington was more like her father than Violet, in her cheek and in her looks. She knew the girl had been desperate to join the dancers' pen for months since she had done so well at the Palais' dance competition last September and, in fairness, Nancy thought it was only right Maisie had a spot. She had worked hard and earned it.

'All right, then.' She nodded. 'We'll start with two afternoons a week and see how it goes.'

Joy spread across Maisie's open face. 'You won't regret it!'

Nancy grinned. 'I'd better not.' Then, glancing at the group, she said, 'Speaking of Christmas, I wondered what you guys were doing?'

At the question, the Millington sisters looked embarrassed.

'I'm going to Temperance's,' Violet said. 'She's asked if I want to spend it with her and her family.'

'And I'll be at home, *not* breaking Mum's heart,' Maisie said, looking resentful. 'Isn't it enough that Mum's lost Roy this year? You could at least sit down at the table with her, Vi.'

A look of fury passed across Violet's face. 'I've told you, I'm going nowhere near that man. While he's still under Betty's roof, I'm not interested.'

'You're so selfish, Violet,' Maisie hissed. '*I* have to put up with Dad after what he did to Ma, why can't you?'

'I'm not saying it's easy, Maisie,' Violet said, her eyes filling with tears. 'You have to do what you have to do. I just can't be near him.'

'Girls, please,' Nancy said, holding up a hand to call for calm. 'The only reason I ask is because I wanna invite you all here in the evening.'

'On Christmas Day?' Maisie quizzed.

'Uh uh.' Nancy nodded. 'As you know, being Jewish we don't celebrate Christmas, but I know how important it is and I know how emotional it can be during the holidays when loved ones aren't with us.'

There was a pause then, as each of the Palais women thought of those that weren't by their sides this holiday season. For Nancy, despite her conflicted feelings about their marriage, Alex would be sorely missed.

'Which is why I thought it would be nice to have a little gathering in the evening,' she went on brightly. 'It will be Ruth and Peter's first Christmas with us, and that's something worth celebrating.'

'Well, I'd like that,' Violet said hesitantly.

'Me, too,' Maisie agreed. 'Thanks, Nancy.'

'My pleasure.' Nancy beamed. A wave of relief pulsed through her. To be honest, the idea had only just come to her, but for some reason it was important to her that the Millington family came together at Christmas. It was a time for healing past wounds and building bridges, and Nancy very much wanted to be a part of that.

'What about Temperance?' she asked suddenly, spotting her chief dance instructor talking to a rather tall man in the corner of the room. 'Will she come?'

'I dunno,' Maisie said with a shrug. 'She might do.'

Nancy watched Temperance, who seemed engrossed in conversation.

'Who is that?' she asked.

'Nigel Henshall,' Violet replied. 'He's that hotelier with a couple of posh places in Piccadilly.'

Nancy frowned. 'What does he want with Temperance?'

Maisie finished selling a pair of dances to a returning customer before replying. 'He comes in quite a bit. They've been talking for a while,' she said, 'Temperance has been teaching his wife to dance.'

'OK.' Nancy nodded, though she frowned as she watched Temperance continue chatting to Mr Henshall. She knew Temperance was heartbroken over the loss of her brother, but she hoped the girl wasn't about to do something daft. She might not be Temperance's mother, but she was her friend, and what happened to the girls at the Palais mattered very much to Nancy and it always would.

Six

It didn't matter where you were in the world, Renee thought as she sat in a cafe opposite the Crystal, eating a slice of bread and dripping. For her, every Saturday evening since she had been old enough to make a living from dancing was the the same.

A quick wash with pitcher and jug, then Renee made sure her dancing shoes were polished and her dress steamed and pressed, before she set off to arrive at the dance hall early to check that the hall was clean and the dancers knew what they were doing for any exhibition dances they might be performing. She would then run through any last-minute choreography. Once she had chatted with the pen manager about how many dances they could accept, Renee would nip out to whatever cafe was closest and treat herself to something to eat – a lukewarm cuppa and a cigarette. It was a ritual she had enjoyed for years.

Sitting by the window and watching the Christmas shoppers scurry through the city, the grey clouds casting a shadow over their movements, Renee felt a pang of sympathy for them. There was nothing in the shops this year, with window displays scant as shopkeepers did their best to make the best of what little they had. As for decorations, there were none of those, either, with all the paper and aluminium going to the war effort.

Renee closed her eyes and thought of her childhood Christmasses. They too had been filled with scraps. There had never been much money to go around, with every penny her father earned going straight from his pocket to the tote. Her poor long-suffering mother, Mavis, had done her best to keep Dad on the straight and narrow. She'd even insisted he hand over his wages so she could take the housekeeping the moment he got home. Even then, Renee's dad had been crafty and simply not gone home until his pay packet had been spent.

Taking a deep inhalation of her cigarette, Renee shook her head. She had no idea how her mother had found the money to bring up her and Lizzie, but then she supposed that behind every mother there was a desire to look after her brood, no matter what. It must have taken its toll, though, since Mavis had dropped dead when Renee was just fourteen years old. From then on Renee's world had become chaos, with her father dragging her towards an uncertain and abusive future, thanks to the gambling habit he couldn't give up, no matter how hard he tried. Renee had tried to blame Ronnie over the years for her father's debts. She had told herself that any man worth his salt would never have allowed a man like her father to get into so much trouble, but deep down Renee knew that the fault lay squarely at her father's door. It was him she had to thank for being forced into a violent, unhappy marriage to settle his debts.

Shaking her head, Renee tried to bring her thoughts back to the present. She looked again at the shoppers staring mournfully into the empty windows, no doubt remembering Christmasses in the Great Depression when things had been scarce. The only ones who had profited back then had been the black marketeers, and no doubt it would be that same band of tawdry men that would profit this Christmas, too. Renee took another drag on her cigarette, as Ronnie invaded her thoughts once more. She knew with certainty that these men would use whatever tactics they wanted to get hold of illegal goodies and sell them to the desperate at inflated prices. Reluctantly, she wondered what Ronnie was doing this Christmas; untouched by the country's scarcity, he'd ensure he had the biggest goose on the table and presents for his nearest and dearest in plentiful supply. There would be no piece of coal thoughtfully wrapped at the bottom of *his* stocking – more likely a nugget of gold!

Just the thought of Ronnie made Renee shudder. She'd hoped that she had successfully managed to lose whatever tail he had on her down in London since she had changed her last name and moved north.

When her sister Lizzie's husband had passed away before the war, Renee had used his death as an excuse to leave her husband high and dry in Liverpool and create a new life for herself, away from his tyranny and his criminal lifestyle. Naturally, she had ended up in London, where Lizzie now lived, and for a time it had been wonderful, the two of them under one roof again just as they had been as children. Ronnie, of course, had expected her to go back but Renee never had, and though Ronnie was not exactly Brain of Britain, he wasn't stupid, either. He'd tracked her all over the country, including London, sending her letters at the Palais. Renee knew that it was only a matter of time before he caught up with her, and when he did she knew there would be hell to pay. The question was, how she would deal with it? It was something that had been running through her mind ever since she'd got to Manchester.

Stubbing her cigarette out, Renee reached for her bag and was about to get to her feet when she saw Janice, the Crystal's MC, walk through the door.

'Hiya, Renee, love.' Janice smiled, ordering herself a cuppa from the man behind the counter. 'Thought the pub would be more your style of an early evening.'

Renee raised an eyebrow. 'You casting aspersions on my good name?'

'Not at all, it's where I'd be if the pub was nearer.' Janice laughed, taking the tea and sitting opposite Renee. 'You don't mind, do you, love?'

Shaking her head, Renee took a moment to observe Janice. She was in her early fifties, with silver hair and a smile that would light up the darkest of coal pits. She had clearly been a beauty in her day, and although she had a husband and children she had devoted herself to a life in entertainment. Janice's passion for people's pleasure shone through every dance she called, and she was as natural an MC as Renee had ever come across. Warm and witty, but with a natural respect that commanded the attention of audiences. Bill Cain could learn more than a thing or two from Janice, Renee thought grimly, as she took a sip of her tea.

'Should be busy tonight,' Renee said, 'just three days before Christmas.'

Janice frowned. 'I'm not sure, to be honest with you, love. With the country the way it is and money in such short supply, along with everything else, most folks could well be at home for the night.'

'You reckon?' Renee asked, a hint of incredulity to her voice.

'I really don't know,' Janice said with a sigh. 'I can't tell what's going to happen one day to the next. After what went on in Liverpool yesterday, I don't think any of us could, or should, predict the future.'

At the mention of her hometown, Renee's face darkened. The news of the previous day's blasts, courtesy of the Jerries, had shocked her far more than anything that had happened in London.

'You grew up there, didn't you?' Janice asked.

'Aye, not far from Toxteth,' Renee replied.

'You got family up there still?'

'None that matters,' Renee said grimly.

For a second, Janice looked surprised at Renee's remarks, then recovered herself. Looking out of the window at the clear skies, she now looked thoughtful.

'It's another good night for a raid off the Jerries,' she offered. 'Some folks are saying Hitler'll have a go round here, next.'

'Never in this world. What's round here for him?' Renee exclaimed.

Janice shrugged. 'We're not far from Liverpool. Perhaps he'll have another go at them, and call on us while he's at it. He's the sort of bloke that likes to spread misery around.'

Renee raised a smile. 'I've met a few blokes like that.'

'Like I say,' Janice said shucking off her grey wool coat, 'I couldn't tell you what's going to happen. But the only thing I do know, is that if I don't call a dance for Emmy Mattherson tonight my life won't be worth living.'

At the mention of the regular customer and her family, Renee chuckled. 'Isn't it her daughter's twenty-first today?'

'It is. And she's booked our only male dancer in the pen for dances with all her family tonight,' Janice finished.

'Oh, Christ. John'll be doing his pieces.' Renee sighed.

She shuddered at the thought of their only male dancer, who at the best of times had a face on him that would make a glass eye cry.

'I'd better get back and check he's all right,' she said, getting to her feet.

She was just about to walk away, when Janice laid a hand on her forearm. 'Oh, I meant to say, have a word with Linda when you get back.'

Renee frowned. Linda was the front-desk manager. 'Why?'

'She said some woman was looking for you earlier.'

'A woman?' Renee frowned. 'Was it a customer?'

Janice shook her head. 'Linda didn't say. She left a message, though, whoever it was. Something about a fella called Ronnie who'll see you later. I'm not sure to be honest, love, Linda's got the details, she can tell you proper like who the woman was and what exactly she said.'

Ronnie. She should have known. At the mention of her husband, Renee's blood ran cold. She'd known it was only a matter of time before he found her, but she had hoped to manage a little longer before she fell into his clutches again. And this was just his style, sending a chilling message through someone else, all wrapped up in the guise of innocence. A sweet enquiry from an unsuspecting woman he'd probably charmed in the pub to do him a favour. Renee supposed he'd got sick of writing letters, or reckoned she'd be wise to them by now so he needed to up his game, change tactics. Let her know without question that he still had a hold over her. That no matter where she went he would always find her.

'You all right, Renee, love?' Janice quizzed, a look of concern flaring across her face.

Renee managed a brief nod of her head. 'Fine, chuck. Just thinking about tonight. I'd better get back. I'll see you over there, yeah?'

And before Janice had a chance to reply, Renee had rushed out of the cafe and onto the rain-soaked street, her heart beating so fast she wondered if she might pass out.

She sniffed. The smell of burning scorched the air, and for a second Renee wondered if it was the stench of Liverpool burning, reminding her she could run, but she could never truly escape the city that still held her in its clutches.

Seven

Back at the Palais, cold winter sunlight streamed through the windows of the dance hall. If Temperance closed her eyes, she could almost pretend she was somewhere else, far away, on holiday with her family. Margate, perhaps. If she tried really hard, she could smell the salt in the air, hear the waves crash against the rocky shoreline and taste the ice cream from the stand on the seafront.

'Oi! Stop bloody daydreaming.' Bill Cain's sharp London undertones cut across her thoughts, bringing her swiftly back to the present.

'Sorry, Mr Cain,' she mumbled, opening her eyes,

'I should think so, an' all,' he said.

As Temperance got to her feet, she saw Peter standing shyly behind Bill, and she gave him a welcoming smile to ease the tension. She knew it was never easy to witness one of the legendary MC's dressing downs.

'Peter's going to start learning the ropes with you today,' Bill barked. 'Make sure you show him everything.'

Temperance frowned. 'But I'm not on the cloakroom, any-more. That's Maisie's job.'

At this rebuke, she saw a look of confusion pass across his face before he growled. 'I know that.'

'So, you want him to help me teach dance?' Temperance asked with a hint of hesitation.

She felt confused. Peter was supposed to be learning the ropes with Maisie and Violet today.

Right on cue, Violet and Maisie walked through the doors and smiled in welcome as they saw Peter.

'You're with us today.' Maisie smiled.

Taking off her hat and coat and hanging them in the booth, Temperance couldn't help but notice how light the younger of the Millingtons seemed these days. Temperance couldn't put her finger on it, but the more Maisie blossomed, the more Violet seemed upset and despondent in contrast. Temperance watched Violet now, pulling off her coat as though it was made of lead not wool, and arching her back.

'Vi, hurry up,' Maisie said bossily to her sister. 'Peter wants to learn the ropes *today*, not next week.'

'All right,' Violet snapped. 'Just give me a minute, I didn't sleep well.'

Maisie winked at her audience before she said, 'Yeah, I'll bet, with all that space to yourself. Your Auntie Winnie's spending a lot of time round yours again, ain't she, Temp?'

'A bit.' Temperance shrugged. 'I think she and Mum are keeping each other company.'

'Unlike old Vi here, who don't want no company,' Maisie tried again.

Peter and Temperance exchanged awkward looks.

'Do you know I've even offered to move in with her, but you won't hear of it, will you, Vi?' Maisie continued.

'Because it's not *my* place, is it?' Violet said, stifling a yawn. 'Come on, Maisie, don't air your dirty drawers in public, it's not fair on poor Peter.'

'I'm fine,' Peter said stiffly.

'Well, I'm not,' Bill thundered, causing Temperance to jump. She had almost forgotten he was there. 'You two are paid to work, not dawdle. Violet, Nancy wants you in the office after you've lent a hand down here.'

Violet looked at him in surprise. 'But I thought there was a problem here that had to be sorted.'

Bill shook his head. 'No. Nancy says there's some paperwork she needs you to go through, before she and your mother go up Howell & Smart's offices later. Needs you to sign something or other.'

'Oh.' Violet looked wrong-footed, but didn't have time to say anything else as Bill left abruptly, muttering under his breath and leaving Peter with them.

'Shall we get you started, then?' Maisie said, as Temperance looked helplessly between Peter and Violet.

It was as the young boy neared the door to the ticket booth that Violet suddenly clamped a hand over her mouth and fled from behind the desk.

'Violet,' Temperance cried as she rushed past her.

Only Maisie rolled her eyes. 'She's been moaning all day every day that she feels sick. Attention-seeking, if you ask me.'

'Maisie!' Temperance said, rounding on her friend. 'Violet looks terrible, how can you talk about your sister like that?'

'Shall I go and get her some water?' Peter asked, looking for all the world as if he wanted to be elsewhere.

Temperance shook her head. 'I'll go. Peter, get Maisie to tell you exactly how she does things so you can help with the tea dance later.'

'But Mr Cain said I was to go with Mrs Millington to Oxford Street this afternoon,' Peter protested, his dark hair falling into his eyes and making him look younger than he really was. For a moment, Temperance wondered if Nancy was right. He suddenly seemed far too young to be in this world of entertainment, with all its foibles.

This time, Maisie shook her head. 'Trust me, you'll be better off here with me. If you think Violet's trouble, you don't want to spend time with my old ma when she's got it about her.'

Not sure whether to laugh or scold, Temperance scurried out of the dance hall and along the corridor towards the ladies toilets. Pushing the door open, she heard the distinctive sound of retching coming from one of the cubicles.

Tapping lightly on the door, Temperance hesitated before she spoke. 'Vi, it's me. Are you all right?'

There was silence, save for the flushing water. Then the sound of Violet getting to her feet, before the door opened and Temperance came face to face with a very green-looking Millington sister.

'What's the matter?' she whispered. 'I know you've just been sick.'

Violet wiped the back of her hand with her mouth. 'It's worse mid-morning. It's why Maisie thinks I'm so grumpy.'

'Maisie doesn't know, then?' Temperance tried again.

Violet shook her head. 'Nobody but you.'

As Violet's eyes rested on hers, Temperance felt a wave of love for her friend. She reached out her arms and pulled her towards her.

'I'll help you, you know I will.'

'Thanks,' Violet said into her shoulder. 'I just feel very alone right now, Temp.'

Temperance clutched Violet tighter in her arms. She didn't deserve to feel like this, no woman did. 'You're not alone, you've got me for a start. I'll make sure you're all right.'

'But I can't keep this a secret for much longer,' Violet said, sobbing now into Temperance's shoulder and soaking her blouse.

Temperance said nothing for a moment and just stroked her friend's head. Violet was in a terrible situation and she didn't envy her. But at the same time, there was something so beautiful and timely about it. To her, it seemed as if her brother was going to live on.

'You know how proud Eamon would be if he could see you now, don't you?' she said, releasing Violet from her arms and clutching her hands.

'He'd be heartbroken he wasn't here to help me,' Violet said, her voice trembling as she spoke. 'He wouldn't have left me in the lurch, like some blokes would.'

'No, he would never have done that,' Temperance said fiercely. She'd known how much honour her brother had, and how much love he had for Violet. He would have seen this as happy news, an excuse for them to get married, because Temperance was certain that was what he'd wanted, and that had been on his mind the moment he had laid eyes on Violet.

'How far along are you?' she asked.

'About four months,' Violet said, her eyes red and swollen from tears. 'I know I'm going to have to tell my family soon, and everyone here.'

As she said the words aloud, Violet's face transformed into a picture of shock and Temperance had to pull her in towards her shoulder again.

'It's gonna be tough, love,' she consoled her. 'But you'll survive. Your family love you, they'll understand.'

At that Violet let out a snort of laughter. 'You've met my mother, Temp. She thought working here was a sin, what's she gonna say about me having a bun in the oven out of wedlock?'

Despite the situation, Temperance found herself laughing. 'But Betty came round to the Palais in the end, didn't she? In fact she came round so much she ended up working here herself.'

'I know, but I think this is a bit different, Temp. She's gonna do her pieces. And gawd knows what Queenie and Maisie will say. I just hope your Auntie Winnie won't fling me out on me ear.'

'She won't,' Temperance assured her. 'Remember, Aunt Winnie runs a theatre up West. She knows more about what goes in life than you think. What matters now is making sure you're all right. What do you need?'

'For Eamon to still be alive,' Violet said, her voice trembling.

'I wish I could bring him back for you,' Temperance said, her own voice faltering as she mentioned her brother's name.

'Is it worth you asking Nancy if you can come in later, that way you don't have to keep throwing up at work?'

Violet shook her head. 'I'm in the office most days, now. I don't think I could get away with it.'

Temperance thought for a moment. 'What if we told Nancy the truth? You have to start telling people soon and Nancy's a woman of the world, she won't kick you out.'

Panic flooded across Violet's face. 'I can't.'

'Then, what's your plan? Keep it a secret, forever and a day? Wear baggy blouses and nip to the loo one day and come back with a baby – shouting, surprise!'

Violet managed a smile at that. 'I can't face it yet.'

'Maybe so, but this baby's coming whether you're ready or not and you're going to have to get yourself in order.'

At the bluntness of Temperance's words, Violet nodded miserably. 'I just don't know where to start. I mean, I can't go home. Where am I gonna live? How am I gonna provide for a kid as well as myself? There's a reason people don't do this on their own – babies belong in families, not to single women,' she said. 'This should be a happy time, but it's such a mess.'

Tears rolled down her face as she slumped to the floor. Temperance sat down beside her and held her hand, leaning her head against Violet's shoulder. It was warm and she smelled of lemons and cinnamon.

'If there's one thing I'm learning in life, Vi, it's that life hardly ever works out how you plan it. But you will be all right. You're going to be this little baby's family,' she said. 'And so will I.'

Snaking a hand around Violet's waist, she gently laid her palm against her friend's stomach and felt content for the first time since Eamon's death. She didn't have much to offer but she would make sure that Violet and her child . . . Temperance's niece or nephew . . . would be well cared for – of that the whole of Hammersmith could be sure.

Eight

Boarding the trolley bus that would take them to the heart of Oxford Street, Nancy gazed out of the grime-smeared window at the scenes of devastation across the city that she had come to call home. Although Hitler had mainly wiped out the east of the city, he hadn't left the west alone. The near-nightly bombing raids had become almost a soundtrack to the evening, and Nancy wondered if or even when they would ever end.

As the bus passed mounds of debris and rubble, she felt a pang of sadness at the bombed-out houses and signs of life called to an abrupt halt. No matter where she fixed her gaze, she could see partially decimated homes, each bearing cracked mirrors or crooked pictures, washing still on the line, amidst the debris waiting for an owner that would never return to come and claim the soot-stained skirts and blouses.

'You think we'll ever get used to this?' Nancy asked suddenly, as the bus rounded the corner towards Marble Arch.

'The bombs?' Betty had a hint of wistfulness to her tone. 'I hope not. If we ever do, it's a sign we've given up, isn't it? That we've got used to Jerry and his madness.'

'I guess you're right,' Nancy replied as the bus pulled up to their stop. 'I just thought that maybe if we could get used to it, then maybe we could all stop living in fear.'

Betty stopped suddenly in the gangway, causing the woman behind her to tsk loudly in her direction.

'You're never afraid of anything, Nancy Blum,' she said, aghast.

Nancy turned her thick work scarf into the collar of her coat as she stepped off the bus and into the cold December air. 'Since Peter and Ruth came to live with us, I feel more afraid than ever, knowing I'm responsible for two little lives. I dunno, honey, the world seems a scarier place, somehow. I want to keep those kids safe, they've already been through so much.'

'Spoken like a true parent,' Betty said.

At the term 'parent' being applied to her, Nancy felt a flush of pleasure. It was a role she hadn't known quite how much she wanted, but now that she was in charge of Peter and Ruth she wanted to give them the world and keep them safe.

'D'you think you ever stop worrying about your kids?' she asked Betty, as they made their way along the debris-strewn road, and she smiled at the team of volunteers helping to sweep and clear the fallout of Hitler's latest attack.

'Never!' declared Betty. 'Being a parent never stops. Not even when they're adults and they leave home.'

'You mean Violet?' Nancy asked, cutting to the core of the matter.

'Of course, Violet,' Betty sighed.

Nancy looked at her newest employee for a second. With the same raven-dark hair and green eyes as her daughter, Nancy could see Betty would have been a knock-out when was younger. She would have had her pick of the men. Why on earth she had settled for someone like George, who was clearly beneath her, Nancy wasn't sure.

'Still trouble there, huh?' she probed softly.

Betty shrugged, her threadbare coat brushing the tips of her earlobes as she did so. 'Violet's always been strong-willed and independent.'

'Oh yeah?'

'Yes. She's always wanted her own way. Always got it, too. Just like her brother.' At the mention of her late son, Roy, Betty's eyes grew misty. 'But I love the bones of her, and sure I wouldn't change a thing about her, even though she drives me potty half the time.'

'And I take it she won't even think about moving back home?' Nancy quizzed.

'No, she won't,' Betty said, stoically. 'And, to be honest, I can't say as I blame her. I blame George myself for what happened to Eamon that dreadful night, so God alone knows how Violet must be feeling. But, anyway, we've other things to consider now . . .' Betty smoothly moved the conversation along to another subject. 'What exactly will Nora Lovell want me to be doing this morning? I'm not expected to turn out a tray of scones with nothing more than a bag of reconstituted egg, am I?'

At the thought, Betty looked so serious and worried, it was all Nancy could do not to fall about laughing.

'Nothing like that, honey, don't worry. They're already impressed with you, and I don't think the cooking you'll be called upon to do would be much more than the home cooking you prepare for your family. This is just a chance to get to know them a little better, that's all. Work out practicalities, that sort of thing.'

Betty gave a tight nod of her head and Nancy felt an almost protective-like streak towards her. To enter the workforce at forty-three was an achievement in itself, never mind with all the problems Betty had to deal with at home. As they sauntered up the road together in companionable silence, each lost in their own thoughts, Nancy wondered what she would have done if it had been Alex who had got another woman pregnant. Would she have stood by him in the way Betty had? To Nancy's surprise, she wasn't sure that she would. It was different for her and Alex, though. Before Ruth and Peter had come to live with them, their family amounted to the mixed bag of characters at the Palais. She didn't think she could have stood the idea of Alex leaving her to go and take care of another woman and child. Worse, still, she wasn't sure if she could or would recover from the shame of having

Alex leave her for another woman, period. She closed her eyes for a second, allowing the torment to tear through her. Betty Millington was a brave woman for staying with him, putting on a front and disguising her pain to protect her family. Nancy wasn't sure Violet quite appreciated that.

Her thoughts turned to Alex again. Wasn't that what she was doing? Their marriage had changed since the early days, and, deep down, Nancy knew that neither of them had been particularly happy, even before Alex had gone off to fight. But then, what did happiness have to do with marriage, she thought, half laughing to herself. Wasn't it more about duty, or loyalty, than expecting to be happy every day? The double standards of the expectations placed on women and men weren't lost on her as she glanced at Betty and saw she was gazing resolutely out of the window. Nancy might not have all the answers about marriage, but she did know a thing or two about Violet, and that she was grieving and angry, as she had every right to be. But she resolved to try and speak to Betty's eldest daughter. Perhaps it would do the girl good to try and see things from someone else's perspective.

Spotting the gleaming, black doors of Howell & Smart up ahead, Nancy slowed her pace and together they walked inside the staff entrance.

'This is nice, isn't it?' Betty muttered, as a uniformed flunky took their names and asked them to take a seat.

'You mean nicer than our staff entrance?' Nancy beamed as they sat down. 'Yes, I should say it is. But have Howell & Smart got a maple-sprung floor?'

'True,' Betty said, laughing. 'And I'll bet they haven't got a replica fountain in ladies casuals, either.'

Stifling a laugh of her own, Nancy recovered in time to see a tall, stiff-backed woman, whose blonde hair was elegantly coiled into a chignon at the nape of her neck.

'Miss Blum, Mrs Millington?' the woman said. 'I'm Nora Lovell, Catering Manager.'

'Pleasure to meet you,' Nancy said getting to her feet.

'Likewise,' Betty said.

'Come on up,' Nora replied, spinning on her heel and showing the ladies a door to the right. Pushing it open she gestured for the two women to walk up the marble staircase ahead of her.

'First door on the right,' she said. 'I've arranged for tea to be sent through for us all.'

'All?' Betty asked, as Nora led them through a wood-panelled room and into another smaller room.

Nancy looked around and saw a large, heavily varnished oak table with a smiling thick-set man sitting at the head. As the ladies came in, he got to his feet and smiled in welcome.

Nora encouraged Betty and Nancy to take a seat. 'Ladies, please do meet Alan Hopkins. He's the head of the National Restaurant campaign.'

'Pleasure to meet you,' Nancy said, extending her hand.

As Alan shook it and smiled in greeting, Nancy saw him do a double-take at the sight of Betty. She turned to her friend and saw that her cheeks had flamed red, and that she was gazing at the floor rather than at Alan as she held her hand out.

'Betty Dunne, is that you?' Alan said tentatively. 'I almost didn't recognise you.'

Nancy looked at Betty in astonishment. She appeared to be in a state of shock.

'It's Millington, now,' Betty managed. 'Betty Millington.'

'Sorry, but you guys know each other?' Nancy looked at Nora for confirmation, only to find the Howell & Smart catering manager looked equally baffled.

'We used to,' Alan said softly. 'Knew each other as kids.'

'But that was a long time ago,' Betty said, her voice shaking slightly now. 'All in the past, wouldn't you agree?'

This time, her voice had such a firm quality to it that all Alan could do was nod.

'I suppose, I'll . . . have to, Mrs Millington,' he finished.

Nine

Back at the Palais, Temperance was also getting ready for that evening's dance, but unlike Renee she was in no doubt of a busy Saturday night. The pen was already booked out and she had choreographed something special – a new Latin American dance known as the rumba – for Daisy, who was one of the Palais' pen dancers, and Archie, one of their part-time male dancers, to perform during the interval.

There was no denying it, Archie Ledbetter had become a good friend in recent months. As a butcher, he was in a reserved occupation so hadn't been called up for war. Temperance knew that like Eamon, who as a dockyard worker had also been in a reserved occupation, the guilt over the fact he hadn't served alongside men of his own age ate away at Archie every day. Like her brother, Archie had tried to counteract that guilt by volunteering for the fire service, but she knew it wasn't enough. After Eamon had died, Archie felt an even bigger sense of guilt that he was still living and his friend was not. With Temperance's help, Archie had channelled his emotions into dance, and he was often as excited as she was at the idea of trying something new. When Temperance had read about the rumba in the *Dancing Times,* Archie had been as keen as she was. They both knew the lively movements and upbeat music would be just the thing for people to forget their troubles and get in the mood to celebrate the festive season.

As Temperance sat on the steps of the Palais' foyer, the blackout blinds already drawn for the night and the sound of the orchestra warming up, providing the soundtrack to her thoughts, she allowed her mind to wander back to her own family at Christmas, to her childhood memories of her father telling terrible jokes at the dinner table, and her mum proudly serving the goose she had saved every penny of her housekeeping to buy. Then there was Eamon, her wonderful, precious older brother, who would take care to think about what she needed and bought her the most thoughtful of gifts. Usually it was a tangerine, or a new Agatha Christie mystery he knew she would love. At the thought of Christmas without her brother, Temperance felt a wave of panic. How would she go on without him? Losing her father had been bad enough, but now Eamon. How her heart hadn't broken with grief, Temperance wasn't sure. She knew there were thousands worse off than her. Some who had endured having their entire families wiped out. You only had to look around the streets of London, at the bombed-out shells of houses, families snuffed out before they had even had a chance to say their goodbyes.

Temperance kept trying to remind herself of all she had to be grateful for. At least she still had some family left. She had a home and a job she adored. And a little nephew or niece on the way, who would continue Eamon's legacy.

Since finding Violet throwing up in the ladies, Temperance hadn't stopped worrying. She knew her friend had a tough road ahead of her as an unwed mother. Then there was money. Temperance knew how much Violet made, and it was scarcely enough to feed herself, never mind a baby. At the moment Violet was lodging at Aunt Winnie's for a pittance, but Temperance worried that her aunt would give up her flat and move in with her and her mother permanently to help Enid save money, and then where would Violet and the baby be?

Leaning back against one of the pillars, she heard a rattling at the doors.

'We're closed!' Temperance shouted impatiently. 'We open in an hour.'

'Temperance love,' the voice called again. 'It's me, Queenie. Let me in, I'm freezing me proverbials off out here.'

Walking across the floor to the heavy, double-fronted doors, Temperance slid the bolt open and ushered Violet's grandmother inside.

'What are you doing here?' she asked, shutting the door quickly to stop the light escaping.

Queenie shot her a withering look. 'I'm here to see the king. What do you think I'm doing here?'

'Well you're a bit early for the dance,' Temperance said, shooting the gold-plated clock above the Palais' main entrance a knowing stare.

'I know that,' Queenie said, patting her grey curls. 'I want a word with Violet. Seeing as this place is the only chance I get to see her.'

Temperance frowned, creases forming across her otherwise smooth skin. 'Does she really never come home?'

'Never,' Queenie affirmed, crossing her arms across her ample bosom. 'And I know something's up with that girl. More than the fact she's lost her first love.' She paused, peering closely at Temperance's face, before adding, 'And there's something up with you, too. I can tell just by looking at your face. Those frown lines'll become permanent if you're not careful. What's the matter with you?'

It was impossible not to smile. Even when the Millington matriarch was being rude.

'I'm fine.' The lie tripped easily from her tongue.

'And I'm the Queen of Sheba. Come on, out with it,' Queenie snapped.

Pausing for a moment, Temperance took in the old woman's firm stance and thought, to hell with it. She needed to confide in someone about her troubles.

'I'm a bit worried about money, I s'pose. Christmas just brings it home how poor we are.'

'Why?' Queenie asked, patting her grey curls. 'Enid'll do a spread with what she can.'

'I know that,' Temperance said with a shrug. 'But with Eamon gone, it's hard to keep up. Even with the money from my promotion, we're struggling.'

Pursing her lips, Queenie sighed and her eyes brimmed with concern. 'Has your mother said anything?'

'Course not,' Temperance scoffed. 'She's far too proud for that. But I can see the worry in her eyes. And I know it's a lot for her to bear on top of her grief over Eamon and Dad . . .'

As her voice trailed off, Temperance felt as if a weight had been lifted off her shoulders. She hadn't been as truthful with Queenie as she'd have liked, but it was a start. The fact she had left out her biggest concern, namely Violet and how she was going to manage, didn't matter. Just talking about some of her problems helped her feel unburdened.

'You could always try and get another job,' Queenie suggested.

'Where would I find time to do something on top of these hours and my WVS work?' Temperance gasped.

'Sorry, Temp, love, you're right,' Queenie said, falling silent for a moment as she looked sheepishly around the foyer. 'But what if you did something that was a little bit less than part-time?'

'Whatever d'you mean?' Temperance asked, confused.

Queenie looked shifty as she glanced over each shoulder. 'Well, there are other ways to make a bit on the side.'

'Like?' Temperance had a feeling she knew what Queenie meant, but she didn't want to make it easy for the Millington matriarch. When Violet and Maisie had first started working at the Palais, they had been full of tales of how their grandmother sold stolen goods down Bradmore Lane Market. One week it was tea towels, another it was stockings. Queenie didn't discriminate with what she sold, and was also surprisingly good at keeping an eye out for the police. Temperance had no idea how much Queenie made, but she did know that she was always generous with her granddaughters, often slipping them a little extra for a trip to the pictures. And she didn't scrimp on the port and lemons she treated herself to when she was enjoying a tea dance at the Palais, either.

She was about to open her mouth to dismiss Queenie's idea, when something inside Temperance stirred. What if this was the answer to all her problems?

'Have you got something in mind?' she asked, whispering over the strains of the violinist clearly now practising scales.

Queenie took a step closer and Temperance could smell her Lily of the Valley perfume.

'As it happens, I do. How d'you feel about eggs?'

'Eggs?' Temperance echoed in confusion. 'I mean, they're all right. Nice with a toast soldier.'

Queenie rolled her eyes. 'Never mind bleedin' soldiers. They're rationed, ain't they, girl? But I know a bloke who's got a good layer. People are crying out for a bit extra. I was going to take the job on myself, but if you're keen I could pass it onto you. If you think it'll help you out, like.'

As Queenie stopped speaking, Temperance saw her cheeks flush – she could see that the matriarch was pleased with her offer of friendship.

'That's very kind of you, Queenie.' Temperance smiled. 'But where would I sell them? I couldn't really go door-to-door, could I? Someone might grass me up.'

'For the love of everything holy,' Queenie said, sighing as she looked heavenwards. 'I worry about your bleedin' generation. If it was down to you lot for us to survive the war, we'd all be in trouble. What's wrong with you?'

'Nothing's wrong with me,' Temperance exclaimed, feeling

exasperated. 'But I've never dabbled in selling knock-off goods.'

'All right, all right, keep your knickers on,' Queenie said in hushed tone, raising her hands up and down in a bid to mollify the younger woman. 'Sorry, I shouldn't have said that. But it's simple. You just need one buyer to take the lot off you a couple of times a week.'

'But who would I find? I can't really ask the Palais punters.'

'No, but ain't you mates with that posh hotelier?' Queenie put in.

'Nigel Henshall?' Temperance gasped. 'I can't ask him.'

'Why not?' Queenie leaned against the pillar and cocked her head to one side as she regarded Temperance. 'Rich bloke like that's going to be crying out for rations, and he'll have a couple of pennies to drop your way.'

Opening her mouth about to protest, Temperance stopped herself for the second time since Queenie had walked through the doors. It was true she had built up a relationship with Nigel. He was ever so grateful that she could teach his wife how to dance, and in a funny way the two of them had bonded. He had only been moaning to her the other day about how it was becoming harder and harder to get the stocks they needed. What if she could make his life easier? In turn, he could make hers and Violet's much easier, too. Was it too risky? What if she'd misjudged their relationship? Moaning about lack of stock was one thing, but accepting black-market goods was quite another. Could she possibly talk to Nigel about it beforehand? What if he said no?

But then she remembered how he always had a kind word for her. And she knew that even if he did say no, she could always say there had been some confusion –and Nigel would want to believe the best of her. For a moment, Temperance felt a flash of fear, but then she thought of Violet. Her need was greater – she had to do this for her friend, and for her brother.

Turning back to Queenie, Temperance smiled. 'When can I start?'

Queenie's face broke out into a broad smile. 'Meet me by the south entrance of Ravenscourt Park, the day after Boxing Day – after the tea dance. I'll give you your first batch then.'

Ten

As Renee walked along the Manchester Canal the following Sunday lunchtime, she wrapped her scarf tightly around her neck to protect herself from the arctic chill. There were many things she preferred about the north – the people for one. Despite what anyone said, northerners were friendly, warmer, with a sense of humour that was as sharp as a tack. Southerners were all right, but the north was where she felt right at home, and always would. That said, there was a hell of a lot to be said for the southern weather. She quickened her pace, determined to escape the cold that was quickly seeping through her fingers and toes.

As was so often the case these days, Renee had no idea how the day would evolve. Since moving to Manchester, she usually spent her Sundays enjoying whatever pie was on offer at the local pub near her Deansgate flat, and afterwards taking a trip to the Gaiety and spending the afternoon at the pictures.

She knew people thought she was lonely, but the truth was she loved this chance to spend time with herself. Alone time was something she had never really enjoyed before. As a child she'd constantly been picking up after her father and sister, and then as an adult, as Ronnie's wife, she'd been at his beck and call. These precious Sundays, when she was free to do just as she pleased all day, were fast becoming her favourite times of the week and she cherished every single one.

When Renee was living with Ronnie, she had always been on edge, wondering when he'd lose his temper and how. In

London, living with her sister, Lizzie – a widower who earned pin money doing odd jobs to get by – Renee always felt as if she had to take care of her sister. Now, there was just her to think about, and it was a luxury, but one she knew wouldn't last forever. Ronnie would catch up with her, eventually. He had come close in London, seeking her out, sending her those letters at the Palais, letting her know she was in his sights.

And now, though it looked like Ronnie might have tracked her down in Manchester, Renee was determined to try and enjoy the calm. She knew that the girls at the Crystal worried about her. Unlike the motley collection of lost souls at the Palais, the Crystal Girls all had families of their own, or parents, uncles, aunts and grandparents at home. Renee was the only one that lived alone, and it had taken her a long time to get the girls to understand that she was happy. Being alone was something of a novelty and she was even looking forward to spending Christmas by herself. She'd been to the butcher and treated herself to an extra slice of bacon, intending to cook herself the biggest, greasiest bacon butty she could on her one-ringed stove, and then sit in the bath all afternoon with the latest copy of the *Picture Post* – she couldn't wait.

There were just three days to go until her extra day off, and Renee felt restless. An early blackout from noon had been announced and so she'd got up late. Feeling hungry, she'd ventured out to her local pub for an early lunch. To her surprise, the landlord had shut for the day.

'Paul, open up will yer?' she called, spotting him through the window.

'We're closed today,' Paul replied, coming to the door.

'Why?'

The landlord pointed to the blackout blinds he was in the middle of lowering. 'Early blackout means Hitler's on his way here, love. I'm going down the shelter, you should do the same.'

'Not at this time,' Renee gasped. 'We'll be there for hours.'

'And I'll bet the folks of Liverpool wished they had that choice,' Paul put in sagely. 'Poor devils. That city's broken, and now it's our turn. I'm not giving him the satisfaction of claiming my life.'

'Give over,' Renee said, her stomach growling for one of his meat and potato pies. 'Manchester's a lot better protected.'

Everyone knew that the factory roofs in Trafford Park had been painted green to make them look like fields, whilst another factory in Newton Heath had its walls painted to look like terraced houses, even adding real gardens to complete the effect. Large fires were regularly lit on the moors or mosses on the outskirts of the city, to try and convince the Jerries the real fire was elsewhere. And if that wasn't enough, a generator was used at regular intervals to belch thick black smoke across the city, giving the illusion of clouds.

'They reckon Hitler's on his way,' the pub landlord said warningly. 'Get yourself to safety. I want you in here for lunch next week!'

Renee gave Paul a weak smile as she bade him goodbye. She understood his fear. While there had, of course, been raids on the city, the people of Manchester hadn't seen anything like the scale of the bombs dropped in London and Liverpool.

Up until today, Hitler had largely left them alone. There had been a stray bomb in Wythenshawe, and a row of shops in Ancoats had been taken out earlier that month, but other than that Manchester had remained unscathed. People were optimistic. Shops were open, albeit without much to sell, but folks were ready for Christmas, a chance to hold their loved ones in their arms and forget the horrors of the past year.

Only glancing upwards, Renee shivered. The day was crisp and clear. Not only that, there had been a full moon for over a week – helping the Jerries navigate when night fell. People had been expecting Hitler for days, and Renee felt a sense of despair as she looked up at the cloudless sky, as if half expecting Jerry to arrive that moment.

But despite the threat of enemy attack, Renee couldn't face the idea of spending the day rattling around in her flat with just her own thoughts for company. And so she decided to walk along the canal.

As she walked, she tried to push her worries about the hell Hitler might unleash to the back of the mind. She did have bigger problems to worry about closer to home, after all. Such as Ronnie catching up with her. Renee needed to decide what she should do next.

Linda hadn't been able to give her much more information than Janice had passed on in the cafe. Other than to say a youngish woman with thick, fair hair had called in. Pleasant-enough-looking, Linda had said, echoing what Janice had told her, that the woman wanted Renee to know that Ronnie was passing through Manchester and he'd call in to see her soon.

'An old friend from home, is he?' Linda had asked.

As Renee had nodded mutely, Linda had smiled and said, 'That's nice.'

Nice?

Renee had wanted to scream. Typical Ronnie to send such a threatening message in such a seemingly non-threatening way.

But that was Ronnie all over. She knew how he worked. He was a master at his craft. He knew all the avenues, had fingers in every pie. Word was, he even had a racket down in London – charging desperate folk for admission to the tube stations when they sought shelter from Jerry's never-ending bombing campaign.

Renee now shook her head in disgust. The worst day of her life had been her wedding day when she'd been forced to shackle herself to that man. Praise God, for her Catholic upbringing forced herself to feel some guilt, but there were times she couldn't understand just why Hitler had managed to bomb so many thousands of others but had left Ronnie Newsham well alone – where was the justice in that?

As she continued walking, she turned her face up to the sunshine and allowed the warmth to seep into her skin. She wouldn't go down without a fight, of that Ronnie Newsham could be sure.

Turning down Winser Street, Renee spotted a familiar figure coming towards her.

'Renee, flower!' Janice cried joyfully. 'Y'all right?'

Dressed in a dark-green wool coat and a brightly coloured scarf wrapped tightly around her head, Janice definitely wasn't allowing Hitler to upend *her* day.

Renee smiled. 'All right, Janice. You not at home with the kids, then?'

Janice's grown-up children always called in for lunch every Sunday. It was something Janice frequently complained about, but it was also something she enjoyed, and everyone at the Crystal knew how devoted she was to her family.

'Our Doris is out with her in-laws, Elsie's gone to a WVS meeting and Bobby's doing summat with his Local Defence Volunteer group, in case Hitler comes calling tonight.'

Janice's tone hardened with her mention of Hitler.

'So, you've got your glad rags on and are cavorting about the streets of Manchester, eh?' Renee was determined to recapture Janice's playful tone.

'Summat like that,' Janice replied. 'An afternoon to myself is a rare thing. What are you up to, lady?'

'Same as you.' Renee smiled. 'Enjoying an afternoon to myself. I usually go to the pub, but Paul's shut up for the day, he's worried about the early blackout.'

'On your own!' Janice exclaimed clearly more concerned about Renee's moral standing than whether Jerry was paying them a call.

Renee laughed at Janice's outrage. 'Shocking, isn't it? Woman on her own in a pub! Whatever next? A fella doing his own washing up?'

At that they both laughed.

'Well, if you're at a loose end, d'you fancy coming up the pictures with me?' Janice asked.

Renee thought for a moment. She didn't have anything else to do.

'Go on then.' She smiled.

And together the two women walked through the streets of Manchester, hoping an afternoon in Hollywood would take away the horrors of what lay in store in the North West.

Eleven

The sound of 'Away in a Manger' blared from the little Bakelite radio in the office and Nancy smiled. She had always loved Christmas carols and this was one of her favourites. It reminded her of when she and her brothers and sisters had gone around the Brooklyn neighbourhood she had grown up singing carols in the lead-up to Christmas.

At first people were confused as to why a Jewish family were singing carols at all, but Nancy's mother, who had long memories of the Great Depression, had simply said you had to take your joy where you could find it, and that Christmas may not be a Jewish holiday but it was certainly synonymous with joy.

It had always been such a happy time, and at the memory of it, Nancy realised she missed her family more and more these days. When she had moved to London, she hadn't been upset that she hardly ever saw them. She had been so lost in her love of a new city, a new adventure, and then, when she married Alex, a new love. But these days, her family felt further away than they ever had. Her cousin, Rosa, who had fled from Munich almost a year ago, was still missing, and Nancy wondered how long it would be before she would see her parents and siblings again. Her sister, Esther, had recently had a baby boy and the thought of never meeting her little nephew plagued Nancy in her waking moments.

'Oi, Dolly Daydreamer,' Edna called from the other end of the office. 'I asked you a question.'

Nancy's head snapped up and she looked apologetically at the Palais' dance doyenne.

'Sorry, Edna, honey. Miles away.'

Edna looked at her sharply. 'I can see that. Just because you're going cavorting about with the likes of Howell & Smart, don't think you can shirk your responsibilities here.'

Nancy's wistful mood evaporated, and, feeling a flash of fury, she got to her feet and leaned over the desk. 'Edna, sweetheart, I think you'll find it was my idea to work today. And I am sorry you've had to come in,' Nancy glanced apologetically at Betty, who was working her way through the roster of dancers for the Christmas and New Year period, 'but if you'd prefer to stay home and wait for Bill to call on you, then that's fine with me.'

At the suggestion, Edna flushed bright red. 'I have never waited in for a man in all my life.'

Nancy smirked as she sat back in her chair. 'If you say so.'

'I do say so. I don't know what's got into you today, Nancy Blum, but I do know I won't stand for your cheek.'

'Nothing's gotten into me.' Nancy glared at her mother-in-law and felt another wave of frustration. 'I'm going down to the dance hall to see how Temperance is getting along.'

Edna glared. 'What's Temperance doing on the dance floor?'

A sinking feeling snaked through Nancy. She was so tired, work was mounting up, girls were going off sick, two more of the men in the stores had been called up, and now Edna was going out of her way to make life difficult. Which was why she hadn't told Edna that Temperance was choreographing the big Christmas Eve number this afternoon.

'I think she's just going through the running order of songs with Harry Leder,' Betty put in smoothly.

Nancy turned towards Betty and felt affection flood through her. In that moment she could kiss Betty for her quick thinking.

'Oh, right,' Edna said, looking mollified and sitting back down.

'Edna, you don't have to stay,' Nancy tried again. 'If you want to get home then I understand. You've been a great help this morning helping me, but, honestly, you're fine.'

'It's no trouble,' Edna said.

'I know that,' Nancy replied, her patience beginning to wear thin. 'But the thing is, what would really be a great help is if you could take the kids out. They've been stuck in the Palais all week with me trying to keep everything together.'

At the idea of spending time with Peter and Ruth, Edna visibly brightened. 'Oh. Perhaps I could take them up to Oxford Street. We could have a look in Liberty's window. I used to do that when Alex was a boy. He loved it up there.'

Nancy's face broke into a wide smile. 'That sounds perfect. They've never been.'

Edna clapped her hands together as she gathered her coat and bag from behind her chair. 'I wonder if Bill would like to come.'

Resisting the temptation to roll her eyes, Nancy nodded. 'He's in the basement with Eric. I think they're looking at ways to make our shelter more comfortable.'

Looking like an excited child on Christmas morning, Edna rushed out the door and Nancy shook her head.

'She's just lonely, you know,' Betty said quietly.

'I know,' Nancy said. 'But she doesn't make life easy for herself the way she talks to us all.'

'She'll never change,' Betty said, her brunette curls bouncing. 'The best thing we can do is keep her occupied.'

'Speaking of occupied, did I mention that we're meeting Alan and Nora just after the New Year? Is 2nd January all right for you?' Nancy said, slipping on her cardigan.

As she glanced at Betty, she was surprised to see a look of fear pass across her features. 'Is that all right?'

'Course,' Betty said hurriedly, and Nancy was reminded of their recent encounter at Howell & Smart.

'You never mentioned you knew Alan,' she ventured. 'Did you go to school together?'

'Something like that,' Betty mumbled.

'Well, he certainly seemed happy to see you,' Nancy said cheerfully.

'Sure, I dunno.'

'Well, it'll be nice for you to have an old friend to spend time with,' Nancy tried again. 'Though I must say, I don't think I'd wanna bump into any of *my* old school friends. With my big nose and pigtails, I wasn't exactly Miss Popularity.'

As Nancy smiled, she couldn't miss the look of worry cross Betty's face.

'What's wrong, honey?'

Betty gave her a wan smile. 'I'm sorry. Bit maudlin with it being Christmas.'

'Why?'

'I was hoping to spend time with Violet at some point, seeing as I won't see her for her lunch.'

'You'll see her Christmas night, too,' Nancy added carefully.

'I know,' Betty said with a sad look on her face. 'It'll just be hard this first one without her and Roy.'

Nancy nodded. She understood full well what it was like to be without a loved one. This year she was determined to look on the bright side, with Ruth and Peter to share Christmas with.

'Chin up, honey,' she said now. 'The first one is the hardest. Least you've still got Maisie and Queenie.'

Betty laughed. 'I think we'll always have Queenie. You know, there was a time in my life I thought I had the worst mother-in-law in the world, and I cursed the day she ever came to live with us. But now,' Betty's face softened, 'I think I wouldn't be without her.'

'I hope you're not telling me that you think one day I'll feel that way about Edna.'

Picking up her paperwork, Betty gave a slight shrug of her shoulders. 'It's not for me to say, love. But p'raps we're not all quite as lucky.'

Shaking her head with mirth, Nancy crossed the floor. Then, with one hand on the doorknob, said, 'Don't stay all day if you don't want to, Betty, honey. You work hard enough.'

'And where else would I want to be?' Betty half whispered under her breath.

Saying nothing, Nancy made her way downstairs and crossed the gilded foyer. Rounding the corner past the ladies bathroom, she had almost reached the dance hall when she spotted Violet looking out of the window.

She stopped for a moment to observe her. The girl looked ill. Her pale skin was almost grey, and the spark she'd arrived at the Palais with had disappeared. As Nancy watched Violet staring out at Brook Green Road, she felt a pang of worry. This wasn't the same girl she'd hired in the spring. And yes, she knew that Violet had suffered a terrible tragedy but there was something else wrong, Nancy could tell.

'Violet, honey,' she ventured, taking a cautious step towards the girl. 'What are you doing?'

At the sound of her voice, Violet jumped. Nancy felt a fresh pang of concern as she watched her try and plaster on a smile. 'Oh, sorry, Nancy. I was just watching people outside go about their business. Hard to believe it's Christmas in three days' time.'

Nancy nodded. 'You looking forward to it?'

'Oh, yes,' Violet breathed, looking for all the world as if she was trying to do her best to make herself believe the words she was saying. 'The Palais looks set to be magical. Temperance is working so hard to make Christmas Eve a success.'

'And what about the big day? You're not going to be with

your mom . . .' Nancy let her voice trail off, waiting for Violet to fill in the blank.

'No, but I'll be with Winnie and Temperance. I'll feel closer to Eamon that way. And then of course we'll all be here with you on Christmas night,' Violet finished brightly.

Nancy still wasn't convinced by the tone of Violet's voice. 'Honey, it will be wonderful to have you. I can't tell you how much it means to me that you'll be with me to celebrate my first Christmas with Peter and Ruth.'

'What about Alex?' Violet asked. 'You must be sorry he's not going to be here.'

The question blindsided Nancy for a moment. Of course she was sorry her husband was away . . . Wasn't she? The conflict must have shown on her face as Violet added, 'It's hard, isn't it, when you've been with someone a long time and then they go away. I guess it must feel a little like Alex is a stranger sometimes.'

A sense of relief and guilt flooded through Nancy. 'You know, that's exactly how it feels sometimes. How did you get such a wise head on young shoulders?'

Violet hung her head. 'I think that's the last thing I am.'

Nancy let Violet's words hang in the air before she spoke a second or two later. 'What's going on? You're not yourself, and don't tell me it's just grief, it's something else.'

Looking at Violet more closely, Nancy could see she was halfway right.

'Is it the Palais? Has Bill upset you?'

Violet shook her head.

'Your mom? Your dad?'

Still another shake of the head.

'Then, what?' Nancy couldn't keep the frustration from her voice. She wanted to help all the girls that worked under her care. They were known locally as The Good Time Girls, but Violet looked the very opposite of that.

'I'm expecting,' Violet said abruptly.

The confession nearly knocked Nancy off her feet.

'You're what?' she whispered.

Violet lifted her head and met Nancy's concerned gaze. 'I'm pregnant, and I haven't a clue what my life's going to look like in a few months' time.'

Looking at Violet, seeing the tears now roll from her eyes, Nancy felt a flash of tenderness.

'Does your mom know?'

At the question, Violet laughed. 'Betty? Christ, no! She'd disown me.'

'I'm not sure.' Nancy pursed her lips for a moment and thought. 'She's changed ever such a lot lately.'

'I don't think she's changed enough to welcome an unmarried daughter complete with bastard child into the fold, do you?'

At the bitterness in Violet's tone, Nancy winced. 'It may not be as bad as you think.'

'No, it'll be worse,' Violet said morosely.

'What do you want to do?' Nancy tried again.

Alarm and anger flowed across Violet's features. 'I'm not going to one of those mother and baby places and giving my baby up.'

'Nobody's asking you to.' Nancy ventured a step closer to Violet and slid an arm around her shoulders. The girl felt cold, Nancy thought. She pulled Violet towards her and felt a flood of motherly concern for her friend. It was one thing to be grieving for her lost lover, but quite another to be going through something as traumatic as having a baby alone.

'You know I'll help you, don't you?' Nancy said suddenly. 'Whatever you need.'

At the offer of help Violet turned to look at Nancy, a mixture of hope and gratitude in her eyes. 'I need Eamon.'

Nancy pulled Violet in towards her once more. 'That's the

one thing I can't do anything about, honey. But anything else, you only have to ask. This baby,' she added softly, glancing down and noticing for the first time Violet's gently rounded tummy, 'is one of us now, whatever happens.'

Twelve

Nestled in a red velvet seat at the Gaiety, Renee felt a sense of peace descend over her as she watched Fred Astaire on the big screen. Glancing across at Janice, she saw her friend was enjoying *Broadway Melody of 1940* as much as she was. It was just the thing to take their minds off whatever hell was being unleashed outside.

Sinking down into her chair, Renee reached for a Craven A, lit it and inhaled deeply before glancing around the theatre. It seemed a lot of women had a similar idea to her and Janice, judging by the full rows. However, as she watched them light cigarette after cigarette, it was possible that they weren't as engrossed in Fred's exploits on screen as they should have been.

Renee wasn't sure if she was imagining things, but it seemed as if the volume was even louder than usual. Anxiously, she fixed her gaze on the screen. Whatever was happening outside was outside of her control, like so many other things in her life.

A few minutes later, the film stopped and the stark letters of the air-raid warning appeared on the screen.

'Here we go,' Janice muttered under her breath.

Renee said nothing and glanced at her watch. In the gloom she could just make out that it was just after half past six. More than time for Hitler's Junkers to make an appearance.

'Do you want to find shelter, or take your chances?' Janice whispered.

Looking around her, Renee couldn't see anyone else getting up, and she smiled. It was typical of people to want to see the rest of the film they had paid for, regardless of how bad things were outside.

'I'm happy to stay, queen,' she said with a touch of determination.

'Me an' all,' Janice said firmly.

Like everyone else, they turned back to face the screen and waited for the projectionist to restart the reel. As Fred Astaire reappeared back on the screen, Renee tried to lose herself in the story. But no matter how hard she tried, she couldn't stop wondering what Hitler's lot were up to outside. It was strange. She wasn't usually this troubled by an air raid, preferring to either find shelter and wait for it all to be over, or carry on with whatever task she was involved in. But this time felt different. Ominous, somehow. Renee wasn't sure if it was because it was three days before Christmas or because the attack was possibly going to be so much worse if Liverpool was anything to go by.

An hour later, and as the end titles rolled, Renee and Janice got to their feet.

'Ready to see what fresh hell's waiting for us this time round?' Janice asked, in a forced jovial tone.

Renee gave her a brave smile. In a way, she was relieved to find out just how bad the devastation was.

With the ushers' warnings to head to safety as soon as possible ringing in their ears, Janice and Rene stepped out into the cool moonlit air.

Immediately, the eerie sound of a low whine rang out overhead.

'You hear that?' Janice hissed, above the unmistakable din of the Luftwaffe.

'Impossible not to,' Renee joked, doing her best to remain light. 'We'd better find a shelter.'

Janice wrinkled her upturned nose. 'I hate them places. You never know what you're going to find. I'd rather find shelter in the basement of the Crystal.'

'It's not open,' Renee ventured.

Janice reached into her handbag and jangled a set of keys.

'Lucky I can get us in then. Come on, it's only ten minutes away.'

Reluctantly, Renee agreed and with heads bent low, they hurried through the throngs of streets towards Deansgate, the sound of the Junkers overhead getting louder and louder as every minute passed.

Renee could feel her heart banging against her chest. She told herself it was the brisk pace they were walking at, but inside a very real fear began to unfurl.

Just then, the sound of three bangs erupted overhead as an ARP warden rounded the corner.

'What are you doing out here?' he growled. 'Find a shelter now. There's one next door to the Kings Head just up the road.'

'We're going, officer,' Janice called sweetly.

As the ARP hurried away, seemingly satisfied, the two women continued through the throng of empty streets, Renee opened her mouth to speak, but her words were drowned out by the persistent sounds of the Luftwaffe overhead.

All around her, the scent of smoke filled her lungs and nostrils. Lifting her head, Renee couldn't miss the fires up ahead surging through the streets. As Janice charged ahead, Renee stopped for a moment to take in the scene, her heart in her mouth.

She felt as if she were witnessing the beginning of the end of the world. From her position at the top of Princess Street, she could see a series of small fires up ahead in Albert Square. And above her, the Junkers were growing in number, each one clearly using the fires to guide them into unloading more bombs on the more iconic and important parts of the city.

Renee tried to scream at the top of her lungs to stop Janice from running any further. But she could see her MC was determined to reach the Crystal, and that Janice wouldn't let any amount of Jerries stop her in her quest.

She ran up ahead, trying to catch up with her friend, with the roar of planes overhead growing louder. Renee didn't think she had ever felt fear like this, but she was determined to rise above it.

Watching Janice turn left down Lloyd Street and pass St Peter's Square, Renee felt as if her lungs were on fire. The Crystal was just a few yards away now, tucked at the bottom of Deansgate. Renee quickened her pace and eventually caught up with Janice.

'What are you doing?' she gasped, breathless.

'What do you think I'm doing?' Janice hissed as another German plane flew perilously overhead. 'Getting to bloody safety.'

Renee glanced upwards. The plane was so close she was sure she could see the pilot's face. In that moment she felt a rush of anger. How dare these Jerries try to run them out of their city.

'What if we don't go to the Crystal?' Renee said suddenly.

Janice looked at her in surprise. 'What the hell do you mean?'

Renee pointed to the fires snaking their way along the north-east end of Deansgate. Teams of firemen were doing battle with the blaze, while volunteers were doing their best to help the injured.

'We need to help, not hide,' Renee said, feeling a fire of her own burn inside her. She pointed up at the bombers, circling the city now like vultures. 'The Jerries will destroy us all if they have their way. How about we lessen the damage?'

Janice's eyes gleamed like sapphires in the orange light as she nodded. 'I'm in, love. We'll show bloody Jerry what we're made of.'

Together, the two women ran towards Albert Square. As they did so, Renee tried to make sense of the whirlwind of activity around her. The quiet she and Janice had felt moments earlier was now replaced by the sounds of hundreds of people rushing through the streets. Volunteer firemen were doing their best to put out the blazes with stirrup pumps, while teams of Civil Defence Volunteers and the WVS were helping to escort those caught up in the blasts to safety.

From her position by the Town Hall, Renee could see that up to the cathedral, the Luftwaffe had achieved what they had wanted. The north-east end of Deansgate, up to what looked to be as far as Victoria Station, was on fire.

Spurred on by their achievements, Junker after Junker flew past them, and as the sounds of fireworks ricocheted in the sky, Renee felt a renewed sense of urgency to help.

'How bad is it?' she asked a passing fireman.

The fireman shook his head. 'Bad. A gas main's been ruptured at St Mary's Gate, which has made the fires wore. And of course half the lads are still in Liverpool helping over there. We've got more than threehundred fellas working away.'

At the news, Renee's heart sank. Manchester would be destroyed.

'Tell us what you want us to do,' she said bluntly.

'Help us clear the area, free the wreckage, and get as many people as you can to safety. And, above all else,' the fireman warned, 'stay safe.'

For hours, Renee and Janice toiled long into the night. Together, they helped clear the wreckage, lead those who had lost their homes to safety, send messenger boys on errands across the city with news of the loss of loved ones, and help the WVS make endless cups of tea for those dealing with loss, shock and injury. As Renee worked, she prayed to God she would never see another night like this one. The devastation would haunt her for years to come. The piled-up bodies, the screams of mothers who had seen their children killed in front of them, the stench of charred flesh, the air black with smoke. It was as if she had found herself in hell. But Renee never complained; she knew she was lucky compared to some of the poor unfortunate souls who had seen their lives ruined in one deadly night, because it was clear that the Jerries were determined to try and destroy this city, just as they had tried to wreak havoc on London and Liverpool.

Every so often, Renee would stop what she was doing and look at the scores of other people working around her. The firemen working that night were heroes. Not only were they down in manpower, most of their vehicles were in Merseyside. Instead, many were using improvised private cars and vans, doing their best to deal with the devastation with whatever they could use.

Just four hours after the fires in Albert Square, the whole cathedral and Corn Exchange area were ablaze. Not only that, the Royal Exchange building on the corner of Cross Street and Market Street had been hit, as had the Victoria Buildings, Miller Street, Victoria Street, and the Exchange Hotel in Fennel Street. Word had also spread that the iconic Victoria Hotel in Deansgate had fallen to the fires and almost all the residents had been evacuated to the nearby Grosvenor Hotel, where there was an extensive shelter in the basement.

At just after six-thirty, the all-clear sounded, and as dawn broke, Renee was exhausted. As she sank back onto a pile of rubble, drinking a cup of tea handed to her by a kindly WVS volunteer, she thought she might cry.

'What a bloody night,' Janice said, sitting beside her friend and taking a sip of her own tea. 'What's the betting Jerry'll be back tonight?'

Renee had been thinking exactly the same thing herself. This was just a temporary respite. Hitler's mob would be back, the full moon assured her of it.

'Let's just hope we can get some of the firemen back from Liverpool,' she said. 'It'll be tough on these lads to do the same again tonight.'

There was no denying that the firemen were exhausted. They had worked wonders with very little, yet the decimation wasn't lost on them.

Renee looked at Janice's soot-smeared face. The beautiful scarf she'd had tied around her head had become a tourniquet for one of the walking wounded, and her clothes were cut to shreds. Renee looked down at her own clothes, taking in her own torn skirt, and shoes that were now somehow minus their heels. Still, she thought as she surveyed the scene in front of her, clothing was the last thing that mattered now. With a heavy heart, Renee couldn't tear her eyes away as the early morning dawn shone a light on the scene of devastation – all the iconic landmarks wiped away, as if they had never been there at all. Those caught up in the blasts weren't thinking of all they had lost, they were thinking about how they were going to get to work. Even though Hitler had done his best to unleash terror across the city, Mancunians everywhere were dusting themselves off and readying themselves to make use of the partial bus service still operating.

Thinking to do the same herself, Renee was getting to her feet when suddenly there was a loud cry.

'The cathedral!' came a voice. 'It's ruined.'

'Surely not,' Janice cried. 'The filthy bastards.'

But it was true. Although Hitler hadn't completely destroyed the city's beloved cathedral, one of the last high-explosive bombs to fall before the all-clear had hit it, causing horrific damage. All the windows and doors had been blown out – ornaments, pews and furnishings destroyed – and the high altar still visible beneath ten feet of rubble.

As the news travelled, Renee felt a pang of sorrow for her friend. Janice was Manchester born and bred. This would be hard for her. Tentatively, Renee reached an arm around her and pulled Janice in towards her. As she did so, she allowed her eyes to travel towards the end of Deansgate, where she lived and worked. In that moment she realised it wasn't just the cathedral that had been destroyed. Her home was gone, and with it the Crystal. All reduced to nothing but a pile of ash and rubble. As she felt Janice's hot breath against her shoulder, Renee tried to stem the tears that threatened to flow. She knew it was selfish, there were so many people worse off than her. So many who had endured so much suffering in one night. But her new start, her home, had been wiped out in an instant. Ronnie might be on her tail, but it had still been home until she chose to move on. She ran a sooty hand across her face, as Janice got shakily to her feet and asked a nearby fireman about the devastation. To the emergency services, the Crystal would be just another casualty, Renee thought, wondering how many poor souls had been caught up in the explosions. The cathedral would have been closed, but what about those who had been nearby?

Suddenly, Renee felt the first flash of brightness she'd had since Hitler started dropping bombs. What if her own life had been snuffed out, like so many others that night? What if, finally, she had a chance to escape Ronnie, and like a phoenix from the flames, rise up and start all over again, with the past wiped clean?

Thirteen

Christmas Day dawned clear but bright, and in Hammersmith Betty found herself putting the finishing touches to the table, while everyone bar Queenie sat in the good front room. There wasn't much to go round this year, but Betty had saved all her ration coupons to buy a chicken and somehow, by miracle of miracles, Queenie had managed to get her hands on a glut of carrots, potatoes and parsnips.

Despite not getting home until just after ten the previous night, Betty had got up at the break of dawn to wash and prepare the food. Then she'd made sure that Maisie's stocking was hanging on the mantlepiece, stuffed with a piece of coal rather than a tangerine this year. She knew her daughter wouldn't appreciate it, but the ever-present mother in Betty wanted to make sure her daughter might have a drop of warmth over the winter. To sweeten the lack of gifts, she had found a pretty piece of ribbon in the practice rooms of the Palais a few days earlier, which Nancy had assured her she was welcome to take, agreeing it would make a handsome belt for one of Maisie's dance dresses.

Looking at the lone stocking now, Betty tried to ignore the feelings of sadness that threatened to overwhelm her. This Christmas would be her first without Roy and Violet, and she couldn't fight how much she missed them. Losing her boy earlier in the year had broken her heart, and though she knew she would never get over it, she had slowly come to terms with his death, each day getting a little bit easier to bear the pain.

But then Violet had left, and although Betty understood why, this day was bringing home to her how much she had lost that year – and how much she could still lose.

Now, as she glanced at her Christmas table, Betty did her best to focus on the places she had set, rather than the two places that she hadn't. She would make the most of this year, be grateful for the fact that her husband had been returned to her in one piece, rather than smashed to smithereens like so many of the poor souls caught up in Dunkirk back in May. Things might be difficult with George, but he was still her husband. Her family before the eyes of God. She had to be grateful for her lot and accept that marriage had its ups and downs, though it wasn't easy. Up until recently, Betty had become very good at forgetting her marital concerns, but since bumping into Alan at Howell & Smart, she had felt unsettled, concerned about where this trip down Memory Lane might take her. It was almost as if this brush from the past had reminded her of the girl she used to be.

Determined to do better, when she'd arrived home that day, she had found George slumped on the settee in the good front room, tucking into the beer she had put away especially for Christmas.

Usually she would have been irritated, but instead she simply removed the bottle from her husband's hand, set it down on the table and gently shook him awake. As he made his way upstairs to bed, cursing under his breath at being disturbed, Betty knew he would be grumpy from lack of sleep. But no matter his mood, she was determined Christmas Day would be a happy one. Even without two of her children at the table.

Listening to him now, stamping about upstairs, no doubt with a hangover as filthy as his morals, she heard Queenie give out to him about the stench on his breath.

Betty laughed and reached for yesterday's paper. As she did so her stomach lurched as she took in the headline – *Raider*

Down at Manchester. Hitler had been up to no good again, bombing seven bells out of the northern city. She read on about the atrocities, in which 684 people had died.

Betty immediately thought of Renee. She often prayed for her friend at church, and hoped the Liverpudlian had been spared now. Anger and fear coursed through her as she read the article again. She hoped the filthy Jerry would be strung up for his crimes.

Pressing the newspaper to her chest, Betty felt the familiar threat of tears. When would this war end? Like so many up and down the country, she had hoped that when Churchill became prime minister the war would be resolved. Instead, things had only got worse. Now Churchill was begging the Italians to rise up and overthrow Mussolini. Betty almost laughed to herself. As if that would ever happen. It showed how desperate the prime minster was.

Since the first barrel-load of hate that Hitler had dropped on London that fateful Saturday night in September, the bombs had become almost a nightly affair. Betty knew that Hitler's aim was to terrify the British people, but he had underestimated their strength.

'Tea, Ma?' Maisie said brightly, interrupting her thoughts and filling the kettle with water and setting it on the range. Betty nodded, surprised her youngest was offering to help.

'Bloody good job,' Maisie said with spirit as she glanced at the paper. 'That bloody raider wants stringing up!'

'Maisie!' Betty snapped. 'I shall wash your mouth out with carbolic, lady. A bit of respect – it's Christmas.'

Maisie shrugged and rested against the stove. 'Sorry, Ma.'

Looking at her daughter's contrite face, Betty softened. If she could extend an olive branch to her philandering husband, she could certainly do the same for her daughter.

'So, what time shall we go to Nancy's do you think?' she asked a few moments later, when the kettle had boiled.

'You're still going, then?' her husband's voice boomed as he walked through the doorway.

'Course,' Maisie said, poured the tea. 'I can't wait. She's asked us all.'

'Not quite all,' Betty put in quickly. 'Just staff.'

George raised an eyebrow and sat awkwardly at the table. As he reached for a cup with his one remaining arm, he sent himself off balance and slopped the tea in the pot all over the table, causing Betty to wince. As she got up to help him, he smacked her hand away and she silently seethed. Before his accident, Betty would have snapped back and all hell would have no doubt broken loose. Yet lately, she no longer had the time or the energy to fight with him. As his wife, she had a duty to ensure George was cared for after his terrible ordeal. But since the truth had come out that he had got another woman pregnant, and duped her into thinking he loved her and would leave his wife for her, Betty would never feel the same about her husband again. George had always been on the untrustworthy side, but that had been Betty's own private cross to bear.

Not anymore. She looked at him now and felt a knot of despair rising in her stomach. She didn't hate George in the way Violet did. Instead, she felt pure indifference. Betty was sure that was far worse.

'So, you're leaving me alone again,' George growled, attempting to mop up the mess. 'And on Christmas night, too.'

'Don't be like that, Dad,' Maisie said cheerily. 'You'll be passed out on the bed by five, after the King's speech, you won't even know we're gone.'

'You little—' George snapped, a look of outrage on his face that Maisie had cheeked him.

'George, that's enough,' Betty said quietly.

To her surprise, George said nothing, and turned back to the fresh tea that Betty had poured for him.

'Anyway, you'll have to get used to me not being about as

much. I'm helping out at that fancy department store up West, with their new restaurants campaign, remember?'

George grunted. 'So you're telling me you're gonna be too busy cooking and sorting for everyone else to look after me.'

Betty inwardly groaned. She should have known he wouldn't be pleased for her. George had always seen her as little more than a skivvy, and for years she had felt as if that was a role she deserved. Not these days, though. These days she had more about her, and she knew what she was worth. Thanklessly and wordlessly, she looked after a man she no longer loved, working tirelessly to put bread on the table and contribute to the war effort with the WVS, and now this new campaign with Howell & Smart.

Any other husband would have been proud, pleased for her, even. But not George. He had such little respect for her, he always had.

'Well, I think it's brilliant, Ma,' Maisie said now, interrupting the silence. 'When you're a bit more established and need volunteers I'll come and help you.'

Betty looked at her youngest daughter in surprise, something not lost on Maisie who laughed.

'We should all be doing our bit. Look at what's happened in Liverpool, Coventry and now Manchester. People are going to be grateful for a hot meal when they've got nothing. I want to be a part of that, and Nan will, too.'

'Thanks, love,' Betty managed. 'I'd really appreciate your help when we're settled.'

'As long as the punters don't mind wearing their food instead of eating it, eh, girl?' George guffawed as he looked at his youngest daughter. 'You're a clumsy cow at the best of times.'

They both shot him a look of disdain, and Maisie turned her back on her father.

'Anything I can help you with now, Ma?' she asked.

'Well, if you don't mind waking your nan and letting her know lunch is nearly ready, that would be grand.'

'Done,' Maisie said skipping out of the kitchen.

'I still can't believe you're going to leave me here, on me tod,' George growled as he prodded at the paper. 'It ain't right.'

Irritation flared again. 'Yes, well. There's been a lot gone on round here that's *not right,* George Millington. I'm going.'

Ignoring the wounded look he gave her, Betty turned back to the table and surveyed it one last time.

The world, his daughters and his wife were changing. George would have to get used to it.

Fourteen

'Should we really be doing this?' Peter asked, glancing at his sister, his eyes filled with worry. 'We're Jewish. We've never celebrated Christmas before. I'm not sure Mother and Papa would approve. We never even *knew* anyone who celebrated Christmas at home.'

Nancy felt a wave of fondness for her charge. She had begun to realise that Peter felt anxious about a lot of things, wanting to control almost everything in his world.

She was just about to reply, when Edna got to her feet from her place at the Palais bar and sniffed. 'It's not traditional, dear, no. And Christmas is certainly something we never celebrated until Nancy came along with her funny American ways—'

'But when there's so much hardship in the world, it's nice to celebrate the happy moments when we can,' Nancy cut in smoothly, shooting daggers at Edna over the top of Peter's dark head. 'It doesn't mean we're any less Jewish.'

Ignoring Nancy, Edna looked pointedly at her empty glass and jiggled the ice cubes. Taking the hint, Nancy reached for the gin bottle behind the bar, filled her mother-in-law's glass and then poured a measure each into Queenie's, Betty's and Maisie's glasses. The Millington trio had been the first of her guests to arrive an hour ago. They had been early, but as Betty looked particularly grim-faced, Nancy hadn't had the heart to say anything and had instead welcomed them all inside.

'Such a shame Alex couldn't be here,' Edna said, her eyes misting over.

'But I thought you said you didn't celebrate Christmas, and it's just Nancy and her funny American ways?' Ruth said, innocently.

Queenie rocked with laughter in her chair. 'Out of the mouths of babes, eh?'

Ruth looked confused. 'What did I say?'

'Nothing,' Nancy said, doing her best to hide a smirk.

While Peter was frequently prone to anxiety, Ruth had comic timing that was often pure genius. 'Why don't you check to see what Christmas records we have for the gramophone player,' Nancy suggested to both kids now.

As Ruth and Peter skipped off, Edna turned to Nancy. 'I do wonder if Alex is all right. This is his first Christmas without his family. Who knows where he is and who he'll be celebrating with.'

She looked pained at the thought, and Queenie nodded sympathetically.

'It's the first for a lot of us without loved ones. At least your Alex is alive.'

'Hardly the point,' Edna snapped, closing down Queenie's attempts at festive spirit.

Nancy resisted the urge to roll her eyes. Queenie and Edna never got on.

'I'm sure he'll be grand, love,' Betty said with a kind glance. 'From what Nancy has told me of your son, he wasn't one to get too sentimental about things.'

'True,' Edna conceded. Her eyes glazed over and Nancy felt a wave of sympathy for her. She was close to Alex, too close in Nancy's opinion, but today wasn't the day to think like that. It was a time for charity and kindness.

'Anyway, it's the here and now we should think about,' Maisie said loftily as she took a large gulp of her gin. 'Happy to be around loved ones.'

Betty raised an eyebrow. 'Are you going to say that to Violet when she arrives?'

Maisie looked hurt. 'Of course. Me and Vi made up long

ago. You know, I feel sorry for her. She's been so grief-stricken since Eamon died.'

'As has Temperance,' Nancy sighed.

'It's different, I suppose,' Maisie said, her face clouding.

'I'm ever so worried about Violet,' Betty put in.

'She never smiles no more,' Queenie added, as a look of sadness passed her lined face.

In that moment, Nancy longed to tell them what was wrong with Violet, knowing how much family support could mean in a crisis. But it wasn't her secret to share. She knew why Violet felt she couldn't say a word, but looking at these women before her, concern etched across all of their faces, Nancy felt she owed it to them and to Violet to try.

'Well, perhaps we can spread a bit of Christmas cheer Violet's way today, huh?' she said.

'Not if you keep serving up tiny measures like these ones, love,' Queenie said.

As she passed the glass across the bar, Nancy caught the twinkle in the older woman's eye and was grateful to her for changing the subject.

Refilling her glass, Edna checked her watch.

'What time are you expecting everyone else?'

Nancy checked her watch. 'In about ten minutes, I said anytime after five.'

'I told you we were early,' Betty hissed at Queenie. 'I am sorry, Nancy.'

'Not at all,' Nancy soothed. 'Happy to have you.'

'George was in a right mood. Fell asleep as soon as the King's speech was over. We thought it better to leave him with the company of beer,' Queenie explained.

'Gran!' Maisie growled. 'Don't tell Nancy that.'

'Why?' Queenie shrugged. 'It's the truth ain't it? That good for nothing son of mine don't deserve company on Christmas, not after all his carry-on.'

Nancy winced. She knew George had his faults, but it must be hard as his mother to recognise them. Sometimes people were simply bad and there was nothing you could do about it, no matter how good a parent you were. And despite the fact Queenie tried to laugh off George's faults, Nancy could tell that she was hurt and disappointed by the way her son had turned out.

'Betty, did you tell Queenie about the old friend of yours that you ran into at Howell & Smart the other day?' Nancy said, keen to change the subject.

'No!' Maisie exclaimed.

'Who's this, then?' Queenie asked, eyes twinkling.

'Alan Hopkins,' Nancy said smoothly. 'You two were old school friends, weren't you?'

'Something like that,' Betty mumbled.

'Alan Hopkins?' Queenie gasped. 'Well there's a name I haven't heard in years, eh, Bet? I expect that gave you a surprise.' Shooting her daughter-in-law a kindly smile, she turned back to Nancy. 'Nice thing you did here today. Thanks for the invitation.'

'It was,' Edna agreed. 'Inviting lost souls over today. Christmas Day can be such a difficult day for some.'

'Thanks,' Nancy said, delighted for once to be on the receiving end of a compliment from Edna.

'It was kind of you,' Betty added, lifting her glass by way of thanks. 'We're very glad to be here.'

As Queenie and Maisie murmured their thanks, Edna ran a hand over her grey curls and coughed.

'And I do hope you don't mind but I invited Bill to come along. He wanted to join me in raising a toast to Alex, wherever he may be.'

Nancy gritted her teeth. She should have known Edna wasn't being nice without good reason. Still, she could hardly object. Even though she disliked the Palais' resident MC for the way he had bullied Temperance recently, she decided to be charitable. It was Christmas, after all, and she knew Edna would be missing her son.

'Sure, honey,' she said, giving Edna a lipsticked rictus grin.

Fortunately, she was saved from further pretence by the arrival of Violet through the double doors.

Flanked by Winnie Adams, Temperance's grandmother, Nancy could see the girl still looked pale. She glanced at Betty and saw the worry flash across her features.

'Sweetheart,' Betty said, getting to her feet. 'Happy Christmas.'

'Happy Christmas,' Violet managed, doing her best to smile.

'Vi! Winnie!' Nancy said in welcome. 'Merry Christmas.'

'Very kind of you to invite us,' Winnie said warmly. 'Temperance and Enid will be along in a minute. Temperance wanted to change her top.'

Glancing around the bar, Winnie took a seat beside Edna. 'I've never seen the place so empty. It's almost like a different world. My theatre's like that when there's nobody in it.'

Edna giggled, the effects of the gin clearly beginning to show. 'I feel a bit like that. Must say I rather like it.'

'I must admit, I do, too.' Winnie laughed.

Nancy shook her head. 'What would you like to drink?'

'I'll take a port if you have one, Nancy,' Winnie put in. 'And if you have a stout, give one to Violet. She's barely eaten a thing all day, complaining she doesn't feel well.'

Nancy looked sharply at Violet, who was now being fussed over by Betty. The girl had to eat. She was about to suggest as much in a roundabout way when in walked Archie, with Bill and two of their dancers, Helena and Daisy.

'Evening all, Happy Christmas,' Archie called cheerfully.

Nancy smiled and rushed to greet her guests. Archie was always a ray of sunshine and she enjoyed his company. Though she had a feeling, looking at the boy in his best suit, that he hadn't dressed up for her.

'Temperance not here yet?' he asked, his cheeks flushing slightly red.

Nancy smiled. It wasn't lost on her that the butcher's boy was sweet on Temperance and had been for some time.

'She'll be along in a minute, sweetheart,' Winnie called cheerfully from the bar.

'I dunno why you're so interested in her,' Bill said quietly, so that Winnie wouldn't hear. 'You can do better.'

Archie rounded on him before Nancy had a chance to. 'It might be Christmas Day, Bill, and that's about the only thing stopping me from punching you on the nose, but any more of that talk . . .'

Before Bill could answer, Archie moved towards Nancy and kissed her on both cheeks, before handing her a waxed paper package.

'What's this?'

Tapping the side of his nose, Archie winked.

'Mince pies!' Nancy gasped, as she undid the string. 'Where the hell did you get all these?'

With rations the way they were, getting hold of anything sweet had been a challenge and one Nancy had been desperate to rise to. She knew that she wouldn't be able to give Peter and Ruth a traditional English Christmas, but she had done her best. Taking a leaf out of Betty's book, the three of them had made paper chains from newspaper Nancy had felt bad about saving, and they'd decorated the bar with sprigs of mistletoe she'd found during a walk in Ravenscourt Park one day.

Not only that, Nancy had borrowed some Christmas ornaments from one of the dancers, who had been kind enough to let her decorate the upstairs living room and the mantlepiece in the bar area. There had of course been no Christmas tree to be had, what with all available wood going to the war effort, but the Christmas effect was, even if she said so herself, enchanting.

'Don't ask,' Archie said now in a stage whisper. 'Let's just say me dad knows a fella what knows a fella that could help me ma make her famous pies.'

Laughing so hard her curls bounced against her shoulders, Nancy beckoned the children towards her.

'Look at these.'

'What you got there?' Bill asked, craning his neck over Archie's shoulder.

Nancy ignored him, instead holding out the pies to Ruth and Peter. 'Here, guys, take one.'

'What are they?' Ruth asked, cautiously helping herself.

'The food of the gods,' Bill said reaching out to take one from the packet.

'That's bloody typical of you, Bill Cain. Snatching the food from the mouths of children,' called a voice from the back of the bar.

At the familiar tone, Nancy looked up and gasped in shock. 'Renee?'

Dressed in a fur stole and matching hat, Renee Hammond smiled as she sashayed through the bar.

'Happy Christmas, everyone.' She beamed.

Fifteen

'What the hell are *you* doing here?' Edna growled, getting to her feet and walking towards Renee. 'Thieves aren't welcome in my dance hall.'

At the sight of the old Palais matriarch coming towards her, despite her quaking nerves, Renee held her ground. After everything she had witnessed in the past few days, a confrontation with Edna Goldstein was a walk in the park.

'I think I'm saying Merry Christmas to me old pals at the Palais, chuck,' she replied coolly. 'That all right with you?'

'You've got a flaming cheek,' Edna roared. 'After what you did to us.'

'Quite right,' Bill thundered, siding with Edna. His eyes were flinty with hatred, and Renee knew the old MC would love nothing more than to see her crumple before him.

Briefly, she felt her resolve weaken. She had been in two minds about whether or not to come back to the Palais after the Manchester Blitz. But once the idea that Ronnie might believe she was dead had staunchly taken hold, Renee wanted to get her new life underway. So she had refused Janice's offer of the chance to stay with her, asking only one thing – that if anyone came looking for her, Janice was to tell them Renee had died along with any other poor soul that happened to be in the Deansgate area.

Confused, but knowing it better not to ask questions, Janice had agreed. And it was then, as Renee thought about where she could go, it suddenly dawned on her that the only place she wanted to be was the Hammersmith Palais de Danse. Strange as it sounded, after the way she had stolen from them, she wanted to be among her friends. After Hitler had raided Manchester that night, he had returned again, wreaking havoc across the North West. Like so many others caught up in the attacks, Renee had lost her home and her job, but she had survived.

With a few borrowed clothes from Janice, Renee had boarded bus after bus going south, and then finally a train to London, on which she had plenty of time to think. She hoped that her friends would have forgiven her by now. That they understood why she had been stealing drink and fags. It was her sister Lizzie who'd come up with the idea to try and make extra money so that they could repay Renee's husband Ronnie the debt her father owed and secure her freedom. Looking back now, it had been a laughable idea. The plan to sell knock-off booze and fags up Bradmore Lane Market. What had she and Lizzie been thinking? They'd have needed to make thousands – that was assuming Ronnie would even accept the money and let the debt and Renee go. In her heart of hearts, Renee had known Ronnie would never leave her alone. But for a while, it gave her and Lizzie hope they could lead a normal life without Ronnie in it.

'Leave her alone,' Nancy said now, as she guided Renee to the bar and gestured for her to sit next to Violet. Renee glanced at the younger girl and did a double-take. She looked like death warmed up. Turning to Betty she watched Violet's mother give a brief shake of her head, advising her to say nothing. Renee got the message and pulled her stole around her neck.

'It's nice to see you, Renee,' Violet managed, giving her a half-smile. 'I was so worried about you with the raids.'

'We all were,' Nancy put in.

'Yes, we thought you were dead,' Bill chimed cheerfully.

'Some of us hoped you were,' Edna muttered savagely.

Fortunately, Renee was saved from having to answer Edna, as Queenie returned from the toilets with Maisie in tow.

'Well, blow me down with a feather,' Queenie gasped. 'I had you down as brown bread.'

'You weren't the only one,' Edna growled.

'I swear to all that's holy, lady, if you mention me being dead one more time it'll be you getting ready to meet your maker, not me,' Renee thundered before turning back to Queenie. 'It'll take more than a couple of nights with Hitler to see me off, queen,' she added, her tone warm now as she allowed herself to be pulled into Queenie's arms for a hug.

'I can see that,' the older woman replied brightly. 'It's good to see you. You back with us for long?'

Renee looked at Nancy with undisguised hope in her eyes. 'All depends.'

'You can stay with us. There's room at the flat,' Nancy put in.

'Over my dead body,' Edna growled.

'I'm glad we're finally talking about your death rather than mine,' Renee shot back.

'It'll be Nancy's life in danger if she allows you to set one foot back in here,' Bill grunted.

'Can we please stop talking about death,' Betty cried. 'This is Christmas Day!'

At the outburst, Bill looked genuinely contrite. He crossed over towards Betty and bowed his head slightly in shame.

'Sorry, Mrs Millington.'

Renee felt a flash of guilt. She had wreaked havoc on these people.

'I'm sorry,' she said with genuine contrition. 'I wasn't thinking.'

'Don't be daft,' Temperance said firmly. 'You come and sit down. We're glad you're here, aren't we?'

Out of the corner of her eye, Renee couldn't miss the look of warning Temperance gave the others as she guided her to a chair beside the fireplace.

'What can I get you to drink, honey?' Nancy asked gently.

'Anything that's wet,' Renee said gratefully.

Sinking back into the warmth of the chair, she looked at the familiar group around her and smiled. She hadn't realised how much she needed to see the faces of those she loved. The last few days had begun to take their toll and it was only now, in the company of friends, that she was beginning to realise how much.

'How bad is it in Manchester?' Violet asked, pulling her into the present moment.

'Bad.' Renee sighed. 'Hitler did a bloody good job of knackering people's Christmas.'

'He's done a good job of knackering our lives, full stop,' Betty muttered.

'It's true,' Maisie put in. 'All I got was coal in my stocking.'

'You ungrateful so-and-so,' Betty exclaimed. 'You know how tight things are at the moment.'

'And I got you a new book,' Queenie put in. 'I'll have it back if you don't want it.'

Maisie looked shamefaced. 'Sorry.'

'I should think so,' Betty said with a shake of her head. 'Just because you're dancing the odd dance here now in the pen, don't you start getting ideas above your station.'

At the mention of the dance pen, Renee's ears pricked up. It was good to talk about something normal.

'You're dancing here now, eh, Maisie?'

Maisie flushed with pride. 'Just a couple of days a week,' she said. Then, as if suddenly remembering the hell Renee had been through, asked, 'What about the dance hall where you work?'

'Did work,' Renee replied grimly. 'It's gone. As has my flat.'

Taking a much-needed sip from the glass of gin that Nancy handed to her, Renee allowed the warmth of the alcohol to soothe her soul.

'I'm sorry,' Edna managed charitably.

Renee gave a brief nod of her head, touched by the older woman's recognition of hard times.

'Me, too. Good bunch up there. Even had a female MC,' she said, pointedly looking at Bill.

Bill shook his head. 'That's not right. How's a woman MC going to break up a fight between a pair of lads?'

'Well, you manage all right,' Queenie scoffed, 'and you're an old fella.'

'Good point,' Winnie added, with a smirk.

Renee hid a chuckle, while Bill looked menacingly at Queenie and Winnie, who didn't take a blind bit of notice as they continued drinking.

'How did you get here?' Violet asked her. 'Was it hard?'

Renee nodded. 'Yes. I had to take a lot of buses, then finally I got on a train to London at Nantwich.'

'What made you want to come back here?' Betty asked now.

'I just needed to be somewhere familiar, with folk I know,' Renee admitted. 'I first came for Lizzie all that time ago, and along the way I made a lot of friends.'

'Friends you stole from,' Edna put in quietly, earning herself a look of reprisal from Betty.

'Christmas is a time for forgiveness, Edna,' she said.

Edna only raised an eyebrow, threw back her drink, then said, 'Good job I'm Jewish then.'

Renee choked back another laugh. The old woman aways liked the last word, she was glad that hadn't changed.

'Will you stay?' Betty pressed. 'I'm sure there's still a job for you here isn't there?'

Turning to Nancy, Renee saw the manager nod.

'There's always a place for you here,' Nancy promised.

Bill thumped his fist so loudly against the bar that he made everyone jump.

'I can't listen to any more of this. I'm here to create some nice memories for these kids, not listen to a thief whinge about not having a job no more. I'm off.'

And with that he crashed through the door and left.

'You might wanna make an entrance more often, Reen, if it clears Bill from a room,' Queenie said drily.

Everyone laughed except for Edna, and Renee felt another wave of guilt at all she had done to the girls at the Palais. It was wrong of her to come back and expect a warm welcome. Not after that.

'What about Ronnie?' Nancy asked. 'Does he know you're in Manchester?' Reluctantly, Renee nodded.

'He sent some woman to tell me that he'd see me soon,' she admitted. 'Typical calling card.'

Renee saw Nancy pause and take stock, about to open her mouth and ask something, when Violet beat her to it.

'Is Ronnie alive?' she asked bluntly.

At the question, Renee bit her lip. She had been wondering the same thing herself.

'I don't know,' she said, wearily.

'Question is, does he know *you're* alive?' Nancy said.

'I'm hoping not,' Renee said carefully. 'I've asked Janice to tell anyone that comes looking that I'm long gone. I'm hoping it might buy me a bit of time at least.'

She glanced at the floor. If he wasn't dead, it was still only a matter of time before Ronnie discovered that she wasn't, but a few weeks' respite while she gathered herself together might make the world of difference.

'So, where's all your things?' Ruth asked from her place by the fire.

Renee smiled at the girl. She had never met Ruth and Peter before, and was immediately charmed by their innocence.

'That's all gone, too, sweetheart,' she said.

Immediately, Ruth got to her feet and, to Renee's surprise, wrapped an arm around her shoulders. 'I'm sorry,' she said. 'That's horrible.'

'That is horrible,' Peter agreed, from his chair opposite

them. 'But clothes and things aren't important. It's people that count. We found that out when we left our family.'

Ruth nodded. 'People are all that matter.'

Surprised to find she was blinking back tears, Renee looked at the two children and then up at Nancy, who was looking anxious.

'Where did you find two such wise kids?' Renee asked.

Nancy smiled. 'I have no idea, but I know we all got lucky the day I found 'em.'

'I'll drink to that,' Edna said, raising her glass.

Renee smiled. She didn't know what the future held for her, but whatever lay in store she was beginning to realise the true spirit of Christmas and she was determined to make this fresh start a powerful one.

Sixteen

From her position at the bar, Temperance watched Renee chat to the dancers in the pen and felt a mix of fear and joy seep through her soul. Naturally, she was overjoyed to see her friend, and even more delighted that Renee had escaped the Manchester Blitz unscathed. Yet, equally, she was worried what Renee's return meant for her. Did it mean that she was now out of a job? Would Renee be wanting to see her back in the cloakroom? Or worse, would there be no job at all for Temperance now that Peter was beginning his apprenticeship? What were Renee's plans, and where would they leave her?

It had been two days since Christmas, and Renee showed no signs of leaving. In fact, she seemed to have got her feet further under the table. Although nothing official had been said, Renee had just picked up where she'd left off, organising dance rotas and the pen, such as it was these days, and she had wasted no time experimenting with tempos to create new exhibition dances. So far, Renee hadn't tried to interfere in the dance lessons Temperance ran, but surely it was just a matter of time.

Anxiously gnawing at her nails, out of the corner of her eyes, Temperance saw Archie approaching.

'You all right?' he asked.

Temperance glanced at him and felt a wave of affection. Since she had been attacked that fateful night in October when they had held the infamous Palais dance contest, Archie had always kept an eye out for her, and she liked it. Now, dressed in a pair of navy trousers and a crisp white shirt with a navy tie, he looked just the right side of smart for Nancy's festivities.

Temperance nodded and gave him a wan smile. 'Fine.'

Archie gave her a small frown of understanding in return. 'Not worried about her ladyship coming back, are you?'

Gazing at Archie in dismay, she worried her emotions were written all over her face.

'Don't worry.' Archie grimaced, guessing what was the matter. 'I'd feel just the same if it was me. For what it's worth I don't think Nancy would ever get rid of you. You must know how important you are to her.'

'I do know.' Temperance let out a sigh. 'But the Palais won't need two dance teachers, in fact they probably won't need any teachers at all, soon. The dance authority is on about suspending lessons and exams until the war is over.'

Watching him scratching his chin thoughtfully, Temperance could see that Archie was searching for the right thing to say, and she felt a flash of affection for her friend. She gave him what she hoped was a reassuring smile – after all, she was taking matters into her own hands. She was meeting Queenie's egg man later that night after work, hoping that with his help she would be able to find the extra money to help out Violet. And though Violet hadn't found the courage to tell her family about her pregnancy at Christmas, remaining tight-lipped instead, Temperance was grateful that at least Nancy knew the truth.

Apart from the support she'd need before she had the baby, Temperance was well aware of the bigger problems Violet might face further down the road. Not only was she expecting a baby out of wedlock, she was also expecting a mixed-race baby. With a heavy heart Temperance thought of the prejudices her own mother had faced – and she had been a respectable married woman.

'I've lost you again,' Archie said, giving her a playful nudge.

Temperance looked at him, feeling lost for a moment before she spoke.

'Sorry, Archie, I'm a bit at sixes and sevens at the moment.'

'Anything I can help with?' Concern was etched across his face.

Temperance shook her head. 'I'm fine. Anyway, I've been meaning to ask about your dad. How is he?'

At the mention of his father, a look of worry flickered across Archie's angular features. Alf had suffered a severe bout of flu over Christmas and was struggling to regain his health. Consequently, Archie had stepped into the breach to run the butcher's alone.

Temperance admired Archie. He was a good man who never shied away from responsibility, and he had been a good friend to her since Eamon had died, frequently offering her the chance to talk and express her grief, if she wanted. So far, Temperance had refrained. Merely taking comfort from the fact he was there.

'Fancy a drink after your shift?' he asked. 'We could pop into the local? Landlord's having a bit of a sing-song tonight.'

She felt warmth flood through her heart. There really was nothing she would have liked more. But she had to meet Queenie; so much seemed to depend on it.

'I'm busy, sorry,' she said. And seeing a flicker of regret pass across his face, felt a stab of guilt. 'I've got the night off next Friday, though . . . If you've nothing else on, that is?'

Seeing Archie's face instinctively light up, she knew she had said the right thing.

'How do you fancy a Chinese meal? We could go up West?'

At the idea, Temperance nodded. 'I finish at seven.'

'I'll see you then.' Archie beamed.

Watching him walk away, Temperance felt some of the heaviness in her heart lift. She felt as if she had something of her own to look forward to.

Standing in the cold of Ravenscroft Park, Temperance waited anxiously for Queenie. It was quarter past seven, where the hell was she? Stamping up and down to try to keep out the chill, she blew on her fingers. It was freezing out. Just as she was about to give up on the idea, she saw the glow of a cigarette and braced herself for Queenie's entrance.

'All right, darlin'?' Queenie called.

Temperance could see the outline of a man she didn't recognise standing beside Queenie.

'This is Dave,' Queenie said, a hint of irritation in her voice. 'He wanted to meet you.'

'Wanted to check you're up to the job, and talk terms,' Dave grunted. 'Queenie says you ain't never done this before.'

'Well . . . no . . .' Temperance began, before Queenie interjected.

'We've been through this, Dave,' she hissed. 'She's one of my girls, you can trust her.'

'And it's my right to check she ain't gonna grass,' Dave countered.

At the gruffness of his tone, Temperance shuddered. She had always done her best to walk on the right side of the law, terrified that the consequences would be so much worse for someone like her than for others. Her father had drummed it into her since she was a kid, what would happen to her as a coloured kid if she ended up in trouble with the police.

'People expect us to fail,' he had said one day. 'You must always show that you not only meet the bar, but you rise above it.'

At the thought of her precious father, Temperance felt a flash of guilt. What would he say if he could see her now? Meeting black marketeers in dark corners of London to make a bit extra for her family. Would he be proud of her courage and ingenuity, or would he be ashamed? In that moment Temperance didn't want to answer that question and instead focused on the duo in front of her.

'I ain't gonna grass,' she said, firmly. 'I'm here to make money, nothing else.'

Dave chuckled, his cigarette glow showing off a row of rotten brown teeth. 'A girl after me own heart.'

Just then, she heard the rustling of a paper bag and felt something pressed into her hands.

'Two dozen there,' Dave said. 'I want half of whatever you make.'

'Half?' Temperance gasped. She looked at Queenie for confirmation, who simply shrugged her shoulders.

'You didn't think you'd be getting eggs for nothing, did you, girl?' Queenie said, in a kindly tone.

Temperance said nothing. Truth was, she hadn't really given it much thought. But half seemed ever such a lot. She did a quick mental calculation. How many eggs was she going to have to sell to help Violet, as well as her own family? More than she had anticipated, she realised, grimly.

'Fine,' she said, seizing the bag.

'I'll meet you back here on Saturday,' Dave said. ' And I'll give you another batch.'

'What if I don't sell them?' Temperance suddenly thought.

At the suggestion, Dave broke out into a laugh that Temperance knew didn't meet his eyes.

'Sweetheart, I still get my money, don't matter to me whether you sell 'em or not. So that's four shillings plus another two profit.'

Temperance stared at him aghast. Four shillings for two dozen eggs and another two on top. Did he think she was made of money? But even in the half light, Temperance could tell that saying no wasn't an option. Instead, she fished her purse out of her bag and handed Dave a fistful of coins.

'I won't check 'em,' he said cheerfully. 'I'm sure you're good for it. See you on Saturday.'

As Temperance watched him walk away, she felt a stab of anxiety eat away at her. Just what had she got herself into?

Seventeen

Nerves jangled away inside Betty as she arrived for work early in the New Year. Today was the day she was meeting with Alan and Nora, and she'd barely slept a wink in anticipation. Alan Hopkins. Who'd have thought he would have reappeared in her life? Just saying his name in her head felt dangerous. For years now, she had done her best to forget about Alan, believing it to be the best thing for everyone if his name was consigned to the history books. But now fate had played a hand and delivered Alan to her, and Betty couldn't help feeling conflicted.

She cast her mind back to how she and Alan had been friends as children. He'd always had the power to make her feel confident, capable, as though she was good enough for anyone and everyone – in stark contrast to her husband's attitude. But equally, Alan had left her suddenly and in the lurch. There had been no real rhyme or reason for his disappearance and the abrupt end to their relationship, and Betty would be lying if she said she hadn't lain in bed over the years, George fast asleep beside her, wanting the truth from Alan.

Now he had popped back up like a jack-in-a-box, as if nothing had ever happened between them. But would she get the answers she had spent decades hoping for? Just the thought of discovering the truth after all these years left butterflies flapping away in her stomach. Taking a deep breath, she patted her hair into place and had just about steeled herself when the toilet door burst open and Maisie appeared. Her youngest daughter stopped and stared at her mother's reflection as if trying to work something out.

'You look different?' she managed at last. 'You changed your hair?'

Betty laughed. 'I had it washed and set at the hairdresser's last night.'

Maisie's eyes went out on stalks. 'You did what?'

'Little present to myself. Thought I deserved it.'

Privately, Betty thought Maisie did, too, but wasn't about to say so. Instead she said, 'Have you seen Violet lately? She barely said two words to us at Nancy's Christmas do.'

Maisie walked towards the sink and splashed cold water onto her wrists. 'You know our Vi, she's always been uptight!'

'Maisie Millington, you take that back immediately,' Betty gasped, making a sign of the cross with her right hand against her chest. 'Your sister's always known what she wants that's all. Ambitious, I think is the word, not uptight.'

Maisie sighed as she wiped her hands. 'She'll be all right. Nancy's taking a special interest in her now so perhaps that will help.'

Betty's eyes narrowed. 'What do you mean, Nancy's taking a special interest?'

'She's got her doing more work in the office. Says Peter can learn the ropes downstairs and Violet can take on more of the admin. Nancy's invited her to the synagogue as well.'

'What? Why?' Betty demanded. 'Violet's not Jewish.'

She was as troubled as anyone else about the changes in her daughter, but felt uneasy about someone else becoming involved in her family's problems. It was for them as a family to sort out, not a stranger.

Although Betty could hardly describe Nancy as a stranger. The New Yorker had been good to the Millingtons, offering them all a hand when they needed it. But even so, what did Nancy know that she didn't?

As if sensing her mother was in turmoil, Maisie laid a hand on her shoulder. 'Look, Ma, Nancy's just trying to help. Sometimes it's easier to talk to people that aren't family.'

'So, you agree that something's up with Violet?' Betty said sharply.

There was a pause before Maisie spoke. 'Of course. But I think it's just grief. First we lost Roy, and then, just as she was getting back on her feet, she lost Eamon. That's a lot of heartache.'

Miserably, Betty nodded. She knew just how Violet felt. There had been days when she hadn't wanted to get up at all after Roy had died, and if she was truthful there were still days now when all she wanted to do was scream at the world. The nightly raids were a constant reminder of all she had endured, not to mention the terror that Roy must have felt as Hitler bombed his ship.

'Maybe I ought to talk to her . . .' she mused.

'And say what?' Maisie said, quickly. 'She's probably just as upset with you as she is with Dad.'

Shock pierced Betty's heart. 'Why?'

'Because you're still with him. After all he's done and you've just forgiven him.'

'I'm a married woman,' Betty snapped. 'I took vows, before God. What am I supposed to do? Leave him to his own devices? Throw him out on the streets? Turn my back on him while he's injured? Sure, that's not very Christian, Maisie.'

Hands on hips, Maisie looked her mother up and down before she spoke in a calm tone. 'What Dad did wasn't very Christian, and yet you keep defending him. The question is, why, Ma?'

With that she turned slowly on her heel and made her way outside. Leaving Betty alone with her thoughts.

Later that afternoon, Betty sat in the reception area of Howell & Smart, fiddling with her cup and saucer. Maisie's question had been going round and round in her head all day. She was right. George's behaviour hadn't been very Christian. When did things go so wrong between them? They had been friends once upon a time. Betty smiled as she remembered how carefree George had once been. Their fathers had been pals, and Betty's family had often gone out on family picnics and days out to the beach with the Millingtons. By the time he proposed, Betty knew George inside out. She knew he liked to gamble, that he had an eye for the ladies, and that he wouldn't be faithful to her. But, still, she'd been convinced that through it all he'd be her friend, and he knew she'd turn a blind eye to any extra-marital dalliances, whereas some women might not. Given that her choices had seemed very limited back then, Betty had been grateful for his offer, and accepted his proposal.

'Betty?' A bright voice boomed in the reception area, pulling her back to the present.

Lifting her head, she smiled and then faltered slightly as she saw it was Alan Hopkins standing before her.

For just a second, the years rolled away and she saw him as the milk boy that always called at their street every morning. When they had been nothing more than children, without a care in the world.

Reminding herself she wasn't a kid anymore, Betty rose to her feet and revived her smile. She was determined to play the part of a professional woman and not let Alan derail her.

'Alan, hello.'

But as she stood there looking at him, for a second she felt her resolve fail. He was every bit as handsome as he'd been when they were young, with all of life's possibilities laid out before them.

'Pleasure to see you again,' he said softly. 'Shall we go upstairs?'

As he led the way, Betty was sure the sound of her heart galloping now against her chest must be audible to everyone in the store.

Following Alan up the stairs to the same meeting room as last time, she listened to his easy chat about the store and the weather, all the while doing her best to concentrate on the business in hand, and not how differently her life could have turned out.

Following him into the room, she was surprised to see it was empty, save for a tea tray in the centre of the dark wooden table, laid out for two.

'Is Mrs Lovell not joining us?' she asked, feeling nervous.

Alan shook his head as he gestured for her to sit down. 'Nora's had to go across to our Harlesden branch today to deal with a last-minute emergency, so it's just you and me, I'm afraid.'

Betty nodded, sinking into the chair opposite him and allowing him to pour out her tea. Automatically, he reached for the sugar and was about to drop a lump in when Betty shook her head.

'I don't take sugar,' she said, adding, 'not anymore.'

Alan looked at her in surprise and smiled before giving a tiny shake of his head. 'Of course, I'm sorry. Old habits and all that.'

'Quite,' Betty said, feeling a little prim as he slid the cup towards her.

She took a sip and felt Alan's sparking blue eyes boring into her.

'You've changed,' he said softly.

Betty laughed. 'Haven't we all?'

She looked at him over the rim of her cup. He still had the same spark, the same energy he'd had all those years ago when he'd delivered the milk to the Dunne house.

He had of course put on a few pounds, and his hair was more salt and pepper these days. But just the sight of him had the power to take her back to when she was no more than a child with dreams of her own.

'How's your mother?' Alan asked.

Betty nodded. 'Fine. Lives in Kent now with her sister.'

Alan nodded. 'And you. What have you been doing in the . . . How many years has it been since we saw one another?'

'Twenty-two,' Betty said abruptly.

Alan nodded. 'It doesn't feel like that long. I still think of you as the girl who showed me the magic of swimming in the Serpentine on a cold day.'

At the memory, Betty gasped. It had been a beautiful sunny but crisp April day. She and Alan had been for a walk and the sight of the water had been tempting. She had felt like a devil as she waded through the water, his hand in hers.

Betty's temples began to throb. She couldn't go back to the past. Not now, not after so long.

'So, where shall we start today?' she asked brightly, determined to push away any nostalgic thoughts and concentrate firmly on business. 'Should we perhaps discuss recipes? I'm sure Nora would want to keep things basic but simple?'

Alan nodded. 'Yes, she's come up with a few here in this folder. Here, take a look and see what you think?'

As he passed her the folder across the table she felt his fingers brush against hers and it was as though an electric charge had pulsed through her body. She looked up at Alan and saw from the look on his face that he had felt it, too.

'Thank you,' she said stiffly.

Aware that her cheeks were burning against her skin, she leafed through the folder and saw recipes for simple soups and stews, as well as classic pies.

'All very filling but easy recipes,' she said.

'That's Nora's plan,' Alan said. 'She wants to serve uncomplicated food at prices people can afford, so they can be sure they're getting a good meal when they're in crisis.'

Immediately Betty's thoughts turned to the events, just four days ago, when Hitler had delivered another barrel load of hate, this time on the City of London. The financial district was consumed by fire after the Jerries dropped over 20,000 incendiaries and 120 tons of high explosives. The Guildhall and the area around St Paul's Cathedral was a sea of flames, and although the precious cathedral was spared thanks to the change in weather, 160 people were killed. It had been a devastating night and Betty had felt helpless. Looking at the folder before her, she felt a fresh sense of resolve.

'I can't wait to get started,' she said with a note of triumph.

'And I can't wait to spend more time with you, Betty Dunne,' Alan said softly. 'Here's to new beginnings and old friends.'

As he raised his cup and touched it against hers, Betty locked eyes with him. They had never been friends, and Alan knew it. But perhaps fate had delivered her an opportunity to finally right some past wrongs, and that was something she certainly would raise a glass to.

Eighteen

'Will you get your bleedin' hands off my notes,' Bill Cain shouted. Snatching the sheaf of papers from Renee's grasp so roughly that she almost fell backwards with surprise.

'You only had to ask,' she fired at him. 'I'm trying to help.'

Bill leaned forward and pressed his face close to Renee's. 'The only way you can help is by clearing off. You ain't welcome here, you little thief. When are you gonna get that through your thick skull?'

'The moment you accept the fact that you're no spring chicken, Bill,' Renee replied in a bored tone as she leaned against the Palais bar, hands folded. 'Look at you. False teeth, a wig, who d'you think you are, Rockefeller? Or some dirty old sod who's trying to keep up with the young girls that come in here? The sooner you're put out to pasture the better.'

Bill scowled, and Renee felt a flash of satisfaction. She was sick and tired of men pushing her about, dictating what she did and how she lived her life. If it wasn't her father with his poor choices, it was Ronnie, and later, at the dance halls, the punters – who all wanted to lead and expected Renee to capitulate. Now, here was Bill Cain pushing her around. She had always disliked Bill and hated the way he threw his weight about and bullied the female staff. The worst thing was that he had got away with it for so long. Now he was trying it on with her, using the fact she she been caught thieving as a weak spot. Well, no matter what he did, Renee wasn't having it.

But as he pushed past her, she sank onto the windowsill

opposite the replica fountain and allowed herself to take a deep breath and think. So far, her plan to start afresh was working. Ronnie certainly hadn't caught up with her, but the hideousness of all she had endured in Manchester, as well as losing her home, her job and her possessions, made her feel as if her real life was on hold.

After all, despite her determination to make a go of things she was living in borrowed clothes, sleeping on Nancy's camp bed in her good front room, and concerned that she was outstaying her welcome at a job that wasn't really hers.

Hearing the sound of footsteps, Renee got to her feet and pretended to be busy sequencing a reverse turn, as Violet and Temperance walked through the doors.

'Hiya, Vi, Temp,' she called brightly.

Just for a second, she saw Temperance's face fall before she smiled.

'All right, Reen?' Temp asked. 'What are you up to?'

'Just trying to work out some new sequences for the exhibition dance on Saturday night. Start the New Year off with a bang, like.'

Temperance nodded looking miserable, and Renee felt concerned. The Temperance of old, the girl she had become so fond of both here and in her letters, seemed to have disappeared before her eyes since Renee had returned, and she couldn't understand why. Had Temperance suddenly become shy?

'Here,' she said now, stepping back and gesturing for the two girls to take to the floor. 'I'm working on a new quickstep variation. Thought we could get Daisy and Archie to have a go at it on Saturday. The timing's very simple. Instead of quick, quick, slow, I thought we could try slow, slow, quick—'

Temperance managed a smile. 'Sounds good, Renee. Let me know if I can help.'

'You can always help, queen. You've probably got more of an idea than me these days,' Renee added.

'If you say so.' And with that Temperance walked past her and out into the corridor.

'What's got into her?' Renee asked, as the door banged shut.

She turned to Violet and saw that she looked uncomfortable.

'Come on, out with it, queen,' said Renee.

'She's worried she's going to be out of a job,' Violet said flatly. 'Now that you're back.'

Confusion passed across Renee's face. 'What does me coming back have to do with anything?'

'Well, she's dance instructor now, isn't she?' Violet said uneasily. 'Chief dance instructor. Now you're back, that position might not be hers any longer.'

Realisation hit Renee. '*That's* what she's worried about? Losing her job?'

Violet nodded. 'She's the main breadwinner, now that Eamon's gone. She's scared she won't find work elsewhere. All this,' Violet held her arms open and gestured to the vastness of the dance hall they were stood in, 'it's her dream.'

There was a pause as Renee took in what Violet had shared with her, then she shook her head, sadly. 'Dozy mare. Course I'm not here for her job. I'll talk to her, make things right.'

A look of relief passed across Violet's face. 'I think that would be a good idea. I'm worried she's going to do something daft to make ends meet.'

'What do you mean, "daft"?' Renee asked, a little more sharply than she intended.

Violet shrugged. 'Not sure. I know she's been hanging about with Queenie a bit more than usual. And Queenie, well, she's no stranger to making a bit extra.'

Renee nodded grimly. Queenie Millington was as tough as old boots. She'd been round the block and then some over her lifetime, and she could see off dodgy fellas and rough-as-old boots crooks with a blink of an eye. Renee had no doubt Queenie could hold her own, but Temperance was another matter. She was young and still had a lot to learn.

'So, you think that's what Temperance is doing since I've come back?' she asked bluntly. 'Making money on the side like Queenie does?'

'I dunno,' Violet admitted. 'But she's not been herself, I know that.'

Renee nodded. She would sort this mess immediately. Temperance was her friend, or at least she always had been. The last thing she wanted was to make her feel as if she had to start making extra hanging about with fellas like her husband. The thought made Renee shudder. She'd rather live on the streets herself than see Temperance turn to anything like that.

She turned to Violet and saw the girl looked ashen. A look she had perpetually worn since Renee had returned.

'And how are you?' she asked quietly.

Violet gave her a smile that didn't reach her eyes. 'Fine.'

Reaching inside the pocket of her cherry-red skirt, Renee pulled out her cigarettes and lit one. 'You don't look fine to me, chuck. You look peaky . . . pale, like.'

Violet laughed. 'That how you greet all your friends, is it? You won't win any popularity contests with compliments like that.'

'You can't kid a kidder,' Renee said. She took a long pull on her cigarette then observed Violet again, who met her gaze with a steely one of her own. Renee wasn't going to get any more out of her, that was obvious.

'How are you, Renee?' Violet said. 'Must be hard for you being back.'

Renee nodded. 'It's not easy, starting again.'

'But it's the right thing, isn't it?' Violet said. 'A chance to escape your Ronnie once and for all.'

Renee laughed. 'I'll never escape that man. I've resigned myself to it. All I can do is enjoy the peace while it lasts.'

Violet shook her head. 'Can't you go to the police or something, Renee? It's not right you should be suffering like this.'

'The police?' Renee echoed. 'Are you having a laugh? The police are in Ronnie's back pocket. If I went to them, they'd no doubt let him know straightaway, I'd be walking into a trap.'

'Is that really true?' Violet sighed, sadly. 'There must be something you can do?'

'I wish there was,' Renee said, wanting to change the subject. 'Anyway, how are things at home . . . with your dad, and everything?'

Violet's expression hardened as she shook her head. 'I wouldn't know. I don't spend much time with Betty and George at the moment, but Maisie says Mum's changed towards him. She's colder somehow. Like she's sick of him.'

Renee thought of George's 'indiscretion' and felt solidarity with Betty. 'Well I can't say as I blame her,' she replied. 'I'd be fuming an' all if my husband had got another woman in the family way.'

'It's more than that,' Violet said. 'It's as if she's indifferent towards him. Like she's just going through the motions.'

Renee nodded. 'She's had a lot to cope with. It's probably her way of dealing with it all.'

'Who can say?'

'Would you be pleased if Betty finally booted your dad out? It's not as if he doesn't deserve it.'

At that, Violet threw her head back and laughed. 'Betty'd never do that. She's made a vow in the eyes of God. That means more than anything else in the world to her.'

'I'm sure that's not true,' Renee said carefully, noting that Violet still insisted on calling her parents by their Christian names rather than Mum and Dad. When she'd asked Vi about it months ago, she'd been told it was something she had always done because she'd never felt close to either of her parents. Renee had hoped that might change and was sad to see that it hadn't.

'It is,' Violet replied sadly. 'For Betty, doing God's will is the only thing that matters. She'd never leave George, more's the pity.'

'You ever got on with your old man?' Renee asked.

Violet considered the question before giving a brief shake of her head. 'We've never seen eye to eye. Roy neither. We hated George's belligerence, the way he treated Betty. But Roy was much better at holding his temper, doing his best to keep the peace with George, than I ever was.'

Renee nodded. 'Betty's had it tough of late. I'm not saying you haven't, either, Vi,' she added hurriedly, seeing a wounded look pass across Violet's face. 'Just that she could do with some good luck.'

'She could,' Violet agreed 'Maybe this new job with the National Restaurants will do her some good. Bit of a change at the very least, more time away from George.'

Stubbing out her cigarette, Renee smiled. 'Stranger things have happened, kid.'

Nineteen

As Bill and Edna stood shoulder to shoulder, Nancy felt weariness come over her. Something she was feeling increasingly more of with every passing day.

'So, let me get this right,' she said at last. 'You have delivered a ten-point plan on why we ought to kick Renee out of the Palais.'

'Correct,' Edna said sharply.

She gave the collar of her Chanel jacket a little tug and Nancy felt the woman's familiar hostile stare bore into her.

'But, why?' she asked, impatiently, determined not to let Edna derail her. 'With everything going on in the world, why are you two devoting yourselves to getting rid of one of the finest professional dancers in Britain?'

'Because it's not right that she's here,' Bill hissed. 'Renee stole from us. She has no respect for the Palais.'

'No, Bill, she has no respect for you. And I'll admit I'm struggling to find an ounce of respect for you myself, right now.'

Jabbing at the piece of paper in front of her, Nancy felt a sudden urge to get it off her desk, as though it was poisonous.

The year had only just got underway, and already the world had gone to hell in a handcart, as the expression went. Not only had the Nazis devastated Cardiff, Bristol and attacked Dublin, but there were rumours abounding that Hitler was encouraging the Japanese to start a war on America so they would be too preoccupied to become involved in his war on Europe. People were being bombed out of their homes, loved ones were dying by the hour, food shortages, not to mention the promise of more rationing, were all a daily source of worry. And yet here were Bill and Edna, both of whom Nancy could only describe as idiots, wanting to wage war on poor Renee.

Reaching for the sheet of paper containing their plan, she tore it into shreds and tossed it into the wastepaper bin underneath her desk, before eyeing Bill and Edna coldly.

'I've said it before and I'll say it again. Have you two really got nothing better to do than torment Renee? She has been through enough.'

'She wanted to destroy *my* Palais!' Edna snarled.

'Honey,' Nancy replied in a bored tone, 'it's not your Palais. And it certainly isn't *yours*,' she added, looking at Bill.

Looking at the anger written across their faces, she tried another tactic.

'Look, I understand you're both angry with Renee,' she said, her tone gentler now. 'I was myself when I found out what she'd done. Hell, I even slapped her across the face. But she's more than paid her dues now. She's apologised, and she only did it because she was desperate—'

'Because she married that thug!' Edna blasted.

'Which,' Nancy continued, ignoring Edna's outburst, 'is why she needs our help and support. At a time like this with everything going on in the world, don't you think we should be offering the milk of human kindness and turning the other cheek? It's not beyond you, surely? I mean look at how kind you both are to Peter and Ruth.'

At the mention of the children, their faces softened.

'It's not their fault what they've been through, poor little mites.' Edna said. 'They must miss their mum and dad dreadfully.'

'And all their little pals,' Bill added. 'Breaks your heart.' He sniffed. 'But Renee Hammond has brought this all on herself. And we aren't the only ones who don't want her here.'

'The bar staff don't respect her,' Edna offered.

Nancy felt bewildered by their double standards.

'If you mean Sybil Hancock, she and Renee have been at war longer than Britain has with the Jerries,' Nancy replied.

'And Alex certainly wouldn't want her here, either.' Edna sniffed.

Nancy felt her hackles rise. 'How do you know that?'

'He told me so.' Edna examined her manicured nails. 'In his last letter. Said it was no good for morale, Renee coming back to work here.'

Nancy narrowed her eyes. She was sure Edna was lying. Not only would her mother-in-law have been lucky to have received a letter this quickly after Christmas, since the post from overseas notoriously took weeks, but Nancy was sure Alex would never have said something like that. He had always been such a compassionate man, or at least he had when they'd first met. Perhaps war had changed her husband? she thought. It had certainly changed her. She was sharper now, less tolerant.

'And then there's you,' Bill pointed out sharply.

'What about me?' Nancy replied, her brown eyes narrowing as she looked from him to Edna.

'None of the staff respects you, either,' Bill put in. 'The dancers think it's odd that you don't know a quickstep from a foxtrot – and the punters ain't keen, either.'

'Bill . . .' Edna said, a surprising note of caution to her voice. But Bill was on a roll.

'The punters hate you cause you're a Yank! Here's us Brits doing our bit for the war effort, even the bleedin' Canadians have pitched up, but you Yanks are too good to get involved. It ain't right you're in charge of one of the biggest dance halls in Europe.'

'Bill, please,' Edna tried again, 'that's enough. No need to insult Nancy.'

But the man's face was a picture of anger, with his pinched expression and flushed cheeks. Nancy recognised the look from when he was ready to do battle with troublesome punters.

'There's every need. We've gone on like this long enough, and she needs to hear the truth. We don't just want Renee gone, we want you gone, an' all.'

At this, Nancy's mouth flew open in shock.

Trembling, she leaned back in her wooden chair and eyed her mother-in-law and the MC. She had known them almost as long as she had been in London – and there had once been a time when she hoped they might turn out to treat her as family. But deep down she had known that would never happen, not even when she and Alex started courting and announced their engagement. If anything, their hatred for her had only grown. They hated the fact that she was American, an outsider not good enough for Alex, the boy that had grown up in the Palais. They had just about disguised their disgust when she and Alex got married, but she'd always known how Edna and Bill really felt about her. And that when Alex's back was turned they would strike and want to see her out of a job, because they hated her running the Palais. For Bill it went even deeper than the fact she was American, it was the idea of a woman being in charge that enraged him. Nancy telling Bill what to do irritated him no end.

'So, the gloves are finally off, huh?' she said at last. 'You've wanted me gone for a long time and this is how you do it – through Renee.'

'It's not like that, Nancy,' Edna said uncomfortably, while Bill just looked triumphant, a smug gleam in his eye. 'We just think that what with the burglaries last year, and the fact you've welcomed Renee back—'

'Not to mention you've promoted that black girl,' Bill muttered.

'We think it shows poor judgement. That you're not fit to be a manager. At least not yet,' Edna said, her voice cold.

Nancy shook her head and stood up.

'The fact you still refer to Temperance that way, rather than by her name, shows how ignorant you both really are.' She shouted.

As they stared at her, dispassionately, Nancy was so consumed with anger that she felt like sweeping the morning mail off her desk and thumping it. How dare they? She had single-handedly taken charge of this sinking ship after Alex had gone. The Palais had been her home from home when she'd arrived in England. It was the place she'd found love, and a job she adored – from the very core of her soul – and to have these two suggest otherwise made her sick to her stomach.

'Now, listen to me. You might think I exercise poor judgement, but have either of you stayed up until the small hours trying to balance the books?' Nancy hissed. 'Have *you* tried to work out how to ensure everyone keep their jobs when there is less and less money coming through the door? Are *you* constantly thinking up ways to help people forget their troubles with themed nights and events? And have either of you seen a woman in crisis and offered a hand instead of turning your back? I mean, I might be a Yank, but I'm doing my bit for the war effort. I help out with the WVS, I've taken in two Kinder Transport kids and given them a home, a family. What have you two done? Neither one of you volunteers, citing the fact you're too busy or too old.' She gave Bill a pointed glare. 'And yet you've the nerve to lecture me about my poor judgement. We're at war here, the sooner you two realise that instead of bitching and whining, the world might be a better place.'

Just then there was a knock at the door.

'Come in,' Nancy barked.

Renee's face appeared hesitantly around the door.

'Sorry, am I interrupting?'

'No,' Nancy snapped, her eyes never leaving Edna and Bill. 'We're done here.'

Taking their cue to leave, the two shuffled past Renee and out of the office. Only Bill paused at the doorway.

'This ain't over, Nancy,' Bill growled. 'We meant what we said.'

And then, with a pointed glance at Renee, he followed Edna down the stairs.

Once they were gone, Nancy sank back in her chair and allowed herself to breathe.

'What the hell was all that about?' Renee asked, going to sit in the chair opposite Nancy. She reached for a cigarette and offered one to Nancy, who to her surprise took it immediately. Nancy rarely smoked but in this moment felt she needed it.

'You don't wanna know,' she muttered darkly, blowing a series of smoke rings into the air.

'Fair enough,' Renee replied.

Nancy was grateful Renee didn't press her. She felt exhausted after her tirade.

'What can I do for you, honey?' she asked instead.

'A couple of things,' Renee said. 'Firstly, your Peter and Ruth have expressed an interest in dance lessons.'

'Have they?' Nancy felt surprised. In the few weeks they had been living with her at the Palais they had only wanted to watch the dancers, not learn any of the steps.

'I think Peter's soft on Temperance.' Renee grinned. 'He's hoping to join her classes. And it seems whatever Peter wants to do, Ruth wants the same.'

Nancy smiled. She had been just the same with her sister. They had always been close, and when Esther had left the States for England, naturally Nancy followed.

'Well, that sounds nice,' Nancy managed. 'They must be feeling a little more at home. So, what's the problem?' she asked, getting to the heart of the matter.

Renee paused and Nancy could see she was nervous.

'The thing is Peter only wants lessons off Temperance,' she said uneasily.

'Well, she *is* the dance instructor,' Nancy reminded her.

Renee nodded. 'As she should be, and she's more than earned

that job. But what I'm wondering is where does that leave me? I've been here over two weeks now, and it's been lovely being back, helping out 'n'that. But do you need me? I know those two old crones don't want me knocking about.'

'Ignore them.'

'It's not them that bother me . . .' Renee paused. 'But you do, Nancy. I don't want to make your life difficult,' she said, carefully.

'I want you here,' Nancy said firmly. 'There's always a place for you at the Palais, I told you that when you left.'

'Sure?'

'More than sure,' Nancy said. 'And you're welcome to stay with me as long as you want, as well.'

Nancy couldn't miss the look of relief that passed her old friend's face, and she felt a rush of pleasure. It was nice to do something of genuine help.

'So, what do you want me to do exactly?' Renee asked again. 'I mean, Temp's looking after the pen and the lessons, I don't want to tread on her toes.'

Renee's words hung in the air as Nancy realised that she was pointing out that there was no real role for her.

She thought quickly, and then it came to her.

'Honey, how do you feel about a dual role?'

'How d'you mean?' A look of nervousness flashed across Renee's face.

'I mean, it's been pointed out to me that the fact that I'm American is a problem, so it might be better if I'm not the face of the Palais for a while. I want you to do my old job as front-desk manager and also be chief dancer. Helena's role was only ever temporary. She never wanted to be chief dancer longterm, not with two kids at home, so she won't mind you taking that role back on.'

'Really?' Renee looked delighted.

'Really,' Nancy promised.

She stubbed her cigarette out and as Renee got up to leave,

turned her attention to the morning's mail. There were the usual bills and pamphlets, but at the back stood what was obviously a Christmas card, written in a hand that was familiar to Nancy now, but that was not addressed to her. She felt the hairs on the back of her neck stand on end as she studied the envelope, knowing without a shadow of a doubt it was from Ronnie Newsham. So much for him believing that Renee had died in the Manchester blitz. Nancy shivered, aware that Renee was still loitering. She was about to hand her the card, but when she glanced at Renee's smiling face, quickly changed her mind. Instead, Nancy discreetly set the mail down and bid Renee goodbye. The mail from Ronnie could very well mean her friend was in danger, but she couldn't give Renee anything else to worry about. And so, like many other problems these days, Nancy resolved to keep this one to herself, at least until she could do something to help.

Twenty

17th January 1941

Standing with her hands folded in front of her chest, Temperance stood at the back of the Palais next to the huge, steel bins, once again shaking with cold. Stamping her feet up and down while Nigel Henshall checked the eggs she had presented him with, she tried to shake off her nerves.

This was the second batch she had been able to obtain for Nigel, and he was meticulous in examining the produce. She understood why, of course she did. Nigel was running a high-end hotel, the last thing he needed was shoddy goods.

But equally, as she glanced over her right and left shoulders, her fingers practically blue with cold, she did wish he'd hurry up. Not only was it freezing, but the afternoon tea dance was due to begin in ten minutes, and questions would be asked if she wasn't there to welcome the dancers out onto the floor.

'Everything all right?' she asked nervously.

The hotelier's head snapped up and he gave her a warm smile.

'These are really excellent, Temperance. Perfectly brown . . . And chef was impressed with the golden yolks of the last batch.'

Temperance tried to look pleased as she rubbed her hands together to keep warm.

Nigel shot her an apologetic grin. 'Not easy, all this subterfuge is it?'

'No,' Temperance admitted.

Thankfully, the only person that ever really came out the back was Eric the storesman, when he brought out the bins. Like most entertainment venues, the style and glamour of the Palais was kept strictly front of house.

Rolling over the top of the brown paper bag, Nigel grinned again and fished in the pocket of his trousers for a fistful of change. 'Eight shillings we said?'

'That's right.'

Guilt ate away at Temperance at the price for the eggs. Not that she was making much out of it herself, it was all going to Queenie's egg man. But nobody could complain about that right now. Times were hard, you had to take what you could, when you could.

As the hotelier handed her the money, he paused. 'You don't seem the type to sell black-market goods, Temperance, if you don't mind me saying.'

'I don't mind.' Temperance shrugged as she placed the money carefully in her purse. 'No. I've never done this before.'

Nigel put his hands in his pocket and jiggled his leftover change. 'I can tell.' He paused, this time there was genuine concern in his eyes. 'Do you really need the money that badly? You seem such a good girl, Temperance.'

Temperance bristled at the well intentioned remark. She couldn't tell anyone just how much she needed this money. That it wasn't for her, it was for Violet. Who knew what pressure she would be under when word spread that she was having an illegitimate child. Temperance knew of one girl at school who'd been in the same predicament. She had been shunned so badly she'd been cast out of her home and her job, leaving her penniless. Temperance wouldn't allow that to happen to Violet, not when she was her friend, and she had meant so much to Eamon.

'We all do what we need to do for our families,' she said evenly.

Nigel nodded. 'Yes, of course. Well, look, if you can get me more eggs like that on a regular basis, I'll take every one. The customers love them.'

'Good.' Temperance gave him a smile now.

'And if I do take them all, I wonder if there's any chance of a discount?'

Shaking her head, Temperance set her mouth in a hard line. 'Sorry, Mr Henshall. No discount.'

Nigel chuckled. 'Good for you, Temperance. All right, you've got a deal.'

With that he tipped his hat and then walked past the bins and back down the alley. As he disappeared, Temperance let out a sigh of relief. She had to get better at this if she was going to keep selling eggs. From the moment she picked the eggs up to the moment she sold them, her nerves were a mess. She was not cut out for a life of crime.

Just as she turned to go, she saw the door of the Palais open and Archie appear. At the sight of Temperance, he froze in shock.

'Temp! What are you doing out here?'

Dressed in his butcher's overalls rather than his dance clothes, he looked as if he had just arrived fresh from work.

'I could ask you the same question,' she said, flustered. 'You're supposed to be on the floor, ready to welcome guests.'

Archie looked sheepish. 'I know, I'm sorry, I'm running late.'

'Are we still on for tonight?' she asked more softly.

As he looked into her brown eyes, she felt a flush of warmth towards him. 'Yes.'

'Good. I'm looking forward to it.'

'Me, too,' he replied.

Later that night, as she sat opposite Archie in a restaurant in the heart of Chinatown, a bowl of vegetable chow mein between them, Temperance did her best to push all thoughts of black-market goods, thefts, Dave Price and Nigel Henshall firmly from her mind. Instead she promised herself she would sort the 'egg situation', as she now thought of it, and concentrate on the boy sitting in front of her, who was currently regaling her with stories of his life.

'I can't believe you did that,' she gasped now after one of his childhood anecdotes. She set down her port and lemon.

Archie laughed. 'I wanted to be a cowboy, what else could I do?'

Temperance shook her head. 'I don't know many lads who'd actually write a letter addressed to cowboys in Montana and tell them he wanted to join them one day.' She smiled. 'I take it your letter got there?'

Leaning back in his chair, Archie scratched his chin thoughtfully. 'The letter didn't just arrive, it caused quite a stir in the community.'

'How do you mean?' Temperance leaned forward in her chair, agog.

'Well, the entire town got involved, they sent me a cowboy outfit which was the perfect size for a seven-year-old. Then they put together a training guide on how to be a cowboy. They even sent me a couple of American candy bars.'

'No.' Temperance was on the edge of her seat. 'What was the chocolate like?'

Archie wrinkled his nose disapprovingly. 'Not as good as British chocolate.'

Temperance laughed again and felt a pulse of delight as Archie slid his hand across the table and rested it on hers.

His hand stayed there all night as they continued to swap stories. And she was delighted to lear more about Archie's relentless ingenuity. After he grew out of his desire to be a cowboy, Archie wanted to be an accountant and he'd even trained with a company who had an office at the bottom of Bradmore Lane. But after two years of working away after school and every Saturday, Archie realised his rightful place was with his father and so he'd turned to the family business instead and learned the family craft of butchery.

'And your dad wasn't upset you weren't initially going to follow him into the business?' Temperance asked.

Forking a noodle into his mouth, Archie laughed and shook his head. 'Why would he be? Just 'cos he was a butcher, didn't mean I had to be.'

Temperance reached for her water glass. It seemed strange, but then, was it really? Her father had never pressured her or Eamon to do anything – and he certainly never expected Eamon to become a tanner like him.

'I don't know,' she said at last. 'I s'pose being a butcher is one of those jobs that's meant to carry on through the generations.'

'I s'pose so,' Archie agreed. 'Not sure why. I mean if my kids wanted to do something different, I wouldn't make them cut up meat all their lives.'

The warm fizzy feeling grew in Temperance's tummy. There was something so wonderfully relaxing about being in Archie's company, she could spend all day with him.

'Anyway, enough about me,' Archie said. 'What about you?'

'What about me? I didn't spend my childhood writing to cowboys in America.'

'No, but tell me more about you. I want to know everything,' Archie grinned, helping himself to a fortune cookie from the plate in the middle of the table.

As he broke it in two and read the slip of paper inside, she saw his cheeks bloom red.

'But you know everything,' Temperance said. 'There isn't much to tell.'

'Don't believe you.' Archie grinned. 'I don't know what you were doing round the back of the bins earlier with that hotelier, for example.'

'Oh, nothing.' Temperance felt herself growing hot. She'd hoped Archie hadn't taken much notice of what she was doing there. 'Just getting some air . . . Mr Henshall was feeling a bit nauseous.'

'So you took him out by the bins?' Archie raised an eyebrow.

Temperance gave a nervous laugh. 'Seemed like a good idea at the time.'

'Well, remind me not to ask you to look after me if I feel sick,' Archie joked.

'I'd do better than that for you,' Temperance grinned. 'Mum used to be a nurse, remember, she taught me how to look after people you care about.'

A broad smile spread across Archie's face. 'So . . . You care about me?'

Realising what she had said, Temperance felt that warm fizzy feeling turn to panic.

'Because I care about you, Temp,' Archie said softly. 'You mean a lot to me.'

And with that he slid his hand across the table and reached for Temperance's. As he rested his palm on top of hers, Temperance felt the warm feeling inside her stomach settle and a growing sense of calm take its place. Looking into Archie's eyes, she saw there was only kindness and affection there, and in that moment she wanted nothing more than to stare into those pools of blue all day.

'Shall we go?' Archie said softly. 'I ought to get you home.'

Temperance nodded. Ordinarily she would have felt reluctant, but she knew instinctively that this wouldn't be the last of their evenings together.

After helping Temperance on with her coat, they made their way out into the cold night air. As Archie reached for her hand, she smiled and slid her slender palm into his warm grip but when he turned to smile at her, she caught the clench of his jaw.

'Is everything all right?'

Archie smiled in gratitude. 'It's fine. Just trouble at work.'

'Anything I can help with?'

'Not unless you can catch thieves?'

'Thieves?' Temperance echoed.

Archie shrugged. 'Since Dad's been off, some scrote's been nicking our supplies. Rations, you know, that we get sent for our shoppers.'

Temperance's chest felt tight. 'What sorts of things?'

'Eggs, bacon, you name it, some toe-rag's been stealing it from us,' Archie sighed. 'And I bet it's someone that knows we're short-staffed because Dad's ill.'

He shook his head in disgust and stubbed his cigarette out onto the floor. 'These people make me sick. We're all doing the best we can at the moment, yet there's always someone that wants to take advantage. I've had to let customers down and we're out of pocket. Not only have we got no stock to sell, but our customers are threatening to register their ration books elsewhere.'

'I'm sorry,' Temperance managed, a lump of fear forming in her throat. She'd had no idea of the impact of her egg thefts. She shook her head, she had no proof Dave Price was getting his eggs from Archie's business – it could be an arrangement he had with one of the farmers and nothing to do with Archie at all.

'Hey, it's not your fault,' Archie said softly. 'It'll work itself out, always does.'

Guilt tore through her, as they made their way through the blackout, walking through Leicester Square and down Piccadilly towards their bus stop. When they were almost at Green Park, Temperance stopped and turned to Archie.

'What did your fortune say?' she asked.

'What?' he laughed.

'Your cookie.'

Temperance could hardly make out his features but she could tell by his pause that he was agonising over whether or not to tell her.

'It said "The love of your life is right in front of your eyes",' he finally admitted, softly.

As the words spilled from his lips, Temperance's heart-rate quickened. In that moment she desperately wanted that to be true.

Twenty-One

As January swiftly marched into February, Renee found herself immersed in plans for the upcoming Valentine's Dance. All thoughts of how she wasn't needed, or was stepping on toes, vanished in an instant the moment Nancy announced her role with everyone at the Palais.

Naysayers had been silenced at an impromptu staff meeting a fortnight earlier, when they had been told without question that Renee was not only front-desk manager, she was also in charge of dance operations – meaning anything to do with dancing fell under her charge.

It had been precisely what the Palais and Renee had needed as almost everyone got behind the redhead. Apart from Bill and Edna, of course, and Renee's old enemy Sybil Hancock, who had gone out of her way to be rude to her since her arrival back in London.

That morning, as Renee stood in the bar trying to find out if there was any way they could arrange some Valentine's decorations above the bar area, Sybil had been deliberately difficult.

'I told you, we've got to keep the bar clear for the drinks,' Sybil said again, and her pretty mouth set in a hard line.

'And I've told you we need to get a theme up here to get people in the mood,' Renee tried again.

'What's the theme, then?' Sybil asked, a wicked glint in her eye. 'Free drinks all night? It's not like you to pay your way, after all?'

Anger flooded through Renee, but she managed to swallow it down. Largely because she felt she deserved the jibe.

'I'm not asking for much,' she said. 'Mainly because there isn't much—'

'Specially not after you nicked it all,' Sybil fired back.

Renee's patience wore thin. 'Come at me again like that, lady, and you'll regret it. I don't answer to you.'

'You don't answer to nobody.'

'You won't answer at all when I crown you!'

Shoulders squared, Renee rounded on Sybil and watched with satisfaction as the barmaid took a step back.

'I'll see what I can do,' she said sulkily.

'Make sure you do,' Renee snapped.

Turning on her heel and walking out of the bar, Renee crossed through the foyer and out into the street. She needed a breath of fresh air after that exchange. Although she took a small amount of pleasure in winning a row with the Palais barmaid, guilt ate away at her for what she had done. She knew she deserved the relentless jibes from Sybil, or indeed anyone that cared to make them, but she had made some amends for what she had done. After Lizzie had died, Renee had been able to repay the Palais – though of course it had been hard since she'd been so consumed with grief. The money didn't make up for the betrayal, she knew that, and that it would take some time before she earned the forgiveness of everyone at the Palais.

Leaning up against the wall outside, Renee reached in her pocket for a cigarette. It was cold outside, as expected for the beginning of February, but it was good to breathe in a lungful of fresh air and pause.

Things had been difficult over the last few weeks. Not only was Renee busy pouring her heart and soul into the dance, but living with Nancy, Peter and Ruth was highly charged. The flat was cramped with the four of them, and Renee couldn't help thinking that it wasn't good for the children, who were still getting to know their new foster mum, to have to deal with Renee's troubles as well.

Although she hadn't told Nancy, Renee had been looking for somewhere else to live, but with half of London seemingly bombed out, pickings were slim.

Inhaling sharply on her cigarette, her gaze turned towards the nearby news stand. The papers were full of reports of how the British had successfully bombed the German city of Dusseldorf, killing thirty-five people. Cries of 'our brave boys' and 'sticking it to Jerry' screamed from the front pages, but it was still an atrocity. Germany bombed Britain, and then Britain retaliated. As far as Renee could make out, that wasn't a war anyone would win.

Tearing her eyes away from the newspapers, she saw Betty, with a man she didn't recognise, walking towards the cafe across the road. Heads bent, they looked engrossed in conversation. Renee waved, but Betty didn't see her.

Curious, Renee watched them together. Betty led such an ordered, proper life, and Renee was pretty sure she wasn't the type to have male friends. But looking at the way the man she was with took Betty's elbow and steered her into the cafe, Renee had a feeling they were more then just acquaintances, they had to be friends.

Just then, turning at the the sound of footsteps behind her, Renee saw Nancy and Violet together. At the sight of Renee, Nancy looked surprised, but quickly composed herself.

'Morning.' Renee smiled.

'What are you doing out here?' Nancy gasped. 'It's freezing.'

'Could ask you the same question?' Renee said wryly.

She glanced from Nancy to Violet and saw the girl looked positively green.

'Violet! You look like you should be wrapped up in bed not standing outside in the chill, propping up street corners.'

'I'm fine,' Violet said, though her teeth were chattering with cold.

Renee said nothing and inhaled another lungful of smoke. If that was what 'fine' looked like, Renee could only hope the girl never got properly ill.

'Honey,' Nancy said quietly, looking squarely at Violet. 'You're going to have to start telling people, sometime. You might as well start with Renee.'

Renee raised a perfectly pencilled eyebrow. 'Should I be flattered?'

'I didn't mean it like that.' Nancy shook her head. 'I guess I meant that you're open-minded.'

Renee took another pull of her cigarette. 'You mean I've been around a bit?' she said, good-naturedly.

Violet gave a weak smile at the joke. Nervously, she glanced back at Nancy and then seemed to steel herself.

'You're right.' She took a deep breath and then looked up at Renee, a hint of determination spreading across her face. 'Well . . . I'm pregnant.'

'Ah . . .' Renee nodded her eyes flitting over Violet's stomach. Truth be told, she wasn't surprised. True, Violet had been knocked sideways by Eamon's death, and Renee knew that grief affected folk in different ways, but she didn't think throwing up regular as clockwork was one of them.

She gave Violet a warm smile.

'Well congratulations, queen,' she said.

Violet looked bewildered. 'Congratulations?'

'It's happy news, isn't it?' Renee flicked the cigarette butt to the floor and stubbed it out with her foot, all the while making it look as fancy as a reverse turn. 'A baby, new start, new life and all that.'

'But . . . it'll be a bastard,' Violet whispered, glancing around her as if someone might hear. 'And what will people say about me?'

Renee wrinkled her nose. 'As someone that's been on the receiving end of gossip often enough myself, I can tell you that today's news is tomorrow's chip paper. Or at least it was before Hitler had us rationing potatoes an'all.'

Violet laughed.

'At the end of the day, chuck, folks will always talk. But in my experience, they soon move onto something else. All that matters now is that you and that kiddie are all right, happy and healthy – don't let anyone tell you different. Are you going to have it easy? No, course not. But don't let other people's opinions spoil your joy.'

'I told you she'd understand.' Nancy grinned at Violet, giving the girl a playful nudge.

'Look, I do understand,' Renee went on, gently. 'You've been a bit daft getting caught out like, but you're not the first and you certainly won't be the last. And I don't know anything about changing nappies, but I'll help you in any other way I can.'

Violet now gave her a warm, relieved smile, and Renee felt a sudden rush of tenderness for her. She'd seen many a girl in the family way, at dance halls up and down the country, but she was surprised it had happened to Violet. Renee had always thought of the girl as more vocation-minded, and the type to want a family within wedlock. In truth, Renee had always considered Violet to be more like her, though the one thing Renee had been sure of was that she never fell pregnant with Ronnie's child, and he was her husband. The very thought now made her shudder. She had made plenty of mistakes in her life, but praise everything holy she'd never been pregnant.

'I take it your mam doesn't know?' Renee asked, Betty popping into her mind.

At the question, Violet shook her head, vehemently. 'You know what she's like.'

Renee nodded, but after seeing Betty with that chap earlier she wasn't sure that she did. It looked as if Violet's mum had secrets of her own.

'I want to wait until things are more sorted before I tell her. She'll worry less if I tell her I've got a plan.'

'Sounds like a good idea.' Renee smiled. This was more like the Violet of old.

'I know I've been stupid, Renee,' Violet blurted. 'But I want this child. It's the last bit of Eamon I'll ever have, and I want to give it the world.'

'I know you do, chuck,' Renee said affectionately. 'And I know you'll be a good mum. Your heart's full of love, that's a very good place to start.'

At the compliment, Violet flushed with pleasure and Renee felt pleased she had been able to say something to the girl that made her happy in that moment.

She pulled the collar of her blouse tighter around her neck and made to go back inside. But as she did so a figure with his back to her, standing beside the news stand, caused her to pause.

Dressed in a thick, wool coat and trilby, it was almost impossible to make out any distinguishing features. But the broadness of his shoulders, the thickness of his neck and the way he tapped one foot on the floor whilst he flicked through the paper made a violent shiver fly down Renee's spine.

After all she had been through, all the hope she'd for her future, was the rest of her life about to be wiped out in a heart-beat? Because standing not fifty feet from her was the man she loathed more than anyone else in the world, Ronnie Newsham, his eyes fixed on the paper he was reading.

It had been three years since she'd laid eyes on him, but she'd know him in an instant. For a moment, panic gripped her. Ronnie had finally found her. Despite the fact she had hoped he'd think she'd been killed, he had found her. Renee should be running, as far as she could away from him. But staring at him as he continued to leaf casually through the newspaper – as if he had all the time in the world – it occurred to her that for once she might have the upper hand. Unless she was mistaken, he hadn't seen her yet. And that meant Renee had power. The question was, how could she best use it to her advantage?

Twenty-Two

'I'm telling you here and now, I did no such thing.' Betty grinned as she waved her finger at Alan, who was seated across the table from her.

The manager of Howell & Smart simply raised an eyebrow as he picked up his steaming cup of tea. 'I think you'll find, Betty Dunne, that you did run down my alleyway in your bloomers. It's a memory that's etched firmly in my mind.'

He set his cup down, then, and gave Betty a look that – to her shame – still made her stomach flutter.

She blushed, but refused to look away. 'If I did, it's only because my old ma was getting at me about something or other. She was a devil that woman, may the Lord forgive me.'

With that she made the sign of the cross against her good green coat and shook her head gently. 'I was a different person then. Different times.'

'I think we both were,' Alan said gently.

At the admission, Betty laughed. 'I should say so. You used to be a common or garden thief! Now look at you. Manager at one of the smartest department stores in the country.'

Now it was Alan's turn to look embarrassed. 'I couldn't go around picking locks forever.'

'Not if you valued your life, you couldn't,' Betty responded. 'Didn't your father ever teach you not to mess up where you eat?'

'He did, but he was also cursed with a lazy streak, which he passed on to me,' Alan replied, with searing honesty.

'I can't argue with that.' Betty sighed and pushed her uneaten piece of toast away from her. They were sitting in the cafe across the road from the Palais, and as usual the forthright but friendly cafe manager, Marge, had burnt the toast. And, as usual, Betty didn't have the heart to say a word. The poor woman had been rushed off her feet since all her staff had joined the munitions factory around the corner to help the war effort. Since then Marge had been swamped. Betty had half thought about suggesting to Nancy that Ruth lend Marge a hand, but it wasn't her place to interfere.

'Where have you gone?' Alan asked, peering at her. 'You always used to do that.'

'Do what?' Betty asked coming back to the present.

'Drift off halfway through a conversation, into your own private world,' Alan said softly.

Startled, Betty looked at him in surprise. 'You remember that?'

'I remember everything about you, Betty, you're hard to forget.'

Alan fixed his gaze on her again, and as she took in his tender smile and the kindness in his blue eyes, the years seemed to melt away. His once thick, dark hair now contained more than a little salt and was thinning, but the laughter lines around his eyes at least showed there had been joy in his life. Age didn't matter anymore, as Betty remembered how simply good it was to be in his company, how he still made her feel alive.

'Do you ever think about what life might have been like for us if we'd stayed together?' Alan asked now.

Betty shook her head, sure that her flaming cheeks were giving her away. She thought of the nights she had lain in bed wanting answers after he'd vanished from her life. The times she'd wished things had been different, that she and Alan had never parted ways. What would life have looked like then?

She shook her head again. 'What good would wondering about that do? You and me were over a long time ago, Alan.

Better to think about the present rather than disappear down memory lane with a pair of rose-tinted spectacles.'

'You always were a pragmatist.'

'And you were always a dreamer,' Betty replied.

Nonetheless, she picked up her cup and tried to still her racing heart. She and Alan were over and had been for a long time, she told herself. Her heart had been broken and there had been days she thought it would never heal, but then she had met George and life had changed. Slowly, her every waking moment was no longer taken up with thoughts of Alan, though she'd still allowed herself to think of him when she was alone at night and the house was quiet. She wondered if he really was the same person he'd been back then. Most of all, she wanted to know what Alan had done after he'd returned from service in the war – and about his wife.

'What did you do when you got back from the war?' she asked. 'I heard you moved to Wales.'

Alan nodded. 'I did. I was a teacher for a while, but then I moved back to London and gave up teaching. Which is when I joined Howell & Smart.'

Teaching sounded like a wonderful job to Betty, and she was curious.

'Why did you give up teaching?'

'Various reasons, but mostly because Vera wanted to leave Wales.'

And there it was. At the mention of his wife's name, Betty felt her stomach drop like a ship's anchor.

'Your wife?' Betty managed. She glanced at the curled up piece of toast on her plate and pushed it further away, its charred edges making her feel nauseous. She had of course heard a while ago through the Hammersmith grapevine that Alan had got married to a woman called Vera, but she had refused to dwell on the woman who'd finally captured his heart. Or at least she'd not dwelled on it often.

'Yes,' he said. 'She lives in Canada now.'

Betty raised an eyebrow. 'What the blazes is she doing in Canada?'

'Escaping from the war,' he said. 'But mainly getting away from me.' He brushed an imaginary piece of lint from his tweed jacket and Betty could see that despite his nonchalance he found the conversation difficult. 'Things hadn't been too good with us, not for a while.'

'I'm sorry,' Betty said.

'So am I. But we were never really right for each other. Of course, we did a good job of pretending we loved each other, but slowly the cracks started to show. And, if truth be told, we had nothing in common. The war was a good opportunity for us to take a break from each other.'

Betty nodded.

'Yes, marriage is difficult, or at least it can be.'

'Sounds like you know that from experience?' Alan said.

Betty laughed, sadly. 'I suppose I do. George and me, well we've had our own ups and downs.' She blinked, not wanting to talk about George. 'And do you have any children?' she asked, steering the conversation back to Alan.

'Yes. Susan and Robert. They're teenagers now. They went to Canada with Vera.'

Betty couldn't avoid the look of sad pride on Alan's face at the mention of his kids. 'I miss them, but I know it's better for them to be with their mother. They're fifteen and sixteen and they are helping Vera with a new business she's setting up.'

'What's that?' Betty asked politely, though she didn't really care what Vera was doing.

'She's set up a professional maid service. Helping rich folks with their domestic duties.'

'I can't imagine there's a lot of call for something like that around here,' Betty remarked archly.

'Which is just one of the reasons we're better off apart than together,' said Alan. 'I don't want a life in Canada, and Vera's business would never succeed here. And at least this way, there is an air of respectability to our separation. And, as terrible as the war is, it's focused our minds.'

'To want more freedoms, you mean?' Betty smiled. She agreed with him. Since war broke out attitudes had changed, with many fearing that today may very well be their last day, so what the hell? Live the life you want to live? Though the downside of this, she considered, was that crime rates had soared across the country.

'And you?' Alan asked now. 'I know about George of course. Ups and downs aside, are you two still happy?'

Betty stared at him. Sudden anger unfurled within her as she thought how dare he ask her this question, when her life was the way it was because of him.

'We're very happy, thank you,' she said, tightly. 'Twenty-one years married now.'

'Congratulations.'

'Thank you,' Betty said again, stiffly. 'Course it's not been easy for him, he lost an arm in France, when the Jerries . . .'

There was no need for Betty to finish her sentence. Everyone knew what had happened to the British soldiers in France.

'I'm sorry,' was all Alan said, though she could tell that he meant it. 'And what about your children? I know about Violet. Oh, and Roy, of course . . .' Now it was his turn to trail off. 'I . . . was very sorry to hear he'd died, Bet.'

She nodded, touched, but she still wasn't going to make this easy for him.

'Did you and George have any more kids?' he continued.

'Yes, Maisie, a couple of years younger than the twins,' Betty said, a hint of pride to her voice.

'Wonderful.' Alan's voice radiated goodwill for her and Betty fought against the grief resurging inside her, and that the biggest tragedy of her life had been losing her boy.

'You know an awful lot about my family,' she said, instead.

'Queenie's mates with my old ma's cousin. News trickles through the family.'

'Of course.' Betty rolled her eyes. 'Queenie's got her fingers in that many pies it's a wonder she hasn't grown a few more fingers.'

At that, they both chuckled, but Alan's smile stayed fixed on his face.

'I've been wondering if it's fate that's placed you in my path again,' he said.

'How d'you mean?'

'Well, you being the one to help Nora with this new scheme. Walking into our offices after not seeing one another for nigh on twenty years. I wonder if fate's trying to tell us something.'

Betty paused for a moment. This conversation was beginning to feel dangerous.

'I don't believe in fate,' she said firmly. 'Or raking over the past.'

'But I have been thinking about it, Bet,' Alan said, and he suddenly reached for her hand across the table and as he placed his smooth palm on her long fingers she felt a jolt surge through her. 'I've wondered what you were doing, and wished things had worked out differently. Now you're here in front of me after all these years and I can hardly believe my luck. I want to get to know you, again. Is that all right?'

Betty's heart continued to thud dangerously against her chest. In that moment it was all she wanted, but to admit it seemed like an act of treachery. She knew what Alan meant and she had a horrible feeling that she knew where this would end. But, as always, when it came to Alan Hopkins she was powerless to resist.

Twenty-Three

The panic Renee felt at her near-miss with Ronnie stayed with her for the next fortnight. No matter how much she threw herself into the Valentine's Dance, helped Ruth with her home-work or Peter learn more about life working, not to mention running a dance hall, she couldn't shake the fear that Ronnie was out there waiting to strike.

So many times since, she'd wanted to confide in someone but had resisted. She didn't want anyone else worrying about all the trouble Ronnie might bring when he did find her, which she knew he would, when he was ready.

The only advantage she had over Ronnie was that he didn't know she had seen him. She just had to keep her wits about her, stand her ground when he finally did appear.

At least that was the plan. How much she would be able to stick to it, she wasn't sure. Especially when her patience was being tried at every turn lately, by of all people, Temperance and Archie.

Watching the two of them on the dance floor together today, lovebirds mooning at each other, Renee's patience had been tested to the limit. She was trying to prepare Archie and Helena for the Valentine's dance in the evening, but every time she gave an instruction Archie would look longingly at Temperance and she would give him a round of applause.

Helena was getting fed up, too, shooting filthy looks at Temperance, and slipping off her shoes.

'What the hell are you doing, lady?' Renee snapped at her.

'Going back to the pen,' Helena said moodily. 'I don't mind him making eyes at Temperance, but I do object to having to lead him round the sodding floor because of it.'

'Hey, come on, I'm not that bad,' Archie protested.

'Not that bad,' Helena echoed in disgust. 'You've kicked me in the shins twice, and nearly tripped me over.'

At this admonishment, Archie hung his head in embarrassment, and even Temperance looked guilty.

'Sorry,' they murmured in unison.

'Don't be sorry,' Renee trilled. 'Just be professional.'

'I'll leave you to it.' Temperance jumped to her feet, but Helena shook her head.

'No. You should dance with Archie.'

Panic washed over Temperance's face. 'I can't do that.'

'Why not?' Renee said, her voice taut with impatience. 'You and Archie won the pairing at the dance contest in September, Temp. Time to repeat your success.'

'But it's different now,' Temperance said.

'What?' Helena laughed. 'Because you're sweethearts?'

Archie nodded. 'It might affect our dancing.'

'I've got news for you, chuck,' Renee said. 'The fact you're courting's already affecting your dancing, you might as well make the most of it.'

Helena rolled her eyes. 'I'll expect tips tonight, since I'm giving up my place.'

'And I'll make sure you get 'em,' Renee promised.

With that, Helena sashayed away, leaving Temperance and Archie on the floor staring longingly into each other's eyes.

Renee clicked her fingers, summoning the couple's attention.

'Save that for your own time, not now. I want you ready, you hear me?'

Meekly, they both nodded, and as Renee cued up the music she watched eagle-eyed as the two readied themselves for the rumba Renee was instructing them in. As soon as they began to move, any worries she'd had of pairing them up fell away. Archie and Temperance were so in tune with one another, able to predict one another's moves in a way that was so seamless, it reminded Renee of how she and her old partner, Alf Monroe, used to dance together.

At the thought of times past, a lump formed in Renee's throat. There had been nothing between her and Alf – who'd been camp as Christmas, as the old expression went – but there had been the same shared affection and genuine love of dancing that Renee could see between Temperance and Archie. She and Alf were naturals together, each lost in the other and the music as they used to glide around the floor. The army had seconded Alf to an office position in London, but then last November he had been posted to Egypt, as part of the Western Desert Campaign, and she hadn't heard from him since before the New Year.

Seeing the door open out of the corner of her eye, Renee saw Peter standing mesmerised at the doorway. Smiling, she walked over to him.

'What do you think?' she asked.

'They look incredible,' he marvelled. 'Why don't all dancers look like that? Is it practice?'

Renee smiled. Peter was so enthusiastic, particularly around Temperance.

'That, and natural chemistry,' she said. 'You see, dance isn't just a skill you learn, it's like alchemy – get the right magic ingredients, the right pairing, and you see chemistry happening right in front of your eyes.'

Peter nodded and Renee watched him, seeing that he genuinely seemed to understand this.

'Was there something you wanted, lad?' she asked.

'Oh, yes, sorry.' At the question, Peter shook his head. 'Mr Cain asked if he could see you.'

Renee's heart sank. She had successfully managed to keep out of Bill's way of late, knowing he never had anything good to say.

'Did he say what it was about?'

'No. He just said to come now.'

Renee sighed. Of course he did.

As the music came to a close, she smiled brightly at Temperance and Archie. 'You two are a match made in heaven. Now, believe in yourselves and each other and you'll have them eating out of your hands tonight.'

Turning back to Peter, Renee gave him a warm smile. 'Can you give Temperance a hand tidying up, please?'

Without waiting for an answer, she then hurried out and down the corridor, to find the the second most-hated man in her life.

Bill was waiting for her in the bar.

'What is it you want, Bill?' Renee asked in a bored tone as she approached him.

He picked up a mug of coffee and grunted as he gestured to the bar area behind him.

'Sybil says you're making life difficult for her with all your demands.'

Renee laughed. 'Isn't Sybil old enough to fight her own battles?'

'She's a good worker, is what she is,' Bill replied.

'She's easy on the eye, you mean. And she's got you wrapped around her little finger.' Renee paused. 'What is it they say? "There's no fool like an old fool."'

Bill shrugged. 'There's nothing worse than a jealous old shrew. Your looks are fading, Renee Hammond.'

At that, Renee couldn't help laughing. If there was one thing she wasn't bothered about, it was losing her looks.

'I'll repeat the question in case you've gone soft in the head. What is it you want?'

'I want you to take over the dance lessons for some of our key customers.'

Renee narrowed her eyes. 'Why? Temperance does all the dance lessons.'

'Well, things are changing around here.' Bill leaned back in his chair and eyed her easily. 'And those decisions are to be handled between me and Edna from now on.'

Renee licked her lips and thought for a moment. She knew Bill wanted her to jump in and protest. Start screaming about how Nancy was the manager and how she wasn't going to listen to him. But something told her that was exactly what he wanted – that to say something like that would be playing right into his hands.

'Right, well I'll see what I can do then,' she said. 'Thanks for letting me know, Bill.'

At the politeness of her tone and easy acquiescence, Bill nearly fell off his chair.

'That all you've got to say?'

'I've learned my lesson the hard way,' she said. 'I know where my loyalties lie and that's with the Palais. It's this dance hall that comes first.'

'But . . .' Bill looked furious, and it was all Renee could do to contain herself. The old sod was raging because he'd been spoiling for a fight with her and he wasn't getting one. And if it wasn't so treacherous to Nancy, Renee would have loved nothing more than to wipe the smirk off his face.

'If that's all, Bill, I'll be off. I'll talk to Temperance about me taking over some of her dances and we'll work something out. We won't let you down, Bill. T'ra.'

And with a swing of her hips and an easy smile, Renee left the bar before he had time to say anything else, leaving the MC with the thought she wasn't remotely bothered by the exchange.

Outside in the corridor, it was a different matter. Renee's blood boiled. She had always known Edna and Bill were a dangerous force and now they had teamed up together to try and oust Nancy from her position. It had only been a matter of time. They'd both resented Nancy taking over from Alex.

Edna, because she was jealous that her boy had entrusted the running of the Palais to his wife rather than his mother. Bill, because he believed women belonged at home rather than in senior positions in the workplace, and he'd go out of his way to destroy any one of them who tried to change what he considered to be the natural order of life, which to Bill meant a man in charge at every turn.

Trying to gather herself, Renee looked up to see Nancy at the front desk, merrily laughing with a customer who was enquiring about that afternoon's tea dance. As Renee watched her, she felt guilt eat away at her. This was all her fault. Returning to the Palais had only made matters worse for her, and it had no doubt given Bill and Edna all the ammunition they needed to remove Nancy from her position and take over the running of the place themselves.

It sickened Renee to her core, but she knew that she would always support her friend. Whatever those two schemers had up their sleeves, Nancy Blum could rely on Renee to step up and do whatever was right. This time, Renee wouldn't let her friend down.

Twenty-Four

At the sound of the band tuning up, Nancy walked around the empty dance hall and beamed. She may not be musical, and she sure wasn't no dancer, but there was something about this very special dance hall that touched her soul. Nancy loved nothing more than to spend a precious few moments on the floor just before the customers arrived. It was here she could be herself, lose herself in the possibility of all the dance hall had to offer.

Nancy had always worked in the world of music. Back in Brooklyn, she had managed several music halls, securing the biggest and brightest names of all time. And when the chance came to come to London and work at the Palais, doing much the same but on a larger scale, she couldn't resist. And from the moment she'd walked through those doors over a decade ago, Nancy hadn't looked back.

She still felt the same, in fact she had come to love the Palais more than she'd ever thought possible. The trials of war, Alex being away, and being made to step into the breach to manage the place made her feel alive. Every day, it brought a set of challenges she loved nothing more than to try and solve.

Observing Peter, now, as he learned how to stock the bar, gave Nancy another unexpected flash of pleasure. She was still sure school was the best place for him, but knowing he planned to follow in her footsteps gave her a sense of pride. Perhaps this was what motherhood truly was all about, she thought. Learning to be flexible, to admit when you were wrong. Because watching Peter easily arrange the bottles, ensuring the most expensive brands were displayed more prominently, made her realise he was a natural.

'You'll be running the place, if you carry on like that,' she couldn't resist shouting as he expertly poured a pint of bitter.

At the compliment, Peter beamed from ear to ear and Nancy felt another wave of triumph.

'Though you should probably step away from the bar now, honey. The last thing we need is to get in trouble with the authorities for letting a child near alcohol.'

Peter laughed and nodded. Thanking Sybil with perfect manners, he left the bar and scurried over to Nancy.

'When do I get to work behind the bar for real? That was so much fun!' he declared with all the enthusiasm of a new puppy.

Pulling her surrogate son in towards her, she kissed his mop of dark hair. 'Soon enough. Enjoy being a kid a little while longer, huh?'

For a second he lingered in her arms and Nancy loved the feel of having him there. The opportunity to pour all her love into one human, for just a few moments. But, soon, as though remembering his age and where they were, Peter pulled away from her. Straightening his tie, he looked at the floor a little embarrassed, and Nancy couldn't help grinning to herself. The awkwardness of teenagers to her was too sweet.

'What would you like me to do now?' Peter asked in a sombre tone.

Nancy checked the clock above the door. It was five to seven, the customers would be piling through the doors at any second.

'Why don't you go and greet the customers at front desk? Violet's working this evening, I'm sure she would be grateful for some help – we're expecting a full house tonight,' Nancy suggested.

At the suggestion, Peter lit up. 'You want me front of house?' The boy's enthusiasm was infectious.

'You've more than earned it,' Nancy said warmly.

'I wish Papa could see me now.' Peter beamed, and she watched him hurry off,

Nancy knew she had made the right decision. She looked around and felt truly blessed. Yes, there was tragedy outside these four walls, but inside, the Palais held her heart.

Upstairs, in the office, Betty chewed her lip nervously as Bill and Edna sat before her.

'Why do you have to do this now?' she asked. 'Can't it wait until tomorrow? This is one of the most important nights of the social calendar, and it's all Nancy's doing.'

'That's why we want it done tonight – as soon as possible,' Bill said. 'We can't have Nancy ruin tonight with another of her daft ideas. She's lost the ability to think straight, which is what happens when you put a woman in charge. Didn't you see her earlier? Letting a kid behind the bar? She'll have us shut down.'

As Betty and Edna exchanged furious glances, Bill was reminded of the company he was keeping.

'Not that every woman's like that, of course,' he added smoothly. But the damage was done as Betty's stony expression did not alter.

'I don't usually interfere in managerial matters,' she said. 'But I will say this: what you're doing to poor Nancy is cruel. She's the lifeblood of this place, you both know that.'

'Don't speak to us like that,' Edna, having quickly reverted to siding with Bill, snapped back.

Edna got to her feet, and, as she did so, caught the sleeve of her Chanel jacket on the corner of the chair. Betty couldn't resist smirking as she heard the fabric tear.

'Just go and find Nancy, and tell her we wish to speak with her,' Edna snarled.

Betty shook her head. 'You tell her yourself. I'm not doing your dirty work for you. Now, If you'll excuse me, all this snake-like talk is making me feel sick.'

As Betty stalked out of the room and down the corridor, she collided straight into Violet.

'Sweetheart!' she exclaimed at the sight of her daughter. 'I've not seen you for days. You all right?'

Violet nodded, though her raven hair looked lank, and Betty hid a frown. Violet had been looking under the weather for weeks. She wasn't looking after herself and Betty decided enough was enough. It was time for her to step in.

'Why don't you come round and have your tea with me and Queenie tomorrow?' she said, kindly. 'Your father's out. I've finally got him to join the League of Defence Volunteers.'

Violet raised an eyebrow. 'George has volunteered to do something?'

'I think he thinks this is his way of making amends,' Betty said though gritted teeth.

'Well, I suppose something's better than nothing,' Violet managed, giving her mother a weak smile. Betty wanted nothing more than to pull her daughter into her arms, but Violet's volatile moods these days made her wary.

'So . . . How about six?' she said, more chirpily than she felt. 'I'll see you then?'

'All right.' Violet nodded, and Betty relaxed a little.

'I'll make a pound cake,' she said. 'One of your favourites.'

'There's no need to go to any trouble, Bet,' Violet said softly. 'It'll just be nice to see you and Gran.'

'Likewise.' Betty smiled warmly, though as she watched Violet walk away, her happiness was quickly replaced by anxiety as her conversation with Edna and Bill came back to her. If she had to order Nancy to walk straight into the lion's den, she could at least warn her what those treacherous devils were up to.

With a heavy heart, Betty made her way to the bar area where she knew Nancy would be. Sure enough, knowing they were short-staffed, Nancy was working beside Sybil, helping to pull pints and trading jokes, as if she did this every day of her life.

Waving at her through the fug of cigarette smoke, Betty caught Nancy's attention.

'What is it, honey?' the manager called over the din of customers ordering drinks.

'You got a minute, Nancy?'

Nancy nodded, then, gesturing to Sybil that she was stepping out for a moment, she lifted the bar hatch and joined Betty on the other side.

'Honey, are you OK?' she asked in her thick New York brogue. 'You look worried.'

Betty sighed. 'I am, Nancy . . . Thing is, there's something you ought to know.'

Nancy pursed her lips and leaned back against the bar, arms folded.

'I'm listening.'

'It's Bill and Edna, they're plotting to get you out.'

For a second, Nancy's eyes narrowed, but then she broke into peals of laughter.

'Honey . . . that's old news. They've been trying to get me out since the day I was made manager.'

'It's more than that.' Betty shook her head. 'They've been to the board.'

At the mention of the word 'board', Nancy's eyes widened in fear. 'They've what?'

'They went this afternoon,' Betty continued. 'They've told them you've shown poor judgement by allowing Renee to come back here.'

'But Renee's good,' said Nancy. 'She's practically our star employee. The board knows that.'

'They do know that, but Bill and Edna have made a good fist of throwing doubt on your competence,' Betty continued. 'And they've managed to convince the board that you're not up to your job.' She sighed. 'They've got a new investor who was apparently horrified you let a known thief return to work in a senior position. They've said you can stay on as front-desk manager, but Bill and Edna have temporarily been put in charge. I've been sent down here to fetch you, so they can tell you all this themselves, but I said no. I want no part of it. I think what they've done is awful, Nancy, you deserve far better than this.'

As Nancy took in this information, Betty could practically see the cogs in her brain working as she thought it through.

'So, they've really done it.' Nancy shook her head, the shock visible now across her face. 'They're really going to take away the one thing I love.'

'I'm so sorry, Nancy.'

As Betty laid a comforting hand on her arm, Nancy gave Betty a brave smile.

'Don't be sorry, honey. None of this is your fault, and I appreciate you telling me. No, they may have taken my beloved role away from me, but let's just see if they can do a better job.' She gave a short laugh. 'You know what, Bet. This might be the best entertainment I've had in months, watching those two bitter old codgers try and run this place. Stand back, Betty Millington, things are about to get interesting.'

And to Betty's surprise Nancy stalked off back through the bar. Betty had no idea where she was going, but she did know she had never seen Nancy as fired up. This new investor might have been swayed by Bill and Edna's sob story, but Betty had a feeling they'd come to regret getting one over on Nancy Blum.

Twenty-Five

As Harry Leder's band played an easy standard, Temperance swayed her hips in time to the music as she waited to step onto the dance floor. Not, this time, in her capacity as pen manager, but as an exhibition dancer! To say she was nervous was an understatement. She had only ever danced publicly with Archie once before, at the fundraising competition back in September. And although they had won, she couldn't forget the terrible consequences of that day. She had lost her brother and her world had upended itself in a heartbeat.

Now, as she stood in the corridor waiting to go on with Archie, she felt a mix of emotions coursing through her body. Though she couldn't wait to show off her skills and have Archie hold her in his arms, she was scared of what was waiting for her on the other side.

'It's going to be fine,' Archie promised.

He reached for her hand, lifted it to his lips and kissed her knuckles.

Temperance felt herself blushing. 'You don't know that.'

Archie gave her a teasing frown. 'Temp, I am telling you, lightning doesn't strike twice. You and I are going to walk out there and dance like we've never danced before, and to rapturous applause. Then we're going to have a drink in the bar to celebrate, and that will be it.'

Temperance couldn't help smiling. She had confided her fears to Archie earlier that day, half expecting him to laugh at her. But he hadn't, he had been sweet, kind, understanding and attentive. Archie was convinced that nothing was going to go wrong, that the evening would be nothing short of a success. Temperance really hoped he was right. She glanced at him now. Archie Ledbetter was so easy on the eye, with his filmstar smile and the twinkle in his eyes. The wonderful thing about him was that he didn't seem to know how good-looking he was. Even if he did, Temperance reckoned he was far too modest to exploit it.

She was taking a few calming breaths when the opening notes to the dance she and Archie were performing started to play. Feeling excited butterflies in her stomach, Temperance smiled nervously at Archie as he reached for her hand and then led her across the dance floor.

The first thing she saw was the lights hitting the replica fountain. The next thing was the sheer volume of people. At the sight of so many dancers with smiling faces, Temperance felt the last of her nerves begin to subside. They all wanted her to succeed as much as she did, and it was wonderful for the Palais to have so many faces enjoying a dance. Temperance knew that this was exactly what Nancy had hoped when she'd planned the Valentine's dance.

She searched the sea of faces, hoping to find her manager and friend, but, to her surprise, Nancy was nowhere to be found. Nor was Renee. The only well-wisher she could see easily was Maisie, who gave a her huge thumbs-up amid the applause.

Before she knew it, Archie had wrapped a hand around her waist, and with a tilt of her chin the pair stepped out across the floor in a series of perfectly executed steps. As the music played, Temperance forgot all her niggling concerns and instead focused on the beat and Archie's hand in hers. This was her moment, her time, when she could truly be herself and forget the wold around her. There was no audience, no worries about the war or the Palais, no thoughts of her family or money – there wasn't even Archie. There was just her, the music and her steps.

As she managed the quicktempo change, Temperance thought she heard Archie whisper something in her ear, but she couldn't be sure. All that mattered to her was the music, and so when it came to a stop, she felt bereft. It was a shock to her system, now, seeing all these people, all these lights.

Tuning into the present moment, she felt her heart swell with love as she took in the beaming faces and the applause. Even Sybil was standing behind the bar next to Nancy applauding.

She basked in the applause until it struck her – what was Nancy doing behind the bar? She was usually at the front greeting the customers, weaving her way through the throngs of tables, saying hello to the regulars. But there was no time to dwell, as Archie grabbed Temperance's hand and pulled her to the front of the circle. He took a bow, and gestured for Temperance to do the same. Instead she curtseyed, and enjoyed the cries of 'encore, encore' from the crowd. Shyly, she grinned up at her admirers and was delighted to see that not only were her regulars applauding her efforts, but Renee was now at the back of the room, clapping and cheering the loudest in the room. Temperance grinned up at her friend. Renee had long been her biggest champion, and she owed her so much. As her eyes roamed further across the crowd, she saw that Una, from the League of Coloured People, was also in the audience, and the two grinned at each other. Una was not just a lasting link to her roots, but to her brother – and all Eamon and her father had believed in. Now, Una had a chance to see Temperance in her own right, doing what she loved, understanding that like so many black folk across the country they were about more than just the colour of their skin. After Eamon had died, Temperance had resolved to become more involved in the movement, but so far work had kept her too busy to do more than pop in for the occasional meeting.

She waved at Una, then noticed a movement at the back of the room and spotted a tall, bulky man dart quickly from one side to the other. She fixed her gaze on him; he looked furtive but determined as he weaved his way to the front. There was something about the man that Temperance didn't like. She couldn't put her finger on it

Temperance glanced at Archie to see if he had noticed him, but Archie seemed transfixed on showing off Temperance and all they had achieved. She glanced back at the man, who seemed to be making his way towards the bandstand.

Temperance frowned, what was this man doing? Customers weren't allowed to approach the band, all requests had to be made through the MC. Desperately she searched for Bill, but he was nowhere to be seen either.

She felt uneasy, and in even in the midst of this special moment wished she could go and ask Nancy what was going on. There was a strange energy in the air, and Temperance didn't like it one bit. Turning to Archie, he looked straight at her and somehow knew just what she needed. With a final wave at the crowd, he took her by the hand and together they exited the stage, Temperance's heart thudding as she did so.

The moment they were backstage, Archie looked at her with concern across his features.

'What's wrong, Temp?'

She shook her head. 'I don't know. I saw a man, rushing towards the stage. Nancy was behind the bar . . .' Her sentence faded. Now that she said the words aloud, she could hear how daft she sounded. 'I don't know. Just that something felt wrong back there.'

Archie smiled and pulled her into his arms. Inhaling the scent of the Lifebuoy soap he always used, Temperance allowed herself to relax. Archie always had that effect on her.

'Shall we try and find out who the man is and if everything's OK?'

At Archie's use of 'OK', Temperance couldn't help but smile. He had picked up the Americanism from Nancy, and it sounded strange with his west London accent.

'OK,' Temperance agreed.

Together, they made their way along the corridor and headed towards the main entrance to the dance hall. Weaving their way through the throngs of people around the bar area, Temperance was about to ask Nancy what was going on, when the sight of Harry Leder's conductor – Michael – walking across the stage towards the centre took her by surprise.

None of the band ever addressed the crowd, they were always too busy with the music, and it was an unspoken rule. Nervously, Temperance looked at Nancy, who seemed as surprised as she was.

Smiling out at the crowd, Michael began to address the people gathered around the stage.

'Ladies and gentlemen, I appreciate this is a bit unusual but I've been asked to introduce a very esteemed gentleman tonight,' he began.

At this there was a general hum of curiosity across the audience, as everyone tried to work out who this 'esteemed gentleman' might be.

'I'll leave the talking to the man himself, so please welcome one of our country's finest businessmen to the stage,' said Michael, stepping to the side and gesturing at someone making their way over to him.

With that, there was rapturous applause, while Temperance recognised the same man she had seen darting across the floor earlier, now walking up to the bandstand and onto the stage. He had a hulking presence, a certain menace about him, despite the rictus grin on his face as he joined Mike and slapped him jovially on the back. Temperance felt another shiver of unease travel down her spine.

'Good evening, everyone. Thanks for letting me have a few words. I promise you I won't take up too much of your time, I know you're all eager to get back to the drinking and the dancing.'

At that there was a loud cheer, and the man smiled.

'It's why we're all here, am I right?'

Again there was another loud cheer.

Temperance exchanged bewildered glances with Nancy. The man was charismatic, that was for sure, but what did he want?

'I just wanted to thank you all for giving the Palais the support you do. As a businessman, I am always on the lookout for investments, and it's because of the fantastic support this dance hall receives that I was eager to buy into it. I want to see this place thrive as much as you do. I want you to have somewhere to come where you can relax and escape from the horrors of the world outside. No matter what Jerry does, he can never take this place from us.'

Again, there was another round of applause, while Temperance felt the unease inside her grow. She'd had no idea that the Palais was securing new investment. Truth be told, she had never really taken much interest in the way the place was run, seeing the board of directors as anonymous figures who put their hands in their pockets whenever money was needed, but otherwise stayed invisible. Yet, here was a new man, willing to introduce himself. A first surely?

She looked back again at Nancy and saw that she too looked worried. Was it possible that Nancy hadn't known about this new investor, either?

Casting another glance at the man, who hadn't yet revealed his name, Temperance saw that behind the false smile, there was a cold set to his expression.

'I intend to be at the dance hall a lot,' he continued. 'And I'm always very hands on with my investments, so if you see me around feel free to come and say hello. Oh, and if you ever feel like buying me a drink, then I can assure you I've always got time for anyone who treats me to a pint.'

The man paused to allow the crowd a minute to laugh, but

Temperance didn't join in. She wasn't buying his rehearsed air of nonchalance, not one bit.

'So, thank you, and I'll look forward to seeing a lot more of you.' With that he made to leave the stage, but had got no further than a few steps before he stopped, turned back to the assembled crowd and gave a smiling shake of his head.

'Forgive me. I'd forget me head if it wasn't screwed on. I should introduce myself to you all,' he said, with another insincere laugh. 'I'm Ronnie Newsham, Ron to me pals.'

Twenty-Six

Renee stared in numb horror at the man on stage. The man she knew to be her husband, Ronnie. She knew he would find her, that he would never leave her alone, that he would make her repay her debt. And now that he was stood there, larger than life, fulfilling her worst fears, she almost felt relieved. She had run from him for long enough, and now the time had come to settle this once and for all, and for whatever there was between her and Ronnie to end.

As if reading her mind, Ronnie stepped off the stage and weaved his way through the crowds towards her, where she was rooted to the spot, a rabbit caught in the headlights.

Something took over Renee, then, a courage she'd never felt before, and as he drew ever closer to her, she felt her fear fading, and in its place, a resolve never to cower in front of her tyrannical husband again.

'Ronnie,' she said coolly, as he reached her.

'Renee, flower.' He bent to kiss her ear, and she bit back the revulsion she was feeling, keeping herself straight and proud, though the familiar scent of his musky cologne made her want to gag. She hadn't smelled that fragrance in over three years, and it had always had the power to leave her quaking with fear. Not this time.

'Lovely to see you again,' he said, as if she was some long-lost, aged auntie who'd popped round for a cup of tea.

'I'd like to say the same, but me mam taught me that lying was wrong,' Renee said, her voice steady.

Ronnie threw back his head and laughed, revealing a row of neat, white teeth, interspersed with the odd gold cap. New additions, she noted.

'Oh, Renee, I have missed you,' he purred. 'What were you thinking of, running off like that?' His steely eyes tried to pin her in place.

'I told you, me sister needed me,' she said, refusing to let them.

'For three years?'

He took a step back and looked her up and down. She resisted shivering under his gaze.

'Is there somewhere we could go to talk?' he asked.

The band had started playing again now, and Renee could see that interest in Ronnie had gone as everyone started to dance. She glanced towards the bar, her eyes seeking out Nancy, but her friend had disappeared.

Ronnie's gaze was following hers.

'If you're looking for your mate, she's probably mopping the toilets,' he said, a sneering edge to his voice.

'What?'

With a jerk of his head, Ronnie gestured towards the direction of the ladies toilets.

'Nancy Blum's no longer the manager here. She's had a demotion, I'm afraid. we thought it was time she got back to doing what she's good at. Women ain't cut out for business, everyone knows that. You understand, don't you, Reen?'

He reached forward and cupped her chin, and as she tried to move away, she felt his fingers tighten, pinching her skin.

'The only way you could make money was dancing your pins off. What you thought you were going to do when your good looks faded, I can't imagine. Luckily for you, I'm back now. I'm here to take care of you, as I always have done,' he said, his voice dropping to a menacing whisper. 'We should be together, my love. Till death do us part, remember?'

As if Renee could forget. She'd felt nothing but dread on

her wedding day at the thought of a lifetime of marriage to Ronnie. He hadn't ever wanted her, she was just a prize to him, a warning to others that he had the power to control people's lives whenever he liked. He was as good as killing her, she thought. But instead of strangling her, or ordering one of his henchmen to do it, he was doing it by curtailing her freedom and owning an extra piece of her, every single day.

As he loosened his grip on her face, this time Renee felt the familiar nausea and fear she'd always felt when Ronnie threatened her.

But despite the fear now coursing through her body, Renee was once again determined to stand her ground.

'So that's why you've bought the Palais, is it?' she asked, gesturing around the place she had, up until twenty minutes ago, felt was her second home.

'I haven't bought it, Reen,' Ronnie said softly. 'I've just made an investment.'

She gave a humourless laugh. 'We all know you're calling the shots, Ronnie. You always do.'

He chuckled. 'You know me too well, Renee.'

He took a step back and put his meaty hands in his pockets. 'But this time I really am just an investor. Saw an opportunity to get my wife back, make a few quid and a few changes, settle a few scores.'

Renee's eyes narrowed. 'What do you mean? Settle a few scores?'

'Well, sweetheart. I can't have the woman what took my Renee away from me for so long in a position of management, can I?'

'What do you mean?' she demanded.

'I mean, Nancy made things a bit too easy for you to stay here, didn't she? She ought to have sent you back to me, encouraged you to return, but she didn't. And when you came back here a second time, after those raids in Manchester, she didn't just give you a job she gave you a home.' Anger flashed across

Ronnie's face. 'She knew your rightful place was with me, but she encouraged you to stay here with her. That bitch betrayed me by keeping hold of you, and she's going to get her comeuppance.'

Renee's mind went anxiously to Nancy. Where the hell was she?

As if sensing her concern, Ronnie laughed. 'Don't worry, Renee, flower. She's fine. I'm not kicking her out of her home, I know she's got two kiddies to look after now. Even *I'm* not that much of a bastard.'

'Then what are you going to do to her?' Renee asked. She had to know just how bad Ronnie intended making her friend's life.

He shrugged. 'I'm putting her back where she belongs. She started her working life here as front-desk manager, and that's where she'll end it.'

'And who's taking over the day-to-day running of the place?' she asked.

'Not me!' Ronnie laughed again. 'No, there's a very capable old bloke here who's right up my alley, Bill Cain.'

'The MC!' Renee exclaimed in disbelief.

'That's him.' Ronnie reached inside his jacket pocket. Pulling out a carton of Players he offered one to Renee, who refused it, then lit one up himself. 'Seems a capable chap.'

'A bleedin' idiot, more like.'

'Oh, Reen, you always did have a touch of the dramatics about you.' Ronnie shook his head.

Renee stared at him as he took a long pull on his cigarette. He had aged in the three years since she'd last seen him up close. He was still tall, big built and menacing, but his head was completely shaved now. Renee guessed that either he was balding, or his vanity wouldn't allow him to go grey. He was thicker round the middle, but seeing the flex in his cheek and the set of his angular jawline, she knew that Ronnie was just as strong and capable, just as dangerous as he'd ever been.

'I've missed you,' he said suddenly. 'I know you think me

marrying you was all just a way for your old man to settle his debt. But I never would have married you, Reen, if I hadn't wanted you. And I wanted you for a very long time.'

Renee shook her head. 'You're like a child, Ronnie. You just want what you can't have.'

He said nothing to this at first, just dropped his cigarette to the floor. And Renee winced as he aggressively ground it into the beautiful maple floor with his foot.

'See, unlike a child, I always get what I want, Renee. You should know that by now.'

He stepped towards her, and with a force that she couldn't escape, pressed his lips against hers. Renee knew that to anyone looking on, this would seem a romantic gesture, but she felt the aggression behind his kiss, the determination to make her bend to his will.

As he pulled away, he looked at her with satisfaction in his eyes. He felt he had her just where he wanted her.

'Time for us to go,' he said.

Renee froze. 'I'm working. I don't get off until eleven. It's only nine.'

'Well, since I more or less own the joint now – as your boss, and your husband, I can tell you that you're officially off the clock. Time for you to come home with me, darling. Back to your rightful place with your husband.'

For a moment, Renee felt like screaming. Every fibre of her being wanted to wrestle with Ronnie, make it clear to him that she wasn't that person anymore, that she had changed. But then she caught his clenched jaw again, and she knew it was pointless. Until she miraculously found some way of getting rid of him, any dreams she had of a new life without Ronnie in it, were over.

'Right, then. I'll get my bag,' she said instead.

As she walked away, Renee caught sight of the cut-out hearts above the ticket booth to the dance pen and she grimaced.

If there was one thing she didn't believe in at that particular moment, it was love.

Upstairs, to her relief she saw Nancy's flat was empty. She rushed around packing stockings, underwear, blouses and skirts, but paused when she heard the sound of footsteps behind her.

'You OK?' Nancy's voice asked gently.

Renee turned and saw her friend looked utterly ashen.

'I'm so sorry, queen,' she whispered.

Running towards her, she pulled Nancy into her arms and squeezed her tightly, hoping to shut out all the hurt and pain Ronnie was causing yet again.

'Not your fault, honey,' Nancy said stiffly, as she pulled away. 'I wish there was something we could do.'

Renee shrugged. 'It was good while it lasted. I should have known he'd find me in the end. He always gets what he wants.'

'And is the Palais really what he wants?' Nancy demanded. 'How did he even know we needed the money?'

Renee laughed bitterly. 'Ronnie has spies everywhere.'

'And since when did he become so pally with Bill and Edna?'

'Probably got one of his henchmen to befriend them. He'll get bored of them, and then he'll get rid, when they're no longer of use to him. Happens all the time.'

Nancy sank down onto the battered, brown sofa and put her hands over her face. 'So this is really happening? You're really leaving, to go back with him?'

Renee couldn't miss the tone of incredulity in Nancy's voice. She didn't blame her. She could hardly believe what she was doing, herself.

'I have no choice,' she said, turning back to packing her things. 'If I don't, it will all be so much worse,' she snapped her case shut, 'for all of us.'

'No, Renee . . .' Nancy's eyes were full of tears. But as much as she wanted to stay and tell her everything was going to be all right, Renee knew she would just be putting off the inevitable.

'Take care of yourself, Nancy,' she said, pulling her case upright, then leaning forward and planting a kiss on her friend's cheek. "You mean the world to me.'

And with that, Renee walked out of the flat and made her way down the stairs towards her new life. There was no point crying over what had been lost. It would only make the agony over all that lay ahead all the more unbearable. A lifetime of experience had taught her that.

Twenty-Seven

As Nancy stared out of the community-centre window, she tried hard to shift the misery that had plagued her since the night of the Valentine's Ball. The weather outside was grey and dull, reflecting just how she felt – grey and listless.

Since she had been demoted to front-desk manager, a job she now shared with Violet, Nancy had found herself wanting to stay in bed longer and longer each day, hoping to shut out the world.

She told herself that she was lucky to still have a job. Especially in the industry she loved. But being removed from office without good reason was a particularly bitter pill to swallow.

'Nancy, do you want us to wipe these windows down, too?' Ruth called, pulling her out of her maudlin mood.

'Better had, honey,' Nancy replied, doing her best to keep the warmth in her voice. 'Let a little of the sunshine in.'

'If it ever appears,' Ruth said with a grin.

As the girl turned to the window, Nancy watched her charge whisper something to Betty, and the Millington mother turn around, nod and gesture towards a box in a cupboard by the window.

Wordlessly, Nancy saw Ruth reach for a tin of instant coffee and then before she'd had a chance to realise what she was doing, she'd handed it to her.

'This for me?'

'You're the only one I know that drinks that horrible stuff.' Ruth beamed.

Betty's voice rang out from the other side of the room. 'If I were you I'd need a biscuit to go with it,' she said. 'And I'd probably find one underneath the worktop you're leaning against.'

Nancy laughed. 'You're both too good to me.'

'We try.'

With that, Ruth skipped off back towards the dirty window, and Nancy felt a rush of love for her foster daughter. She and Peter really were the only good things in her life, just now. As she watched Ruth busy herself, Nancy realised that the reason she was so upset that she had been demoted wasn't only because of her personal feelings towards the Palais. It was because now that she was a mother, she wanted to show both kids just how capable a woman could be. She wanted Ruth to have a strong female role model and she wanted Peter to see that women had just as much value in the world as men. But now that message might well be lost. If it had, how could Nancy hope to give them the decent upbringing she was sure their parents would want for them?

Taking a sip of her coffee, Nancy found that, for once she didn't need to wince. It actually wasn't that bad, or maybe she had just got used to awful coffee as the war progressed.

Like her career, the war seemed to be something of a roller coaster. The Germans had exacerbated their bombing campaign, doing their best to decimate Avonmouth in Bristol, Leeds, Liverpool and Birkenhead. In London, the Jerries had not only destroyed the infamous Cafe de Paris – the lifeblood of the city's entertainment scene – but they had also hit Buckingham Palace, truly proving the war touched everyone.

Thankfully, President Roosevelt had finally agreed to back Britain in the war effort with the new Lend and Lease Act, which meant that the US could loan vital war supplies to the Brits. It was a good idea and Nancy was grateful her home country was finally doing something to help put an end to this war. But at the same time, she couldn't help thinking about what would happen afterwards and how they were expected to pay all this money back once the war was over. The economy was likely to be crippled for years.

'You all right, Nancy?' Betty said, as she wended her way towards Nancy, pinny in one hand and clean ladle in the other.

Nancy sighed, securing the head scarf she wore to keep her hair clean from the cooking smells.

'I'm trying to be,' she said. 'Good company helps.'

Betty smiled. 'I know what you mean. Got to take the happy moments where you can find 'em,' she said. 'Especially since Ronnie Newsham took over, and ...'

Nancy nodded, grateful that Betty hadn't finished that sentence with, 'you lost your job'.

'Gotta keep going I guess,' she said.

Betty tied the pinny around her waist and grimaced. 'Even if the world around you is falling apart.'

'Something like that,' Nancy agreed.

'Well, you know I think it's disgraceful, what's happened,' Betty said.

'More disgraceful for you.' Nancy turned to her. 'You're out of a job, Bets!'

The day after Ronnie had taken over, he'd called a staff meeting that Nancy would never forget. Standing at the front of the stage, flanked by Bill Cain and Edna, he had addressed the gathered staff.

'My priority is to get the Palais back to being the talk of the town,' he'd told them. 'But make no mistake, that means change. We've got to cut the dead wood.' Ronnie's gaze swung around the crowd, alighting on a few specific faces. 'You, you, you, and you,' he said gesturing towards two dancers, the junior storesman and Betty. 'You're no longer needed. Get out. As for you,' he'd pointed at Temperance. 'I want you back in the ticket booth where you belong.'

An audible gasp rang out across the room as Betty got to her feet. 'If you want to get rid of me that's fine, but this poor girl, she's the most talented dance teacher we have. She belongs on the dance floor and she's more than proven her worth.'

'I agree.' Renee also got to her feet.

Nancy looked at her. She hadn't seen Renee since she'd left the previous night. She looked all right, Nancy thought. Tired, judging by the shadows under her eyes, but there was still some Renee spirit there, and for that Nancy was grateful.

'Sit down,' Bill snarled, turning to look at both Betty and Renee. 'Your opinions aren't welcome here.'

There was another collective gasp from the others, and sensing dissent, Edna got to her feet. With a smile at Ronnie, she walked to the centre of the stage.

'I know change is hard, everyone, and we all do value your efforts. But Mr Newsham as our newest and largest investor has some requests and suggestions. We will have you back to work as soon as we can.'

Nancy shook her head. She couldn't believe what was happening in front of her eyes. She knew she ought to say something, do something to stop this madness, but she was too shocked, too paralysed with it to open her mouth.

'You,' Ronnie said, pointing at her. She looked up and felt dread course through her veins. 'You'll be back to running the front desk with her,' he gestured at Violet, who blinked in shock.

Nancy's heart thudded. At least Violet wasn't facing the sack.

'When you're not working the front desk, you'll be working with Howell & Smart on their kitchen initiative. We've got to maintain our support for the war.'

After that, there had been a lot of talk from Ronnie about the Blitz spirit, to keep up morale, presumably. But Nancy had tuned out. She looked at Renee, who after her brief burst of spirit, now looked as if she had died.

That meeting had been a month ago and Nancy had largely got used to her new role. It helped that she still had a roof over her head and that Betty had been taken on full-time for the National Restaurant campaign, along with Temperance, on a part-time basis – the reason for this, Nancy guessed, was because Ronnie wanted Temperance at the Palais as little as possible.

Anger shot through Nancy. She knew that many people couldn't get past the colour of Temperance's skin, but at the Palais things had been different. Even Bill Cain had started to drop the racial slurs he'd so frequently used around Temperance.

Standing in the community centre, she watched Betty chop vegetables for the hearty soup they dished out to the needy, which contained as many vegetables and nutrients as Betty could find. She really had come into her own since stepping into the role at Howell & Smart full-time, and Nancy felt like a proud mother hen.

Last night there had been yet another bombing campaign in the West End, with several people and families bombed out of their homes. Betty had scrambled to service like a sergeant major calling in the troops. Now as they opened the doors of the centre, swathes of the needy poured through. Dressed in dirty, badly torn clothes, Nancy saw all walks of life flood through inside. From hard-working moms to city gents, all had one thing in common – they had lost everything, not just a job.

Nancy felt a pang of sorrow as she watched them all take the bowl of soup, grateful for nourishment after yet another night of misery. She knew that Temperance would direct them to the mobile WVS vans outside when they had finished, where they would find help with new clothes and housing, if appropriate. Betty was running a well-oiled machine and Nancy couldn't help think that being fired from the Palais might be the best thing that could have happened to her.

Just then, she saw Alan Hopkins come in. Nancy waved at him, and walked over to welcome him.

'Hey, there,' she said cheerfully.

Alan took off his hat by way of greeting. 'Looks like it's all going well here.'

'It is. As you can see, Betty's running a tight ship.'

Alan turned to gaze at Betty, who was doing her best to comfort a young woman who was sobbing into the sleeve of her jacket, all the while offering her food and keeping the line moving.

'She's a natural,' Alan said warmly.

Nancy looked at him in surprise. 'You and Betty used to know each other, right?'

Alan nodded. 'We were childhood sweethearts once.'

'You courted?' Nancy chuckled. 'Betty is a dark horse.'

A flicker of amusement passed across Alan's face. 'Did she not tell you?'

'She said you were friends. Queenie might have said it was something more.'

'Ah, well, Queenie Millington is a force to be reckoned with herself.'

'How do you know Queenie?'

'She was a friend of my mother's cousin. Queenie knew everyone, even back then.'

'I can imagine.' Nancy said wryly. 'So . . . What happened with you two?'

The flicker of amusement on Alan's face was now replaced with one of regret. 'Oh, you know. We were just kids, really,' he said, casually. 'Wanted different things, I suppose.'

Nancy nodded. She'd had her fair share of young love, and despite mutual declarations of undying devotion, she never met anyone she truly wanted to share her life with until she met Alex.

In that moment Nancy caught sight of Betty strolling towards them and looking flustered.

'I didn't realise you were coming in today,' she addressed Alan.

'It's an impromptu visit,' he said with a grin. 'Actually, I've got an ulterior motive.'

'Oh?'

'I was hoping to take you for lunch after you've finished here.'

'Oh, no.' Betty shook her head. 'I couldn't leave the girls. We've so much to do.'

'It's not all pleasure, I can promise.' Alan chuckled. 'I actually do need to discuss business. We want to set up another restaurant in the north of the city.'

'Oh, right.' Betty looked relieved and pleased.

'So, can I whisk you away?' Alan extended his arm and Nancy grinned.

'You two go have fun,' she said. 'We'll clean this up. Anyway, Violet's coming over later.'

At the mention of her eldest daughter, Betty looked up sharply.

'She's coming here?'

Nancy checked her watch. 'In about ten minutes.'

'Oh, right, well, give her my love, won't you?' Betty said, going across the floor for her coat. 'Shall we go now, Alan, there's a little place around the corner.'

'Sounds good to me. Bye, Nancy.'

As Nancy watched them go, she couldn't help feeling that something wasn't quite right.

Twenty-Eight

Back at the Palais, Renee was doing her best to stay focused on the dance rotas. Yet every time she made some sense of the pairings, she could hear Ronnie either bellowing in the background or walking up and down the dance hall behind her.

Renee had tried to bite her tongue and concentrate on the job in hand, but she could bear it no more.

'What are you *doing?*' she demanded.

Turning to look at him, she saw Ronnie do an angry double-take, and instantly regretted opening her mouth as he strode up to her.

'You talking to me, love? Only, from the way you were speaking, I thought there was a dog in the room.'

Renee took a deep breath. 'Sorry, Ron. I'm just trying to concentrate here, you know.'

Standing too close to her, she felt Ronnie's breath against her face, the rancid smell of the kippers he'd had for breakfast hitting her nostrils. Her stomach turned as he whispered, 'Never were all that bright, were you, Reen?'

He glanced down at the sheet of paper she was holding.

'Dearie me, that'll never do.'

'What's the problem?' she tried to ask in as neutral a tone as possible.

'You've put yourself down to work Saturday night. That's *our* night, Reen. We spend Saturday nights together, don't we?' He kissed her softly but possessively on the cheek, and Renee hid her revulsion at the gesture.

* * *

In the month since Ronnie had returned, Renee had done her best to stay out of his way, citing work as the reason she was busy. But living with him had been hard, as it always had been. Ronnie would never change. And though he had yet to raise a hand to her this time around, she knew it was only a matter of time before the beatings began.

'But we've got no dancers, Ronnie,' she said, patiently now. 'You sacked 'em all, remember?'

'Not all,' Ronnie protested. 'Just the dead wood.'

'You let Temperance go, and Helena. Neither of them is dead wood.'

Ronnie shrugged. 'Helena was gobby, and that other one – her face didn't fit.'

'You mean, she's coloured?' Renee pointed out in a risky tone that brooked no argument. She paused for a second, instinctive indignation rising deeply within her at the Ronnie's prejudice of her friend, the way he treated her because of her skin colour.

'I mean, her *face didn't fit.*' Ronnie gave Renee a hard,warning look. 'Don't question me, love.'

Then, before she could react, he reached behind her and yanked at her chignon. Renee wanted to cry out in pain, but she wasn't going to give him the satisfaction.

'I ain't anywhere near close to forgiving you for running off like that and leaving me all that time.' Ronnie leaned in towards her. 'Now, any more of your lip and I'll be in even less of a forgiving mood – understand?'

Renee held her breath and silently nodded, while Ronnie's face loomed closer to hers.

'I can't hear you, flower.'

'Yes,' she said, in a hoarse whisper.

As he finally moved away from her, Renee heard the sound of footsteps behind them. Glancing around, she felt her heart sink as she saw it was Violet, standing a couple of yards away. How much she'd witnessed, Renee couldn't be sure, but the look on Violet's face said she'd got the gist.

'Violet, sweetheart,' Ronnie said amiably, strolling towards her. 'You got that paperwork I asked you to organise?'

'It's here.' Violet handed him a sheaf of papers, her face now an impassive mask.

'Lovely,' Ronnie said, smiling at her.

With the papers under one arm, he started to walk away, but when he reached the door, he turned back and directed his gaze straight at Renee.

'I mean what I say about Saturday nights, Reen. I want it sorted.'

As the door banged shut behind him, Violet took a seat next to Renee and threaded an arm through hers.

'You, all right?'

'Fine, queen,' Renee said, in a tone she knew was a little too bright and a little too sharp.

Violet looked at her sympathetically. 'You can't kid a kidder, isn't that what you always say?'

Renee gave her a sad smile.

'I'm all right, Vi, nothing I can't handle.'

'What's it been like . . . with Ronnie?' Violet pressed.

Renee shrugged. 'Well, he's got himself a nice house in Fulham, near the river,' she said. 'And that's just about the only good thing about him coming back. I'm not exactly slumming it.' She sighed. 'But Ronnie's biding his time, he's waiting for his moment to make me pay for walking out on him the way I did.'

'He's not . . . hitting you, nothing like that?' The concern in Violet's eyes almost brought tears to Renee's, but she remained emotionless.

'No. He's not doing that.' *Yet*, she thought.

She desperately wanted to change the subject, so turned her attention to Violet's situation, her eyes taking in the girl's rounded stomach.

'You're beginning to show,' she said, smiling.

At this, Violet flushed red, and Renee wrapped an arm around her.

'I sound like a broken record, queen, but you're going to have to tell your mum, soon. You're how many months now?'

'Almost six,' Violet mumbled.

'Sweetheart . . .'

'I just can't,' said Violet. 'Betty will never forgive me, and we've been getting on ever so much better, lately, I don't want to ruin it.'

'Absence makes the heart grow fonder, I suppose,' Renee joked, then started at a noise coming from the ticket booth. Both she and Violet turned to see Temperance, cloth in hand, wiping down the booth desk.

How long had Temperance been there? Had she seen Ronnie grab her hair? Renee winced. She'd thought they were alone. The thought of Temperance witnessing Ronnie's appalling treatment of her only added to the horror of it.

Renee decided to bluff it out.

'Temp! Why don't you come and join us?' she called.

It pained her to see Temperance look hesitant.

'I don't want to get in any trouble,' she said.

'You won't, he's gone off somewhere,' Renee reassured her. 'Come on, just for a minute.'

'All right, then.' Temperance looked relieved, though as she started walking over, Renee could see how the brightness, normally so present in Temperance, had evaporated lately. It wasn't just down to the fact that she'd been demoted. Renee knew it was because the Palais had lost its sparkle in the few weeks since Ronnie had taken it over. He was far too hands-on for an investor, attending staff meetings, involving himself in ideas, though Renee had a feeling that Bill and Edna liked it, especially as it meant the staff were far more deferential.

'Look at the state of us,' Renee joked as Temperance sat down.

Temperance sighed. 'It could be worse. At least I still have a job.'

'And a sweetheart,' Violet pointed out cheerfully.

At the mention of Archie, Temperance blushed, but Renee had to admit she was pleased for her friend. It was obvious how much she and Archie liked one another and it was sweet.

'We're just seeing how it works out,' Temperance mumbled.

'Una says you brought him to an LCP meeting last week,' Violet prompted, with a smile. 'I'd say that sounds serious.'

At that Temperance's face broke out into a wide grin, and she laughed. 'All right. You've got me. I don't know, girls, things with Archie seem so right.'

Resting a hand on her knee, Renee smiled. 'I'm happy for you, love. You deserve it.'

'You really do,' Violet echoed. 'Eamon would want this for you, you know he thought the world of Archie.'

At the mention of Eamon, all three of them fell briefly silent.

'I just wish he was here to help you, Vi,' Temperance said then. 'Eamon would hate to see you in this mess.'

Violet nodded and wiped a tear from her eye. 'I know. It's why this little one is so important to me.' She cradled her stomach so tenderly that Renee felt a lump in her throat. 'I know you all think I've got to tell Betty, and you're right. How she hasn't worked it out already, I'll never know. But that aside, the reason I haven't said anything yet is because I don't want to taint what Eamon and I have created. It feels special. Pure. The moment it's public knowledge, people will start saying things. I'll be called names, and so will this little one, and believe me when I say I'll do anything to keep this one safe. He or she is the most important thing in the world to me.'

Violet looked so fierce, so proud in that moment, that Renee knew she was a born mother. There was nothing she wouldn't do for the child growing inside her. She looked at Temperance, who nodded and smiled.

'We can see that, chuck,' Renee said softly. 'But part of doing what's right for your child is facing up to reality. You've got to do that, love, if you want to give that kiddie the best start in life.'

'We're all here for you,' Temperance added. 'We all know this won't be easy, but it's not just about you know, its about this little one growing inside you.'

'I know,' Violet nodded. 'And I've said I'll go round to Betty's for lunch, soon –when George is out training with the local defence volunteers. I'll tell her then.'

Temperance looked pleased. 'Good.'

As Renee looked at the elder of the Millington sisters, she felt a flash of resolve. If Violet could find the strength to solve her problems, then surely *she* could to do the same?

Twenty-Nine

As March rolled into April, Betty Millington found her emotions running high. She started most days reading the newpaper, anxious at all Hitler was doing to destroy Europe. Only recently, he had begun a bombing campaign in Belfast – successfully invading Yugoslavia and creating the new state of Croatia.

It seemed to Betty that the world was in chaos, but Churchill thought differently. Only the previous week, he'd addressed the House of Commons, insisting that the war was going well, confident that once the Americans were delivering a constant stream of supplies Britain would secure retributive justice.

It all made Betty's head spin. Privately, she thought Churchill had become a warmonger, and he wouldn't necessarily lead Britain to success. But then, as the mother of a child killed in action, some would think Betty wasn't the most independent of judges. The fact was, that as far as Betty was concerned, the last time Britain had been at war with Germany the bottom had dropped out of her world – with a lifetime of consequences. Wasn't it natural she would be cautious?

As the early spring sun beamed down outside, Betty pushed all thoughts of war firmly out of her mind, and tried instead to concentrate on the afternoon's work at the restaurant. Things were going well, so much so that Nora had entrusted her with looking after the Hammersmith branch, while Nora set up new facilities in both Islington and Westminster. Reaching the community centre now, Betty felt a spring in her step.

Pushing the door open, she walked into the restaurant and smiled at Nancy and Ruth, who were laying tables.

'Shouldn't you be at school, miss?' Betty asked Ruth, peeling off her coat and hanging it on the rack by the door.

Ruth shook her head. 'School finished an hour ago. I wanted to help Nancy set up for tonight.'

Betty smiled at her, noting that the two children Nancy had taken in both had impeccable manners. But as she pushed open the door to the kitchen, she felt her pulse quicken at the sight of Alan at the sink doing the washing up.

'What are you doing here?' she exclaimed, taking in his rolled-up sleeves.

Alan turned and grinned. 'Pot washer's not well, so I thought I'd help. We're not too busy at the shop at the moment.'

Betty took off her jacket, then hung it up next to the apron she kept on a hook by the pantry. She took down her pinny and tied it around her waist.

'You make it sound as if you run a corner shop,' she told Alan, 'not one of Oxford's Street's most famous department stores.'

'Retail's retail.' Alan shrugged, earning himself a grin from Betty. He washed and dried the last of the saucepans and then gave her his full attention. 'I thought you might need my services more.'

'Well . . . I just might, at that,' she said, looking round at the mounds of vegetables on the counter that needed chopping for that day's pie-and-soup offer. Temperance was due in later, as were the other two girls who usually helped out. Violet had also offered to stop by and help after work, though privately Betty wasn't sure that was a good idea. Her daughter still looked so tired and unwell all the time. She wasn't unduly worried – knowing how exhausting grief could be. She'd felt it so keenly herself, for months after Roy had died.

Still, there didn't seem to be time for grief, with a war on. It wasn't right, but with so many losing their lives, personal sorrow seemed an indulgence. Not to mention the sheer amount of work she had on. You just had to get on with it, she supposed. But Alan's help was appreciated, even if his presence left her unsettled.

She looked up at him and found his gaze set on her.

'What is it?' she asked. 'Have I something in my hair?'

Alan smiled and shook his head. 'Just marvelling at how you haven't changed a bit.'

Betty felt a blush creep across her cheeks. 'You always did know how to get me in a pickle, Alan Hopkins.'

'I don't mean to,' he said softly. 'I just sometimes can't believe you've come back into my life after all this time.'

He took a step towards her, and Betty felt a pang of guilt. She had to stop this, whatever it was. She and George may not have the best of marriages, but they were still husband and wife; still united in the eyes of God.

'You and me were a long time ago,' she said. 'We're both married now, we shouldn't be talking like this.'

Gazing down at the floor, Alan looked embarrassed, and Betty felt a flash of guilt. He had meant so much to her, once. If she was being truly honest, he still did.

'I've told you my marriage is as good as over,' he said.

'Not in the eyes of the Lord it's not,' Betty said quietly but firmly. 'You took vows, as did I.'

He held her gaze. 'Are you really happy?' he asked. 'The way your husband treats you . . .'

She flinched. 'I don't know what you're—'

'I've heard the stories, Bet, we all have. About George and his carry on. Word gets round . . .'

A heady mix of anger and pride rushed through Betty. She had spent over twenty years being a decent, respectable wife and mother. Alan Hopkins didn't get to tear that down in a few seconds. Not after what he'd done.

'Gossip,' she said fiercely. 'You know nothing about my life.'

'I know you deserve better,' Alan said softly.

'Who do you think you are?' Betty thundered suddenly. 'You weren't around to give me better, were you?' Two years of courting, with promises of a trip up the aisle. Did you got a better offer? Is that why you vanished out of me life?'

'It wasn't like that,' Alan protested. 'You know it wasn't. I loved you, Bet.'

'And I loved you, but it wasn't enough to make you stay.'

'I had to go. We were at war. I was called up, I had to serve my country.' His tone suggested he had been through this many times before – alone, if not in front of Betty.

'I know that,' Betty said furiously. 'But I thought you were coming back for me. When you wrote to me and told me that you weren't, that you were leaving me . . . You must have known how devastated I was.'

He hung his head in sorrow. 'I'm sorry. I was young, and stupid. I thought I was doing the right thing.'

Folding her arms and looking at him incredulously, Betty leaned back against the worktop. 'You thought you were doing the right thing? Alan Hopkins, I gave you my innocence, not three months before you sent me that letter that left me feeling cheap and used. So don't spout on now about how you thought you were "doing the right thing". I want the truth now.'

Alan looked shamefaced. He unrolled his sleeves and adjusted his tie, clearly buying time.

Betty was going nowhere. She had waited a long time for this conversation, dreaming of all the things she wanted to say when she finally confronted the young man who had ruined her life. Now she had the chance, she wasn't going to let him slither away because he felt uncomfortable.

'I'm waiting.'

Lifting his gaze to her, Alan ran a hand through his hair and Betty was shocked to see tears pool in his eyes.

'When I went to war I wanted to do nothing more than serve my country. But the things I saw, Betty. The things I saw men

196

do to each other. No man should ever see that.' He looked out of the window for a moment, and Betty could see his pain. 'I became a coward.'

Confusion crossed Betty's face. 'What do you mean?'

Alan wiped his eyes with the back of his hand. 'War was brutal. I was a kid when I went away. Thought I was going to save the world.' He laughed now, as though at the arrogance of youth. 'But what I saw broke me. I started having chest pains, couldn't breathe. I was plagued with nightmares. The other lads were the same. We all made jokes about it, but the truth was we were tarnished by the brutality of war. I felt like a shell of a man. I couldn't let you see me like that, Betty, you deserved more than I could give you.'

Shock coursed through Betty's veins as she tried to make sense of what Alan was telling her.

'I loved you with all my heart, I promise you that.' He looked back down at the floor as if searching for the right words. 'That day, we were together, when we gave each other everything, it was the best day of my life. It was all I thought about when I returned to the army. But it couldn't change the fact I felt scared, Betty. I was half a man, you didn't need me and I didn't want to ruin your life.'

'But my life was already in tatters,' Betty said. 'I wrote and wrote, but nothing. Then, months later, I ran into your mother, and she told me you had met someone else. Do you have any idea how hurt I was? How that made me feel? Do you know what you put me through, Alan? The humiliation, the shame I felt.'

The pain Betty had been holding onto for years was now unleashed, and rivers of tears streamed down her cheeks. She'd waited so long for this moment, for the chance to tell Alan Hopkins how he had destroyed her life. And now the time had come, she wasn't sure she could stay in control. She felt completely overwhelmed.

'I'm so sorry,' Alan whispered. He took a step towards her

and put his warm hands on hers, which were shaking. 'I really didn't mean to hurt you, Bet. I hated myself for the way I treated you, and I should never have stopped writing to you, but at the time it was the only way I could think of to let you go, rather than be lumbered with me.'

'But I would have helped you,' she said.

Alan shook his head, the tears he had tried to keep at bay now coming.

'Nobody could help me. Not back then. I wasn't myself.'

'I don't understand,' Betty pleaded.

'Betty, I couldn't sleep or eat. I flew into untold rages. I cried, and I'd shake with terror in the street. I wasn't the man you knew, I wasn't good enough for you.'

Sympathy burned, but still Betty couldn't forget the pain and humiliation she had endured.

'Good enough for your new wife, though,' she whispered, pulling her hands free from his.

'Bets, you were already with George by the time I met Vera,' Alan said. 'It was too late.'

Bloody George. If marrying him hadn't meant the arrival of Roy, Violet and Maisie, Betty would be consumed with regret that she'd ever said yes to his proposal.

'I only got with him because you'd left me high and dry. George rescued me,' she found herself lying.

'That what you call it, is it?' Alan shook his head. 'His gambling and the womanising has always been legendary around here.'

'And so it might have been, but he was there,' Betty shot back.

'In a way I never could be,' he whispered. 'I know.'

At that, the two stared into each other's eyes, every moment of the pain and longing that they had endured passing through their veins.

Alan sniffed. 'I've been all over the shop since you came back into my life.'

In spite of her turbulent emotions, Betty found herself resisting a smile. 'Pun intended?' she said, deadpan, and Alan's mouth twitched.

'And I've missed your sense of humour.'

He took a step towards her, and Betty knew she was done for. As Alan leaned forward, put his arms around her and pressed his lips against hers, all thoughts of religion and the sanctity of marriage flew from her mind, as she gave into the sweet, healing kiss of a lost love come back to her.

Thirty

As Temperance crept out of the community kitchen, her heart was thudding. She would never have imagined she'd catch Betty Millington in the arms of another man. And catching her in a passionate embrace with Alan Hopkins had sent her into a tailspin. Trying to calm her beating heart, Temperance took a seat at one of the tables in the community centre's makeshift restaurant in the main hall, trying to make sense of what she had just seen. Was it possible that there had been a mistake? Had Betty hurt herself? *And had Alan kiss it better?*

Temperance shook her head at her stupidity. No. There was only one explanation for what she had seen, but there wasn't time to think about that now. She had to not only get on with this job, she also needed to try and get across to Mr Henshall's hotel for her latest egg drop. Now she had been demoted at the Palais, Temperance was earning even less, and the strain of providing for Violet and her family had never been felt more keenly. She chewed her bottom lip with the worry of it all. She'd wanted to make sure she took her brother's place and provide when he could not, yet Temperance felt she was in a precarious situation. Ever since Archie had talked about someone thieving from his dad's business, what she was doing felt so much worse. But every time she'd tried to end her egg round with Dave, she'd think of Violet. So then she'd told herself that she had no proof Dave was taking eggs from Archie's butcher's, that the eggs she was selling could very well be coming from somewhere else. She'd remind herself that her duty was to her brother, to her family. And that's what Violet and her baby were – family.

And now, as well as providing eggs for Mr Henshall's hotel, Temperance was also supplying them to the hotel across the street. They were, by and large, competitors, but Mr Henshall had insisted that since the war they were all clubbing together, so Temperance was just about managing to make up for losing her job at the Palais.

The extra money she was able to put on the table was going down well at home, with even Aunt Winnie giving Temperance a smile of thanks for all she was doing. But how much longer could she keep this up? The fact was, she hadn't told her family about losing her job as a dance instructor, the position she'd worked so hard for. Her mother was so wrapped up still with the loss of Eamon, Temperance couldn't make it worse for her.

For a moment Temperance's thoughts strayed back to Archie. He was the only drop of sunshine in her dark existence at this moment. He had stood by her, furious for her when he had discovered how she had been treated by Ronnie, and refusing to dance at the Palais himself. Thankfully, she'd managed to calm him down, insisting that any war was better fought from the inside out, and if she ever hoped to make it back inside the Palais then she would need friends to help her get there. Reluctantly, Archie had agreed but she knew he wasn't happy about it.

With the weight of the world seemingly on her shoulders, Temperance rose and shucked off her coat. She only had a few short hours to put in here before she made her way across London to the hotel, the last thing she wanted to do was risk this job as well.

The sudden noise of a clang in the kitchen made her jump. Turning around, she saw Nancy and Ruth were startled, too.

'What the heck is going on in there?' Nancy said exasperated. 'I ought to go and check.'

'No!' Temperance moved quickly towards the kitchen door to thwart them.

Nancy looked at her amused.

'You OK, honey?'

Temperance nodded furiously. 'Just, I know Betty specifically said she didn't want to be disturbed. Something about making a special soup.'

'Oh. All right,' Nancy replied, turning to Ruth. 'Honey, can you make sure that all the cutlery is polished on the tables?'

As Ruth skipped off happily to do as she was told, Nancy rounded on Temperance.

'All right, what's going on?'

Temperance felt her face heat up. She suddenly felt very tired of keeping all these secrets. She was about to say as much when thankfully Violet walked through the doors.

'Hello,' Violet called cheerily.

'Well, hey there.' Nancy grinned as she turned to the girl. 'I didn't know you were working today.'

'I'm not,' Violet replied, walking towards the kitchen. 'I'm here to see Betty.' She gave them a nervous smile. 'I'm going to tell her today. About the baby.'

'Now?' Temperance gasped.

'I keep putting it off,' Violet went on, oblivious to Temperance's agitated state. 'But then this morning I felt the baby kick.'

'Honey, you did?' Nancy crooned. Immediately she rushed over to Violet and rested her hands on her belly hoping to feel something.

'It's not doing it now.' Violet laughed, and in the midst of her nerves, Temperance grinned at the sound of it. She hadn't heard her friend laugh in months. In fact, not since before Eamon passed away, and the surge of happiness that passed through her took her by surprise.

'Well, excuse me,' Nancy giggled. 'What do I know? I don't have kids, remember.'

Though she was making light of it, Temperance couldn't miss the look of sadness that passed across Nancy's face. She reached out a hand and squeezed her friend's forearm.

'You have Peter and Ruth now, though,' she assured her.

Nancy nodded, smiling through slightly teary eyes. 'And I wouldn't be without them.'

In that moment, Temperance realised how very difficult life must be for Nancy now.

'Have you heard from Alex since Ronnie invested?' she asked quietly.

'Oh, yeah.' Nancy let out a bitter laugh. 'I got a letter.'

'What does he say?'

'Here, read for yourself.'

With that Nancy reached across the table for her bag. Fumbling inside she pulled out an envelope and handed it to Temperance.

Looking doubtful, Temperance exchanged a look of concern with Violet.

'Go on,' said Nancy, gesturing at the envelope in her hands.

Reluctantly, Temperance opened it, and with Violet peering over her shoulder, began to read.

April 2nd 1941

Dearest Nancy,

How are you, my darling? I am well, all things considered. We are continuing to do our best to wage war on Jerry. It's all the men can talk about, that we will win and we will ensure our country enjoys the freedoms it always has. We will not let a man like Hitler ride roughshod over those liberties we enjoy. Some days are harder than others, but it's thoughts of you, Mother, the Palais and of course Peter and Ruth that keep me going in my darkest hours. We all need hope in our lives, and for me it's the home comforts of life in London that propel me forwards.

I urge you to do the same, Nancy. I was sorry to

*hear the desperation and anger in your last letter,
my sweet. I can imagine that being demoted after
so many years of loyal service must be a very bitter
pill to swallow and I know how upset you must be.*

*But Nancy, dearest, I firmly believe that Mother
and Bill know what they are doing. They understand the Palais in ways that you and even I, to a
certain extent, do not. The Palais is in their blood
and if they truly believe that Ronnie Newsham
is the best choice for the business then we must
respect that.*

*We are outsiders, Nancy, and though I know we
both truly love the Palais, we must trust in Bill and
Edna and their expertise. And perhaps this is also
a blessing – now that you have Peter and Ruth to
care for? Maybe, my love, this is a sign that you
need to concentrate on the children from now on.
When this godforsaken war is over, and I return,
we can all be together again, with me at the helm,
providing and caring for you all, as it should be.*

Your loving husband,
Alex xxx

As Temperance and Violet both finished reading, Temperance hardly dared look at Nancy. She knew how upsetting it must have felt to receive this letter.

'When did it arrive?' Temperance asked.

'Three days ago,' Nancy replied, her tone even. She shoved her hands in the pockets of her apron and shook her head.

'I'm sorry,' said Violet, gently. 'But maybe it's not that bad. Maybe he's just trying to make you feel better about what's happened. Remind you there are other things in your life beside the Palais.'

'Nuh-huh,' Nancy shook her head. 'This is exactly what Alex

has always wanted. He has always hated me working. When we got married, he asked me to give up my job, but I refused. I told him I loved it too much, and I do . . . I did. And when I got demoted . . . I felt like some of my identity had been taken away.' She looked at them, sadness etched on her face. 'And I felt ashamed, as though those kids won't have anyone to look up to.'

'Nancy, that's ridiculous,' Violet exclaimed. 'The kids don't care about your job, and whether you're manager or a floor sweeper. They'll look up to you because you're you.'

'Violet's right,' Temperance added. 'Jobs don't make you who you are.'

'Maybe not . . . But that job was *part* of who I am,' Nancy said, wiping at her eyes.

As Temperance watched Nancy's tears fall, she felt helpless. Glancing at Violet, she realised it was a feeling she was becoming all too familiar with. Something had to change. But what?

Thirty-One

Across town at the Palais, Renee was applying a final coat of lipstick in the ladies toilets. Peering at herself in the small mirror above the sink, she couldn't help thinking that in the month since Ronnie had appeared, she had aged dramatically. She had lines on top of her laughter lines now, and as for the dark bags under her eyes, well, there was only so much makeup she could apply.

Her life was lived permanently on edge as she waited for Ronnie to strike. He was worse than ever with his smart mouth, and she knew he was just biding his time before he laid a hand on her again. It was all part of his plan. On the surface, their day-to-day life was just like any other married couple's. They shared a home, went to work together, discussed the events of the day. But there was always an overtone of duress to every conversation, to every moment shared. Their relationship was far from normal and Renee wondered how long they could continue.

Shaking her head, Renee shoved her lipstick back in her pocket and marched determinedly out of the toilets and into the corridor, only to run straight into her errant husband.

At the sight of her, Ronnie gave her a smile that didn't reach his eyes.

'Renee, flower. I've been looking for you. Thought you'd run out on me again.'

'Never, Ronnie, love,' Renee replied in as breezy a tone as possible.

'I should hope not.' Ronnie took a step back and observed

his wife. 'You don't want to make a habit of that. Who knows what sort of trouble it might cause.'

Renee smiled calmly at him. She had learned over the years that neutrality was her friend when it came to Ronnie.

'So, you were looking for me, you said?'

Ronnie nodded. 'Ernie Myers is in town on Friday. I want you to show him a good time. Dance with him, make him feel special.'

At the mention of Ernie, Renee inwardly grimaced. He'd been a friend of her husbands since both men had worn short trousers, so Ronnie said. But where her husband at least had some dynamism and a determination to succeed, Ernie was just lazy and lecherous, the type to hitch himself to anyone who'd got the winning card. Ronnie saw this as loyalty, which meant a lot to him, so he had rewarded Ernie over the years, mainly by making him the regional manager of his operations, looking after Ronnie's business enterprises when he couldn't. In return, Ernie always put Ronnie first, and her husband liked that, making sure that Ernie lived a good life – expensive suits, and flash nights out with the best entertainment money could buy, including female attention. This week it looked as if that was going to be from either Renee or a couple of the other Good Time Girls at the Palais. Renee inwardly shuddered. When Ronnie brought his mates into business with him, trouble was never usually far behind, and Ernie Myers was the worst of the lot. She hated the thought of subjecting her friends to charmless groping.

'Come on, Ron. Old Ern's handsy, everyone knows that,' she said, hoping to appeal to Ronnie's jealous side. Did he really want Ern grabbing at her, or worse?

But Ronnie's eyes flashed with anger, and Renee knew she'd misstepped. He took a step towards her and she flinched.

'Ernie's a good pal of mine,' he said quietly. 'Handsy or

not, you and the rest of the girls here will make sure he's well looked after.'

Despair washed over Renee, but she kept quiet, remembering the pain of him yanking at her hair the last time she'd dared to stand up to him.

'I don't want to have to have these conversations with you again, my love,' he said in a low voice. 'You do what I tell you, when I tell you. I'm your husband, Renee, it's time you worked out that what I say goes.'

Then, for just a second, as she stared into his cold, black eyes, Renee fantasised about telling the brute where go. He would thrash her, beat her to within an inch of her life, no doubt. But maybe the satisfaction of letting him know he couldn't always treat her like this would be worth it. But her fantasy quickly vanished, and her sense of rebellion weakened. She had spent three years on the run from her husband, and still he'd found her and managed to control her. With three times her strength and with spies everywhere, Ronnie was never going to be easy to get rid of. All Renee could do was play the long game, and hope for her sake, and more importantly her friends' sakes, that she could find a way to solve this problem.

'Course, Ronnie,' she said instead.

'Sorry, didn't hear you?'

'Yes, Ronnie,' she said loudly.

'Yes, Ronnie, what?'

'Yes, Ronnie. Me and the girls will show Ernie a good time.'

'And?' he persisted, his eyes never leaving hers.

She felt a flash of disgust at the pleasure in his eyes as he made her squirm.

'And, I'm sorry,' she said, fighting the humiliation seeping through her.

For a moment, Ronnie stared into her eyes, then he reached out his hand and lifted her chin, the smell of stale fags on his fingers making her want to wretch.

'Good girl,' he said. 'You know what's best for you.'

She nodded, nausea in her throat.

Then, before she knew it, Ronnie lunged forward and pressed his hot mouth on top of hers, kissing her roughly. As she tasted sour breath and tobacco, Renee felt her stomach turn over and willed for it to be over.

Finally letting her go, Ronnie stepped back, ran his eyes over her body and gave a crude wolf whistle, before turning to walk back down the corridor towards the dance hall.

As she watched him walk away, Renee now felt as though someone's eyes were boring into the back of her head.

Turning, she locked eyes with Sybil, who was standing near the toilets. Renee squared her shoulders and braced herself for whatever pithy quip she suspected the barmaid was about to make, but Sybil remained silent.

The idea of another person witnessing her being treated like that by Ronnie, flooded Renee with shame. And there, reflected back at her in Sybil's brilliant blue eyes, was unmistakable pity. And it was in that moment that Renee realised, if Sybil felt sorry for her she really was in trouble.

Thirty-Two

Nancy wasn't sure how many hours she had spent tossing and turning in the night, but when she woke up the next morning, after little sleep, she felt woozy and confused – and blinded by the shaft of bright spring sunshine coming through the gap in the curtains.

Bed had always been a place of salvation to her after a hard day's work. But since Ronnie had taken over the legendary dance hall and she'd been pushed out of the job she loved, sleep had evaded her. Instead, nights were filled with worry over her future. Though Nancy knew she was still employed at the Palais – something that perhaps had more to do with Edna's grudging pity than Ronnie's generosity, who knew how long for.

Glancing at the clock by her bedside, Nancy saw to her horror that it had gone ten, on a Saturday morning. She should have been up hours ago. She threw back the ivory candlewick bedspread, patted the curlers at the front of her hair and got out of bed.

Hurriedly washing with the pitcher of water that stood on the vanity unit of her bedroom, then quickly dressing in her patched-up tea dress, Nancy tried to focus on the joy still left in her world. She reminded herself of the two wonderful children she had care of, and that she did at least still work at one of the most legendary dance halls in Europe. And, she had friends. Though as her thoughts snapped to Renee, she felt a stab of worry.

The look of bleak despair in Renee's eyes these days was

210

heartbreaking. Gone were the wisecracking quips, and plucky Scouse spirit. Instead Renee now permanently wore the look of the battle-weary, and Nancy so wished there was more she could do to help her friend.

Now, as she walked through the flat to make herself a coffee before starting work, she was surprised to see that Ruth and Peter were nowhere to be found. Puzzled, she drank her coffee quickly, and then left the flat to make her way down to the dance hall, where, to her surprise, the two of them were helping Sybil tidy the bar.

'Here you are!' she called, putting on a bright smile.

At the sound of her voice, all three of them jumped.

'Ruth and Peter were at a loose end this morning. They came down to lend me a hand,' Sybil explained.

'Why didn't you wake me?' Nancy ran a hand through her messy hair.

'We thought you would like to sleep in,' Ruth said kindly, her dark hair bouncing on her shoulders as she spoke.

'Yes, and Mr Newsham has kept us occupied,' Peter added.

At the mention of Ronnie, Nancy felt her hackles rise.

'Mr Newsham, huh?'

As the late April sunshine streamed through the bar, Nancy glanced around. She saw broken glass and upended tables. Chairs battered and scratched.

'What the heck happened here?' she exclaimed.

At the question, Sybil's face fell. 'We had a bit of trouble last night.'

'Trouble?' Nancy echoed.

'Yes, there were a few fellas in last night, getting upset about something and nothing. Mr Newsham took care of it.'

Nancy cast her gaze towards the bar and felt a stab of fury. There had been fights when she was in charge, but nothing like this.

'Peter, Ruth, you can stop cleaning now,' Nancy ordered.

'But we want to help.' Ruth's eyes were wide with confusion.

'And Mr Newsham said it would be good for my training to deal with the messy end of business,' Peter said, continuing to sweep broken glass from the floor.

'Well, I'm telling you to go to the ticket booth and ensure that it's clean and tidy, please,' Nancy instructed.

A flash of petulance passed across Peter's face and Nancy could see that he was considering protest. But he must have changed his mind, because then he only nodded, handing the brush and pan back to Sybil.

Once the children had disappeared, Nancy turned to Sybil.

'What's really going on?' she asked. 'We've never had mess like this on a Saturday morning.'

Sybil looked hesitant. 'Some of Mr Newsham's business friends stayed here late, drinking and things got a bit loud and out of hand . . . there was a fight between a couple of them. '

Nancy gazed angrily around the battered bar. This was wanton vandalism and destruction.

'Did any of the customers see them?' she asked.

'Some,' Sybil admitted. 'Mrs Hawkins and her friends were very upset. They asked Mr Cain to intervene, but he said there was nothing he could do. Instead he got me to send them a round of port and lemons as an apology.'

Nancy groaned. They were going to lose money hand over fist if this carried on. Although she was sure that was of no interest at all to Ronnie Newsham. No, he saw the Palais as nothing more than his personal playground, somewhere to entertain his kingpin mafia pals.

'A lot of people left,' Sybil added. 'Including Mrs Hawkins and her lot – and Mr Humphries and his friends. Walked out on account of the noise and threatening atmosphere.'

'Jeez . . .' Nancy felt sick. 'Where's Mr Newsham now?'

She looked around the bar, half expecting to see Ronnie pop up from behind it.

'Gone across to the cafe, for a cuppa, he said,' Sybil replied. 'Mr Cain's in his office though.' Sybil's face fell. 'Your old office.'

Despite there never having been any love lost between her and Sybil, Nancy felt sorry for her now. It couldn't be easy taking orders from Ronnie.

'Thanks, Sybil,' she said, laying a hand on the girl's forearm and giving her a comforting squeeze.

With that, Nancy walked out of the bar and back out to the foyer. She reached for the coat she always kept behind the front desk. Slipping it on, she was about to march across the road to the cafe when something stopped her in her tracks – the sight of Ronnie sitting in the window with, of all people, George Millington.

As Nancy stared at the unlikely duo, she felt a swirl of confusion. What was going on?

'What are you doing standing out here in the rain?' came a voice.

Whirling round, Nancy saw Edna approaching, umbrella up and wearing a mac – her trademark Chanel just visible underneath.

'Just gathering my thoughts,' Nancy replied.

'In the rain?' Edna enquired.

'Uh-huh.' Nancy nodded. 'Rain brings a little clarity with it, I find.' She looked at Edna. 'And what are you doing here at this time on a Saturday?'

'Ronnie asked me last night if I would pop in a little earlier,' Edna said smoothly. 'He wants me to oversee the organisations for the tea dance.'

'Gonna clean up his mess, too?' Nancy said.

Edna frowned. 'What are you talking about?'

The flicker of confusion in her eyes gave Nancy a stab of satisfaction.

'You didn't hear about the bar brawl Ronnie's friends got into last night at the Palais?'

Edna quickly recovered. 'Oh, that . . .' she said. 'High spirits, I expect. Boys will be boys.'

'Broken glasses? Broken furniture?' Nancy could feel her face becoming warm with rage. 'It's an appalling way to behave. What will our customers think? The Palais has a respectable reputation.'

A dark cloud passed across Edna's face. 'You're making too much of it, Nancy,' she said. 'And I'm sure it won't be a regular occurrence.'

'Are you?' Nancy persisted. 'I'm not. None of our other investors or board members act as if the Palais is something that belongs to them, they treat the place with respect.'

'I can't deny that there aren't . . . teething troubles,' Edna said hesitantly. 'But Ronnie has been a lifeline for the Palais. He's made changes for the better.'

'You mean he's brought in a lot of money and demoted me for no good reason,' Nancy snapped back. 'You know I was a good manager, Edna. Do you really hate me that much you had to bring in that thug to take me down a peg?'

'I don't hate you, and Ronnie Newsham is not a thug,' Edna protested. 'He's—'

Edna broke off abruptly, and that's when the penny dropped. Edna was afraid of Ronnie.'

'Look,' Edna said, trying to regain control. 'We've been losing money hand over fist, and Alex will need a job when he comes home. If the Palais isn't here anymore, what's he going to do?'

Despite her dislike of the woman, Nancy felt herself soften just a little bit. Edna's duplicity had come from a place of love. She was worried about her son.

'You thought bringing Ronnie in as an investor would save Alex's future?' she said.

'So many men are going to come back from the war to nothing,' Edna said. 'I won't risk that for Alex, not for you or anyone else.'

Nancy stared at her. Edna was delusional, that was for sure. But seeing her mother-in-law so determined to protect her family struck a chord. Nancy might well do the same for Peter and Ruth, though she hoped she wouldn't be quite as misguided as Edna if it came to it. One thing was for sure, there would be no convincing Edna that her plan would almost certainly backfire. That didn't mean Nancy was going to go along with her. Her only hope was to open the woman's eyes to the kind of man Ronnie Newsham really was.

She took a deep breath and then gestured towards the cafe, where Ronnie and George were still sitting in the window. 'What do you think's going on there, huh? What would Ronnie want from George Millington? I'd say Betty has enough on her plate at the moment. The last thing she needs is a man like that encouraging her husband to do some of his dirty work for him.'

But if she hoped Edna would feel just as alarmed, she was wrong. Edna just shook her head, and with one hand pulled the collar of her coat up around her neck.

'None of my concern, nor yours, Nancy. And George is a grown man, capable of doing as he wishes.' She fixed her flinty eyes on Nancy. 'The sooner you let it sink in that you're no longer the Palais manager, the better for all of us, dear. Bill, Ronnie and I are running the place now, and that's the end of it.'

With that, her mother-in-law swept past her towards the Palais' entrance. And as she watched her go, Nancy had never felt more alone in the world.

Thirty-Three

The music of Oscar Reyburn never failed to make Temperance smile. And even now, as she worked back in the ticket office and watched Archie and Renee swirl across the dance floor, she felt the power of the music lift her spirits as they moved together. The thing about dancing was that it was all-consuming. You could lose yourself in the music and in the steps, the real world all so very far away.

It was a feeling that Temperance had longed for when her father had passed away, and later when Eamon died. But since meeting Archie, she found that the feeling of wanting to lose herself was different. When she danced with Archie she felt that they were lost in their own private world together. And it was something she wanted more and more of. For Temperance, the biggest casualty of no longer being in charge of dance instruction at the Palais was that she no longer got to work with Archie. That for her was the real disappointment.

That didn't mean she wasn't grateful that Archie still came in on the nights she was working, to keep her company when he could. For Temperance, just seeing him was a treat, and she loved their precious moments together. Even if she was no longer his dance partner, no longer the one he held in his arms. It seemed like her romance with Archie had come into her life just at the right time, like a blessing. The only fly in the ointment was her egg round, a secret she was still keeping from her love. She longed to tell Archie what she was doing, explain why she felt she had to step up to the plate and take these risks for her family and Violet, even if it meant she was hurting him. But every time she saw him, she found it impossible to form the words she knew she had to say.

'Temp, you're going to crease that coat if you don't hang it up,' Maisie said impatiently, bringing her back to the present.

'Eh?'

'The coat.' Maisie tugged it gently from her hands and put it on a hanger. 'What is up with you?'

'Nothing.' Temperance shrugged.

Maisie grinned and gave Temperance a playful nudge. 'You're in love,' she said in a sing-song voice.

'Yes I am,' Temperance said simply. And as she said the words aloud she knew she was proud to call Archie her sweetheart.

As the music came to a close, Archie smiled at Renee and then walked back across the floor towards Temperance.

'I could watch you and Renee all day,' she said, smiling.

Archie leaned across the counter and quickly kissed her cheek. 'You know I'd rather dance with you.'

'You're just saying that, Renee's a pro!' Temperance exclaimed, her eyes landing on the fiery redhead.

'She is,' Archie agreed. 'But she's not you.' He quickly glanced back at Renee and then lowered his voice. 'And between you and me, she doesn't seem herself. I mean, she could dance in her sleep, but there's no joy in her eyes, anymore.'

Temperance nodded. 'I wish there was something we could do,' she said.

'We all do,' Maisie, who'd overheard, broke in. 'This place is going to the dogs and no mistake. And nobody seems to care. Bunch of crooks running the place now.'

'Yes, well, crooks are everywhere. Not just at the Palais,' Archie muttered, darkly. 'Those swines are still nicking from our shop.'

Maisie, who knew about the thefts from the butcher's

business, frowned. 'Thought that had all stopped since your dad came back to work?'

Archie shook his head. 'I wish. If anything, it's got worse. They nicked a pig the other day.'

'A pig!' Maisie screeched. 'However did they get that through the streets of Hammersmith?'

'I wondered that myself,' Archie muttered.

Temperance felt sick. In that moment she wanted to tell Archie who was likely doing this to him and why, but she couldn't, there was too much at stake. Instead, she inwardly cursed herself for her treachery and steered the conversation back to safer territory.

'What can we do about the Palais, though?' she asked. 'Now that Ronnie's taken over.'

'And Edna and Bill are in cahoots,' Maisie muttered, then rolled her eyes. 'Look out. Talk of the devil.'

All three of them watched as Bill Cain took to the stage.

'Thank you, ladies and gentlemen. Please put your hands together for our incredible band.'

The audience clapped politely, and when the sound died down, he continued.

'And a big round of applause for our newest investor, Mr Ronald Newsham, who is with us tonight.'

There was another round of clapping, this time more subdued, which Bill tried to compensate for with a few tired old jokes, none of which raised much of a laugh from the crowd.

'Even the audience have had enough,' Maisie said, with a sigh. 'We're nowhere near as busy tonight as we would usually be. If this keeps up, all our loyal customers'll be decamping across town to that new dance hall in Camden.'

'The regulars don't like all the trouble Ronnie's brought with him,' Temperance said. 'Poor old Peter and Ruth were helping Sybil clean up some broken glass and furniture this morning.'

'Maybe we need a council of war?' Archie suggested.

'A council of what?' Maisie asked, laughing. 'Don't come in here with all your airs and graces.'

Archie smiled. 'I just think we could have a meeting. You know, us, Renee, the dancers, Nancy, Violet—'

'I doubt Violet's going to involve herself,' Maisie put in quickly. 'She's not been herself since Eamon died.' She cast a tender look at Temperance. 'Such a loss for you both.'

Temperance gave her an affectionate smile.

'I think the best thing any of us can do right now is just carry on with our jobs,' she said. 'Help make sure the customers we have got left are as happy as we can make them.'

Archie leaned in and gave her another kiss. 'You always want to do the right thing,' he said softly.

Temperance squeezed his arm as guilt gnawed at her. If only he knew how wrong he was about that.

'I'm going to go and help Sybil clear some glasses,' she said, then, wanting to get away.

Opening the hatch to the cloakroom closet, she made her way to the bar, looking around her. The place was full of louche men, dressed in trilby hats and trench coats, and the air was thick with both cigar and cigarette smoke. With their cruel laughs and arrogance, Temperance wondered how anyone could stand to be in their company.

'Anywhere you'd like me to start clearing?' she said, reaching the bar, where Sybil was adding drinks to a tray.

A look of gratitude passed across Sybil's features.

'Thanks, Temperance.' She jerked her head towards Ronnie's table in the corner. 'Him over there wants serving, if you can stand it?'

Temperance raised an eyebrow. 'That bad?'

'I'm just tired of dodging their greasy hands whenever I go past,' Sybil said with a sigh. 'I'm fine with a bit of innocent flirting with the clientele, but that lot . . . They're not nice.'

Temperance peered through the crowds and gazed at the table. 'Isn't that Betty's George sat between them?'

Sybil raised an eyebrow. 'He's been there all night, hanging on Ronnie's every word.'

'I wonder if Betty knows about it,' Temperance murmured. She swallowed. 'Anyway, here goes.'

As she weaved her way through the throngs of tables, her nerves rattled as she drew close to Ronnie's table.

Head bent low, she made sure she didn't catch the eye of any of the handful of men sat around the table, and instead focused on collecting the glasses. But it was impossible to miss the strands of conversation.

'So what happened then, Ron?' one of the men asked.

Ronnie took a sharp pull on his cigarette and shrugged. 'You don't need me to answer that for you do you, Charlie?'

At that there was a snigger around the table.

'He had to be taught a lesson, one he understands.'

Another snigger.

Ronnie now jerked his head towards George, who was sat looking animated in the centre of the men.

'Let's just say, George here is in better shape than he was when I finished with him.' He thumped Betty's husband on the back. 'Perhaps I ought to send you out as a warning, George, eh? This is what happens to blokes what don't pay up.'

There was another peal of laughter from the men, while George sat there, pathetically puffed up with pride at being included in Ronnie's gang.

'I'll literally be your right-hand man,' he said, gesturing to the stump where his left forearm used to be.

Temperance shuddered, shame on behalf of George heating her face as she reached down to pick up a remaining near-empty glass. But as she did so, one of the men clamped a hand on her forearm.

'Oi!' he snarled. 'I ain't finished with that yet.'

Cheeks flaming, Temperance mumbled a hushed sorry.

'I should bleedin' well think so,' the man continued. 'Ron, you wanna do something about your staff.'

Fear trickled down her spine as Ronnie fixed his cold eyes on her.

'Ignore her, she ain't usually in the bar,' Ronnie said. 'Why aren't you in the ticket booth where you belong?'

At the question, Temperance felt her mouth go dry. She willed herself to speak but found no words would come out.

Desperate for an ally, she looked at George, who studiously avoided her gaze.

'I asked you a question,' Ronnie repeated, his voice low and threatening.

The other men fell silent.

'I'm just helping Sybil out,' she managed at last.

'You were just helping?' Ronnie slammed the table with his fist. 'You weren't helping by taking my friend's drink before he'd finished it. Now he's got your grubby fingerprints all over his glass, he's not going to want to finish it. You,' he said pointing at her with his cigarette, 'owe him another drink.'

There was another silence and Temperance felt herself freeze. She should be used to it, how she was treated because of her skin colour, but it stung.

'I'm sorry, Mr Newsham—' she started nervously, but a familiar voice cut over hers.

'Evening, fellas, how you doin'?' Renee chirruped behind her.

At the sound of her friend's voice, Temperance felt herself relax as the men now all turned to Renee and murmured their greetings.

'So, what's going on here then, eh? Not tormenting this poor girl, are you?' She smiled and rested a hand on Ronnie's shoulder, while casting a fierce look of solidarity at Temperance over his head.

'We were just having a bit of fun, weren't we, boys?' Ronnie said in an easy voice.

Renee laughed, and the men followed suit. Temperance watched them with interest, Renee knew how to handle these men.

'Well, I'm here to spoil your fun,' Renee said easily.

There was a chorus of pantomime jeers as Renee plucked a cigarette from a packet on the table and lit it, taking a long drag before speaking again. 'How about you let Temperance get back to work, and one of you lucky lads has a dance with me.'

Her eyes landed on the man who'd accused Temperance of taking his drink.

'How about you, Ernie?' she said. 'Fancy a waltz around the floor with me?'

Temperance saw the man's eyes light up.

'Don't mind if I do!'

As Ernie got to his feet, Temperance noticed Ronnie's grip on his wife's hand become tighter and tighter. Her knuckles were almost white, she must be in agony, but Renee only kept a smile on her face as she held out her free hand for Ernie to take and lead her across the floor.

Ronnie had no choice but to let her go, but there was a look on his face Temperance didn't like. Murderous was one way of describing it.

With her tray now full of glasses, Temperance slunk away from the table and back across the floor to the bar, relieved to have got away from Ronnie and his thugs. She hoped to God that Archie hadn't seen any of what had just happened, she didn't dare look. And as she turned and watched Renee dancing with Ernie, she thought her heart would break. Although Renee was executing every step perfectly, Archie was right – there was no joy in her movements. Just how long could Renee keep this display up? The strain of it must be killing her.

Thirty-Four

'That smells nice,' George said admiringly as he walked into the kitchen.

'Woolton Pie,' Betty replied, as she pulled the pie from the oven and rested it on the counter. 'Vi's coming round for lunch.'

George grunted. 'Pulling out all the stops for her, I see.'

'There'll be some for you later.'

He let out another grunt. 'Cold, no doubt.'

'We're all having it cold! Your mother's been growing salad potatoes and leaves in the garden. Some of it's ready.'

Betty tried to squash the exasperation she was feeling towards her husband and instead turned to look at him.

'What in heaven's name are you wearing?'

Dressed in a lounge suit and tie with polished shoes, Betty hadn't seen George look so smart since their wedding day.

He straightened his tie. 'Got a meeting.'

Betty raised an eyebrow. 'With Ronnie Newsham, I suppose.'

'What if I am?'

'Ronnie's that bent, he can't lie straight at night,' Betty grumbled.

'He's a businessman what's successful.' George set his gaze on Betty. 'People round here don't like success.'

Betty shook her head. 'That's not what this is about. Ronnie Newsham's trouble. Everyone knows that. Whatever does he want with you?'

'To give me work!' George thundered. 'Look at me.' He gestured to his one remaining arm. 'It's not as though people are queuing up to employ me.'

Betty felt a knot of frustration unfurl in her stomach. Her husband had never been bothered about work, everyone knew that. He'd begged, borrowed and stolen most of his adult life to make ends meet. Even when he had a job, it never lasted very long. Now that Ronnie Newsham was sniffing around him like a dog around scraps, George had suddenly become career-minded.

'Is that why you're hanging about with a thug like that?'

George laughed. 'I don't think you're one to talk about the company I keep. Word about town is that you're hanging about with Alan Hopkins. All these nights you should be here, making my tea and looking after me, and you're out with some old flame. Thought you were better than that, Bet, after what he did to you.'

She bristled. 'It's not what you think.'

George chuckled, softly. 'I'm sure it's not. But, Bet, don't forget how I took you on when nobody else ever would. I don't want you embarrassing me, not now, not after all this time, you hear?'

But there wasn't time to answer as the doorbell rang. Pushing past George, Betty raced to get it and managed to smile in welcome as she saw her eldest daughter standing on her doorstep.

'Vi,' she breathed, holding the door wide open to welcome her daughter inside. 'Come in.'

Violet smiled at her mother and pressed a bunch of stocks into her hands. 'For you.'

'You shouldn't have,' Betty said, taking the flowers gratefully. 'Shall we sit in the garden for a bit? Thought we might eat a bit later.'

As Betty walked down the corridor, she found she felt oddly nervous. It had taken so long to get Violet to agree to come round for lunch, she wanted it to go well. She felt as if she hardly ever saw her daughter these days, and when she did it was only fleetingly at the Palais.

She was about to blame George, but knew that wasn't the only reason she was struggling to find time for her family these days. What with the National Restaurants job and, of course, Alan keeping her busy.

At the thought of Alan, guilt churned. Betty thought she had been clever, but if George now knew she was knocking about with Alan again, she would have to be careful. The last thing she wanted was for anyone else to get wind, and linking her arm through Violet's she realised with a shudder that her daughter was the last person she wanted to hear of Alan's involvement in her life.

They hadn't kissed since that fateful lunchtime in the kitchen, a few weeks earlier. But that didn't mean Alan wasn't always on her mind. She might have pushed him away, citing the fact they were both married, but her heart wanted more, and she wondered how long she would be able to resist temptation, especially when he'd made no secret of his feelings for her.

'Is Queenie in?' Violet asked now, as she wandered out into the garden.

Betty shook her head. 'She's gone to the market.'

'Buying or selling?' Violet asked with a knowing look in her eye.

'When it comes to your grandmother, I've learned not to ask,' Betty replied sagely.

Pulling out a chair from the table, she sat opposite her daughter, who was still dressed in her chunky wool jacket despite the warmth of the day.

'Do you want me to take that for you?' Betty asked, gesturing to the jacket.

Violet shook her head. 'I'm a bit cold.'

Betty peered up at the sunshine. It was late April and unseasonably warm. She looked back at her daughter.

'You all right, Vi?' she asked.

A flicker of alarm passed across Violet's features. 'How do you mean?'

'You don't seem yourself.'

Betty leaned across the wooden table and reached for Violet's hand. As she did so, she couldn't help noticing that Violet's palm was clammy. Worry coursed through her.

'I know losing someone you love is tough, but this grief, Violet, it's taking you over.' Betty's voice was rich with concern.

Violet snatched her hand from her mother's and buried it in her lap. 'I am living my life.'

'You're not.' Betty shook her head. 'You're hiding. You mope about at the Palais—'

'I'm doing my job,' Violet cut in.

'You don't go out with your friends. You just go to work and then you go back to Winnie's. I know, because she's told me.' Once again, Betty reached for Violet's hand, and this time was pleased when her daughter didn't pull away. 'Eamon wouldn't want this.'

There was a silence and for a moment Betty fretted she had gone too far, but something seemed to shift in Violet, who looked her mother in the eyes for the first time in months.

'There's something I need to tell you,' she whispered.

Betty narrowed her eyes. She knew it! A mother's instinct was never usually wrong.

'You're not ill, are you?' she demanded now, thoughts of tuberculosis and scarlet fever tearing through her mind.

Violet shook her head, and Betty saw there was real fear in her daughter's eyes and she clasped her hand tighter, hoping the grip would offer reassurance.

'Tell me?' Betty begged.

'I'm expecting,' Violet said then, abruptly, flatly.

Wide-eyed, Betty stared at her daughter's face for just a second before her eyes travelled down her body and landed on her belly. There, underneath the shapeless tea dress and thick coat, there was a clearly visible bump.

Pulling her hand from Violet's, Betty's hand flew to her mouth as she tried to take in her daughter's news. For months now, she had known something was wrong . . . But pregnant? She had never envisioned this. She hadn't even known that she and Eamon had become that close. But then her mind strayed back to the kiss she and Alan had shared just a few precious weeks ago. Sometimes your innermost secrets remain private.

She looked back at her daughter's face and could see that behind the fear there was determination. In that moment Betty felt proud of her daughter. Violet had always been strong in a way she had never been. A pang of sorrow gnawed away at her, and, dare she admit it, jealousy. If she had found half the strength of her daughter, life could have turned out very differently.

Yet Violet wouldn't have it easy. Not only would she have a tough road ahead of her, giving birth to an illegitimate child and all the stigma that would bring, but the child would be half black and half white. Betty shook her head; it was a good job Violet was so strong – she'd need to be if she and her unborn child were to cope with all that lay ahead.

'How far along are you?' she managed to ask now.

'About eight months,' Violet replied.

Betty's eyes were out on stalks. 'Eight months?'

How could she not have realised?

She thought of the poor relationship she and Violet had endured all these years. But despite their problems, there was one overriding emotion that outweighed everything else – love. And so Betty simply nodded, recognising that at this moment it was support that her daughter needed and nothing else.

'How do you feel about this, Vi?' she asked gently.

Violet thought for a moment, and then Betty watched as a small smile spread across her daughter's face.

'When Eamon died, I thought I would break,' said Violet. 'But then, this miracle happened, something wonderful to come out of this awful pain, Eamon's legacy. But I'm not stupid, Betty, I know how hard this is going to be.'

The bluntness of Violet's words stunned her mother for a moment. She really had thought of everything, but then Violet always did.

'And are you ready?' Betty asked.

At the question Violet looked surprised and then she laughed. 'Is anyone ever ready?'

Betty laughed too and shook her head. 'I certainly wasn't. When you and Roy arrived, I wondered how I'd cope. You were both so much more than I could have expected.'

'In a bad way?' Violet asked in a small voice.

'Never in a bad way,' Betty said fiercely. 'But George wasn't around a lot, and I hadn't realised how lonely bringing up two children would be – and I was a respectable married woman.' Betty bit her lip. She couldn't resist adding that last bit. Because despite how much Betty loved her daughter, she couldn't deny the fact that Violet had committed a sin against God. Violet had to understand that. This was a belief that had been drummed into Betty since childhood.

That didn't mean she wouldn't do anything she could to help Violet. When she herself had found motherhood tough, she'd had Queenie to help her, and no matter how worried she felt for her daughter she wanted Violet to have the same.

'Your grandmother was a rock for me,' Betty said carefully. 'She helped me care for you both, I'd have been lost without her.'

'And your own mother?' Violet asked.

Betty shook her head. 'My mother disapproved of your father. She said she had raised her own family, she wasn't helping me do the same.'

Violet shook her head in disbelief. 'There never was a lot of love lost between you and Nan, was there?'

At the question, Betty thought back to how difficult it had always been with her mother. She hadn't seen her in years, but their dysfunctional relationship had stayed with her. For so long, Betty had wanted things to be different but they never had been. And then history had repeated itself with Violet. Ever since Violet had stopped calling her Mother or Ma when she was small, their relationship had deteriorated. She felt she had let her daughter down, not been there for her enough. Instead she'd paid more attention to Roy. She hadn't earned the term 'Mother' with Violet.

But could this be a chance to help heal the hurts of the past? More than anything, Betty wanted to make amends to Violet. She had lost her son, she wasn't going to lose her daughter, too. No matter what moral sin Violet may have committed falling pregnant out of wedlock, she was Betty's flesh and blood and she loved her.

'I hope you know I'll help you, Vi, we all will.'

And as Betty said the words aloud she saw the relief sweep across her daughter's face.

'Like hell you will,' a voice boomed from behind them.

At the sound of George's voice, Betty's heart sank. She'd thought he had left for his meeting.

'George, please.' Betty got up and walked towards her husband, but the anger in his eyes was unmistakable as he marched past her and up to Violet.

'Did I hear right? You're up the pole carrying some bastard?'

Betty pulled at George's sleeve, urging him away.

To her surprise, Violet got to her feet, her chin lifted in a defiant fashion.

'If you mean, am I carrying the child of the man I loved, the man that died saving *your* life, then yes.'

Betty thought Violet's reminder to George of all Eamon had done for him might have silenced her husband. But, instead, George took a step towards Violet.

'That don't excuse your behaviour,' he growled, turning to his wife. 'Now get out of my house. I never want to see your face round here again.'

Thirty-Five

Back at the Palais, and Renee was making her way around the dance hall checking that everyone was ready for the tea dance. It was ten to three, and they would be welcoming customers through the doors in less than ten minutes.

Since Nancy had been demoted to front-desk manager, Edna was supposed to have taken over much of the running of the place. But the truth was, there was much the dance hall stalwart missed, or didn't understand. Edna had always been and still was an exceptional dancer, but that was where her skills stopped. When it came to managing others and ensuring the smooth running of a dance hall, she was clueless. Ronnie would have had no idea about that when he invested a large stake in the dance hall; he would have merely seen an opportunity to expand his empire, and that he could take advantage of being able to use an entertainment venue whenever he needed. The dance hall wasn't in his blood as it was for her and Nancy, and so many of the others that called the Palais home. Experience told her that Ronnie would pick up and drop the Palais when he'd had enough, it was down to her to try and limit the damage. Which is why she went out of her way and worked an increasing number of hours to make sure that the place ran as smoothly as it could.

Satisfied that all was in order, Renee walked across the dance hall towards the dancers' pen. Temperance wasn't working until tonight, and unofficially Renee had asked her to manage the dancers and the rotas in the way she always had when Ronnie wasn't around.

But without Temperance, it was down to her to make sure that things were in order.

Pushing open the door of the practice room, Renee stood rooted to the floor as she took in the scene before her. The dancers were standing in a semi-circle, listening to Ronnie in rapt attention, while Peter stood beside him, clearly hanging on every word.

Renee's gaze landed on Sybil, who was standing a little further out of the circle, hands in her pockets and what looked like a large smile on her face. Renee felt a pang of exasperation – of course Sybil would be falling for Ronnie's games.

'So, as I said, girls, make sure you show my lads a good time and I'll see you're rewarded for it, all right?' Ronnie said. 'My lads are gentlemen, but they like to feel important, so laugh at their jokes, make 'em feel like they're kings on the dance floor, even if they've got two left feet – and my lad Peter here will reward you with a generous tip at the end of the night.'

At the mention of Peter, Renee's pulse quickened. Bringing the girls into whatever lousy scheme he was planning was one thing, but not Peter. The lad was young, impressionable. He had already been through so much and he deserved better.

As the girls nodded and filed out, Sybil turned back to flash Ronnie a smile and then filed wordlessly past Renee.

Once the room was empty, save for Peter and Ronnie, Renee gave a polite cough. Ronnie looked up.

'Reen!' he exclaimed. 'Didn't see you there. What can I do for you?'

Ignoring her husband, she smiled at Peter. 'Give us a minute, would you, chuck?'

'Of course.' Peter looked at Ronnie for confirmation, who nodded, and Peter smiled as he walked past Renee.

'So what is it, love?' Ronnie said with an amused look on his face.

Taking a deep breath, Renee walked towards her husband and turned to face him. 'I want you to leave Peter alone. He's a young lad trying to find his way in the world.'

'And I'm just trying to help him, Reen,' Ronnie protested, extending his arms wide as if to further highlight his innocence.

Renee stamped her foot with impatience. Ronnie narrowed his eyes.

'You questioning me, sweetheart?' His voice was dangerously low.

'You know I am,' she said. 'You've won, Ronnie. You've got me back, you've got your fingers in the Palais, you've shown everyone round here you're the king of it all – all I ask is that you leave Peter alone.'

Ronnie laughed. 'Worried he might end up like me?'

'Yes,' Renee said, bluntly.

She saw the familiar clench of his jaw and braced herself for whatever was coming next. For weeks now Renee had watched Peter hang on Ronnie's every word. She'd hoped that she was wrong, that Ronnie wasn't grooming the boy to become a new version of him. Guilt coursed through her. She was responsible for this. She had brought Ronnie here and created this devastation. She might not like her husband, but she knew him better than he knew himself and she knew this was how he operated. Peter and Nancy meant far too much to her to let the innocent lad fall into Ronnie's clutches.

For a moment, Ronnie said nothing. Then, to her surprise, he sank to the floor and sat back on his haunches. Running his hands across his heavily pomaded, jet-black hair, Ronnie let out a long sigh before he looked up at her.

'You've always thought ill of me haven't you, Reen? After all I've tried to do for you.'

Renee let out a hollow laugh. 'Ronnie, you've never done anything for me. Except force me to marry you to settle some lousy debt of me dad's when he passed on.'

Ronnie shook his head. 'I wanted to marry you because I loved you, Renee. I saw you in the dance halls when you were a kid. You was head and shoulders above the rest, and I fell for you in a heartbeat. But I knew you never saw me like that. You were too good for me and I knew you looked down on me.'

A sudden memory of the past washed across Renee's senses. She remembered Ronnie always being at the back of a music hall somewhere whenever she danced. She'd known who he was, everyone in the North West knew Ronnie Newsham – as dodgy as a dark winter's night was long. She wanted nothing to do with him, but she knew her father hadn't felt the same way. That his gambling addiction, and Ronnie's leniency to always extend the credit he offered him at any number of totes, led to her father only seeing the good in him.

'How was I supposed to think of you, after what you did to me old man?' she said.

'Your old man knew fine well what he was doing,' Ronnie barked.

Frustration got the better of Renee. 'And you could have cut him off any time you liked. You didn't, and it's thanks to you he ended up killing himself and I became your wife. How did you think that was going to end up? Did you honestly think you and me would end up as love's young dream after a start like that?'

As she finished her outburst, Ronnie stared at her open-mouthed. Then he got to his feet and looked at her with something like incredulity on his face.

'I had hoped you would fall in love with me, Reen, yes,' he said. 'I know I gave you no choice but to marry me, but I only did it because I thought you would come to recognise how much I loved you.'

From nowhere, laughter welled up inside Renee. From the outside she recognised this would look very much like a declaration of love, but she knew Ronnie inside out. This wasn't an expression of love, this was another manipulation. And she wasn't falling for it.

'Ronnie, you and I know I'm wed to you until you've had enough.'

'That's just it, Reen, love.' He moved slowly towards her now. And when he was just inches from her face, he reached out and stroked his smooth palm across her face. 'I'll never get tired of you, and I'll never stop trying to make you love me.'

'And you think this is the best way of doing it?' she asked.

He gripped her chin, pinching the flesh between thumb and forefinger, a slow lazy smile spreading across his face. 'We both know you'll come round in the end.'

From nowhere, courage came to the fore.

'You've had me married to you ten years, Ronnie Newsham. I've run from you, hated you and cursed the day you were born. What the hell makes you think I'll ever love you?'

Ronnie bent down so his face was so close to hers, she could smell the familiar musk of Old Spice on his neck.

'Because I always get my way in the end, Renee, love. You should know that by now.'

And then, before she had a chance to draw breath, Ronnie reared back and with his fist drawn back above his head, he smashed his knuckles squarely into her right eye socket.

Pain and shock ricocheted through her as Ronnie released her and she fell backwards to the ground. Hunched in a ball, she heard the sound of his footsteps walk towards the door. And then a pause.

'Best you don't work the floor till that eye clears up, Reen. People'll think you're a right clumsy cow walking into a door like that. I'll let everyone know you won't be in work for a few days. Maybe with a bit of time to yourself, you might think about your situation a bit – see if you reconsider your feelings.'

Thirty-Six

In the heart of the West End, Temperance tried to still her racing pulse as she watched Mr Henshall and his chef check the eggs she had delivered, as part of her weekly round.

As he held one of the two dozen she had brought up to the light, Temperance felt her legs tremble. She had seen two police officers on her way here, and paranoia told her they were there for her, and her alone.

Sweat gathered on her brow. Times were hard, but surely there was a better way to make a living than selling black-market goods? Queenie's contact had seemed pleased with her work and the money she was making for him, and he'd asked her last week if she wanted to stock up on cheese, as there was talk of that being rationed along with clothes in the not-too-distant future.

Now, as Mr Henshall snapped the cardboard lid shut, he smiled and handed it back to her.

'Apart from two that are cracked, these are wonderful, Temperance. Our guests are delighted with the little extra service we can offer.' He winked at her then, and Temperance felt her legs tremble even more.

'When can we expect some more?' he asked.

Temperance thought for a moment. It was getting harder to juggle clandestine meetings in Ravenscroft Park 'Next week, sometime?'

Mr Henshall frowned. 'The sooner the better, if you can.'

'I'll see what I can do. It's not always easy getting supplies.'

Mr Henshall nodded, his greying hair falling forward into his eyes as he did so. 'Yes, but I imagine with the Palais the way it is now, you could find anther supplier quite easily if that was your problem.'

Temperance frowned. 'I'm sorry, sir, I don't quite follow.'

Mr Henshall rocked back and forth on his heels, looking uncomfortable.

'Since Mr Newsham's involvement, I must say my wife's rather upset that you're no longer able to teach her to dance.'

'I'm sorry.' Temperance frowned. It was one of her greatest regrets, too.

There was silence for a moment as Mr Henshall observed her, and then his face broke out into a fatherly smile.

'You know, Temperance, you're a good girl, and I recognise you may not be working to your full potential under the Palais' new management structure.'

Temperance said nothing and bit her lip. She had always been loyal to the Palais and it didn't feel right to speak out of turn.

'I respect loyalty, Temperance,' Mr Henshall said, correctly understanding her reticence. 'But I want you to know that I'm considering setting up a dance school here.'

'Here?' Temperance echoed.

'That's right.' Mr Henshall gestured around the hotel. 'It won't be anything like what's on offer, or what used to be on offer, at the Palais, but we hope it will be something our guests and any locals in the area might enjoy. Besides, when the Palais is sold I suppose we might be closer for people to consider coming this way.'

Temperance's mind was a blur.

'The Palais is being sold, and you're offering me a job?' she said.

At her forthrightness, Mr Henshall laughed. 'Yes, and yes. Surely you knew?'

Temperance shook her head and Mr Henshall looked concerned.

'Oh, I beg your pardon. I thought it was common knowledge. Mr Newsham took a controlling stake in the business to sell on to another consortium, who want to develop it. Into what, I'm not quite sure, but it seems as though it's all settled. He was in here with a young lad the other week.'

'A young lad?' Temperance echoed.

'That's right, a tall, dark-haired boy. Ronnie said he was his apprentice.' Mr Henshall chuckled. 'I thought he looked a little young, but these days what do I know?'

As he laughed softly at his own joke, Temperance's head began to spin. The Palais was being sold? Ronnie was really involving Peter in his business? She felt sick at the thought of it. Did anyone else at the Palais know? Edna? Bill? Or did they not care?

She felt as if her head was about to explode, as she struggled to make sense of all this information, but it seemed Mr Henshall hadn't quite finished with her yet.

'You're too good a dancer to waste your talents, Temperance. And if you're not being appreciated where you are, I want you to know we'd appreciate you here.'

Temperance looked up at him, trying to take it all in. She was being offered a way back into the dancing she loved. An opportunity to teach again, to do what she was good at. But it would mean leaving the Palais, the place that had always been there for her, and had been her second home when she had needed support through some of the hardest times of her life. But then, she realised, it looked as though the Palais wouldn't be a part of her future anymore . . .

'As I say, I respect your loyalty.' Mr Henshall met her gaze. 'But sometimes you have to be loyal to yourself, and know when to leave.'

* * *

As Temperance cycled back to Hammersmith, the spring evening sunshine making the ride through the park a pleasant one, Mr Henshall's words echoed round and round in her mind. The Palais might well be sold. She had been offered a new job. It still felt too much to take on board. But as her mind strayed to Ronnie and all the new clientele he was bringing into the Palais, she shuddered. Life was changing, she thought as she sailed past Holland Park. Perhaps it was time for her to change too.

She was so deep in thoughts of her future, she was barely concentrating on her journey, but as she turned down the alleyway near Brook Green Road, she nearly collided with a figure marching straight across her path. She braked suddenly, but it was too late and she toppled off her bike crashing into the wall to avoid the pedestrian.

Leg and head throbbing, Temperance sat in the alley trying to get her bearings but all she wanted to do was cry out in pain. Her leg was bleeding, and, much to her dismay, she saw her jumper was covered in egg.

'Oh my god!' She heard a familiar voice exclaim. 'Temperance, are you all right?'

Looking up she came face to face with Violet, who was grappling in her bag for a hankie.

'I'm so sorry,' Violet said, starting to dab at the cut on Temperance's leg. 'I wasn't looking where I was going, my mind was all over the place.'

'Mine too.' Temperance managed a weak smile. As the throbbing in her head began to subside, she took the hankie from Violet and began to dab at her injury herself. She hated the sight of blood, but could see that thankfully the cut wasn't that bad.

She turned to look at her friend and saw her cheeks were pinched and her normally immaculately coiffed hair was sticking up all over the place.

'Violet? What's happened?'

'Oh . . .' Violet rubbed a hand across her face and sank down on the weed-strewn path beside her. 'I told Betty about the baby today.'

Alarm studded Temperance's heart. 'And?'

'She was very good about it,' Violet admitted. 'But George wasn't. He threw me out of the house and said he never wanted to see me again.'

Temperance winced at the admission. She reached out a hand and let her long fingers slip through Violet's. 'I'm so sorry.'

Violet gave her a soft smile. 'Why should you be sorry? This isn't your fault, and the truth is, I don't care what George thinks. But I suppose it gave me a glimpse of the sort of reaction I can expect when this little one finally comes along.'

As Temperance watched Violet stroke her belly she felt a pang of sorrow.

'I don't think you should ever expect to be thrown out of the house.'

Violet grimaced. 'Maybe not, but it's not a surprise. George has got the morals of an alley cat, but heaven forbid his daughter has a baby out of wedlock.'

'Oh, Violet. I really wish I could help you more.'

'You're doing more than enough, Temp,' Violet said. 'But me and this little one, we have to learn to fend for ourselves. I think it's only now I'm beginning to see that.'

'But it doesn't have to be this way,' Temperance said urgently. 'Me, Mum, Auntie Winnie, we're your family too, now. We'll help you.'

Violet started to say something then stopped, peering at Temperance's jumper.

'Temp, why are you covered in egg?'

At the question Temperance felt her cheeks burn as she quickly tried to think of a reason. But as Violet looked searchingly into her eyes, she knew there was no other option but to tell the truth.

'I'm selling eggs on the side,' she admitted. 'To make extra money. For me and the family, but also for you and the baby.'

'Temp, sweetheart, nobody wants you to break the law!' Violet cried, her voice rich with concern. 'No matter how hard things get. Least of all me, least of all Eamon.'

The mention of her brother's name was her undoing, and all the emotion Temperance had been holding onto poured out of her as she gave in to the tears she had been keeping at bay.

As she wept, she was aware of Violet's arm around her shoulders, squeezing her tightly.

'You've been through so much, and you're trying to be so strong, Temperance, but you don't have to be. You need to let other people help you, and you have to give up this egg round. You don't have to make up for the fact that your brother died. You deserve to be happy.'

As Temperance dried her tears she looked at her friend's face and saw genuine affection in her eyes.

'But what will you do? And Ma? Eamon's wage is missed at home now, and Ma has really appreciated the bit extra I can bring in.'

'And how much help do you think you'll be if the police catch you with these eggs?' Violet eyed Temperance's jumper again and shook her head. 'You're far more use to us here as a friend and as an aunt than you would be in prison! Think of yourself now, Temp. Please. It's time.'

Thirty-Seven

As April ended, the new month brought with it a fresh assault from Hitler. The Jerries had increased their attacks, and as May dawned they began a series of devastating attacks on Greenock, Belfast – and a week-long assault on Liverpool.

The bombing campaign was terrifying, with more than six thousand homes demolished by the raids, leaving a serious housing problem for the city. Not only that, but some of Liverpool's most iconic buildings were devastated. The cathedral, Custom House and Bluecoat church were decimated, as was Renee's spirit.

As news of the devastation in the north of the country spread, her mood sank ever lower, and Nancy couldn't help worrying about her as she watched Renee scuttle about the Palais, having recently taken it upon herself to stay behind the scenes and let some of the more experienced dancers take to the floor instead of her. Nancy had tried to ask Renee about it, but every time she broached the subject her friend would simply wave her concerns away.

As Nancy sat at reception waiting for customers to pile through the door, she watched Renee carefully arranging her hair to cover her right eye. Frustration burned through Nancy. It was obvious that Renee had taken another beating.

'They say a steak's good for that,' Nancy called.

Turning round, Renee managed a wry smile. 'Oh, yeah? With a bag of chips?'

The two women exchanged a small smile as Renee went back to trying to hide her face.

'What did you get that one for?' Nancy couldn't stop herself asking.

Renee shrugged. 'Nothing much,' she said. 'As usual.'

A heady mix of anger and frustration rose in Nancy as she saw her friend do battle with her wound.

'That thug ought to be ashamed of himself,' she said. 'I'm serious, Renee, the guy's an animal.'

'Who's an animal?' a voice boomed.

Nancy seethed with anger as she saw Ronnie standing in front of her, dressed in a lounge suit looking as if he was ready to take on the world. She'd had enough.

'You,' she said simply. 'The way you treat people, especially your wife, is disgusting.'

She heard a sharp intake of breath from Renee behind her, before she saw the muscle in Ronnie's cheek twitch.

'Disgusting, is it?'

'That's right.' Nancy suddenly felt very tired of Ronnie.

'Your Peter doesn't seem to think I'm disgusting,' Ronnie said, as he took a step towards her. 'He seems to enjoy having a man about the place.'

'Only because he's yet to see a fine example,' Nancy said. 'I've seen men like you all my life, Ronnie – all cowards. The one thing I know about you is you'll get tired and move on.' She glanced around the Palais and then back at Renee. 'Once you've ripped the life from something and got bored.'

Ronnie raised an eyebrow.

'But when you eventually do get bored, I'll be the one who picks up the pieces, cleans up the mess you left behind.'

Ronnie took another step towards her and Nancy fixed her green eyes on him. To her surprise, she found she wasn't scared. It was as though she had seen the worst possible version of him and there was nothing more to fear. As he neared the desk she saw his demeanour change and she knew he knew she wasn't going to break.

'You're wrong, love.' Ronnie stopped just a few inches from her. 'I'm going nowhere, and I'm becoming rather fond of your Peter.'

When he turned on his heel and walked away, Nancy heard Renee let out a shaky breath.

'You were lucky there, queen,' she said.

'Lucky?' Nancy echoed. She looked at Renee now, at her bruised eye.

'He's had a bad week. You don't want to make him worse,' Renee said, grimly.

'Renee, honey, look at yourself.' Nancy felt frustrated. 'How much worse could he get? He's using your face as a punchbag. That's gotta make you mad.'

'It used to,' Renee said, and Nancy couldn't miss the sadness in her voice. 'But it's easier now to just accept it. One day you will, too.'

Nancy opened her mouth to contradict her, but Renee's listlessness struck her. It was as though a part of her had disappeared. Just where had Renee gone? What had Ronnie done with her friend?

The following morning, Nancy's mind was still full of thoughts of Renee as she made her way across town to the new Islington restaurant. It had only been up and running a week, but she knew Betty had been working great guns alongside Alan and Nora over the past few weeks to get everything ready.

Reaching the community centre, Nancy smiled as she pushed the door open and saw Betty on her hands and knees scrubbing the floor.

'Betty, honey, you've enough on your plate managing this whole thing. Why on earth are you scrubbing floors?'

Betty got to her feet, taking care not to kick over her bucket of filthy water, and gave Nancy a wry smile. 'If you were Renee, no doubt you'd call me a right old scrubber!'

Nancy laughed. 'I'm not so sure she would any longer. She's different. It's like Ronnie's turned the light off inside her since he's come back.'

Arching her back, Betty grimaced. 'Shall we get a cuppa before we open up?'

'I'd rather have a coffee,' Nancy admitted.

'Course you would.' Betty chuckled. 'Come on, we've got five minutes. Let's see what we can find.'

As Betty trundled into the kitchen Nancy couldn't help but admire the hard work that had gone into transforming the community centre. When she had last visited a few weeks ago the place had been musty and stuffed full of old sports equipment. But now, the place looked more of a home for lost treasure than anything else. It had been transformed into a stylish restaurant, with white, freshly starched tablecloths on each of the round tables, framed line drawings on the walls and sparkling cutlery at every setting. It was as good as anywhere up West and Nancy felt proud of her former colleague for creating something so wonderful out of so very little.

'I gotta say I'm very impressed,' Nancy said as she snaked her fingers around a cup of hot coffee. 'This place is beautiful.'

'Thank you.' Betty looked genuinely delighted at the compliment. 'It was all down to Alan and Nora, really. And Temperance, of course. That girl's been a wonder, helping out when she's got a spare minute.'

'You gotta stop doing that, giving everyone else the credit.' Nancy said with a sigh. 'You worked hard for this, Bet. And after the way Ronnie treated you, this is very well deserved.'

At the mention of Ronnie, Betty's face darkened. 'That man is pure evil. I worry about my girls with him in charge.'

'And I worry about Peter,' Nancy admitted in a small voice as she lifted her coffee cup. 'He really looks up to Ronnie, he even went with him to a meeting in London the other day, at some fancy hotel.'

Betty frowned. 'On his own?'

Nancy nodded. 'Peter told me yesterday. What sort of a mother am I if I can't keep an eye on my own kids?'

'Well, if that's the judgement, we're all bad parents. I hardly ever knew what my Roy was up to. But he was a good kid, and Peter's the same,' Betty said, reassuringly.

'You think?' Nancy shook her head. 'I was hoping to use this time to get to know my foster children better, but Peter's always with Ronnie these days.'

Betty waved her concerns away. 'He'll grow out of it. He's confused at the moment. What about Ruth, is she all right?'

At the mention of her foster daughter, Nancy visibly brightened. 'She's lovely. Always so calm and patient. Always offering to help at home.'

'There you are, you see. Not all bad. I would say girls are easier, but it's not always the case.' For a moment Betty paused, and before she spoke again looked at Nancy. 'You know, don't you? About Violet.'

Just for a second, Nancy thought about lying, but she knew there was no point. It might hurt Betty to know that Violet had confided in her first, but there was no sense making a situation worse, so instead Nancy nodded.

'I'm glad she told you. She's been worried,' was all she managed.

'So have I,' Betty admitted. 'I thought she was ill, but a baby . . .'

Her voice trailed off and Nancy seized the moment. 'But a baby will be wonderful, right?'

'Course it will.' Betty's face broke into a wide smile. 'But she's in for a hard time. Queenie wants her to pretend she's looking after it for someone that's been bombed out.'

'You think that would work?'

Betty shrugged. 'It might. At least for now, until we work out what to do next.'

'I heard that George said he wanted nothing more to do with her.'

At the mention of her husband, Betty's face darkened. 'That man can go to hell. He threw her out. And after all his carry-on, as well. Let he who is without sin cast the first stone. I'll never forgive him.'

At the hatred in Betty's voice, Nancy winced. 'I'm sorry.'

'So am I.' Betty sighed. 'I thought that he might have softened after everything he'd been through in Dunkirk, but he's still rotten through and through. And I'd hoped this relationship of his with Ronnie Newsham might have stopped by now, too. Most fellas get bored of George before long, I assumed Ronnie would, too.'

Nancy sighed. 'I don't know what's going on, but something's not right. Ronnie's got both George and Peter under his spell.'

'What the hell does he want with a lad like that?' Betty demanded.

'I'm guessing it's a power thing. I used to see guys like this in Brooklyn. Low-life criminals that would regularly encourage younger or weaker men. It was as if having them around gave these guys a sense of superiority – someone they could twist around their little finger.'

'Until they get tired of them and toss them in the rubbish,' Betty put in.

Nancy nodded. 'That's it exactly, honey. My hope is that Ronnie will get bored before he can do any real damage. Then I'll be there to pick up the pieces.' Nancy paused. 'What about George?'

'Well I'm used to picking up his pieces,' Betty said. 'But I think George is getting back at me.'

'Why?' Nancy frowned. 'After the way you stood by him when he carried on with Renee's sister, that guy owes you his life.'

Betty smiled. 'He hates the fact I've been spending so much time with Alan. He knows it's work, but he also knows we used to be sweethearts. He's jealous.'

'And there's nothing for him to be jealous over, right?' Nancy put in gently.

'Nothing.' Betty nodded quickly.

Just then, Alan burst through the kitchen door armed with a beautiful bunch of daisies. At the sight of Nancy, he stopped suddenly and looked alarmed.

'Mr Hopkins,' Betty said nervously. 'We weren't expecting you today.'

'Oh, well, I was just in the area and thought I'd pop in,' Alan said.

Nancy glanced between the two of them. They were behaving very oddly.

'Nice to see you, Alan, honey. Those for me?' she joked, gesturing at the blooms in his hand.

Alan's cheeks reddened. 'Actually, they were for all of you. To brighten the kitchen while you work.'

He thrust the flowers at Betty, who immediately set to work finding a vase.

'So . . . er . . . How's your Violet doing?' he asked her.

Betty glanced quickly at Nancy. 'Fine, thank you.'

Alan smiled. 'Oh, good. Violet's a nice girl, she's been through so much. It'll be tough for her, no doubt, on her own with a little one, but we'll all help her.'

Nancy's eyes widened. Betty had told Alan about her Violet's pregnancy? Alan was just a work colleague, wasn't he? She watched Betty out of the corner of her eye and could see a mixture of emotions across her face. Pride, gratitude, and, if Nancy wasn't mistaken, affection.

Nancy took another sip of her coffee and tried to work out what she was seeing. Perhaps George really did have something to worry about.

Thirty-Eight

Sitting in the bar of the bustling Palais, Betty tapped her feet as she listened to the guest band playing that evening. At first she had felt nervous walking into the Palais, having not been in since she was sacked. But with Queenie by her side, and a port and lemon in front of her, she had to admit she wasn't having a bad time.

She turned to look at Queenie, who was looking around in disgust. 'This place has gone to the dogs!' she said.

Betty followed her gaze, and saw it was directed at the group of Ronnie's friends in the corner, who were obviously gambling. With fat cigars, greased-back hair and sharp suits, they looked the epitome of sleaze, and George was sat right in the middle.

'He's a disgrace,' Queenie said, taking a sip of her own port and lemon.

Betty placed a hand on Queenie's forearm. 'I know. It's hard, but we've got to hope he sees reason.'

'Pah.' Queenie took another slug of her drink and swivelled back to face Betty. 'I dunno why you wanted to come here. If you wanted to go dancing we should have gone up West to that new dance hall.' She patted the back of her greying curls and sniffed. 'No riff-raff up there.'

'I didn't want to go dancing.' Betty made the sign of the cross against her chest at the very idea. 'I wanted to see what my husband was up to. And also to see how Violet is. I've barely seen her since George threw her out the other week.'

A look of anger passed across Queenie's face. 'I raised that man to have compassion, and look how he treats his own family.' She sighed, then took another sip of her drink. 'I tried talking to Violet last week, about pretending its someone else's kid she's looking after, someone what's been bombed out, but the fact the kiddie'll be mixed race don't make that little white lie easy.'

'None of this will be easy for Violet,' Betty pointed out. 'What did she say?'

'She said she'd think about it,' Queenie said pointedly. 'But I'm telling you, give it a few months after the baby's born, and she'll want to go around singing and dancing that it's hers, and who could blame her? You were the same.'

Betty nodded and sighed, then spotted Renee walk into the bar flanked by Temperance. Spotting Betty and Queenie, the two women stalked over to join them. As they approached, Betty couldn't help notice how terrible they both looked. Temperance looked weighed down by worry, while Renee looked tired – the last edges of purple bruising around her eye, though beginning to fade, still visible. A fresh round of anger threatened to envelop Betty at the thought of the torment Ronnie was inflicting on everyone since his arrival at the Palais.

'Don't normally see you two in here,' Renee said, taking a seat.

'Don't normally see you wearing that much make-up either,' Queenie said, but in a kindly tone.

Renee grimaced. 'Well, when there's a war on you need your war paint.'

'Especially if the war's on the home front,' Queenie said, jerking her head towards the table filled with Ronnie's friends. 'How long do you think they'll be here for? They're ruining the atmosphere.'

Renee shrugged. 'Until Ronnie gets tired and moves on. That's usually how he works.'

Queenie was about to say something, when Violet and Nancy walked through the double doors and crossed the dance floor.

She waved her hand and they smiled and came over to join them all.

'Well, isn't this quite the reunion,' Queenie exclaimed. Getting to her feet she kissed her granddaughter on the cheek and found a chair for her to sit down on. 'Here, Violet, sweetheart, better take the weight off. Your ankles must be giving you a right load of gyp.'

Violet smiled her thanks as she sat in the chair. 'And my back.'

'I was the same,' Betty sympathised. 'But you've not long to go now?'

'A few weeks,' Violet replied.

'You need to take it easy,' Nancy warned. 'I told you to just work the day shifts.'

'He's not going to let me do that.' Violet flicked her eyes towards Ronnie. 'He already told me that just because I was stupid enough to get in the family way he wasn't making exceptions and I had to work the same as everyone else.'

Betty saw Renee's face flush with anger and in a way it was a relief. Renee had been so full of resignation up until this point she thought Ronnie had stolen all her fire.

'He's all heart, my husband. I'm sorry, Vi, love.' Renee's face glowered.

Violet gave a small smile. 'It's fine. Besides, I'd rather be here with all of you than at Winnie's, worrying about the future.'

Concern flashed across Temperance's face. 'There's nothing to worry about.'

Queenie let out a knowing laugh. 'When you're an expectant mother there's plenty to worry about. But Vi, love, your bump's so neat you're hardly showing, and we've sorted out what you can say when the baby comes.'

Violet nodded miserably, then looked around the table. 'I know, and I'm sorry. You've all been such a help. It's just when I'm on my own I can't stop thinking about Eamon, and how sad it is that he's missing all this. We'd planned to be together, forever.'

'And you will be in your hearts,' Nancy said fiercely. 'This little baby is a way of cementing your love.'

'And we will all make sure this little baby knows how much he or she is loved, and would have been loved by their father,' Temperance said softly.

Betty's eyes shone with tears at the kindness her friends were bestowing on her daughter. Wherever would she be without them?

She thought back to when Violet and Roy were born, how alone she had felt, and cast her eyes over to George. Would she have made different decisions if she'd had the love and support Violet was being shown right now?

Picking up her drink, Betty took a large gulp and pushed those thoughts down where they belonged, in the very base of her soul. Then she plastered on a bright smile and turned to the group around her.

'I always think that in times of crisis you need to count your blessings,' she said.

Queenie rolled her eyes. 'Here beginneth the lesson. Amen,' she said, giving a comedic nod of her head and causing Violet to titter and Betty to jab Queenie sharply in the ribs.

'I know you all mock my devotion to God, but he has helped me through some very dark times. Counting my blessings is just one of the ways I can make sense of the bad times.'

'You're right, Betty, love,' Queenie said. 'And your new restaurant, that's a blessing, I'd say.'

Betty flushed with pleasure. 'It's going well. We're having a special do next Saturday at the restaurant in Islington to celebrate. Nothing fancy, we're just encouraging everyone to come along. All the team at Howell & Smart are very pleased.'

'And Alan's especially pleased, am I right, Betty?' Nancy teased.

Betty felt a shiver of both pleasure and discomfort pass through her. 'I don't know what you mean.'

'Oh, come on!' Nancy grinned. 'Those flowers he bought for the restaurant last week, they were for you. You know that as well as I do. The guy can't take his eyes off you. I'd say he's still smitten.'

'He always did have a soft spot for Betty,' Queenie agreed. 'But he's been a daft lad – he didn't know a good thing when he saw it, if you ask me.'

'That's right! I forgot you knew him!' Nancy exclaimed turning to her.

Queenie nodded, and Betty felt a trickle of dread course through her stomach.

'Everyone knew Alan,' Queenie went on. 'He was a proper charmer, and he only had eyes for Bet. Until he got called up.'

'Well, the war has certainly taken its toll on the men,' Nancy said darkly and Betty knew she was thinking about her own relationship with Alex, and how that would fare when or if he ever came home.

'That might be the case, but despite his past behaviour, I don't think Alan ever got over Betty,' Queenie said firmly, turning to her. 'Frankly, Bet, I don't think there's a court in the land that would convict you of adultery if you wanted to give things with Alan another try.'

'And I say you've had enough of that.' Betty snatched the port and lemon from Queenie's hand and smiled brightly at the group. 'Let's turn to more present blessings.'

Temperance nodded. 'Despite everything going on around us I've a lot to be grateful for. My work with the LCP, all of you, and Archie, of course.'

A slow blush crept across her cheeks and Betty couldn't help smile. She remembered only too well that feeling of young love.

'Good on you, sweetheart,' she said. 'You deserve a bit of happiness.'

'And Archie's a lovely lad,' came a voice from behind them.

Betty looked up and saw Sybil with a tray of drinks in her hands. She felt a flash of discomfort. She'd almost forgotten that Sybil and Archie were old flames and Betty desperately hoped that the head barmaid meant what she said.

'I know you all expect me to say something awful, but it's true,' Sybil said now. 'Archie's a decent lad with a good heart, and with so much nastiness out in the world just now it's good to see a bit of happiness. You and Archie suit each other, Temp.'

With that she disappeared with her tray of drinks, leaving the girls open-mouthed with shock.

Renee was the first to speak. 'Never in my life has someone had the power to surprise me like that.'

Nancy chuckled. 'I can't think what's got into her.'

'I can,' Temperance said in a low voice, as she gestured towards the group of men surrounding Ronnie. As Sybil set the drinks down, the whoops and cheers of amusement as she did so could be heard across the room. Cries of 'come on darling, sit on my knee,' and 'come 'ere, gorgeous,' were audible to everyone. Betty glanced at Renee and saw a look of despondency pass across her face. Something had to be done about this. Turning back to look at the men, she was horrified to see George trying to run his hand up Sybil's leg. She was about to turn away when she realised that George's eyes were on her and she felt a stab of despair. In that moment Betty knew that the reason her husband was keen to make himself an acquaintance of Ronnie was mostly to upset her. She glanced at Violet, and in that moment she knew something had to change, if not for her then for her children.

Thirty-Nine

As Temperance stood in Ravenscroft Park at her usual meeting place, waiting for Queenie, she felt nervous. If truth be told, she had felt nervous and on edge for weeks. Since Mr Henshall had told her about the Palais being put up for sale she had felt as if she had another secret to hide. She had always hated secrets and now her life seemed to be overshadowed and overwhelmed by them.

She had wanted to say something to Nancy and Peter when she first discovered what Ronnie was up to. But Peter wasn't easy to catch alone, and Nancy always looked so burdened that she didn't want to bother her. Then there was Renee and Vi, but they, too, had a lot on their plates. Besides, what if Mr Henshall had got it wrong, and she was stirring up trouble for no good reason?'

So Temperance had decided to bide her time. Wait until the right moment. Yet it never seemed to come, and she just felt powerless. But there was one secret she could do something about, and that was this wretched egg round. Since talking to Violet and confiding in her, Temperance could see that she had been irrational. That it wasn't down to her to solve the world's problems, or even those of her friends. She had to let them find their own way, and step in when she could. Yes, she knew that Eamon would want her to stand by Violet, but he wouldn't have expected her to provide for his family, and he certainly wouldn't have wanted her to break the law or jeopardise her own happiness.

Temperance could see now that although she had the best of intentions, she hadn't handled the situation as well as she would have liked, or been true to herself. And so she'd decided to put an end to the egg business, grateful to be getting out before any more damage was caused.

She had offered to do her own dirty work, and tell Dave herself she couldn't carry on selling eggs, but after explaining her predicament to the Millington matriarch at the surprise Palais gathering last week, Queenie had surprisingly offered to join her before they went up to Islington together to work at Betty's new restaurant.

She checked her watch. It was just past seven. The night sky was clear and it looked as if a full moon was setting up home. Despite the warmth of the night, Temperance shivered. These were perfect conditions for a Luftwaffe strike. Despite an almost nightly assault for months, the Jerries had largely left London alone for the past three weeks. Some had thought that perhaps that meant the Blitz was over, but Temperance knew differently. She had a feeling they weren't finished yet. Just last week Hitler had made a speech to the Reichstag declaring that the German Reich were the most superior in the world.

Temperance shuddered at the thought of it. Just looking around her at the war-torn streets of the city she called home. The shelled-out buildings, lives stopped halfway through – was that what superiority did? It was enough to make Temperance's heart break, no matter how much Churchill declared Britain could take it!

She shook her head free of the thoughts. No good at all would come from continuing to think about the state of the world. Instead she wanted to think about tonight and how lovely it would be to be surrounded by friends as they celebrated Betty's success.

All she had to do first was tell Dave she could no longer do her egg round, and then she could look forward to the future.

And there, right on cue, was Queenie walking towards her and waving.

'Temp, love.'

'Queenie.' Temperance rushed forward to kiss her on both cheeks. She glanced down at Queenie's handbag and saw what looked like a full Victoria sandwich tucked inside.

'What on earth have you got there?'

Queenie tapped her nose. 'It's for later, ain't it? I got the eggs off Dave and the sugar . . . well, the less you know about that the better.'

She folded her arms, as if expecting a fight, but Temperance wasn't going to give her one. The older woman was full of heart and joy and always had everyone's best interests at heart, even if she didn't always go about it in the most legal of ways.

'No sign of Dave then?' she asked now.

As Temperance started to shake her head, they both saw him cycling up the road.

'There he is.'

Queenie nodded her approval. 'Good. And don't worry, I'll sweeten him up by telling him I'll take on your round.'

'Why would you do that?' Temperance asked in astonishment.

Queenie patted her arm. 'Because, my love, he won't care who's doing it as long as he's getting his money, and I could do with the extra.' Her face softened. 'It was lovely of you wanting to help your family out like that, Temperance, it really was. But this game, it ain't really you, is it?'

Temperance gave a soft shake of her head. 'But what about Archie?'

Queenie looked blank for a moment. 'What about him?'

'Dave's getting his eggs from him. He's been stealing from the Ledbetters' shop.'

For a moment Queenie looked confused, then she threw her head back and laughed. 'No he ain't! Is this why you wanted to stop, because you think your sweetheart's getting ripped off? Good heavens, what must you have thought of me then, wanting to take on the egg round and rip off a family friend?'

'Then where is he getting them from?' she asked, just as Dave approached.

'Christ, Temperance, I dunno. But it's not from Archie.'

For a moment, Temperance's head spun as she tried to take in all that Quenie had told her. But there was barely time to make sense of any of it as Dave propped his bike against the railings.

'What's all this, then?'

'Temperance is giving up selling eggs and I'm taking her round,' Queenie said.

Dave looked them both up and down, and Temperance tried to draw herself up to her full height so she felt less intimidated.

'But Temperance was selling to a mate of hers.'

'He wasn't a friend,' Temperance put in. 'Besides, look at Queenie, he's hardly going to turn down the chance of extra eggs from her, is he?'

Dave pursed his lips and looked at them both. 'All right. But it'll cost you.'

'What do you mean?' Temperance exclaimed.

'Yes, what do you mean?' Queenie said in a low voice. 'That ain't the usual arrangement. You'd better not be taking advantage, Dave Price. I know your old ma and she'll tan the back of your legs if you're trying something on.'

Now it was Dave's turn to look alarmed, as Queenie waggled her finger in front of his pale face.

'All right, all right. I just don't wanna be out of pocket because you don't wanna do this no more.' He jabbed a finger at Temperance.

'What's all this?' came a voice.

Whirling round, Temperance's heart sank as she saw Archie coming towards them. How much had he heard? She had successfully managed to keep her black-market operation under wraps. She couldn't let him find out now, just as she was ending it.

'Just something Temperance is helping me out with,' Queenie said smoothly. 'How are you, lad?'

But Archie ignored Queenie's question – he was looking at Dave. Dressed in twill trousers with a dab of soot on the collar of his starched white shirt, Temperance guessed Archie was on his way home from a shift with the voluntary fire service.

'That true, is it?' Archie asked Dave. 'She helping out with something?'

'What's it to you?' Dave's lip curled as he spoke.

'She's special, that's what it is to me. And I know you, Dave Price. You're always up to no good. Trying to sell hooky gear everywhere. Wouldn't be surprised if it was you what was nicking out of my shop.'

Dave gave a nervous laugh. 'Nothing to do with me, lad.'

'You'd better not be trying to get my sweetheart to sell your gear.'

Dave chuckled and shook his head. 'You've no idea, you—'

But Temperance cut him off by tugging on Archie's sleeve and saying quickly, 'Come on, let's go.'

But Archie refused to move as Dave rounded on him. 'Thing is, Archie lad, your sweetheart's been selling gear for me for weeks now. And I've been sourcing grub with a bit more quality than your cruddy butcher's. We've gone upmarket with West End hotels.'

Archie's jaw dropped open with shock as he turned back to look at Temperance. 'Is this true?'

Temperance felt panic rise within her as Archie shook his head in disgust.

'After all I've been through, and you do this?' he said. 'How could you?'

With that he turned and walked away.

'Archie!' Temperance started running after him. 'Please.'

As she caught up with him, she pulled gently at his shirt sleeve, only for him to shuck her away.

'Temperance, if you've been involved with blokes like Dave Price, selling god knows what on the side when there's a bleeding war on, when businesses like mine are suffering, well, you're not the person I thought you were.'

'Archie, let me explain,' she said, desperately, but it was no good. Archie turned his back on her and carried on walking back down the road, leaving Temperance alone.

The journey to Islington on the trolley bus felt long. Temperance kept replaying the scene with Archie in her mind, wondering if she could have done something differently. What if she had been honest with Archie? What if Dave had been on time? But more than anything, she wondered how she could make things right with Archie. The idea of losing him made her feel sick.

By the time they arrived at their stop, Temperance had worked herself up into such a state, all she wanted was to go straight over to Archie's and reason with him. Only Queenie kept her from doing so.

'He'll come round,' she promised. 'I know Archie Ledbetter, he's always liked a tantrum. Just give him time.'

'But what if there isn't time?' Temperance thought of Eamon. 'There isn't always the time we want.'

Queenie clasped her liver-spotted hands over Temperance's shaking ones. 'Sweetheart, that's life. It doesn't always work out how we want it to, but I've a good feeling about you and Archie, and it will be all right. Now, we're late for Betty's night, and gawd help us all if we mess things up for her.' She released Temperance's hands and began walking. 'You know she's got a direct telegraph with God. She'll send him down to smite us if we let her down.'

Despite the blatant blasphemy, Temperance couldn't help a smile. And as she trotted along the tree-lined street behind Queenie, she tried to focus on the evening ahead. As well as the locals and the team at Howell & Smart, there would also be local dignitaries in attendance.

If Temperance was honest, she wasn't sure what that actually meant. But she knew enough to recognise that tonight was important to Betty and she wanted to help her succeed.

Reaching the restaurant, she saw the place was already a hive of activity, with Betty directing Violet and Renee towards the kitchen and Nancy and Maisie hurrying about keeping people's drinks topped up.

'There you are,' Betty cried at the sight of them both. 'You're late.'

Queenie rolled her eyes, while Temperance apologised.

'Ever so sorry. We got caught up,'

'Well, you're here now. Can you help Alan in the back kitchen?'

'Alan's in the kitchen, is he? Sounds domestic.'

'He's doing the washing up – one of the girls that was supposed to do it called in sick.' Betty was in a state of stress, and Temperance could see that this wasn't the time to upset her.

Instead she donned a striped apron, nodded hello to the rest of the girls and got to work.

If Temperance had been worried that she was going to spend hours mooning over her row with Archie, she needn't have. There simply wasn't time with so much to do. Not only had Nora Lovell taken over the kitchen, ensuring that hearty bowls of soup and slices of meat pie were distributed in timely fashion, but there were dozens of people stopping in to pay a visit, congratulate the Howell & Smart team, and welcome Betty to the neighbourhood.

By the time they closed the doors it was almost eleven o'clock and Temperance was exhausted.

'Well, I'd say that went very well, chuck,' Renee said, slipping off her own apron and handing it to Betty. 'But – and don't judge me when I say this – me dogs are killing me, and it's just not worth it if there's no dance floor involved.'

The girls laughed, and Temperance felt a stab of delight to see her old friend's sense of humour make a welcome return.

'Thank you for tonight, girls,' Betty said softly. 'I couldn't have done it without you.'

'Where's all the Howell & Smart lot?' Queenie asked.

'Alan's driven them back to headquarters,' Betty explained.

'And where's our nice car ride home after all our efforts?' Nancy teased.

But at the sight of Betty's stricken face, she relented. 'Honey, I'm joking. Though, seriously, I think we might all have to head home now. I need to get back to Peter and Ruth, and check Edna hasn't accidentally given them food poisoning.'

Queenie was wide-eyed. 'You never let her cook for them? That woman burns water!'

Nancy laughed and opened the door, just as a sudden flash of light made her swiftly close it again.

'What was that?' Violet asked, her hands instinctively pressed against her stomach.

'Not sure,' Nancy replied.

Cautiously, she opened the door again, and as she did the sound of loud bangs and explosions greeted her, along with a night sky lit up like firework night.

Shutting the door firmly behind her, Temperance saw the fear in Nancy's eyes.

'Girls, I don't think any of us are going home tonight.'

Forty

Renee wasn't sure what happened the moment Nancy uttered those fateful words, but it felt as if time stood still. For what felt like hours, she thought of all the bombs the city she loved had endured, and the heartache families just like hers had gone through, night after night.

It was then that all thoughts of Ronnie, Violet and even the Palais flew from her mind, as Renee pushed past her friends, flung open the door and made her way out into the night.

The scene just yards away didn't seem real – everywhere was ablaze, with houses, shops and buildings as far as the eye could see a mass of thick, black soot and orange flames.

Volunteer firemen lined every inch of the roads, pumping jets of water into the devastation as quickly as they could to try and control the raging inferno. As Temperance glanced around her, she saw what looked like ARP wardens and women she recognised as volunteers from the WVS helping carry the sick and injured to safety – all accompanied by the ever-present roar of what felt like a real firework display, complete with hisses and bangs exploding through the streets.

Renee watched astounded as rescuers tried to free those trapped under rubble, their screams sending waves of fear down her spine as they begged for help.

There was so much noise, so many acrid smells in the air, that Renee felt as if her senses were already overloaded. For a moment, she was back in Manchester, where she thought she had witnessed the largest scenes of devastation she would ever see in her lifetime. Yet, almost five months later, it was all happening again. How was this possible? How were these the times they were living in?

For a moment, she stood rooted to the spot, unable to move as she tried to take in the scene in front of her. She realised then that she wasn't the same woman she had been in Manchester. Since returning to London and Ronnie's reappearance, Renee had felt gradually worn down by life, her self-confidence ebbing away until she wasn't sure who she was anymore. She talked the talk, all right, it was all part of her bravado, her not wanting anyone to know how she really felt. But looking around her now at what seemed to be an all-too familiar nightmare, all Renee wanted to do was sit down in the debris and let Hitler finish her off. But then she saw a mother begging for someone to help her son, whose right leg had been blown clean off, and something in Renee galvanised. She might be suffering, but right now it was time to put all that aside.

Flying towards an ARP warden, her voice was clear. 'What can I do?' she begged.

'And me,' she heard Nancy's voice add.

Spinning around, Renee saw the Palais' front-desk manager flanked by Betty, Queenie, Violet, Temperance and Maisie.

'This is one of the worst hits Jerry's dropped on us for months,' the warden shouted over the sound of explosives. 'Hitler's bombed the entire city, targeting bridges west of Tower Bridge, and factories on the south of the Thames. The House of Commons has been hit, New Bond Street and Westminster Abbey.'

'Jesus Christ!' Renee exclaimed.

Nancy looked up at the orange sky. 'Then we'd better get to work.'

With that the warden ran towards the mother still sobbing for help for her son.

Renee turned to Violet. 'I think you should be in a shelter.'

A flash of defiance flickered across Violet's face. 'I'm pregnant, not disabled. If you're helping, so am I.'

Any thoughts of arguing flew from Renee's mind as she took in Violet's expression. Instead, she simply nodded in agreement. Like her, Violet had her own private battle to fight in this moment, and Renee wasn't going to get in her way.

'Come on, then,' she said.

With that she walked towards the biggest of the fires in the centre of the street.

The heat from a nearby building ablaze was enough to scorch Renee's skin from just yards away, and she put a hand up against her face to protect it from the fire and soot flying towards her.

In Manchester, she and Janice had found the strength to help those suffering in their darkest of moments, she would find the strength again. Then, out of the corner of her eye, a woman shook her head. As Renee looked at her properly, she could see the tears in her eyes.

'Don't go in there,' the woman begged, her voice thick with emotion. 'They're bringing out the bodies of a family.'

A lump formed in Renee's throat as she watched the woman wipe away the tears with the sleeve of her coat. But Renee had a job to do. She offered the woman a consoling smile, then walked determinedly towards the building. Once inside, she could see how bad the damage was. Debris, soot and rubble everywhere, along with scores of people helping the trapped and wounded. Experience told Renee that, despite their fear, and the chaos, these volunteers would work tirelessly, sticking to a well-executed and clearly defined regimen.

Stepping over a mound of rubble, Renee pushed up her sleeves and joined what appeared to be most of the community to help clear the bricks and beams from what looked like an old paper factory. She toiled away for hours, glimpsing other members of the Good Time Girls doing the same. But even with the comfort of her friends nearby, the work was back-breaking and the cries of despair from those they could rescue and those they couldn't tore at her heart.

Renee could tell that the rest of her friends felt the same. Maisie's tears as she worked, Nancy's grim determination as she helped patch up a wounded young woman, Temperance's efforts in hauling bricks and rubble to free those trapped – and Violet's soothing murmurs, as she consoled an elderly couple who were clearly shellshocked.

Yet Renee knew that this was what pulling together was all about. That even though explosives continued to rain down, their efforts never diminished. She knew without asking that each of her friends thought that risking their own life to save another was worth it.

Despite their determination, it was a long night and as dawn began to break, Renee had to admit she was tired. Standing up to wipe the sweat from her brow, she saw her friends were still hard at work, each one refusing to give up until they had done all they could. She felt a pang of worry and affection for them all.

It was just then that she realised Violet wasn't now amongst the group. Renee narrowed her eyes and picked her way through the rubble, looking for her friend.

'You all right?' Nancy asked, catching sight of Renee scanning the throngs of people.

'Violet. You seen her?'

Nancy frowned. 'Not for a while.' She turned to Betty and Queenie, who were working with the WVS and handing out cups of tea to the volunteers. 'You seen Violet, guys?'

A flash of concern passed across Betty's face, while Queenie shook her head.

'She went back to the new restaurant, to pick up some supplies to help out here.'

'But that was a good hour ago,' Betty said, a hint of panic in her voice. 'She can't still be there.'

'Or can she?' Renee said, standing alongside Temperance. She remembered how uncomfortable Violet had looked all night, how tired she had seemed.

Suddenly, Renee said what they were all thinking. 'I'm going to check on her.'

'Me, too,' Temperance said quickly.

A look of fierce determination crossed Betty's face. 'I'm coming with you.'

All Renee could do was nod. She had seen enough motherly determination for one night to know that there was no argument.

Forty-One

Making her way across the road, flanked by Betty and Renee, Temperance couldn't get to the new restaurant fast enough. But as she did so, her hands flew to her mouth in shock as she took in the scene before her. A bomb had demolished the row of buildings near where the restaurant had stood, and everything was now covered in rubble from the blast.

Temperance's eyes roamed the building in horror as she saw there were just two of the restaurant walls standing. What several hours ago had been the dining area was now engulfed in so many bricks it was unrecognisable.

She turned to Renee and Betty and saw the shock and desperation in their eyes, but Temperance refused to give up hope. It wasn't even guaranteed that Violet was inside. Then, as she turned back to look at the detritus, a figure moving in the rubble caught her eye and she let out a shriek of recognition.

'Violet!' she called at the top of her lungs. 'Violet!'

Without waiting to check if Renee and Betty were behind her, Temperance's body launched into action as she raced towards who she hoped was her friend. But as she did so, the roar of the Luftwaffe overhead caused a shower of bricks to fall, exactly where she had seen that moving figure.

Panic rose inside her as she stood on top of a pile of rubbish. 'Violet!' Temperance screamed. 'Is that you? We're right here.' But there was silence.

With the dust in her eyes, it was hard for Temperance to see much of anything. The despair she felt grew.

'*Violet!*' Temperance bellowed again, with all her might.

She turned to see Renee and Betty bent double, flinging bricks out of their way to try and clear a path. Anxiously, she joined them, all the while shouting Violet's name, only to be met with no response.

'She's got to be here,' Renee said as she furiously flung another brick over her shoulders, as though it was nothing more than a pair of dance shoes.

' I saw her,' Temperance insisted.

'Then why didn't she answer?' Betty cried. 'Violet, darling . . .' She got to her feet and looked around. 'Sweetheart, where are you?'

The agony in Betty's eyes almost broke Temperance's heart in two. But she steadied her resolve and concentrated on removing the rubble that stood between them and the figure she was sure she had seen.

Temperance wasn't sure how long they worked together, three women side by side; it could have been minutes or hours. Time seemed to stand still.

Then, suddenly, she paused. She could hear the sound of voices just beneath her.

'Violet!' she called again, her heart racing with hope. 'We're going to dig you out. Hold on.'

Surrounded by the crackle of burning wood and the near-constant clang of fire engines, Renee, Betty and Temperance worked quickly, scratching hands and ripping nails in the process, but none of them cared.

All that mattered was Violet. Tossing another brick behind her, Temperance felt a wave of exhuastion. And then an image of Eamon's face flooded her mind. He was smiling at her, encouraging her, and she knew that no matter how tired she was, she had to keep going, for his sake as much as Violet's. She owed him that.

Eventually, the three of them made a hole large enough in

the rubble, and Temperance was able to peer inside. But despite the orange glow of the blaze, all she managed to make out was a dark shadow.

Despair burned. This might not even be Violet.

'Sweetheart,' Betty crooned shakily.

Again, silence.

But then, the unmistakable sound of a baby's cry pierced the air.

Renee gasped in shock and pushed her face towards the hole.

'We're all right,' Violet called weakly.

Temperance blinked in shock.

'*We*,' she breathed. 'You've had the baby?'

'Yes.' The calm warmth in Violet's voice was clear.

'Alone?' Betty cried.

Tentatively, Temperance reached an arm through the rubble, wanting nothing more than to lay a reassuring hand on her friend, but she was still too far away.

'Yes, Bet.'

The three women exchanged worried glances. A million questions ran through Temperance's mind, but Renee cut through them all.

'Are you all right?' Renee demanded. 'Is the baby all right?'

This time there was a pause, and Temperance felt panic burst through her as she waited for Violet to answer.

'We're fine,' Violet replied at last. Temperance couldn't miss the hint of bravery in her voice. 'But me and my baby boy are trapped. I don't know how long we can stay in here with all this dust.'

Temperance's heart swelled with love. Violet had a boy! Her nephew.

Tears streamed down her face as a mix of joy and fear pulsed through her tired body. She was elated to meet Eamon's only child, but this was the worst place in the world for a baby to be. Anxiously she looked around her. There was still so much rubble to clear, so much debris between Violet, the baby and safety.

'We'll get you out,' Renee said determinedly. She flung herself at the bricks, hands trembling as she worked determinedly to save her friend and her newborn.

And like a whirling dervish, Temperance cleared as much of the bomb damage as she could, but the harder she and her friends worked, the more rubble and detritus seemed to fall. To Temperance, it felt as if she were losing the battle, and, with her hands sore and battered, she paused for a moment to look around her.

Glancing at the heap of bricks, a sense of despair washed over her. They needed reinforcements. Betty was exhausted, Temperance could see that, whilst Renee was still going, frantically.

Resting for a second on her haunches, Temperance knew they needed help. All this soot wasn't good for a newborn baby's lungs. With a mix of fear and pride, she thought about all that Violet must have gone through. Delivering a baby alone, with nobody to help her. Her friend's strength knew no bounds.

She stopped for a moment and heard the sound of singing. She was about to say something when she peered through the gap in the rubble and felt her eyes fill with tears. Violet was resting her head against the wall, baby clamped to her bosom and softly singing a calypso melody.

In that moment, Temp thought of her own father, remembered how he had sung the same song to her and Eamon in times of crisis. This calypso melody had always had the power to soothe her soul, and for a second she was taken back to the flat she'd shared with her family as a child. Her father singing softly in the corner, her mother Enid, Eamon and her – all dancing in the kitchen to the sweet, sweet sound.

She glanced back at Violet, who had her eyes closed and looked strangely content. Temperance felt Eamon's presence with them as she watched Violet cradling their newborn child.

That, and the familiar melody, gave Temperance renewed vigour, and for the next hour she continued to scoop away handfuls of rubbish with fresh urgency. Nothing mattered anymore but getting Violet and the baby to safety.

Before long, Temperance realised they had almost cleared the remains of the debris. Together with Renee and Betty, she pulled away the last few remaining bricks and came face to face with a soot-covered Violet.

Temperance's heart was in her mouth as she gazed at the tiny bundle wrapped up in a coat in Violet's arms, as she held her baby boy to her chest, instinctively protecting him from the chaos he had been born into.

'Violet, love!' Betty rushed forward to brush the soot from Violet's hair, and looked down at the baby.

'Well, isn't he a little charmer,' she said, tenderly, stroking his soft cheek with her finger for a second, before she snapped back into an emergency mode.

'Let's get you out,' she said gently. 'Can you walk?'

'I think so,' Violet said, shakily.

With Renee's help, Violet got to her feet and Temperance watched her friend's eyes never leave the tiny bundle she clutched against her chest.

Together, they led the group out into the daylight and towards a waiting ambulance. As Violet was greeted by a first-aider, she turned to Temperance and smiled.

'You're an aunt, Temp. Can you believe it?'

Temperance shook her head. And as she glanced down at the baby still cuddled innocently in Violet's arms, the tears she had been keeping at bay came. This was Eamon's son, and she made a silent promise to ensure he felt loved every single day of his life.

As the first-aiders took the baby from Violet and checked his airways, Temperance squeezed her friend's hand.

'How do you feel?'

Violet shook her head. 'So many things. Tired, sore. Shocked that I'm a mother. That I've given birth amongst all this dirt.'

She looked lovingly over at her son, and Temperance could see already how being apart from him for just these few seconds was difficult.

The sound of heavy footsteps hurrying towards them made both Violet and Temperance start, and they turned to see Alan Hopkins approaching, his face filled with alarm.

'Violet,' he said breathlessly. 'I've just heard. Are you all right?'

Violet smiled and nodded. 'A bit tired, but I'm all right.'

'And how's this little one?' He bent down to take in Eamon's features. As he did so, Temperance felt confused. Why was Alan here, and why was he so concerned? He barely knew them, unless he was just expressing concern on behalf of his old flame, Betty.

'A boy?' Alan cooed. 'Will you look at that.' Temperance was sure she saw his eyes brimming with tears, and in her tired state she felt a pang of empathy. They had all worked so hard tonight, it was no wonder they were all so emotional.

Forty-Two

In the days following the raid, it seemed to Nancy that the entire country was in a state of turmoil. The raid on the 10th May had been the biggest the country had ever seen, with over five hundred bombers flying across London, the full moon providing the perfect source of light for their decimation campaign, which had lasted more than seven hours.

Not only had the streets of Islington suffered, but it seemed as though the entirety of Westminster had been destroyed. The House of Commons, Westminster Abbey and the Turner Buildings had been burned, and the odour of soot and rubble lingered for weeks across every corner of the capital, so great was the destruction.

It hadn't helped morale that more than 1,400 Londoners were killed and 2,000 were injured – the highest number of casualties in any single night of The Blitz. As Nancy sat at the front desk of the Palais, flicking through the latest copy of *Picture Post,* she couldn't help feel that more than anything this was a time that people needed a place to come together and remind themselves of the good things in life.

But then, with Ronnie Newsham at the helm, the Palais might well be the last place people wanted to flock to, and she couldn't honestly blame them. Two nights ago, yet another fight had broken out in the bar, and this time Bill had been unable to break it up. She had almost felt sorry for him, as he tried to remonstrate with the two of Ronnie's friends who'd started it, before giving up.

'Daydreaming?' Edna's voice broke her train of thought.

Looking at her mother-in-law, Nancy tried to stave off the familiar feeling of hatred she felt at the sight of her. She couldn't help blame Edna and Bill for all the Palais' troubles. Ronnie was largely to blame. But if they hadn't gone running to him in the first place, then she wouldn't have lost her beloved job and, crucially, the Palais wouldn't be seeing falling customer numbers.

'Yes, of happier times,' Nancy said curtly, pushing away the magazine and folding her arms. 'What about you? Practising for tonight?'

As it was Saturday, she knew Edna would have a dance prepared that she would want to showcase herself, but would no doubt ask Archie and one of the other dancers to perform.

Edna sniffed and pressed her hand to her neck. 'Actually, I've invited young Violet to tea.'

Nancy's eyes were out on stalks. 'You have?'

Edna sniffed again. 'She's just had a child and I thought it would be rather nice to meet him. Even though we didn't even know she was expecting.'

At the last sentence, Edna looked as if she had been slighted and was now expecting Nancy to apologise. Too bad, thought Nancy. Hell would freeze over before she ever said anything remotely like sorry to Edna again.

As if knowing that, Edna lifted her chin. 'Of course, the tea isn't just for Violet. It's for you, too – and Renee, Temperance and Maisie. I've even asked Betty and Queenie to join us.'

'You invited Ronnie as well?' Nancy said sharply, then got to her feet and went to cross over to the bar, aware that Edna was following her down the corridor.

'It's to say thank you,' said Edna. 'For all the hard work you did during the raid. The staff wanted to do it, I wanted to do it. For you, and for Alex.'

Nancy turned to see that there was a softness to her

mother-in-law's eyes, and she knew Alex was the impetus behind this. That being kind to his wife after a crisis was Edna's way of connecting with her son. Nancy surrendered, too worn down by their feud to keep it up any longer. Instead she smiled at Edna, then spotted a large table by the window of the bar laid with the Palais' best crockery. Large plates of fish-paste, cheese and carrot sandwiches stood in the centre; sausage rolls next to them – and someone had made a small trifle which sat beside a pile of rock cakes.

Nancy felt unexpectedly touched. Looking around her she saw all the staff had gathered and were beaming at her.

'Well done, Nancy,' Eric the storesman spoke first, his voice gruff but full of pride. 'You did well the other night.'

Sybil nodded, her smile genuine. 'You all did. You must have been terrified.'

Nancy thought for a moment. Had she been terrified? At the time there hadn't been a moment to think about her own safety. All that had mattered was saving the lives of those they could, of rescuing those in pain and trouble. It was only afterwards that the true horror of it had sunk in. She smiled at the staff now assembled around her, basking in the goodwill on their faces.

'I can't believe you've done all this! You've made an old broad very happy.'

'And me,' Temperance spoke now.

Nancy smiled at her, seeing that she was standing with Maisie and Renee.

'Can you believe this?' Nancy gestured to the food, and saw Renee's eyes were shining with tears.

Renee shook her head. 'You lot'd make a glass eye cry,' she quipped.

The staff smiled. They all knew Renee wasn't one to show her emotions.

'Where's Violet?' Nancy asked, as she and the Good Time Girls took in the spread.

'Here!' a voice called, and Nancy looked up to see a beaming Violet, standing tall and proud, clutching a small bundle in her arms. Nancy let out her second gasp of delight as she took in the new mother.

'Is that . . ?'

'Nancy, meet Eamon Roy,' Violet said quietly, as Nancy came to her and gazed down at the baby boy.

'Oh, my days!' Temperance gasped. 'What a wonderful name.'

Violet looked down at her baby, and then back at the group. 'What else would I call him? It's the perfect way to honour his father and his uncle.'

For a moment there was silence, as everyone in the room looked over at little Eamon, whom Nancy was sure would be as loyal, kind and loving as his father.

'We'll leave you to it,' Edna said quietly. And together with the rest of the staff she walked away, leaving Nancy and the Good Time Girls to enjoy their celebrations, complete with their honorary new member.

An hour later, and the girls were sat around the bar eating sandwiches and enjoying the gossip that always came naturally when they were together. Nancy felt more relaxed than she had in weeks, with her girls around her, and she was delighted that Betty and Queenie had joined them. Betty, Nancy noticed, could hardly take her eyes off her new grandson.

'So how are you finding motherhood?' Nancy asked Violet.

Violet pressed a kiss on Eamon's forehead before she spoke. 'It's hard, but it's wonderful. I've never known love like it. I'd do anything for this child.'

Betty nodded tearfully in understanding. 'That's motherhood, sweetheart. I felt that way the moment all you children were born. Couldn't take my eyes off you.'

'Some say you still can't,' Maisie said with a groan. 'You stopped me stepping out with Jimmy Michaels last week.'

'Jimmy Michaels has the morals of an alleycat and you can do better,' Betty shot back.

'He's all right, Ma,' Maisie protested. 'Besides, I'm not looking to marry the fella. We was only going up the pictures.'

'Even so.' Betty shuffled uncomfortably in her seat. 'You can do better.'

'Must have been scary, Violet,' Sybil said, who at Nancy's invitation had come to join them. 'Giving birth alone like that.'

'You know, I didn't feel alone,' said Violet wistfully. 'Eamon was by my side, and in my heart.'

'When did you realise . . . that the baby was coming?'

'I'd had stomach cramps all day, thought it was something I'd eaten,' Violet began.

Renee held up a half-eaten meat-paste sandwich and grimaced, making everyone laugh, before Violet continued.

'Then, when the bombs started going off and we began helping people, I just got on with it . . . It was when I went back to the restaurant to get supplies that my waters broke and I knew what was happening.'

'Oh, Vi,' Maisie said, reaching for her sister's arm and giving it a gentle squeeze. 'You must have been frightened?'

Violet shook her head. 'The thing is, there wasn't time to be afraid.'

Betty choked back a sob of pride, and Nancy brushed away her own emotion and gave her arm a squeeze.

'You all right?' Queenie asked Betty, gently.

Betty nodded. 'I just thank God that Violet and little Eamon are all right.' She drew the sign of the cross against her chest.

'You going to have him christened, honey?' Nancy asked Violet.

'Of course,' Betty answered for her.

Violet groaned. 'Eamon's just been born. Give me a chance.'

'You ain't got time to think in your situation,' Queenie put in. 'Which is why I've thought for you.' Queenie paused for a moment as the girls looked at her, expectantly.

'Well, out with it then,' Renee said, briskly. 'Or are you waiting for a drum roll first?'

The girls laughed, and Queenie dusted some crumbs from her blouse.

'As I've suggested already, I reckon we say that Violet rescued this little mite during the raid. She can say that the child is motherless and her last dying words to Violet were for her to take care of this child.'

'You're not serious,' Nancy gasped. 'Who's going to believe that?'

Queenie tapped the side of her nose. 'People believe what they want to believe. She turned to Violet again. 'Have you come round to the idea, Vi?'

Nancy could see the girl was unsure, and she didn't blame her. Of course she would want to claim baby Eamon as her own, because he was.

Looking around her, Nancy could see the sorrow in the other women's eyes. By rights, Eamon and Violet would have been welcoming this child into the world together as husband and wife. But the world was cruel, and Violet's sweetheart was dead – now she had to face lying about the true parentage of their child.

'Honey, you don't have to decide right now,' she assured her.

Violet shook her head. 'No, it's all right. Nan, you're right. This had to be thought of, and it's a good idea.'

'It is.' Betty smiled warmly. 'Things have changed since my day. We'll all know the truth, Violet. You're this little lad's mother, no matter what anyone says. Sometimes we have to tell lies to protect our children . . .' She paused, and Nancy noticed that Queenie's eyes were boring into Betty.

She frowned. What was going on? Betty's face was now a picture of consternation

'Betty, honey are you all right?' she asked.

Betty nodded a little numbly, and then glanced at Queenie,

who gave a nod of what looked like reassurance, and said, 'It's time, love.'

Betty took a deep breath and turned to Violet. 'Sweetheart, there's something I should have told you a long time ago.'

Concern coursed across Violet's face. 'What is it?'

'Well, the truth is . . .' Betty faltered at this point, as though she couldn't get the words out.

'Go on, Bet, love,' Queenie encouraged. 'Violet will understand.'

'Understand what?'

As Violet looked increasingly perturbed, Betty swallowed before she continued.

'The truth is, there's a reason you and your father have never got on very well . . . And perhaps why you and I have always had our difficulties. And that is that George isn't your real father. I'm sorry, Violet. I've wanted to tell you for years, but I thought it was better this way.'

For a moment nobody spoke and then Violet asked a little numbly, 'So . . . Who is my father?'

There was another pause, in which Nancy, for one, had already worked out the answer.

'Alan Hopkins,' Betty whispered.

As she stared at her daughter, wanting the ground to open up and swallow her, she wondered what on earth she had done?

'Alan?' Violet took this in, her face reflecting a hundred different emotions at once, and for a while the silence in the room was deafening. Finally, the new mother let out a long breath, looked down at her baby and then back up at Betty.

'It's all right, Ma,' she whispered. 'Deep down, I think I always knew George wasn't my dad. That there had to be a reason he and I never got along. Now it all makes more sense. It's because I'm not his flesh and blood.'

'George did try, Violet. He took me on when nobody else

would,' said Betty. 'When I was at risk of going to a mother and baby home for unwed mothers. He felt sorry for me and didn't want to see me lose my respectability.' Betty wiped at the tears on her face.

'I'm so sorry, Betty,' Violet whispered. 'You did your best. And he did, too, in his way.'

The rest of the Good Time Girls remained silent, letting the magnitude of Betty's confession sink in.

Betty hoped she had said enough now. There was no need to explain that George's kindness had had consquences. He'd known full well that Betty would let him get away with murder after he'd taken her and her illegitimate twins on, passing the children off as his own.

'So why did Alan leave you in the lurch?' Violet's voice was cooler now, Betty noticed. 'Why did he leave you when you were carrying his baby?'

Betty winced. So much had changed now, life really was too short for resentment – if nothing else, this war had taught them all that.

'He didn't have much choice,' Betty explained. 'The night I fell pregnant with you and Roy was the night before he went to join the fighting. But we were in love, you were conceived out of love, Vi.'

She allowed herself for a brief moment to recall the sweetness of the one night she and Alan had spent together.

'And then what happened?' Renee said gently.

Betty blinked and returned to the present. 'War changed him. It left him shaken with horror at all he had seen. His mind . . . well, like a lot of those boys, he suffered with it.'

The Good Time Girls nodded in sympathy. They all knew of men who had gone off to war and come back different, changed by all they had witnessed.

'I wrote to him and told him I was expecting, but he was really suffering out there. He told me was frightened of the man he'd become,' Betty said, through tears. 'And that his child deserved better. He said he'd only keep you down.'

'And he thought it better to leave you alone?' Violet cried. 'With two children, not one.'

Betty laid a hand on Violet's forearm. 'He didn't know until much later that I'd had twins. And he was very poorly.'

'But he's not anymore,' Violet said quietly, a flash of anger in her eyes that Betty recognised as pure Alan.

There was another pause as Betty struggled to justify how Alan's behaviour looked to Violet. Then she looked around at her friends, and saw that their eyes were brimming with support for her.

'He wants to make amends, if you'll let him,' she said. 'And who amongst us here in this room can honestly say we've never made a mistake?'

Forty-Three

As the dancers twirled like whirling dervishes around the floor, in time to the strict tempo of Oscar Reyburn, Temperance stood at the side of the dance floor, her eyes fixed on Archie.

Since the night of the raid, when he had caught her giving up her black-market egg round, they had barely seen one another. Certainly Temperance had tried to find time to see him – calling on him at the butcher's where he had been too busy to see her. And afterwards at his home, where though he had welcomed her inside, he had treated her with an indifference she had never experienced before.

She was hurt, but she was also angry. Yes, she had done wrong, but she hadn't stolen from Archie and he had made no attempt to hear her out, to find out why she had done what she had done.

The cries of baby Eamon stirring beside her, brought Temperance back to the present moment. She turned to Violet, who was rocking the large pram with one hand.

'He's been so good all day,' Temperance said softly.

'He's good every day.' Violet beamed as she continued to nudge the pram. 'Your mum's doting on him.'

Temperance laughed. It was true, Enid was besotted with Eamon, not that she wasn't herself.

'And I've even seen Auntie Winnie giving him a cuddle,' she said.

'Every chance she can get,' Violet said, chuckling, her eyes never leaving her child. 'She's been round to the flat every day asking if I need anything. As has Queenie, of course.'

At the mention of Queenie, Temperance took a breath. 'Have you given any more thought to her suggestion?'

Violet let out a long sigh. 'I have. And she's right. I've already been telling people I helped out a young mother in the raids. That sadly she didn't survive and that I couldn't bear to leave this little mite.'

'And how do you feel about that?' Temperance pressed.

At the question, Violet turned to face her friend, her brown eyes flashing with mixed emotions.

'It's the only way I get to protect my little boy,' she said softly.

Temperance frowned. There had been something troubling her about this plan.

'And don't you think people are going to be suspicious when you tell them what your baby's called?'

At the question Violet's eyes flashed with anger. 'I shall tell them that this precious baby, this beautiful gift, has been named in honour of the man I love.'

'Well you've got it all worked out I see.' Temperance raised a smile and Violet's face relaxed and she returned Temperance's grin.

'Sorry. But Maisie asked this the other day and I've a feeling it might be a question that keeps coming up.'

As the music ended, Violet glanced around at the dancers walking towards them off the floor. Temperance could see the curious glances being shot their way and her heart ached with despair for all three of them. She was so proud to be an aunt to this beautiful, precious boy, who already reminded her so much of her beloved brother that it nearly broke her not to be able to shout from the rooftops and celebrate the unexpected joy that had come into her life.

She snuck another look at Archie, who was walking off

the floor with Helena by his side. She tried to smile at him as she caught his eye, but the smile he returned was forced. Temperance's heart ached with the mess she'd made of their relationship.

'Archie still not talking to you, then?' Violet said.

'You saw that?'

'Impossible to miss,' Violet replied, while beside her Eamon was still sleeping, in spite of the loud music around them. Temperance smiled at the memory of her brother, who had once slept through an entire lightning storm.

'Why don't you talk to him?' Violet suggested.

'You think I haven't tried?' Temperance shrugged. 'He's avoiding me.'

'Daft bugger,' Violet said under her breath. 'Archie Ledbetter's always been stubborn. But he will come round, you know.'

Temperance felt another ache in her chest. 'Will he?'

'Course he will,' Violet scoffed. 'He just takes his time. I remember when Maisie pushed him off his bike as a kid. He had scuffed knees and bruised pride. Took him weeks to forgive her, but he did in the end.'

'How?' Temperance asked, hoping for inspiration.

'I think Maisie helped it along a bit by giving him a good talking-to. She told him if he didn't pack it in she'd push him in the Thames.' Violet snorted. 'She wouldn't have. But Maisie can be quite threatening when she puts her mind to it.'

Temperance giggled. She could imagine Violet's forthright sister doing just that. And then, with a start, she remembered that Maisie was Violet's half sister.

As though reading her mind, Violet spoke up.

'Maisie's still my sister,' she said softly. 'My full sister, no matter what anyone else says.'

Temperance reached out a hand and patted Violet's arm. 'You've had such an up and down couple of weeks.'

Violet looked down at baby Eamon and nodded. 'You can

say that again. There's been a lot to take in, Temp.' She paused. 'I mean, for so long, I've detested George, but he's the man who raised me.'

'He still is that man,' Temperance pointed out.

'True. But knowing he's not my father, my real father anyway, makes so much more sense to me. Why me and him always butted heads. Can't help thinking he must have resented me for so long.'

'Or, he thought he was doing his best,' Temperance offered. 'Like me doing that egg round.'

'You can't compare your bit of daftness at getting involved in an illegal egg round with George bringing up me and Roy as his own.' Violet laughed. 'I keep wondering what Roy would say.'

Temperance reached out a hand and squeezed her friend's arm.

'I'm sure he'd be reeling, too.'

Violet lifted her chin and Temperance saw her eyes brimming with tears.

'Have you seen Alan?' Temperance asked.

Violet shook her head.

'No, but I keep thinking back to when he came rushing over to me after I'd just given birth. He was just so smitten with Eamon. At the time I thought it was strange, but now I know why he was so emotional!'

'Because he's the child's grandfather,' Temperance mused.

Violet sighed. 'Exactly. And I have no idea what that means for any of us.'

'Whatever it means, baby Eamon is surrounded by love,' Temperance reminded her. She looked at the gentle slope of Eamon's nose and the soft curve of his cheek and felt her own heart swell with joy at the sight of her nephew. She didn't think she would ever tire of looking at him.

She looked at Violet. 'So what do you want to do now?'

'I want to give this little lad the world, and that means the chance to embrace all the family he has,' Violet replied calmly.

'And that includes getting to know Alan. As your father, I mean?'

'I don't know yet.' Violet sighed. 'He hasn't said he wants to forge a relationship with me, and despite his feelings and belief about the man he had turned into, I'm still struggling with how he could have thought that it was a better choice to just abandon me and Roy, not to mention Betty.'

'But he didn't know Betty would marry George,' Temperance said carefully.

'No, but he must have known the shame being an unwed mother would bring,' Violet said. She smiled down at her son. 'When I think about Eamon, I know he would never leave his child, no matter what.'

'But you just said you want to give this little one the world,' Temperance put in. 'And maybe part of that world is giving him another granddad who will love him.'

Violet fell silent for a moment, clearly mulling the idea over in her mind. She shook her head.

'I don't know, Temp. It all feels too much to think about at the moment. I go from being at peace with it, to feeling confused and angry.'

Temperance nodded. 'What about George? Does he know that you know the truth?'

Violet shook her head. 'But I'm glad I do.'

Temperance's heart went out to her. She hoped her friend could find a way to forgive, and to properly look forward to the future.

She was about to say as much when the sight of Archie walking straight at them sent butterflies in her stomach flying.

'He's coming over,' she squeaked.

'So, talk to him,' Violet hissed.

But Temperance couldn't face it. And, unable to bear being treated with indifference by the man she loved, she turned to flee.

Only, just as she did so, she ran straight into Ronnie.

'Watch yourself,' he snapped.

'Sorry, Mr Newsham,' she murmured, gazing at the floor and wanting nothing more than for the ground to swallow her whole.

He jabbed her sharply in the chest, and she noticed that Archie was glaring at him.

'Don't you touch her,' Archie thundered.

Ronnie sneered. 'Who the hell are you to tell me what to do? You work for me.'

'No, I don't.' Archie took a step towards Ronnie and squared up to him. 'If you remember, I resigned from this place the moment you took over because I knew you'd ruin it. I've been helping the girls in the pen as a favour to them, not you.'

Ronnie leaned in towards Archie. 'Watch yourself, sonny.'

'Or what?' Archie growled. 'You'll get one of your henchmen to remind me who you are?'

'Who says I haven't already?' Ronnie said, engigmatically, and stood back, running his tongue over his teeth. 'How's business these days, by the way? You still got a problem with thieves? You wanna nip that in the bud, son, sooner rather than later.'

Archie narrowed his eyes. 'You—'

'You need to be careful,' Ronnie said in a harsh whisper. 'Start upsetting folk, and there's a chance they'll want pay-back. And I'd hate to see a nice little business like yours go under.'

Temperance held her breath. Ronnie had been behind the thefts? But why? What had Archie ever done to him? She sighed. She could guess. Archie had stood up to him, when most other people had bowed and nodded. She watched now, wondering if the man she knew she loved would lose his cool. But Archie merely shook his head and pushed past Ronnie without looking back. As she watched him walk away, Temperance felt her heart swell with even more love and admiration for his courage. She knew she would do anything to earn his forgiveness.

Forty-Four

Watching the exchange with Archie and Ronnie with a growing sense of trepidation, Renee curled her fists. Ronnie's behaviour was getting worse and he was becoming more and more difficult to live with. She had seen this before and knew that he more than likely had a plan up his sleeve that was about to come to fruition, no doubt causing untold amounts of destruction.

As Archie went past her, flashing a grim smile in her direction, Renee knew it was time to try and do something. She had spent too long living in Ronnie's shadow, and now he was back in her life, and seemingly for good, she had to try and make this work for the sake of the Palais as well as herself.

The question was, how? Ronnie wouldn't respond well to being ambushed and she knew she needed time. The only trouble was, she thought, as Nancy walked into the dance hall with Ruth and Peter trailing behind her, Renee wasn't sure she had enough time.

'All right, queen?' she said as Nancy approached.

'Hey, honey,' Nancy said in a low voice.

Renee frowned. Her friend had looked exhausted ever since The Blitz a fortnight ago. Nancy seemed broken, and guilt tore at Renee. This was something else she was responsible for – Nancy's unhappiness. If she hadn't inadvertently led Ronnie to the Palais by coming back here, then Nancy would no doubt still be in her rightful place as manager.

To her dismay, Renee caught Peter looking at Ronnie as if he were a god.

'Can I go and talk to Uncle Ronnie, Nancy?' the lad asked politely.

Nancy nodded, but reluctantly. 'Sure. But be mindful of his time.'

Once Peter was gone, Renee looked aghast at Nancy. 'You're all right with that?'

'Course not,' Nancy said with a sigh. 'But the boy's so smitten. If I say no, he'll only go behind my back. He needs a father figure in his life, and at the moment he sees Ronnie as providing that.'

Reaching into her pocket for a cigarette, Renee lit one up furiously and smiled at Ruth. 'What about you, sweetheart? You don't want to learn from your uncle Ronnie?'

Ruth gave a shy shake of her head. 'I'd rather learn from Temperance. She's so good at dancing.'

'She is that, love.' Renee smiled as she took a pull on her cigarette.

'It's Nancy's birthday next week,' Ruth said, with a beam. 'Temperance said she'd teach me a special dance to show her.'

'You don't have to do that, honey,' Nancy said kindly. Renee watched her run a hand over Ruth's hair and saw how the girl was now almost at Nancy's shoulders. She was growing up fast.

'We want to!' Ruth declared. 'And then at your party I want to show it off as your present.'

Realising what she'd said, the girl flushed red and clamped a hand over her mouth.

'I'm sorry,' she said through her fingers.

Nancy smiled. 'It's OK. I knew already about the party. Why don't you go find Temperance and ask her to show you a few steps so you're ready, huh?'

With that, Ruth gambolled away like a lamb and Renee raised an eyebrow.

'You didn't know about that do next week at all, did you?'

'No idea.' Nancy giggled. 'I guess it was meant to be a surprise, huh?'

'Well, it was.' Renee shrugged. 'It was Maisie's idea. She thought it would cheer you up.'

'I'm not unhappy,' Nancy said, unconvincingly.

'But you're not exactly over the moon are you, chuck?'

'Are you, Renee?' Nancy said quietly.

Renee fell silent, and both women's eyes fell on Ronnie, who was now clapping Peter on the back.

'Something has to be done about that,' Renee said.

'I've tried,' Nancy said in a low voice.

The familiar feeling of guilt nibbled away at Renee once more.

'I'm sorry,' Renee said.

Nancy looked at her in surprise.

'But, honey, none of this is your fault.'

Taking a last pull on her cigarette, Renee stubbed it out in the ashtray beside her. Nancy was wrong. This was her fault and she had to fix it. She sighed, moving the conversation along to Nancy's husband.

'Have you heard from Alex lately?'

A cloud crossed Nancy's face.

'No. Not for a month now.'

Renee felt a flash of concern. Since the huge raids a couple of weeks ago, Hitler hadn't sent over any more bombers. For some, that was a sign the war was over, but Renee wasn't so sure. The papers had been full of reports of Hitler's assault on Greece, with the battle of Crete underway. To Renee that meant, if anything, the Jerries were escalating operations rather than slowing down.

'I'm sure Alex is all right, love,' she said, trying to reassure Nancy. 'He's probably busy, and it's difficult for him to put pen to paper.'

Nancy smiled, but Renee could see it didn't reach her eyes. 'Maybe.'

Renee was about to press further but was stopped by the sight of her ex-husband approaching her.

'Renee, a word,' he said.

Walking briskly past her, it was clear she was expected to follow him.

Shooting Nancy a grimace, Renee traipsed after him and out of the dance hall, into the corridor. Glancing around, she saw there was nobody else around and relief flooded through her. She could tell by the look on Ronnie's face that he was in a foul mood: the last thing she wanted was more witnesses to whatever he might say or do.

'Everything all right, Ron?'

Ronnie narrowed his eyes. 'No, Reen, everything is not all right. What's all this about a party for Nancy next week?'

'You know about that? It's supposed to be a surprise.' Renee tried to keep her voice steady.

Ronnie leaned forward and put his hand on the wall, trapping Renee. 'It's my dance hall. I've a right to know what's going on. You should have spoken to me. I've got people coming, important people and they don't want to hear you lot screaming and gossiping.'

Her heart racing, Renee tried to smile. 'We didn't want to trouble you, Ron. Just doing something nice for Nancy, that's all. We've all been through so much, what with the raid.'

'I don't like it,' Ronnie said sneeringly. 'You're already working too much with that slapper Violet off work cos of that bastard child of hers.'

At the use of the words 'slapper' and 'bastard', Renee flinched. 'The little boy's not her kid,' she protested. 'She's taken it in, off a young mother who died during the raids.'

Ronnie let out a hollow laugh. 'You think I was born bleedin' yesterday? That kid's hers, and her being off looking after it means you're spending more time here when you should be with me.'

'Just trying to make sure your investment makes a decent return, Ronnie,' she said coolly.

Ronnie thumped the wall with his fist, causing her to jump. 'Pull the other one. I don't like being lied to, Renee. And I don't like you doing all this work. Your place is by my side and don't you bleedin' forget it.'

Anger burned inside Renee, and, before she had chance to think about what she was doing, she pulled back her shoulders and looked him directly in the eyes.

'How could I ever forget it, Ronnie?' she said. 'You're on me back every bleedin' five minutes. There are other people in my life, besides you. My friend Nancy, for one, who you've bullied and demeaned and got rid of, more for your own amusement than anything else. Call yourself a businessman? This place thrived under her, and now it's going to the dogs. The way you're going with all your dodgy cronies, this place'll go under and you'll be forever known as Ronnie Newsham – the bloke that finally killed off the Palais.'

As she finished, Renee felt a sense of euphoria, but that quickly evaporated as anger flashed across Ronnie's face, and she braced herself for a beating. But instead she was dumbfounded when Ronnie laughed.

'You might be right, love. But not before I've sodding well sold the place.'

He leaned in towards her with his mouth open, his teeth jutting menacingly, as if he were a savage wolf ready to attack.

'What do you mean?' she asked, her voice faltering. 'Sell the place?'

'I mean I've been deliberately running this place into the ground since I took over. Makes it easier for the board to see my way of thinking. This place has now been sold to a consortium, which makes me a tidy profit.'

Renee stared at her husband in disbelief. 'You invested in this place to ruin it, to sell it off?'

Ronnie winked. 'That was the plan.'

He looked around him and sneered. 'This place is a hole.

Best thing for it is to sell it on. And that means when the deal's gone through at Nancy's birthday party next week, you won't need to work no more. You can be by my side for good, love, being the perfect wife for once.'

He bent and kissed her softly on the cheek, then walked away. Shocked, Renee leaned back against the wall, tears pooling in her eyes as the sound of the band playing a quickstep providing the perfect soundtrack to her thoughts, and the only comfort to her in that moment. The spirit of the music could always be relied on to transport Renee, to take her back to the dance floor – the only place she ever felt safe.

Forty-Five

Across town, in the offices of Howell & Smart, Betty sat opposite Alan and Nora. Even though they were each dressed in smart, business clothing, their hair and skin immaculate, nothing could detract from the sorrow written across their faces.

The loss of their newest and finest National Restaurant had clearly cut each of them to the quick, and Betty felt their grief. She had helped launch the restaurant and felt the weight of responsibility as she helped source ingredients, forge relationships with the community and see how much of a difference they were making to those around them.

To see all that decimated over one long, cruel night, was devastating. Only Alan and Nora understood just how much she had lost.

'So, what now?' she asked, her face grave.

'We rebuild,' Nora said brightly.

'As simple as that?' Betty asked, unconvinced.

'Well, not quite as simple as that,' Alan said with a smile. 'But we have seen first-hand how successful the National Restaurants campaign is.'

'And, more than that, how needed it is in communities everywhere,' Nora added.

She glanced at Alan, and Betty watched him nod in agreement.

'Which is why we've decided to change things a little,' Nora continued.

Betty felt a flash of concern. In her experience, change was rarely a good thing.

'Change things?' she asked.

'Yes,' Alan broke in now, his voice as smooth as silk. 'As you know, we have a number of department stores across the country. Our store in Liverpool was decimated in the raids, but our store in Birmingham is thriving – unlike the people of that city.'

'Birmingham, Liverpool, Plymouth, the list is endless, really,' Nora put in. 'But these cities have been hit almost as hard as London, and we want to help.'

'It's why, with the support of head office, Howell & Smart will be launching National Restaurants nationwide,' Alan said triumphantly. 'Our next restaurant will be in Birmingham and I will be overseeing the operation.'

'In fact, Alan will be overseeing all our new restaurants,' Nora added with a small flourish. 'I have decided to retire.'

Shock coursed through Betty as she tried to take in all this new information. New restaurants? New cities? Nora retiring. Alan moving. What did this mean for her? Were Howell & Smart putting her out to pasture, too?

'We quite understand this is a lot to take in,' Nora said gently, seeing the look on Betty's face. 'But you have been such a key part of operations we very much hope you will continue with us.'

'Continue?'

'Yes,' Alan said firmly. 'In Birmingham. We want to make you manager of the new restaurant. And, as we expand, we want to send you around the country to ensure all the restaurants meet our same exacting standards.'

Betty let out a gasp of shock. She couldn't believe what she was hearing. The chance of a new job. The chance to start again? But then, how could she leave? Her home was in London. Her husband? Her family? Her loyalties lay here.

'You will, of course be compensated financially,' Nora said, punctuating her thoughts. 'And we do understand you have family here. Would your husband be open to relocating with you to Birmingham?'

At the question Betty nearly choked. The idea of George relocating anywhere outside of Hammersmith was a joke. She didn't think he'd ever been further than Cricklewood and that had only been because he'd got on the wrong bus.

She recovered herself, looking down at her reflection in the highly polished mahogany table. There was so much quality in this store, she realised. She had never thought of it before.

'You don't have to decide immediately, of course,' Nora continued. 'There's a lot to discuss, so I'll leave you and Alan to chat this through a little further.'

As Nora stood up she rested a hand on Betty's shoulder and gave it a squeeze. 'Whatever you decide to do, I want you to know just how much we value you and all your efforts here.'

As Nora left the room, Betty turned to face Alan. her heart pounding.

'How long have you known about this?' she demanded.

'It was always the plan,' Alan admitted. 'But since the bombing of the Islington restaurant, we decided to bring plans forwards a little.'

'And was the plan always to include me?'

'Not at first,' Alan said. 'But after the raid, and Nora's retirement, I thought you'd be the perfect choice to fill Nora's role.'

'And what other role would you have me fill?' Betty asked, angry now. She felt as if her life were being decided for her, that she had no say in the matter. 'That of your hussy? Am I also to set up a love nest with you? Was that part of your plan?'

As she fired questions at him, Alan looked aghast. He got up and immediately walked around to Betty's side of the table. Bending down, he reached for her hands and looked into her eyes.

'Betty, my love, no. I know you're still married. I know that the love we've rekindled isn't to be confused with the work we do here. Whatever you can give me, whatever love you can bestow upon me, I'm just grateful that you're back in my life.'

As she looked up at him she saw the sincerity in his eyes. She loved him, she had never stopped. But life had got in the way since their love affair. She was a mother, and a grandmother now, a wife – a woman with responsibilities. Leaving London felt impossible.

As if reading her mind, Alan took a seat next to her, his hands wrapped around hers.

'How's Violet now?' he asked in a low voice.

At the question, Betty first smiled, and then remembered what she had revealed to Violet about her real father.

'I told her the truth,' she said. 'That you're her father, not George.'

'Really?' Alan looked shocked. 'What did she say? Does she hate me?'

Betty paused for a moment. Her daughter didn't tend to run away with her emotions, but she had just given birth and her hormones weren't exactly as they should be. She had only yesterday tried to ask Vi if she wanted a relationship with Alan, but Violet had shrugged and said she wanted to focus on the baby rather than any more turmoil in her life.

'I think she's a bit shocked and confused at the minute,' Betty said carefully. 'She doesn't hate you, Alan. She's curious. But she's had such a poor relationship with George all her life, she's not sure what a decent father looks like.'

Alan nodded. 'I can understand that. But I'd love to be a part of Violet's life, if I can be. I missed out on the chance to get to know my son, I don't want to lose out on the same with my daughter.'

At the mention of Roy, Betty's eyes brimmed with tears. As she'd watched Roy grow up, it had been hard to avoid how much he looked like Alan. The fact hadn't been lost on George, either.

'I know,' Betty said gently. 'But we have to tread carefully, and we must be mindful of George.'

'George!' Alan scoffed. 'After all he's done.'

'He gave me and the kids respectability, once,' Betty said. 'I may not like the man, but I owe him for that. If he hadn't come along I could have ended up in the workhouse and Roy and Violet would have been brought up by God knows who. No, George raised your children when you couldn't, Alan, never forget that.'

He nodded and hung his head in shame. 'I got everything so wrong, Bet,' he whispered. 'I was so broken from the last war, I couldn't think straight. But I want to make things up to you and Violet now. I want us all to have a second chance.'

'And you think that a job in Birmingham and a life with you is that second chance?' Betty asked.

Alan's cheeks flushed red and Betty could see that he hadn't thought any of the of practicalities through.

'I want you to leave George,' he said. 'And be with me.'

As much as she had dreamed of these words for years, Betty wasn't a naïve young girl any longer.

'I can't leave him,' she said. 'And I certainly can't leave Violet. Not now. Not when she needs me.'

'She could come, too,' Alan whispered. 'Think about it. It would be a new life away from prying eyes. And George may have taken on the twins, but how fair has he been to you all these years? He's cheated, he's gambled, and it's you who's had to prop *him* up, not the other way around.'

'I made vows before God,' Betty insisted.

A loud sigh now escaped her lips. She hadn't slept properly since the night of the raid and she was too tired now to deal with all this. She thought back to the day Violet had discovered the truth about her parentage. Betty had half expected Violet to scream and shout. Call her names, but she hadn't. She had simply nodded and calmly admitted that it all made sense, why George had never wanted to have anything to do with her, not really.

'Can I at least talk to Violet?' Alan said, interrupting her thoughts. 'Please, Betty, at least give me that opportunity. Then perhaps we can decide on the future and if you want to have a place with me in Birmingham.'

Betty was silent. She was busy thinking that if she did turn down this opportunity with Alan, she could be out of a job. Not to mention the idea of spending her days with George made her feel desperate.

'You won't lose your job here,' Alan assured her, reading her mind. 'I promise you that. But, Betty, please give me the chance to talk to my daughter. That's all I want. I promise I won't make any trouble.'

Betty heaved a sigh. She knew that was true. Unlike her husband, Alan always knew how to conduct himself in public.

'Well, we're having a party for Nancy's birthday next Friday,' she said. 'Why don't you come along? Violet will be there, and perhaps you can talk to her then.'

A broad smile broke across Alan's face. 'Thank you,' he said. 'That means the world.'

She got to her feet, and gazed at him, this man she adored. But he didn't understand her. She had already sinned in the eyes of God by forging a fresh relationship with Alan. Though it would pain her, she had to put an end to it. Violet had enough problems raising an illegitimate child, the last thing she needed was her mother carrying on as an adulteress.

Forty-Six

It might have been almost the end of May, but the cold rain pounding against the roof of the Palais made it feel more like the middle of winter.

Perched on a stool at the front desk, Nancy pulled her cardigan tighter around her. It was the usual late-afternoon lull between the tea and evening dances, but rather than go up to the flat and spend time with the kids, Nancy had decided to stay at work and try to quieten her mind, that was racing with a gazillion thoughts she couldn't quite hold onto.

Now, as she stared out at the deserted foyer, she pulled open the desk drawer and reached for an envelope. She didn't need to pull it out and read it, she already knew the contents by heart, but somehow hearing from her mother gave her comfort. Nancy wasn't sure if her low mood was down to her birthday coming up in two days' time, or that she hadn't heard from Alex in weeks – or that the war was worsening in Greece, with Hitler now having sunk two British destroyers and another two cruisers off the coast of Crete, making his intentions clear.

No matter how often Mr Churchill insisted that Britain would seize the day, Nancy was beginning to lose hope. Selfishly, she had hoped that when she took in Peter and Ruth she would feel as if she were doing more to help the war effort. But the kids, as lovely as they were, seemed content to make their own way in the world. Ruth was always so busy at school and Peter was, unfortunately, continuing to hang on Ronnie Newsham's every word.

Just the thought of that man made Nancy's blood boil. Apart from anything else, if he hadn't come along, Betty wouldn't have been fired and now facing the choice of a future in Birmingham.

Nancy had been astonished when Betty had confided in her about it. Nancy hadn't known how to advise her, although privately she believed that starting afresh away from George would be the making of Betty. Like everyone else she had been astonished to discover Violet's true parentage, but equally Nancy understood. It was the only reason why someone as moral and decent as Betty had found herself married to someone like George.

She could hear him now in the bar behind her, laughing and joking with Ronnie and his cronies. Ronnie supplying free drinks that the Palais would have to foot the bill for.

Shaking her head she turned her attentions back to her mother's letter, the words having a soothing effect on her soul.

5th May 1941

Dear Nancy,

It's so good to hear from you, sweetheart! Your father and I were delighted to get your letter. Though I'll admit you didn't sound yourself. We're worried about you, honey. Not for the first time I wish you lived around the corner and we could set the world to rights like we always do, with a hot cup of coffee and a pastry from Madam Zelda's. But it's not to be so, honey, just know that you are always in my thoughts and I carry you in my heart every day.

I can't imagine what life is like for you in England right now, but your father says the war is worsening and that will mean everyone there's got to start showing a bit of metal. For you, my girl, I know that will be no problem! You're by

303

far the strongest of your siblings, but I also know that you're the child that keeps her feelings closest to her chest. You don't need to, honey. I'm your mother, you can tell me anything. I can't promise I'll always understand, but I will listen.

This Ronnie guy that's taken over the Palais sounds like a piece of work! I can't believe you're letting him run wild like this – this isn't your style at all, honey. I know that no matter how difficult a bind you think you're in, you of anyone will be the one to solve it. You are the Palais, sweetheart. You always have been. Your sister Esther always reminds us how gifted you were, running those music halls here at home.

As for Edna. You know I've never cared for her. I know it's not my place to talk about her like that, especially when I know so little about her and we only met that one time years ago. But, sweetheart, she's never had your best interests at heart. I can't understand why you're letting her ride roughshod over you like this. Her place as your mother-in-law and her place at the Palais are two very separate things. If she can't see that, she needs to be reminded.

It was lovely of you to tell me all about Ruth and Peter. I can't wait to see them and welcome them into the family proper! Your father and I are hoping that when this godawful war is over, we can take a trip and come see you! We can think of nothing better than getting to know our new grandkids and seeing you again. And Alex, too, of course, who we know you must miss so much, honey.

I know life is hard for you right now, but even

*though you are far apart from us and Alex, know
that true love in all its forms is always with you
and always in your heart. You are the smartest,
kindest kid I know, Nancy – you hang in there and
things will get better soon, I promise.*
    Your loving Mom XX

As Nancy finished reading her mom's letter, she felt a tear slide down her face. How she'd missed her. And she didn't just miss her family, she missed the States where everything made more sense and she wasn't made to feel like a constant outsider. Nancy shook her head bitterly. She was just feeling sorry for herself. She had a lot of friends, a husband, a job and two adorable children. Life was good, or at least it could be.

As Nancy heard the sound of Ronnie's voice reverberating through the wall, she remembered her mother's words of wisdom. She was strong, she had courage. If there were problems to resolve, Nancy could tackle them head on.

When she saw a beaming George stride out of the dance hall and into the foyer, Nancy decided to seize the moment.

'Hey, George,' she called.

Dressed in what had now become his trademark style of trilby hat and charcoal lounge suit, George spun around and gave Nancy a smile.

'Hello, love. How's tricks?'

'OK,' Nancy replied, doing her best as she always did not to look directly at the gaping fabric where his arm should have been.

'What can I do you for?' George asked, now taking a step towards her.

As he looked at her expectantly, Nancy felt her resolve crumble. What should she say? *'Don't get involved in Ronnie Newsham's business anymore? In case you didn't already know, he's a bad guy.'* George Millington already knew all that, and he didn't give a monkey's. She'd have to find another way to reach him.

'I just wanted to check you were all right. You know, with the possibility of Betty leaving?'

Nancy knew Betty had brought up the idea with George, and that she was treading on thin ice by mentioning it now. And, predictably, a storm cloud passed across his face.

'Betty's going nowhere. I've told her,' he said. 'She's my wife and her place is by my side. Besides,' he tapped his nose, 'thanks to Ronnie, and the new business deal he's got me involved in, I'll soon be making more than enough money for the two of us. So she can forget all that nonsense about working and stay at home where she belongs.'

Nancy winced, certain that the last place Betty wanted to be was at home by George's side all day.

'What's this business deal?' she asked casually.

'Oh, something and nothing.' George puffed himself up with pride. 'Something Ronnie needs my help with. I'm going to introduce him to a few of my contacts.'

Nancy said nothing. The only contacts George had were the tote men, but perhaps that was who Ronnie needed.

'And when it pays out in a few days' time, me and Betty will be sorted once and for all,' he added.

Nancy's mind whirred.

'I didn't know about that,' she said. 'Sounds great.'

George grinned. 'Ronnie's promised me I'll get back ten times me investment.'

At the mention of money, Nancy's heart sank. Just what had George gotten himself into? And, worse, did Betty know anything about it? In that moment she felt helpless, her mother's words about strength and loyalty echoing through her mind.

Forty-Seven

When Temperance woke abruptly just before dawn, she was astonished to hear the sound of what she thought was heavy rain. Pulling the heavy candlewick bedspread from her bed, she got up and walked towards the window. As she got nearer, she realised it sounded more like heavy gunfire than rain.

But then, interspersed with the rapid fire against the window-pane, she heard someone calling her name.

'Temperance,' a voice hissed. '*Temmmmp*.'

She smiled. She knew all too well who it was. But tempted as she was to throw the curtains back and beam out of the window, she knew that she mustn't. Strict blackout protocols were in place until daylight proper, and Temperance didn't want to put anyone at risk.

Instead, taking care not to wake her mother or her aunt, she padded down the stairs and, reaching the front door, flung it open. There was Archie, standing in his butcher's overalls, ready to start the day.

'What are you doing here?' She pulled her housecoat around her, suddenly aware in all the excitement that she was dressed in her nightclothes.

Archie beamed and said nothing. Instead he handed her a parcel wrapped in greaseproof paper.

She sniffed it appreciatively, and for a second she was sure she was still upstairs in bed dreaming.

'Is this what I think it is?' Temperance managed now, hoping desperately it was true.

'If you think it's a bacon sandwich, then yes,' Archie whispered. 'Made by my own fair hand this morning. We had some leftover bacon and I thought you might like it.'

Temperance raised an eyebrow. They both knew there was no such thing as leftover bacon, not anymore.

'All right, it's out of my rations,' he said, looking shamefaced. 'And it's an apology.'

'Whatever for?' Temperance gasped.

'For not being very understanding when I found out about your egg round,' he mumbled, shifting from foot to foot. 'I let my own emotions about the theft from the butcher's cloud my judgement, and I'm sorry.'

Temperance shook her head. 'It was stupid of me to carry on with the eggs for so long when someone was stealing from you.'

'Well, that wasn't down to you.' Archie's face was grim.

'Ronnie?' Temperance asked.

Archie lifted his gaze and shrugged. 'I don't know for sure. But the thieving seems to have stopped since he implied it was down to him.' He shrugged. 'But maybe that was his way of keeping me in line, in case he needs me later on at the Palais.'

At the mention of the Palais and her beloved dance hall, Temperance felt an all-too-familiar knot of fear. She hadn't said a word since Mr Henshall had told her he suspected the Palais was up for sale, but the worry of it was weighing her down.

'Archie . . .' she said, hesitantly. 'I don't want to keep anything else from you.'

'All right.' Archie turned and looked at her. 'What's the matter?'

'It's the Palais. I think Ronnie's selling it, Mr Newsham told me a few weeks ago.'

'Selling it?' Archie gasped. 'He's surely got that wrong.'

Temperance shrugged, then relayed all that the hotelier had told her.

When she had finished, Archie looked flabbergasted.

'I can't believe it. We have to stop him.'

'How?' Temperance cried. 'Ronnie's always got his mob about to protect him. And the board sound as if they've agreed it.'

Archie sighed heavily in frustration. 'I can't believe that rotten git has been deliberately creating trouble at the Palais, practically dragging it down to bankruptcy. And now the board will think there's no choice but to sell it.'

'I can believe it,' Temperance said quietly. After all, Ronnie Newsham was rotten to the core. She shook her head. Thoughts of Ronnie and all the harm he inflicted were making her miserable, and she had good things, better things, to think about. Like Archie.

She leaned forward and ran a finger along his forearm.

'So, do you forgive me?' she asked shyly.

'Course I do,' Archie whispered, turning towards her, his eyes brimming with sincerity.

He took a step forward and clasped her hands in his. 'I'd forgive you anything, Temp. And I know you had your reasons for what you did. Can you tell me what they were?'

She looked deep into his eyes. In some ways she and Archie were so similar, in others they were worlds apart.

She sank down onto the step and took a deep breath.

'Because, apart from my family, I wanted to help provide for Violet and the new baby. And even though Mum had help from the government after Eamon died, and Aunt Winnie brings some money in from the theatre, there wasn't enough to go round for everyone.'

'Oh, Temperance.' He looked at her tenderly.

'See, when I found out Vi was expecting,' she continued, 'I felt so strongly that I had to step in for Eamon – provide for Vi and the baby when he couldn't. It was bad enough my nephew would be growing up without a father, I didn't want him to go without what he needed.'

'But, Temp, that's not all down to you. Vi's family would have helped.'

'You don't understand,' she said. 'I'm black, as was my brother of course, and little Eamon will be growing up different. Mixed race.' She paused. 'And coloured people get treated differently, they don't have the chances that white people have. They're looked down on. You must have seen it. The looks, the whispers, when we're together?'

'I . . . I just focused on being with you,' he said, though she could see a hint of guilt in his eyes.

'Because you're white, Archie, that's why you don't notice it, maybe. But this might affect you, too. Mixed-race couples aren't given an easy time, quite the opposite.' She sighed. 'And Violet's baby being mixed race, too . . . Well, that means they're both in for a struggle in society, and anything I could do to take the pressure off—'

'I'm so sorry,' Archie cut her off. 'I didn't think. I understand now.'

She reached out and squeezed his hand.

'And you know I don't care what colour you are, you must know that,' he said.

'Of course I know that. But, Archie, I've been bullied and spat at, threatened and beaten, and all because of the colour of my skin.' She paused and ran a hand over her face, the level of confession exhausting her. 'So that's why, when I saw a chance to make a bit extra, I took it.'

Archie nodded and picked up her fingers, pressing them to his lips, his eyes filled with tenderness.

'I love you. You're wonderful, Temperance, with the kindest heart.'

His words made Temperance's heart leap with joy, and she leaned forward and kissed him. As she lost herself in his touch time seemed to stand still, and eventually, as they pulled apart, Temperance was aware of the greasy package that had become squashed between them.

'Whoops.' She laughed.

'It'll still taste good,' Archie said. 'I promise.'

Temperance unwrapped the sandwich and allowed the scent of bacon against soft bread to assault her tastebuds. She offered him half, only for him to look hesitant.

'I made it for you.'

'And I'm offering you half,' she insisted. 'We're a team.'

With a smile, Archie took the sandwich, and together they sat on Temperance's front step, munching happily as the sun came out. Then, resting her head against his shoulder, Temperance felt happiness like she'd never felt before, and knew that there was no place she would ever rather be.

Later that afternoon, as she cleared away after the tea dance, the joy Temperance felt first thing that morning was still with her. In fact she was wearing a smile so wide not even Bill Cain's perpetual moaning about Nancy's birthday party later that night – and how it was taking away key staff – couldn't dampen her mood. Instead she found herself dreaming about a future with Archie, and what that would look like. She was so lost in her daydreams that she barely noticed Betty tugging at her sleeve as she tidied and sorted coat hangers.

'Oh, Betty!' she said, taking in the sight of her. Betty looked just as cheerful as she did, she noticed.

'You were miles away, love,' Betty said. 'I didn't want to interrupt you, but can you give us a hand to set the bar up for Nancy? She'll be along in a minute – Edna's sent her to the shops on a false errand.'

Temperance chuckled. 'Nancy knows full well what's happening tonight.'

'I know that,' Betty said as they strolled across the maple-sprung floor towards the bar. 'But Edna's laying on a fuss, mostly for the kids.'

'Really?'

'Edna loves the bones of them kiddies,' Betty said earnestly. 'Would do anything for them.'

'Shame that won't stretch to getting rid of Ronnie Newsham, once and for all,' Temperance growled. 'Edna brought him in here, she should be the one to get rid of him.'

'Can't say as I disagree,' Betty admitted. 'He's up there now, holding court with all his cronies. If you didn't know better, you'd think this was a party for him.'

Sure enough, as Temperance and Betty walked into the bar, she could see Ronnie standing tall in the middle of the room. Dressed in a suit and a crisp white shirt, with the trilby he hadn't bothered to remove, Temperance could see he was in his element with all his hangers-on around him, including George.

'And, like I said, boys,' Ronnie said now, his voice bellowing as he looked at each of his pals. 'Tonight we celebrate. Your money's a sure thing. We'll all sign on the dotted line in a bit.'

At that there was a loud cheer, with George cheering the loudest of all.

Temperance chanced a glance at Betty, but if she was troubled by her husband's immersion into Ronnie's clan, she didn't show it.

Instead, Betty led Temperance towards the back of the bar, where there was a hive of activity, as the girls sliced sandwiches into little squares and fixed the drinks.

'Temp, love,' Violet cooed.

'Where's Eamon?' Temperance asked as Violet pulled her in for a hug.

'Your mum's got him,' Violet said. 'She offered to take him tonight. It was a last-minute thing, otherwise I wouldn't have made it here tonight. It was kind of her.'

'It was,' Temperance agreed.

'Actually she offered to take him for me full-time.'

'Full-time?' Temperance echoed.

Violet nodded. 'So's I can come back to work. I don't know

what to say. Doesn't feel right to ask someone else to look after him when he's so young.'

'But you're doing this alone, Vi,' Temperance said softly. 'You'll need money, and a job.'

'Too right you will,' Queenie, who was slicing cucumbers, put in. 'Raising kids ain't only a thankless task, it's an expensive one. You'll want all the pennies you can lay your hands on for when the little bleeder's crying for new shoes.'

'Gran!' Violet admonished. But Temperance knew Queenie doted on Eamon, just as everyone else did.

'Is Alan coming tonight?' Temperance asked Betty, as she reached for a chopping board and started to help Renee make up paste sandwiches.

'I don't know.' Betty looked flushed, and for a second Temperance felt guilty. She hadn't forgotten what she had seen all those weeks ago.

'Ain't you heard?' Renee said with a wink. 'Alan wants to take Betty up to Birmingham. Get her to start afresh.'

'No!' Temperance gaped at Betty. 'You're not going.'

'Why shouldn't she?' Violet put in. 'What's she going to do? Grow old with George over there? Alan didn't say it out loud when I saw him for lunch, but I know he thinks it's just what you need, Betty.'

'Oh, yes?' said Queenie. 'When did you start meeting Alan for lunch, Vi?'

At the question, Violet's cheeks flamed. 'I've been getting to know him. Slowly, not rushing it. But he is my father.'

Queenie nodded with approval.

'Alan's always been a good lad,' she said. 'Apart from when he lost his sense of reason.'

'Alan feels horrible about that,' said Vi, then looked at her mother. 'And I know he wants to make it up to you.'

'Violet, please,' Betty hissed. 'Your father's just over there . . .'

'He's not my father,' Violet shrugged.

'But he is mine,' Maisie said firmly. 'And, despite what Alan's done for you recently, George has been the one that put clothes on your back.'

'And sold 'em when he needed money for the bookies,' Queenie quipped. 'Don't you all look at me like that. I know he's my son, but I'm entitled to say what I think.'

Maisie shook her head, her features full of despair. 'I know Dad's made mistakes, but if he knew about any of this . . . Well, it's not right.'

Violet rolled her eyes as she reached for another slice of bread. 'George is far too busy worrying about Ronnie's latest get-rich-quick scheme to know anything about Alan. Or care.'

'And for that reason alone, he needs his bumps felt,' Renee said quietly.

'Do you know what this scheme is?' Betty asked her, but Renee shook her head.

'I've learned the hard way never to ask questions about Ronnie's business affairs,' she said tightly.

As she spoke, Temperance couldn't miss the shadow of a new bruise on Renee's jaw. She shuddered. Renee deserved so much better than Ronnie, and Temperance wanted to help her get rid of him.

'I know what Ronnie's planning,' she said loudly. 'He wants to sell the Palais.'

Forty-Eight

The sounds of a big band bellowed from the gramophone player in the corner of the bar and Nancy tried her best to immerse herself in the party. All her friends were here to toast her special day – including, importantly, the kids, who had been so generous she had been astonished. That morning, not only had Ruth presented her with a cake that she and Peter had saved up their ration coupons to buy ingredients for, but they had also gone around everyone at the Palais and got them to sign a card – even Ronnie.

She watched Ronnie now, holding court as usual, and tried to fight the anger that burned in her at the sight of him. She'd been racking her brains trying to think of how to stop him selling her beloved Palais, but so far it felt impossible.

She glanced towards Renee, who looked as stunning as usual – dressed in a green shot silk dress that perfectly set off her flaming-red hair – and teetering on red heels. How Renee ever managed to dance in shoes like that, Nancy had no idea, but she knew her friend would carry it off with aplomb later.

'Will that man ever shut up?' Edna groaned loudly beside her now, interrupting Nancy's train of thought. 'It's all I've heard all day.'

Amused, Nancy glanced at her mother-in-law, who was drinking a gimlet. Judging by the outburst she wondered if she might have had one too many.

'I'm going to have a word with him,' Bill thundered. 'He's dragged all his rough mates in again, drinking the profits dry.

These are lads I'd normally throw out as soon as they came in, and they're not welcome here.'

'Well it's all your own bleedin' fault,' Queenie said, who was sitting next to Nancy. Her hat was a little left of centre and Nancy laughed to herself as she realised Violet and Maisie's grandmother had also had one too many. 'If you hadn't got him in here, and booted out Nancy and our Betty, then you wouldn't be in this mess and the Palais wouldn't be being sold from under us.'

'Oh, what do you know, Queenie Millington?' growled Bill Cain.

Queenie arched an eyebrow. 'More than you ever will, Bill Cain. This is your doing and you need to fix it.'

'That's assuming they want it fixed, Queenie, honey.' Nancy swirled her gin and tonic around her glass and fixed her gaze on the Millington matriarch. 'They might like the chaos Ronnie Newsham brings with him.'

'Don't be so bloody daft,' Bill spat. 'We had you demoted, because you didn't have the first idea what you were doing.'

'Unlike you, I suppose. You clearly make very rational decisions,' Nancy said drily, just as one of Ronnie's friends broke wind, very loudly and deliberately, to the amusement of the others in his group. 'This whole state of affairs is all down to you. How could you have been so stupid?'

'Don't you blame us for Ronnie Newsham's misdeeds. We couldn't have known what he was planning,' Edna snapped.

Nancy shook her head. 'He's known across the country as a ruthless crook, and you thought getting into bed with him would get one over on me without thinking of the consequences. You're pathetic, and I can't wait to find out what your precious son thinks about your decisions, now that they've come back and bitten you on the ass.'

There was silence as Nancy's words sank in. She waited for a comeback from Bill, but there was none.

A pink-faced Edna turn to Queenie. 'That's your son sat with that group. Aren't you going to say something?'

'Not on your nelly.' Queenie laughed again 'That boy's old enough and ugly enough to look after himself. As long as he don't involve me, Betty or the kids, I don't care what he gets up to.'

'But he's your son,' Edna said in protestation now.

'And she's *your* daughter-in-law,' Queenie said, jerking her head towards Nancy. 'And look how you've treated her. You should've looked out for your family rather than worked against 'em. You've only got yourself to blame, Edna Goldstein.'

'We were looking out for the Palais. And I was looking out for my family,' Edna retorted. 'For my son, Alex.' Her face had turned puce as she jabbed the table pointedly with her index finger.

'And in the process caused more harm than good,' Queenie persisted. 'Sometimes the kindest thing you can do for your kids is stand well back and let 'em find their own way.'

Bill started to speak, but his words were drowned out by the arrival of clearly another of Ronnie's friends, dressed in a suit identical to Ronnie's, and Nancy sighed. Didn't they have the imagination to dress slightly differently from each other? Or was it a uniform of the underworld?

'Ronnie! You toe-rag,' the man thundered at him. 'How's tricks?'

Immediately, Ronnie stopped talking and turned to see the man that had just arrived. Beaming, he broke away from the group and gave the chap a hearty slap on the back as the room fell silent.

'Mick, you old slag. Didn't think you were coming.'

Mick shrugged, then puffed himself up in his regulation, underworld uniform. 'Bit of business to sort out.'

Seeing him closer up, Nancy could see that Mick's face was riddled with scars and she had a feeling that he was more than Ronnie's business partner – he was someone Ronnie commanded to do his dirty work.

'Course.' Ronnie nodded. 'Come and meet the boys, then we'll sign.' He gestured around him to the Palais. 'And then this will be all yours.'

As he dragged Mick past the group, the women exchanged grim looks, even Edna looked dismayed, and Nancy shuddered, before her determination to try and enjoy her evening resumed. She turned back to face the group and saw Violet had now joined them. Her face was full of worry.

'What's wrong, honey?'

'Alan's turned up,' she hissed.

'And?' Nancy said frowning. 'You two have gotten to know each other now. Don't tell me you've gone shy again?'

'It's not that,' said Violet, glancing nervously over at George. 'What's he going to do, now Alan's here?'

'George won't say nothing,' Queenie said confidently. 'Look at him, he's too wrapped up in Ronnie to pay any attention to what you're doing.'

'Come on. Let's go over and talk to Alan,' Nancy suggested to Violet. 'I could do with a change of conversation.'

Getting up, she threaded her arm through Violet's and together they walked towards Alan, who was standing next to Betty. Nancy smiled at the sight of them. They were made for each other, she could see that. The way their body language mirrored each other's, the way they couldn't take their eyes off one another. She was sure she and Alex had once looked at one another like that. Would they ever again?

Her eyes landed on Peter and Ruth and Nancy felt a fresh surge of hope. The kids had given her and Alex a reason to connect, to find their way back to one another again.

She was about to wave at them, when she heard Ronnie behind her.

'Peter, me old pal,' he called cheerfully. 'Come and meet the lads.'

Alarm pulsed through her. Every instinct bristled as

she wanted nothing more than to pull Peter from Ronnie's clutches.

Before she knew what she was doing, she called out, 'Peter.'

He looked around, embarrassed by the attention.

'Uncle Ronnie needs me,' he said coolly. 'I'll see you later, Nancy.'

With that he walked off with Ronnie, and Nancy felt as if she was losing the only battle that truly mattered now – to be a decent parent to two children who had lost a family.

'Leave it, Nancy,' Violet said softly beside her. 'Peter will come round.'

'Violet, Nancy,' she heard Alan greet them in warm tones. 'How are you? How's Eamon?'

Violet nodded. 'He's well. Temperance's mum's looking after him.'

At the statement, Betty coloured. 'You know I wish I could help out more. George has put his foot down.'

'He's refusing to have me and the baby in the house,' Violet added. 'Not that I care. I never want to have anything to do with that man again. Not after what he did to Eamon's father.'

'And I can understand that,' Betty said quietly. 'But we've Maisie to think of, and appearances.'

Betty glanced around the bar now, clearly worried about who was listening to their conversation, and Nancy felt bad for her friend. But Betty had a solid network here, people who'd stand by her, no matter what.

She was about to say as much when Alan spoke up.

'Which is why all three of you should come to Birmingham,' he said. 'Betty can help me set up the new restaurants, nationally. And you'd have a new start and family around you, Violet.' He looked at her now, as though the full scale of the plan was coming together in his mind. 'You wouldn't have to pretend anymore. You could claim Eamon as your own.'

'It's not that simple.' Betty shook her head.

'But it could be,' Violet said, a little excited. 'It could be perfect for all of us.'

Betty shook her head and turned to Nancy. 'I think we're getting away from the point of the evening, which is to wish Nancy a happy birthday.'

Nancy held her glass of aloft. 'Thanks for coming.'

'Wouldn't have missed it,' Betty said warmly. 'You've been a brick to us. We'd have been lost without you. And no matter what the future holds for us, I want you to know that.'

Feeling her cheeks flame with embarrassment, Nancy suddenly heard the sounds of a scuffle behind her. Spinning around, to her horror, she saw that Ronnie had pinned Mick up against the wall and was holding a piece of broken glass to his throat, while Peter looked on, terror darting across his eyes.

'You cheating bastard,' Ronnie growled. 'Are you really that stupid to have tried to trick me? I'll kill you.'

'No, honest, Ron, it weren't like that.'

Mick was red in the face and floundering. Nancy didn't care about Mick, though, she only cared about the boy she thought of as her son.

She rushed towards the scene only for Renee to reach her husband's side before she had the chance.

'Come on now, Ronnie. Leave him be for now,' Renee coaxed. 'It's Nancy's birthday.'

'And what's that got to do with it?' Ronnie said, his voice low as he pressed the cut glass into Mick's face and blood began to trickle downwards.

Nancy could take no more and hurtled to Peter's side.

'You can do whatever you like to your thugs,' she growled. 'But you will not behave like this in front of my boy.' She pulled Peter fiercely towards her.

Just like that, Ronnie let Mick go, and the man slid to the floor like a sack of potatoes. His face was grey as he clutched his cut cheek, blood seeping now into his white starched collar with alarming speed.

Then Ronnie whirled around to face Nancy, who was still holding onto Peter. He jabbed the piece of broken glass towards her face.

'Don't you tell me what to do, or you'll pay like he has,' Ronnie roared. 'And as for that boy, he needs the guidance of a man, not some stupid Yank like you.'

Before Nancy could come back at him, Peter chimed in.

'Don't you talk like that to Nancy. She's been nothing but good to me and my sister.'

A look of surprise passed Ronnie's face, and then he laughed.

'You mean well, lad,' he said. 'And you should stick up for family. Only she's not your family, is she? Not your flesh and blood.'

Nancy felt a mixture of rage and humiliation flood through her. In a sense, he was right, wasn't he? She could never replace Peter and Ruth's parents. She staggered a little on her feet. Her heart had had just about as much as it could take, lately, and her dreams had disappeared.

It was only Peter wriggling out of her grasp that pulled her back into the moment.

'Nancy's every bit of family that matters,' Peter said fiercely. 'And I don't like you being mean to her.'

'You cheeky little bastard,' said Ronnie, but then he too, stumbled a little, and surprisingly, waved Peter away like he was insignificant. The brute was half cut, or more, thought Nancy. She flashed a look at Peter, thinking she'd never loved him more. He was a brave boy, and a better man than Ronnie could ever be.

Then she caught sight of George, who, to her astonishment, was cowering behind Peter. In that moment, she could see that whatever respect George thought he could expect from Betty had gone in a flash. A grown man hiding behind a child told you everything you needed to know about who he really was.

Leaning forward, she kissed the top of Peter's head. 'Honey, I want you to go and sit with Queenie, OK? I'm just going to sort this out here and I'll join you.'

She fixed her eyes on Ronnie, the man who'd come to ruin so many lives, and the jagged bit of glass in his hand. She looked at Renee and together they looked at the floor – there was blood everywhere.

'I'll go to the office and get something to wipe up the blood,' Renee said.

But as Renee started to head out of the bar, her husband started up again: like a cornered beast, he was raging with frustration.

He swung round and kicked Mick hard in the ribcage. 'You and I are nowhere near finished yet,' he snarled, as Mick howled in pain.

With a look of sheer hatred at Nancy, Ronnie then marched out of the room after his wife, and Nancy felt a trickle of dread course down her spine. Given the mood Ronnie was in, there was no telling what he might do to Renee – she had stood up to protect one family member already, now it was time to do the same for another.

She managed to smile politely at the group, and then made her way after Ronnie. He wasn't going to hurt her friend again, not if she could help it.

Forty-Nine

Renee had lost count of the number of times she had walked down this corridor. But today the journey from the dance hall to the office upstairs felt different, charged somehow. She had a horrible feeling of foreboding.

'Renee, get back here,' Ronnie's voice was harsh and clear in the deserted corridor. 'Don't you walk away from me without my permission. You'll regret it.'

She didn't doubt that much was true. But whilst she had seen Ronnie commit plenty of violence in the years she had been married to him and the years she hadn't, she had never seen so much blood course from one man's face as she had Mick's. She had to do something, no matter what the consequences might be for her.

Scurrying into the office she snapped on the light and headed for the cupboard in the corner, where Nancy used to always keep items such as bandages and iodine. To her relief they were still there and as she gathered them up and spun around, she came face to face with her husband.

He smiled nastily, and Renee winced.

'How many times are you going to keep embarrassing me?' Ronnie grabbed her roughly by the arm.

'That man needs help, Ron. He might have nicked an artery.'

She held her breath, careful even in that moment, with her pulse racing, not to blame Ronnie for Mick's current state. She knew that would only fan the flames of his hatred further.

'And what business is it of yours? I keep you around to look pretty and open your legs when I tell you, not to shove your nose in my business.' He leered at her as he looked her up and down, in a way that made Renee want to throw up. 'And at the moment you ain't doing a good job of either one of those things.'

He shook her roughly again, and pushed her to floor. To her surprise and disgust, Renee found tears were rolling down her face, dripping onto her dress.

'Don't bleedin' cry now,' Ronnie snarled. 'We're just getting to the good bit.'

'You don't scare me,' she said, through her tears.

Ronnie kneeled either side of her and pinned her arms to the floor with his hands. He pressed his face into hers and gave her a broad smile that didn't reach his eyes.

'I think we both know that's not true.'

Renee tried to steady her breathing, but as she saw Ronnie draw back his right arm and curl his fingers into a tight ball she knew what was coming. Sure enough, as his bony knuckles connected with her jaw she did what she always did and tried to wrestle free. But he was too strong for her, sat on top of her hips and pushing her to the floor. Determined, she tried to use her legs to wrestle free, but the only thing she managed to free were her shoes.

'Stop it, Ronnie. Please,' she begged, as he launched the first punch.

There was a pause in between blows, as Ronnie spat out a short, sarcastic laugh. '*Please, Ronnie, stop,*' he mimicked. 'I'll stop when you learn the lesson that so far doesn't seem to have got through.'

He raised his hand again and this time belted her across her nose. She felt the pain flood through her entire face, and the blood trickle out of her nostrils, but even in that moment she felt a renewed sense of defiance. What was the point of always trying to remain on his good side? She got a beating and worse, either way. Suddenly she didn't care anymore, and opened her eyes wide and grinned, even though she thought she might pass out with the pain of it.

Her swift change in attitude rocked Ronnie. He stopped hitting her and just stared in astonishment at her.

'You're pathetic, you know that,' she said.

'You filthy whore,' Ronnie roared. And with that he started to loosen his belt buckle and unbutton his fly. Fear once more began to unfurl through her. She knew what was coming. It wouldn't be the first time he had forced himself on her, but he had never done it when she'd been quite so bloodied and bruised.

'Ronnie . . .' she protested, but all her strength was leaving her.

'Forget it, darlin'.' His face was so close she could feel his breath on her cheeks. 'You've had this coming for a while.'

As he pinned her to the ground, she kicked out again. But she was no match for Ronnie. She felt him inch his fingers up her thigh and rip at her stockings.

She clenched her hands, so tight that her long red nails dug into the flesh in her palm. In that moment she was grateful for the pain, grateful for the fact it gave her something else to think about other than Ronnie pulling up her dress.

'You know what, Renee,' he whispered in her ear as he pushed himself inside of her. 'I reckon my mates would be very impressed if they could see me now.'

For a second, she thought about screaming, but knew there was no point. Nobody was coming to save her. And Ronnie's mates were making so much noise in the bar they would drown out any noise she could make. Instead she allowed her eyes to land on her precious high-heeled shoes in the corner. Beautiful and red, they were her favourites. She had bought them because they reminded her of the dancing shoe Christmas tree decoration her mother had bought for her, years ago. They were so precious to her, and when this ordeal was over she would put them on again, and they would give her the comfort she knew she'd need.

But then, as though she was dreaming, she watched a manicured hand pick them up.

As Nancy walked into the office, her heart was in her mouth
at the scene playing out before her. Ronnie had pinned Renee
to the floor and was having his way with her, while she cried
out in pain, blood seeping from her cut face and battered
nose.

The monster was even laughing, as if it was all just a game.

A fizzing cocktail of emotions charged through Nancy's
body – shock and disbelief, then came rage – and the moment
that arrived, Nancy felt it like a tidal wave.

Scanning the room, she searched desperately for a weapon.
And then she saw them – Renee's upturned spike-heeled shoes.

Calmly, silently, Nancy padded quietly across the room,
picked them up and then turned and walked just as soundlessly
over to Ronnie with his back to her, the crimson red of Renee's
heel leading the way. Over Ronnie's head, she locked eyes with
Renee, who managed to nod, her eyes flashing. Nancy knew
what her friend wanted her to do.

'Ronnie, no,' Renee screamed loudly to distract him.

Nancy braced herself, creeping closer to Ronnie until she
was just inches from the back of his head. Then she raised her
arm, and was just about to strike him with the heel of Renee's
shoe, when the bastard turned round.

Seeing Nancy, he paused for a second in disbelief, and then
his gaze turned to the shoe hovering over him. As quick as a
cat, Ronnie got to his knees and began to stand.

'You pair of bitches,' he snarled. 'I'll kill you both.'

But Nancy felt another wave of red mist descend. Without
even stopping for thought, she brought the heel of Renee's shoe
up and stabbed it right into Ronnie's face.

As the heel connected with his flesh and bone, he cried
out in agony.

Nancy felt no sympathy, only tried to pull the shoe out of his face to land another blow. But it was stuck.

Panic rose. She hadn't caused enough damage to hurt him properly, to make him stop what he was doing to Renee.

She cast her eyes around the office once more, searching for anything that would help her land the damage she so desperately needed, but there was nothing.

Apart from the paperweight.

As her eyes gleamed at the sight of it, Ronnie clocked it at the same time. And as Nancy lunged for it, so did he. Triumphant, his fingers encircled it, but just as he began to lift it and Nancy's life flashed before her eyes, she saw Renee, risen to her feet right behind him, holding her other shoe aloft.

Nancy remained poker-faced as Renee plunged the heel firmly into Ronnie's head, and gasped as blood gushed from his skull. Ronnie staggered around to face Renee, clutching at his head.

'What have you done?' he roared.

'What I should have done years ago,' she replied, eyes brimming with hate.

Renee raised the other shoe, and was about to deliver a second assault when her husband made a sudden movement, lunging for the shoe. But the blood in his eyes meant he couldn't see, and he only stumbled backward and forward as he did so.

With an agonised moan, he lost his footing and fell backwards towards the desk, hitting his head against the corner and slumping to the floor.

Renee and Nancy rushed forwards to stand over him. Together they watched as the life began drain from Ronnie's body.

Nancy saw that the cold, smug arrogance in his eyes was now replaced with mortal fear. And as he gasped his final breaths, she didn't feel one ounce of sorrow. Merely satisfaction that a man who had caused so much pain and misery was now getting his just desserts.

And, sure enough, Ronnie's eyes closed, as his body slumped, defeated.

'Tell me he's dead,' said Renee, her voice quivering with shock. Nancy slid her arm around Renee's waist and squeezed it tight. 'He's dead. I promise you, honey. It's over now.'

Fifty

A month after Ronnie's death, Renee together with Temperance, Nancy and Violet found herself in the upstairs office of the Palais sorting through what felt like a mountain of paperwork. Leaning back in the hard, wooden chair opposite Nancy's desk she rubbed the knot in her neck and surveyed their progress. Despite the fact they had been sifting through files for the past three days, it still seemed as though they had a lot to do.

'We must be nearly finished now, Nancy, surely?' she begged. 'If I look at one more sheet of paper, I'll turn into one.'

Nancy looked up from the desk and shook her head. 'Not even close.'

'Do you really think this will make a difference?' Temperance asked, her features looking slightly defeated. 'Maybe they'll just sell to someone else, anyway, if their mind's made up.'

'They can't, not without Ronnie's share sorted,' Nancy said firmly. 'Either that or they have to vote to redistribute, if his affairs are held in probate for a long time.'

'Is that likely?' Temperance asked, turning to Renee.

The dancer shrugged. 'I'm not a solicitor, how should I know? Mind, I'm not averse to having a go if it means I could make half what they do!'

Violet tittered, and Nancy shook her head in mirth. Then Renee clapped her hands together.

'Look, this is all well and good but Temp and I need to get on with organising rosters for the weekend's dances. We can't be up here all day.'

Putting down the folder she had been holding, Nancy frowned. 'I know it's frustrating, but, guys, we have to keep going. Now that we're not selling, the bank and the board want a complete statement of all our work, and it looks as if, while Ronnie was in charge, nothing got done.'

'You mean Edna and Bill did nothing either,' Violet grumbled.

Renee laughed. The girl had a point – Bill and Edna certainly hadn't helped things, but then, given the fact Ronnie had been deliberately trying to destroy the Palais for his own ends, having two inefficient and belligerent individuals run the place was probably just what he wanted.

As an image of her husband's face came to mind, Renee shuddered. He might be six feet under, but even from beyond the grave he still had the power to terrify her. Realising he truly had gone, once and for all, was going to take some getting used to.

After he had died in the very office Renee sat in now, she had been shaken. Not only because her husband was dead, but because she was terrified the police would arrest her and Nancy. And that her life would be over; she'd be thrown in prison and hanged.

But Nancy and the rest of her friends had a plan. When the police came, they calmly told the officers that Ronnie and Mick had been fighting in the office, and Mick had obviously used the heels that Renee kept there to attack Ronnie, who'd just glassed the poor bloke. Then Mick had done one, Renee said. Because he was nowhere to be seen . . . Only Ronnie, who was already dead when they found him . . . 'Well, there was nothing anyone could have done,' Renee told the officer, sadly, claiming to have been in the toilet while it was all going on, a claim backed up by Temperance and Betty who said they had seen her enter the toilets at that time Mick and Ronnie were fighting.

The police had believed their story without question. And

it had helped when Ronnie's pal, Mick, who had supposedly been the backer behind the consortium primed to take over the Palais had mysteriously gone missing a week later, according to the police, who had clearly had their eye on Ronnie Newsham and his dodgy business cronies for a while. Renee didn't want to ask many questions as to what had happened. In her experience, knowing too much about Ronnie's affairs could only lead to trouble.

She had played the doting wife card one last time at his funeral a fortnight ago. Unlike Eamon's and Lizzie's funerals, there were scarcely more than a handful of mourners. In fact, the Good Time Girls plus Bill, Edna and a couple of Ronnie's friend had made up the congregation. Missed, he wouldn't be, but Renee didn't think Ronnie would care. He'd never had a lot of time for the dead, believing it was how you lived your life that mattered. Looking around the near-empty church, it was clear he hadn't lived a life filled with love and respect, he had hurt almost everyone he had encountered, so it was only right that his misdeeds caught up with him as he was laid to rest.

Rest. What an odd idea, Renee thought, as she threw a clod of earth onto his coffin. If she was honest, she hoped her former husband didn't get a minute's peace, wherever he ended up.

Without Ronnie in her life, Renee had started to rebuild. The first thing she had done was move out of the house she had lived in with Ronnie and move straight back in with Nancy and the kids. Yes, it was cramped and noisy, but Renee had never felt more at home.

The next thing she, Nancy, Temperance and Violet had done was go to the board and convince them not to look for another buyer. It seemed a reasonable request, but the board were uncertain, wanting an accurate statement of accounts, and to be brought up to date with the Palais' affairs before a new investor to replace Ronnie could be found. The four of them had agreed, and for the past few days the Good Time Girls had been holed up in the office looking through every scrap of paper that would prove to the board that the Palais was still a good investment and it made sense to keep it going.

And then, in the meantime, Renee had returned to her role as chief dancer. She had left the instruction to Temperance, not wanting to step on her toes, but the idea of dancing freely as she used to had been too tempting, and so she had quickly and quietly taken up the reins, surprised to find, after everything that happened over the past few weeks, that she could still lose herself in the power of the music, the steps that make up a Viennese waltz or a lively tango.

She had to admit that she was still struggling to live a life without worry, without constantly looking over her shoulder, but she was content to take it one day at a time.

Just then, a sharp knock pulled her swiftly back into the present. Looking up, Renee saw Peter poke his head around the door.

'Hey, honey.' Nancy beamed.

Peter returned her smile and Renee felt a flash of fondness for the boy. Without Ronnie around now, the boy had been thriving.

'We've got a solicitor and a vicar here, Nancy, for Renee,' he said gruffly.

'Mr Aiden? But why would he bring a vicar?' Renee got to her feet and arched her aching back.

'Maybe things have changed?' Nancy said archly.

'Shall I show them in or do you want to go somewhere more private?' Peter asked, looking shy for a second.

Renee shook her head.

Despite her nonchalance, her heart was pounding. Yes, she and Nancy had got away with Ronnie's death as far as the police were concerned. But what if someone on a higher level knew? She glanced briefly upwards, and in her head crossed her heart. She hadn't thought about religion in years, but if there was a god, Renee couldn't help hoping he'd show mercy for the crimes she had committed.

'Whatever they have to say can be said in front of everyone. Show them in.'

And so, just moments later, Renee found herself facing a tall, grey-haired but kindly man she knew to be Mr Aiden, the man who had looked after Ronnie's business interests for decades. Beside him stood a smaller, older gentleman with blond hair, sparkling eyes and a smile so warm she felt instantly at ease.

'What a surprise to see you both,' Renee said now. She poured them a cup of tea from a pot Peter had magically appeared with.

'Well, we have managed to make greater headway into Mr Newsham's affairs than I expected. He was good at planning as you know, Mrs Newsham, and the various loose ends have actually turned out to be easier to solve than anticipated.'

Nancy nodded in approval. 'Sounds like good news.'

'It is. I always think it's good news when the family gets the will resolved, it means you can all move on.'

Renee paused for a moment. Mr Aiden was right. All she wanted now was to move on with her life and forget Ronnie had ever been a part of it.

'To business.' Mr Aiden took a sip of tea from his cup, then rifled through a folder full of papers. 'So, as I'm sure you know, the majority of Mr Newsham's business interests have already been resolved with his immediate family member taking ownership.'

Renee exchanged a look with Nancy. 'What do you mean, "resolved", like?'

'Ah.' Mr Aiden looked troubled. 'Mr Newsham said he was going to speak to you about this, er, rather delicate matter. I'm not sure it's my place to say.'

'Honey, you're the only one that can say,' Nancy said firmly. 'So please, enlighten us.'

Mr Aiden pushed his horn-rimmed glasses up his nose and nodded. 'All right. Mr Newsham has left his clothing stores, the properties he owned in the North West and, of course, the Palais de Danse, to Roger Newsham.'

'Who the hell is Roger Newsham?' Renee asked. She had never heard of him.

'Roger is Ronnie's much older half brother, I believe,' the vicar said.

Renee's jaw dropped. Ronnie had never mentioned anything about a brother, half or otherwise, before. Her mind went into overdrive. What else had he been keeping from her? What other secrets were going to crawl out of the woodwork and surprise her? She tried to steady her breath. She had hoped that with Ronnie gone she was free to start again, but his legacy seemed to cause continued pain and anguish.

'I take it this is news to you?' Mr Aiden said, grimly.

Renee nodded. 'I had no idea.'

'Well, be consoled that arrangements with Mr Newsham have already been settled. He hadn't seen Ronnie for twenty years or so, and was saddened to learn of his death and surprised to learn of his inheritance.'

'I bet he was,' Renee said.

'He is, er . . . how shall I put it,' Mr Aiden said delicately. 'Quite different to Mr Ronnie Newsham. Roger is a practising vicar.'

At that Renee's eyes strayed to the other vicar beside Mr Aiden, and her hands flew to her mouth.

'You?' she gasped, through manicured fingers.

Roger smiled and nodded. 'I'm sorry to ambush you like this, but given the way Ronnie left everything to me I wanted to be here when Mr Aiden explained. It didn't seem right, somehow, that Ronnie would leave you with nothing. I can only imagine how he treated you over the years.'

Renee just gaped at him.

'Which is why I want to transfer the Palais to you,' Roger said, 'as soon as possible.'

'Really?' She rested her hands on her lap and looked at Roger properly. 'Are you sure? Ronnie obviously wanted you to inherit.'

Roger laughed. 'I doubt that very much. I rather think he was using me to get to you, Renee. There's a very good reason I haven't seen my brother in many years, and that's because he's a bad egg, through and through. Capable of nothing but hurting everyone around him. He never brought any good into the world, he simply didn't know how to.' Roger shook his head. 'I believe the Palais should go to you. It's only right, and I do sincerely hope you'll accept. I've always followed your career, Renee, I know dancing is in your soul.'

Renee blinked at him in astonishment. 'Have you?'

Roger chuckled. 'Of course. You couldn't come from the North West and not have heard of the great Renee Hammond. That's why I think this place should be yours.'

Wordlessly, Renee found herself nodding.

'Thank you,' was all she could manage.

Raising his tea cup towards her, Roger smiled. 'Let's hope its the beginning of a new chapter – for all of us.'

Nancy smiled. 'It's more than a new chapter, it's the chance to start again, for the Palais to turn a corner.' She swallowed, knowing that Alex would be just as thrilled as her.

As the girls around her cheered and gasped in shock, thoughts rushed around Renee's head like spinning plates. She, Renee Hammond, had a controlling stake in the Palais. She would be the one to say how it was run? She clapped her hands to her mouth, unable to believe that Ronnie's final, cruel twist had been turned on its head. Finally, Renee could stop running, the Palais was her home.

Epilogue

Christmas Eve 1941

As Renee stood in the centre of the bar, the Christmas tree towering above her, she looked up and smiled as she placed the finishing touch – a huge gold star made from greaseproof paper.

It had been a gift from Ruth last week, who had found the soaked paper in the bin and dried it out, determined to make something beautiful for her second Christmas at the Palais.

Now, as Renee took a step back to admire the view, she felt a stab of pleasure. This Christmas really would be perfect, Renee was determined.

In the time she had become a major shareholder, she had worked hard to secure the support of the board members who'd thankfully recognised her background in dance was an asset. As such she had thrown herself into the role, convincing the board and everyone around her that the Palais was of huge benefit to the community. But there were still some changes that she'd had to deal with. Firstly, to the surprise of everyone, Bill and Edna had retired. There had been no hard feelings, they had both just felt it was time. And Renee was glad. Not just because she had found the two of them hard to get on with, but because she wanted to ring in new changes at the dance hall.

The first thing Renee did was reinstate Nancy back into her role as deputy manager. Renee knew she was good at many things, but organisation wasn't one of them. Instead she would return to her first love as chief dancer, with the coveted deputy position going to Temperance, who had been delighted.

Violet had been promoted to deputy manager, with the proviso she could bring Eamon in whenever she wanted. Meanwhile, Maisie had been promoted to ticket and cloakroom supervisor.

There were still some other ideas up her sleeve, and she had a special surprise that she hoped to reveal later on that night.

'It looks wonderful, Renee,' Peter breathed as he sidled up to her. 'I can't believe what you've done with the place.'

'Thanks, chuck,' Renee breathed, struggling to keep her emotions under control. 'We've all worked hard, you especially. We deserve some fun tonight.'

At the compliment, Peter coloured, and Renee nudged him. The boy was showing real potential since Ronnie had gone. In the days that followed Ronnie's death, Renee and Nancy had tried to convince Peter to go back to school, but he was determined to carry on with his apprenticeship. And so Renee had taken it upon herself to ensure Peter got an excellent grounding in the dance hall business and had even insisted on him learning to dance, with his beloved Temperance teaching him the basics.

'Did I just hear you mention the word "fun"?' Violet grinned, holding baby Eamon with Betty and Alan coming up behind.

Renee returned her grin and held her arms out for a cuddle. 'What are you doing here?'

'He's got a tooth coming through.' Violet grimaced. 'Nancy said I could bring him and put him upstairs, if that's all right?'

'Course it is!' Renee exclaimed as she blew a raspberry to a smiling Eamon. Jiggling him in her arms, she felt a maternal stirring she had never experienced before. In the years she had been married to Ronnie she had never considered motherhood, not wanting to bring a child into the dangerous world he created. But now he was gone, Renee felt something inside her shift.

'Ah, you look like a natural,' Alan said easily.

'Alan! What are you doing here? Birmingham sick of you already?'

At the joke, Alan laughed, and Renee couldn't miss the tiredness etched across his face.

'A rare few days off for Christmas. Thought it would be nice to pop back and see everyone.'

'You were a very welcome surprise,' Violet said earnestly.

Renee could see the affection mirrored in father and daughter and smiled. Glancing at Betty, she was sorry to see her friend looked worried and confused.

'It's lovely to have Alan back.' Betty nodded now. 'But it's only a flying visit. He has work to do, Vi, we must remember that. Birmingham needs him.'

Alan smiled. 'I wouldn't go that far. It's been tough, getting used to a new city. But the scheme is going very well. And of course I'm still hoping to convince Betty to come up to the Midlands and help me get the scheme off the ground.'

'You know I can't,' Betty said firmly. 'My duty is here.'

'Your *duty* has hardly been seen for several weeks,' Violet put in bluntly.

'You mean George?' Renee asked.

Betty shrugged by way of reply. 'He always does this.'

'When he's got a new floozy on the go,' Violet spat angrily. 'How many more times, Betty? Just make a new life for yourself!'

Renee sighed as she handed Eamon back to Violet and glanced at Peter who was looking decidedly awkward.

'Peter, love, you couldn't ask the band to start playing some Christmas tunes, could you? Really get everyone in the mood as they enter the dance hall.'

Peter nodded and walked away.

As he did so, Renee couldn't miss the sense of despair that had fallen on the group. She frowned; this wasn't the Christmas spirit she had hoped to create.

'Now then.' She clapped her hands together. 'I wanted to talk to you about something, Betty Millington – and with Alan here we can perhaps get his opinion.'

'Oh?' Betty frowned and Queenie rolled her eyes.

'Give over, Bet. It might be good news.' She looked pleadingly at Renee. 'It is good news, ain't it?'

'I think so, yes.' Renee nodded. 'Betty, I want you to oversee our catering arrangements. I want us to get back to offering proper food, but in the spirit of wartime I'd like us to continue the National Restaurant scheme you were pioneering for the residents of Hammersmith. We can afford to open our doors to those in need.'

'Oh my days!' Betty gasped. 'Are you sure?'

'Never been more sure,' Renee promised. 'You're the one to look after it all. What do you think?'

'I think you're made for the job,' Alan interjected, sadly.

Betty looked at him fondly. 'I think so, too. It's right for me to be here doing something of service.'

'For the moment, service is what our lives are about,' Nancy said, carefully.

Just as Renee was about to reply, the sounds of the band playing 'Jingle Bells' echoed through the bar.

'Happy Christmas!' a pair of voices chorused from the entrance.

Glancing up, Renee's face broke into a genuine smile at the sight of Temperance and Archie, arms entwined.

They were made for each other, anyone could see that, and Renee was delighted that in recent months their relationship had gone from strength to strength.

'Happy Christmas,' Queenie said, leaning in to kiss Archie on the cheek.

'Steady, Gran!' Violet giggled.

'Steady nothing.' Queenie winked and gestured to the sprig of mistletoe above her head. 'Just welcoming Archie into the fold in true Christmas spirit.'

Everyone laughed, and Violet rolled her eyes.

'So how about a toast, to a new start?'

'I'll drink to that,' Archie said.

He handed Temperance a glass and Renee couldn't miss the way he touched his own glass to hers. She hoped they would be making an announcement of their own very soon.

Raising her glass aloft, Renee spoke. 'To new starts.'

'To new starts!' everyone chorused.

'Wait a minute. Why starts?' Temperance asked, fixing her gaze on Renee. 'What are you up to?'

Renee grinned. 'I never could pull the wool over your eyes, Temperance Adams. You're right. I have got another surprise. I've finally solved our MC problem.'

Excitement bubbled amongst the group.

'Oh, Renee, I hoped you were going to let me have a go,' Archie quipped.

Renee chuckled. 'That won't be necessary, chuck.'

'It certainly won't,' came a voice.

At the sound, Renee looked up and felt a stab of relief, her best party trick was right on time.

'Everyone, I'd like you to give a very warm welcome to our new MC – Janice Dobson. Janice, meet everyone.'

As everyone nodded and smiled at Janice, Renee felt relief course through her. She had kept Janice's appointment to herself, unsure it would even go ahead until a few days ago.

Despite the fact that she and Bill had never seen eye to eye it had still been a huge blow to Renee when he had handed in his notice as MC. For weeks she had panicked, wondering how on earth the Palais would cope. Then she had a brainwave, and remembered that since the Manchester raids, a very good friend and very talented MC was still looking for work. She had taken the train to Manchester a fortnight ago, and been delighted when Janice had agreed to join her at the Palais and make a new start in Hammersmith at Christmas.

'Where's your husband and kids?' Queenie asked bluntly, but not unkindly.

'Me kids have been called up and me husband is busy with the Home Guard. He's given me his blessing,' Janice explained.

'A husband's blessing to start somewhere else,' Renee heard Alan murmur in Betty's ear. 'See, pigs do fly.'

Betty remained tight-lipped and Renee could sense her discomfort, so instead did her best to change the subject.

'Well, I hope Janice is here to stay, and the Palais' future is distinctly female. So, everyone, on this very special Christmas Eve, I wonder if you'd all now raise a toast with me to a brand new start at the Palais. Here's to a very merry Christmas and the start of a female future.'

'A merry Christmas and a female future!' everyone chorused.

And as Renee looked around the room, the band now playing 'Winter Wonderland', she realised she was on the brink of something powerful. Her eyes came to rest on the little red dancing shoe that had been given to her by her mother. Reaching forward, she stroked the decoration gingerly. It was a little scratched in places, the heel slightly bent, but it had survived. Just as she had promised herself she would do all those years ago.

In fact, Renee hadn't just survived, she had thrived. It had taken some doing, and she would never have done it without the help of her friends, but she was still here, she was still standing, and she was going to live her life to the fullest now that she was free.

Acknowledgements

Every book ever written is a team effort and I'd be lost without the people who helped bring this book to life. First up, my incredible editor Hannah Smith who has such wonderful vision and nous and amazingly always knows just how to bring a book to life – this book is as much Hannah's effort as mine, so thank you.

Equally, my wonderful agent, Kate Burke from Blake Friedmann, is a shining presence in every one of my books and I would be lost without her. I'd also like to thank the entire Embla team – Emilie, Jen and Jane. Thank you for taking a chance on me and giving me the opportunity to write these stories.

Not being around during wartime, I'm indebted to the endlessly patient team at Fulham and Hammersmith Historical Society and everyone from the Hammersmith Palais – Old Skool and You're Probably from W12 if . . . social media groups – you've all been brilliantly helpful as I've tried to paint a wartime picture of the Palais and Hammersmith. Any mistakes within this book are entirely my own.

I must also extend a huge thanks to my family and friends who I know must be so sick of me talking about wartime, but never, ever complain. Thanks for the endless supply of tea, the ideas and the biscuits when you sense I'm in need of a sugar hit.

Most important, of course, are all you lovely readers, as without you there would be no book. You make my day when you get in touch and it really is a true pleasure to hear from you all. Thanks for reading this. There are a lot of sagas out there and I'm honoured you have chosen to read this one.

About the Author

With a passion for reading from practically the moment she was born, it was inevitable Fiona would become a writer. Sure enough, after studying English Literature at university, Fiona became a local and national journalist before making her move to books where she began ghost writing fiction for celebrities (too famous to name, of course). One day, some bright spark suggested she write her own stories and, suddenly, an idea was born. She lives in Berkshire with her husband and two cats, and has an unhealthy attitude towards exercise and chocolate – believing one must surely cancel out the other.

About Embla Books

Embla Books is a digital-first publisher of standout commercial adult fiction. Passionate about storytelling, the team at Embla publish books that will make you 'laugh, love, look over your shoulder and lose sleep'. Launched by Bonnier Books UK in 2021, the imprint is named after the first woman from the creation myth in Norse mythology, who was carved by the gods from a tree trunk found on the seashore – an image of the kind of creative work and crafting that writers do, and a symbol of how stories shape our lives.

Find out about some of our other books and stay in touch:

Twitter, Facebook, Instagram: @emblabooks
Newsletter: https://bit.ly/emblanewsletter